Critical acclai

Have a L

Jacquelin Thomas

"Touching and refreshing . . . a solid contribution to quality Christian fiction titles written by and for African-Americans."

—*Publishers Weekly,* on *Singsation*

ReShonda Tate Billingsley

"Amen to *Let the Church Say Amen*. . . . A well-written novel. . . . [It] teaches that while God should come first in your life, family comes before the church. I applaud Billingsley. . . ."

—*Indianapolis Recorder*

J. D. Mason

"Unforgettable . . . emotionally charged and breathtakingly poignant. J. D. Mason does a wonderful job of combining strong characterization, humor, and witty dialogue."

—*QBR, The Black Book Review,* on *And on the Eighth Day She Rested*

Sandra Kitt

"Kitt continues to shatter stereotypes and open doors for writers and readers of popular women's fiction."

—*Minneapolis Star Tribune*

ALSO BY THESE AUTHORS

Jacquelin Thomas

Samson

The Ideal Wife

ReShonda Tate Billingsley

A Family Affair

The Secret She Kept

J. D. Mason

Beautiful, Dirty, Rich

Drop Dead, Gorgeous

Sandra Kitt

Promises in Paradise

For All We Know

Have a Little Faith

Jacquelin THOMAS

ReShonda Tate BILLINGSLEY

J. D. MASON

Sandra KITT

POCKET BOOKS

New York London Toronto Sydney New Delhi

Pocket Books
A Division of Simon & Schuster, Inc.
1230 Avenue of the Americas
New York, NY 10020

This Pocket Books paperback edition October 2013

Manufactured in the United States of America

10 9 8 7 6 5 4 3 2 1

ISBN 978-1-4767-4063-8
ISBN 978-1-4165-2508-0 (ebook)

Contents

Signs of Light
Jacquelin Thomas 1

Faith Will Overcome
ReShonda Tate Billingsley 109

Maybelline
J. D. Mason 229

Survival Instincts
Sandra Kitt 333

Signs of Light

Jacquelin Thomas

Chapter One

Lorna Hamilton peered out the storefront window of Nana's Gourmet Bakery, watching people leisurely making their way along North Main Street in downtown Woodlake, North Carolina. She scrunched up her face as she eyed the two women standing just beyond the entrance of her bakery.

"Doris, just look at them," she grumbled to the employee standing beside her. "They just left the hair salon across the street. Hair all done up, and look at those bloodred nails . . . long as all get-out. They getting all fixed up on our tax dollars. Money s'posed to be for the kids."

Doris nodded in agreement, muttering, "A bunch

of lazy good-for-nothings, if you ask me. Don't wanna work—just wanna lay around getting a check. I *have* a job and can't get no help to pay for childcare. Social Services got me on a waiting list. People like them don't have job the first and can get childcare. It's not fair at all."

One of the women outside turned in their direction, as if she could hear them talking.

Lorna quickly averted her gaze. She and Doris pretended like they were discussing the elegant wedding cake displayed in the window.

Outside the shop, one of the women waved off her friend, then walked toward the entrance.

"I don't know why she keeps coming in here," Lorna uttered. "She don't ever buy nothing."

Despite her personal feelings, Lorna's mouth turned upward into a smile as soon as the young woman entered through the double doors. "Good afternoon," she greeted. "What can I get for you today?"

"I'm just looking." The girl grunted, switching her Gucci handbag from one shoulder to the other.

Lorna couldn't help but wonder how she got anything done with those long nails of hers. Long and frosted in a soft pink color.

Lorna didn't take her eyes off the bubble-gum popping, weave-wearing, designer-bag-toting welfare recipient walking back and forth eyeing the cakes and cheesecakes through the marble and glass display counter.

The woman's two-toned copper-colored weave was styled high, and instead of the conservative suits and comfortable shoes most women who worked downtown wore, she had on a pair of denim jeans that rested low on her hips, paired with a pink tank that looked two sizes too small. Assorted rings adorned her fingers, while a thick gold necklace hung around her neck. The focal point of her bare midriff was her belly ring.

Unconsciously, Lorna compared herself to the young woman. She was pleased that at forty-two she could still catch the eye of men half her age. Her caramel complexion was smooth and even-toned. For work, her long, sandy brown hair had been styled into an old-fashioned bun and covered with a hairnet. She'd been spared the subtle signs of aging—tiny pouches beneath her dark brown eyes, stretch marks, sagging breasts and cellulite. With a measure of pride, Lorna credited her youthful appearance to having never worn makeup and strong family genetics. Her late grandmother had never had wrinkles and looked years younger than her advanced age of eighty-two.

"You have any more of the chocolate cream cheesecake?"

Lorna's head snapped up from staring down at the

young woman's French-manicured toenails and high-heeled sandals. "I'm out. Sorry."

"When do you think you might have some more?"

"Maybe tomorrow," Lorna replied. "The chocolate cream cheesecake never lasts long. Most of my customers special order it, or they purchase a whole one."

"How much for a whole chocolate cream cheesecake then?"

"Twenty-six dollars for a two-pound cheesecake," Lorna quoted. "Thirty-six dollars for three pounds and forty-four for a four-pound cheesecake."

Frowning, the young woman muttered, *"For cheesecake* . . . Y'all too high for me. I can make a whole one at home for about three dollars. Just get one of them kits in the grocery store."

Then go get one, Lorna wanted to shout. *It won't come close to one of mine.*

A few minutes later, the woman left the shop, still grumbling about the price.

Lorna turned to Doris. "This is a gourmet bakery. She know good and well she wasn't gonna buy a thing when she walked herself into this shop. Coming in here, wasting my time."

"Here comes that Melita Dawson," Doris announced. "With her nasty attitude."

Lorna groaned. "Not today." Melita was their most difficult customer.

"How y'all doin?" Melita said as she stepped into the bakery.

"We're just fine," Lorna responded. "How are you?"

"I'd be okay if your employee wasn't staring at me like I'm from the moon." Melita folded her arms across her chest, eyeballing Doris. "You sho' must like what you see. Take a picture—it'll last longer."

Doris opened her mouth to respond, but Lorna quickly cut her off by asking, "What can I get for you, Melita?" To Doris, she said, "Could you check on the cupcakes in the oven for me?"

Melita waited until Doris was out of sight, then said, "My boo wants me to pick him up four slices of your white chocolate and strawberry cheesecake. You got any? The last time I came through you didn't. He was hot when I got home and didn't have no cheesecake with me."

"We have plenty today. Will there be anything else?"

"Let me think on it for a moment."

Melita strutted around the shop, fingering the straps of her Louis Vuitton purse. Lorna noticed that Melita wore matching shoes and had on a necklace with the initials LV. Everything the woman had on seemed to have somebody else's name on it, yet she'd never known Melita to hold down a job. Lorna had met Melita years ago when she and her mother had lived across the street from Nana's.

Even as a young child, Melita had been hard to control. Her mother had finally given up and thrown Melita out of the house when she was around fifteen or sixteen.

"Do you have any pecan pie?"

"I do," Lorna responded. "Would you like a slice?"

"Naw. I want to buy a whole one."

"How's your mother doing?" Lorna inquired as she packaged up Melita's selections.

"I guess she all right. We ain't speaking right now. She always trying to be up in my business, like she know what's good for me. Humph. I'm grown."

"It's because she loves you, Melita. Your mother only wants the best for you."

"What she thinks is best, you mean. I don't need her to try and raise me now. I'm—"

"Grown," Lorna finished for her. "Yes, you've said that."

Melita glared at her. "Why everybody always trying to take her side? Miss Lorna, I don't ask my mama for nothin'. I take care of my three children myself."

"Are you working?"

"No."

"Then you're not really taking care of your children by yourself, dear. You're getting assistance from the government."

"You know what I mean."

Lorna met the young woman's gaze straight on. "Melita, you have a good head on your shoulders. Why don't you at least take some classes and get a trade?"

"I hate school, Miss Lorna. I ain't going to no school. That's out of the question."

"Then why don't you get a job?"

"My boo takes care of me and my children."

"What happens if you two break up?"

Melita frowned. "You sound just like Mama. Y'all just don't understand."

"Melita, if you don't get a job soon, you're gonna lose your day-care assistance. You know that, don't you?"

"I just got it extended for another thirty days," Melita responded with a smirk. "I do enough looking to satisfy my worker. I can't help it if no one will hire me."

Lorna wanted to strangle Melita. Here was a young, able-bodied woman who could go out and work, but what did she do? *Nothing*. Because of her cheating, someone who was really deserving of childcare assistance couldn't get it and was placed on a waiting list.

Lorna totaled Melita's purchases. "Twenty-four dollars and fifteen cents is your total."

Melita handed her a hundred-dollar bill.

"Why you looking at that money like that?" she demanded. "It's real."

"I check all the money that comes across my counter."

"Miss Lorna, don't try to be funny with me."

Placing her hands on her hips, Lorna eyed the young woman. "Melita, why do you always come in my shop with an attitude? Every time you come in here you try to start something."

"No, I don't," Melita shot back. "Y'all just think y'all better than me and always giving me those funny looks. You need to leave me alone. You ain't seen me with an attitude. Humph. I can show you attitude."

Lorna made change and handed it to Melita. "You have a nice day."

"Just because you own this ba—"

Lorna cut her off by saying, "Bye, Melita." Her tone left no room for argument.

Melita left, muttering a string of curses on her way out of the shop.

Doris walked out of the kitchen, saying, "One day, I'ma take that girl by the throat and swing her all over this shop. She gets on my nerves with that mouth of hers. Acting like the world owe her something when all she do is sit on her rump collecting a check and getting money from that thug of a boyfriend."

Lorna was in full agreement. "I can't count how many girls just like her come in here. I'm sick and tired of our tax dollars going to folks like that."

They fell silent when another customer entered

the shop pushing a stroller. Lorna's gaze traveled to the little bald-headed boy with big brown eyes and dimpled cheeks. She estimated his age to be no more than four or five. His sickly appearance was a sharp contrast to the healthy glow of the deep mahogany complexion of his mother. She was thin but didn't look like she'd missed any meals.

Another one of *those* women, Lorna surmised. She probably spent her check on her waist-length braids, ugly gold earrings and bracelets dangling on her arm. From the looks of it, she spent more on herself than that poor child.

"Can I help you with anything?" Doris inquired.

"Just looking," the girl mumbled.

Lorna suspected as much.

A few minutes later, the young woman checked her watch, and said, "Oops, we gotta go, Kendall. It's almost time for the bus."

The little boy gave Lorna a warm smile and slight wave before his mother whirled the stroller around and headed toward the door.

Doris backed away from the display she'd been working on. "What do you think?"

Lorna eyed the blueberry tangerine fruit cheesecake. It was their featured cheesecake for the week. "Let's place it beside the white chocolate raspberry cheesecake and garnish it with some lemon," she suggested.

She glanced across the street to the empty space facing her. Up until a few months ago, it had been a deli shop. Now people were heading in the other direction in search of food for lunch.

Lorna was thankful for her faithful customers, because they provided steady business for her bakery. Not only did she offer assorted donuts, breads, cakes, cheesecakes and cookies, she also sold gourmet coffees, candies, jarred fruits and vegetables.

A customer strolled inside, forcing Lorna away from her musings.

"Hello," she greeted with a smile. "What can I get for you today?"

"I need to pick out a wedding cake. I'm getting married next month."

Lorna quickly assessed the woman standing on the other side of her counter. She wore a navy blue pantsuit and low-heeled pumps. On her shoulder, she carried a basic navy purse—one without a designer logo. Her blond hair was pulled back into a severe ponytail.

Lorna guessed she worked in one of the nearby law firms. "Are you looking for something really fancy or more along simple lines?"

"Simple but elegant."

After going through Lorna's portfolio, the bride-to-be selected a cake with faux-embroidery details hand-painted with edible gold leaves, piped in royal blue icing on rolled fondant. She wanted Lorna to use a bouquet of gum-paste flowers for the topper.

Right before her customer left, more people began to head into the shop.

Without looking at the clock, Lorna knew it was noon. This was when Nana's Gourmet Bakery was its busiest. Doris usually left around one p.m., when either Charlotte or Kevin, her part-time employees, arrived.

Promptly at five-thirty, Lorna began closing up her shop. While Charlotte cleaned up, Lorna wrote out the deposit slip.

It was almost six-thirty when Lorna and Charlotte finally emerged from the shop and headed to their cars.

Lorna drove past the Family and Children Services building located in the heart of downtown Woodlake, just one block from her bakery. The bus stop at the corner was crowded with women, men and children leaving the social services building. Lorna couldn't understand why anyone would *want* a life like that. These people seemed satisfied living off of a check and food stamps. She just didn't get it. And she resented the fact that she couldn't conceive a child while these *other* women had babies all day long.

Lorna pulled into the parking lot of her bank and drove up to the night deposit slot. After making sure her surroundings were safe, Lorna quickly made her deposit.

Back on the streets and heading home, Lorna's mind wandered back to her musings. She wanted a family more than anything in life. She'd tried adoption once, but the birth mother had changed her mind and come back for the child. Lorna refused to go through that heartache again.

Lorna was an only child and had been raised by her aunt after her parents' death. During the summer months, she'd lived with her grandmother, whom she affectionately called Nana, in Woodlake.

Lorna loved Woodlake, a town for all seasons. The falls were spectacular, the winters compared to scenes from Currier and Ives, the springs an explosion of wildflowers, and the summer months like today, the tenth of June, warm and comfortable.

When Nana had suffered her first stroke, Lorna had packed up and left Philadelphia, where she'd been living, without a second thought. She'd eventually sold her house, and she'd decided to stay in Woodlake after Nana's death ten years ago from a second stroke.

In honor of her grandmother, Lorna had opened Nana's Gourmet Bakery. The corner shop was successful—so much so that rumors were circulating that her recipes were closely guarded secrets passed from her grandmother, who used to sell her treats out of the house.

But there were no secrets to Lorna's baking. She

just followed Nana's advice to take time to nurture each batch of dough as if it were her first.

Business was going so well for Lorna that she was considering opening up a second shop on the other side of town. She had one full-time and two part-time employees. She could afford to hire more employees to run the shop, but Lorna loved doing most of the baking herself. It was her passion. If she went through with opening another shop, Lorna would promote Doris to manager and hire another full-time person. Doris was the first employee of Nana's and Lorna trusted her.

It went without saying that Lorna was pleased with her accomplishments. The only thing missing in her life was the presence of a family.

She had no one to share in her success.

Lorna loved to walk through the rooms of her house, admiring the creative blending of the past with the present.

Nana had left her house to Lorna, who, throughout the years, had taken her time redecorating the rooms, making them her own. She'd added rich, vibrant color to the walls and contemporary art pieces to accent the traditional furnishings.

She was proud of her home and her business. Proud that she hadn't had to ask anybody for a thing.

"God bless the child that's got his own," Nana used to say to her, and Lorna took it to heart. She didn't want anything handed to her. Lorna insisted on making her own way.

She picked up a pillow with hand-embroidered stitching across the front and sat down on the sofa in its place. Lorna's fingers moved lightly across the silk fabric, her mind traveling back to the day she'd purchased the new living room furniture.

It was the day she'd met Walter Reynolds, the owner of Reynolds Furniture Store.

Lorna had been attracted to him from the first moment they'd met. Standing at six feet three inches, with a smooth, tawny complexion, Walter kept his head and face shaved. His greenish gray eyes were the one feature most often remarked on, but what she loved most about him was his deep, sexy laugh. His laughter could ignite a fire within her.

He was fifty years old and divorced, with two children in college. From what Lorna could tell, he was a good father and son. Walter had been his mother's primary caregiver until her death two months ago.

She'd been dating Walter for two years now. He'd never brought up the subject of marriage outside of complaining about how horrible his previous wife had been. Lorna enjoyed Walter's companionship but wasn't sure she could give up on the idea of getting married.

Lorna wanted a family. Her aunt passed last year, leaving her with no other close family ties. She was barren and had accepted that fact as best she could, that there would be no children for her.

Hopefully, she could still have a husband. Lorna didn't want to go through the rest of her life alone. Surely this was not what God intended.

Lorna prayed it wasn't.

Chapter Two

Lorna's routine was as regular as the days of the week.

The first thing she always did each morning upon arriving at the bakery was check her calendar, noting any special order due dates. After that, Lorna did a quick inventory to see if she needed to order any supplies.

This morning was no exception.

Although the shop didn't open for another three hours, coming in around 4:30 a.m. gave Lorna and Doris enough time to prepare the donuts, pastries and other goodies her customers enjoyed as they made their way to work in the surrounding office buildings.

Since the bakery was located one block away from Family and Children Services, many of the caseworkers frequented her shop, and Lorna knew quite a few of them by name.

She often donated donuts and cookies for the children in child protective services. She also donated cakes and specialty breads to various other charities and fund-raisers to show how much she cared for her community.

Though this morning started like all the others, a series of mishaps put Lorna in a sour mood.

First, she cut her finger opening a box. She quickly rushed off to the bathroom to clean and bandage the wound. Before she could finish, the shrill ringing of a bell sounded, signifying the entrance of a customer. Since Doris was kneading dough for sticky buns, Lorna rushed back to the front of the store to greet the customer.

On her way, she knocked over a half-full bag of sugar, wasting it all over the kitchen floor. She muttered a curse.

"I'll sweep the sugar up," Doris stated. "Don't worry about it."

Nursing the bandaged finger, Lorna strode up to the marble and glass counter.

Her expression became strained when she spotted the thin young woman who had been in the day before with the little boy.

"Can I help you?" Lorna asked, brushing off a thin layer of flour from her apron.

"Good morning," the girl greeted in response. "I was wondering if I could order a birthday cake for my son. He'll be three soon."

"Yeah." Lorna grunted. "You can order a cake. How soon do you need it?"

"His birthday is in three weeks."

"No problem. All I need is at least forty-eight-hours' notice." Lorna grabbed a pad and pencil. "What type of theme do you have in mind for the cake?"

The girl moved closer and lowered her voice although there was no one else in the shop at the moment. "There's one other thing. Would you be willing to take my EBT card as payment? I don't have any money right now and my son is sick. I—"

Releasing an audible sigh, Lorna laid down the pen and pad. "I don't accept food stamps, miss. You'll need to go somewhere else for that."

"You don't have to be so rude."

"Not trying to be," Lorna shot back. "I just have to be clear—I'm not an authorized retailer and I don't have the right type of equipment to accept EBT cards. I suggest you go to the Food Lion down Anderson Street and get your cake."

Lorna was a bit shaken by the sight of tears rolling down the woman's face. She hadn't meant to come off so short with her, but after a frustrating morning, she wasn't in the mood to deal with another welfare mother.

Without another word, the young woman turned and walked to the door. She rushed out so quickly that she tripped and almost fell down face-first onto the sidewalk.

She gathered herself, wiping away her tears. She never once glanced back to see if Lorna was watching her.

Lorna walked to the door and watched the slender young woman toss her braids over her shoulders and cross the street, her head held high, to the bus stop. She felt a thread of guilt over making her cry, but she forced it from her mind. She didn't want to feel bad over her actions, so she tried to convince herself that the girl was just looking for another handout.

She didn't accept food stamps and never would. The lazy woman needed to get herself a job. What kind of place did she think this was?

Still, she couldn't forget the look on that girl's face. It haunted her for the rest of the day.

Over dinner that evening, Lorna told Walter about the young woman and her request.

"Maybe you should consider accepting EBT cards," he suggested. "Sounds like good business to me. You're not that far from Family and Children Services, so you're gonna get some of the clients in your store."

"I'm fine with that as long as they bring cash.

Nana's Gourmet Bakery is first class. We're not just some . . . some bread store. I don't want to go through the whole process of applying to see if my shop will be approved—it's just too much of a hassle for me. I'm fine with the way things are. I don't need to accept food stamps."

He didn't respond.

"What?" Lorna prompted. "You have something on your mind. Say it."

"Honey, we've talked about this before. With you, the topic always ends up on how many children a woman on welfare should have based on stereotypical perceptions of women on assistance. I have to tell you—you come off a little judgmental. There really is a need for the program, you know."

"I know there is a need, Walter," Lorna shot back. "I don't have a problem with there being a need—I just think that there are too many people trying to beat the system. The people that truly need help can't get any because of these people lying and scheming instead of working—these women having baby after baby after baby. A lot of these young girls *can* work, they just don't want to work. They want a handout."

"I agree with you to a certain extent. But even if some of these young mothers got jobs, they still wouldn't make enough to live on, much less take care of their children. Housing, for one, isn't cheap."

"Then work two jobs," Lorna responded. "I did it. It didn't kill me."

"Then you take them away from their children," Walter pointed out. "How much time can you spend with your child if you're working all the time?"

Lorna felt a thread of irritation. Walter didn't agree with her. They never saw eye to eye on issues like welfare and unemployment.

She believed welfare benefits made people lazy and unmotivated to work, while Walter believed that the benefits afforded families a chance to avoid other issues like being homeless or not being able to feed their children. He believed welfare allowed families the chance to stay afloat. However, like Lorna, Walter didn't believe it to be a long-term solution.

"What's going on in that busy brain of yours?" Walter queried.

"Just thinking about what I have to do tomorrow. I have a wedding Saturday afternoon. I'm doing three cakes for the bride and groom."

"Speaking of weddings . . . my ex is getting married next month in Las Vegas," Walter announced. "I feel sorry for the dude."

"Why is that?"

"That woman is gonna drive him crazy. Maggie is moody and she knows nothing about saving a dollar. She'll drive him crazy and run the man into the poorhouse."

"You married her—she must not have been too bad." Silently, Lorna wondered if Walter still loved his ex-wife. He talked about her constantly.

"She was the same back then, too. I guess I thought I could change her."

"Walter, do you still love her?" Lorna blurted.

He blinked twice. "Huh?"

"I asked if you still loved Maggie." Lorna wasn't sure she was ready to hear the answer. She would be crushed if Walter told her he did.

"No. Why would you ask me something like that?"

"I don't know," Lorna began. "Maybe because you talk about her so much."

"I don't talk about Maggie that much."

"Yeah . . . you do, Walter. She comes up every time we're together. I know how vain she is and how much she loves to spend money even though she's an accountant. I know that even though you hated being married to her, Maggie is your accountant because you trust her. Walter, I know what the woman likes and dislikes. I know how long she's been dating Charles . . . I even know the first time Charles spent the night at her house. *Why? Because you've told me.*"

After a tense moment of silence, he said, "I'm sorry about that."

"It's clear to me that you still care a great deal about Maggie. Just be honest and admit it."

"I don't hate the woman. We just couldn't make it as a couple. We have children together and so I'm concerned about the men she brings into their life."

"Your children are both in college and they live in the dorms," Lorna pointed out.

"You're right," Walter acknowledged. "I apologize." He reached over and took her hand. "Can we get back to enjoying our evening?"

Smiling, Lorna nodded.

After they finished their meal, she said, "I thought we'd go back to my house for dessert. I made something special just for you."

Walter's eyes lit up. "Not the caramel hazelnut cheesecake?"

She nodded.

When Walter let out a loud whoop in the restaurant, Lorna hid her face in embarrassment. "Control yourself," she whispered. "People are gonna think you're losing your mind, Walter."

He laughed. "Honey, you make me crazy."

Lorna released a soft sigh. "Let's get out of here."

Twenty minutes later, they were walking through her front door.

"We'll have our coffee and dessert in the keeping room," Lorna announced.

While Walter made himself comfortable, Lorna cut two slices of cheesecake and made a pot of hazelnut coffee.

She joined him on the sofa after bringing in a tray laden with dessert, silverware and coffee and setting it down on the wicker-and-glass table.

Walter loved her caramel hazelnut cheesecake and nearly swallowed it whole. Lorna had already packaged up the rest of it for him to take home.

Secretly, she hoped Walter was coming around to the idea of marriage, because she didn't intend to stay single for the rest of her life. She was smart, a great cook and, like him, owned her own business and several properties. They could be a great team together. If only Walter could see it for himself.

Lorna wouldn't push for now, but she would not wait forever.

Chapter Three

On the fourth of July, Lorna decided to spend her morning checking out the holiday sales at the mall. She'd grab something to eat at one of the restaurants, then do a little window shopping.

Straight ahead, she spotted a young woman with long braids pushing a stroller toward her. Lorna recognized her as the same woman who'd come into the bakery wanting to pay for a birthday cake with food stamps. EBT card, she amended. Even food stamps were now paperless.

The little boy's pallor hadn't changed. He looked *very* sick, Lorna noted.

When she neared them, Lorna opened her mouth to speak, but the girl dropped her head and pretended she didn't see her.

But the little boy waved and turned around in the stroller, saying something to his mother.

Lorna couldn't hear what he was saying, but she was sure it had something to do with her.

As if drawn by some unseen force, Lorna turned around and followed them into Dillard's Department store.

Lorna ventured over to the children's section when the young woman stopped in the aisle to talk to another mother.

All these young girls with babies, thought Lorna. Don't they know anything about birth control?

"Shonda . . . girl, you were on my mind," she heard her say. "Where you been?"

"Hey, Brittany. Hey there, Kendall."

Lorna fingered the delicate lace trim of a beautiful satin christening gown as she eavesdropped on their conversation. She made a mental note that the young woman's name was Brittany.

"How ya been doin'?"

"I'm doing okay," Brittany responded. "Just tired."

"You dealing with a lot."

Lorna stole a peek at the children. Brittany's son was smiling and talking to the other child, a little girl.

She turned her attention back to the two women.

"What are you gonna do for Kendall's birthday? Is he still going to the doctor?"

Shaking her head sadly, Brittany confessed, "He's in between treatments now. I'm glad because I'd hate for him to get treated on his birthday. I don't know what I'ma do for his birthday. I just don't have the money right now to have a party."

Lorna felt a tremor of regret over how she'd treated Brittany. She'd had no idea the little boy was so ill. When Brittany had mentioned that her son was sick, Lorna had just assumed she'd been lying—trying to use sympathy to get a cake.

The two women talked for a few minutes more before Brittany said, "Shonda, give me a call later. I need to get Kendall home. He's getting tired."

The women embraced before going their separate ways.

Brittany peered down at her yawning son. He gave her a tiny smile before settling back in his seat and closing his eyes. "Let's go home, little man. It's almost time for your nap."

Lorna gazed at the little boy, who still held onto his red truck even in sleep.

Brittany planted a kiss on her son's forehead before pushing the stroller toward the mall exit doors.

"Lorna . . ."

Surprised, she turned around. "Hey, Walter. What are you doing here? I thought you hated the mall."

"I . . . I came out here to pick up a couple of suits," he said, nervously.

Lorna met his gaze. "What's wrong with you?"

Before he could respond, Lorna heard a woman's voice behind her and turned.

"Walter, honey . . . I was just looking for you . . ."

Stunned, Lorna looked over her shoulder at Walter. He was here with another woman. "Walter?"

He gave a slight shrug in response.

Lorna turned to face the woman standing in front of her. She looked to be no more than thirty years old. She tossed her long curly mane over her shoulders and eyed Lorna from head to toe.

After a moment, she held out her hand. "I'm Jasminah, a good friend of Walter's. You are . . ."

Shaking Jasminah's hand, Lorna found her voice. "I'm Lorna. It's nice to meet you." After sending a sharp glance over her shoulder to Walter, who was looking quite uncomfortable with the situation, she faced Jasminah once more. "Very nice to meet you."

Lorna pretended to check her watch. "Well, I must be going. You both enjoy your day." She heard Walter call her name, but she kept going. Tears were forming in her eyes, and she refused to give him the satisfaction of seeing how much he'd hurt her.

As she neared the exit doors, Lorna broke into a run, wanting to put a wide gap between herself and Walter.

Her heart was broken.

Lorna had never considered the possibility that Walter was seeing another woman. She'd foolishly believed she was the only one in his life.

"I can't believe I was so stupid," she whispered while unlocking her car door. She climbed into her car and turned on the engine. With tears rolling down her face, she drove out of the parking lot.

A kind of numbness, like a blanket of warm air, soon engulfed her. Maybe this was just a bad dream. Walter wouldn't deceive her like this.

Not the Walter she knew.

But then, maybe the truth was that she didn't know him at all.

Walter showed up at her door an hour later. The first words out of his mouth were, "It's not what you're thinking, Lorna."

Folding her arms across her chest, she asked, "What am I thinking, Walter?"

"You think I'm involved with Jasminah."

Lorna took a deep breath. "Aren't you?" The words came out in a harsh whisper.

He didn't respond.

"Walter, I don't think we should do this. It's not like we're committed to one anoth—"

"Lorna, I care a great deal for you," Walter quickly interjected. "I haven't seen Jasminah in months. She called me last night, and when I mentioned going shopping today, she invited herself along. I'm sorry."

"You don't have anything to be sorry about."

"I hurt you. I can see it on your face. Honey, I made a mistake." Walter wrapped his arms around her. "A big mistake."

Lorna shrugged off his embrace. "I can't do this right now. Walter, you're single. Do whatever you want to do. I have no control over you, and like I said—we're not exclusive. Basically, we're just friends."

"It's more than that and you know it."

She stared at him, aghast. "*What* I know is that you never once mentioned you were seeing someone else. We've been going out for over two years."

Walter stood with his head bent as if in contemplation, lightly stroking the bridge of his nose between his thumb and forefinger. "What do you want from me, Lorna? I need to know."

She didn't hesitate. "I want you to leave."

"Lorna . . . What about the barbeque? I told Chris and Janie we were coming. C'mon, babe . . . we—"

She cut him off. "No, Walter. I . . . please, just leave."

He studied her a moment before doing as she requested.

Lorna burst into tears after Walter left. She'd wasted so much time with him. How could she have been so stupid?

But what if he was telling the truth?

The fact remained that he'd been seeing someone during the first year of their relationship and he'd kept it a secret. He'd still betrayed her.

When the telephone rang half an hour later, Lorna glanced at the caller ID.

It was Walter.

She didn't answer. As far as she was concerned there was nothing left to talk about.

Lorna turned off the ringer and spent the rest of the day in bed, just staring off into space.

She'd invested her emotions in a man who didn't deserve her, but her heart refused to evict him. She loved him more than she'd ever loved another man.

She wasn't sure she would ever get over Walter, but she had to try.

Chapter Four

Miss Lorna, you gon' be able to come to my wedding?"

"I don't know, Amanda. I have two other weddings to attend that day. I'm gonna try, though," Lorna said, escorting her customer to the door.

She didn't want Amanda hanging around the shop running her mouth about her upcoming wedding. Lately, that's all the girl could talk about—you'd think she was the only bride-to-be in the entire world.

Ever since Lorna's breakup with Walter a couple of days ago, her mood veered to anger whenever anyone mentioned getting married.

"Now you have a nice day and tell your parents hello for me."

"I will. Mama's planning to drop by the bakery because she wants to show you the flowers she wants you to put on the wedding cake. She says only fresh flowers will do."

"Okay then." Lorna urged Amanda out the door. "I'll see you next time. Drive safe."

"Miss Lorna, I really want you to come," Amanda pleaded in that whining voice of hers. "Mama says my wedding gon' be the talk of the town."

"I'm certainly gonna try. You don't want to be late for your fitting. Your wedding dress has got to be perfect . . . can't walk down the aisle looking like anything."

"Miss Lorna, you right about that. I wanna look good in my dress."

"Then you better hurry." Lorna practically pushed the girl to her car. "The last thing I need in my face right now is some blushing bride . . . ," she mumbled, walking back into the shop.

Doris and Kevin eyed her but didn't say a word. They knew it was better to keep quiet whenever Lorna was in a funk.

From the window, Lorna spied one of the caseworkers, Claire Johnson, walking with Brittany. When they neared the bakery, the two women split up.

Claire strolled into the bakery. "Hey, Miss Lorna. How you doing?"

"I'm doing okay," she responded, trying to muster

up some cheer. "Can't complain, I guess. Claire, what can I get for you today?"

"I'm craving your white chocolate cheesecake. I'd like two slices, please. I know my coworker is gonna want some, too."

"I saw you walking with Brittany. How is her little boy doing?"

"I didn't know you knew Brittany. She's such a sweet girl. Out of all my clients, I like her the best. I never have any problems out of her. That lil' boy of hers—Kendall . . . now that's a little sweetheart. He's doing as well as can be expected."

"He's very sick," Lorna murmured.

"Yeah," Claire agreed. "I keep him in my prayers. I really admire Brittany's strength and determination. She had to give up her job and her dream to go to college so that she could take care of her son."

"She wanted to go to college?"

Claire nodded. "All she's ever wanted to do. I'm telling you, Miss Lorna, this girl truly wants to make her way in the world. Just needs someone to give her a chance. A real chance."

From the way Claire talked, Brittany wasn't lazy or trying to get a free ride. Lorna desperately wanted to know more about Kendall's condition, but didn't want to press Claire for more information. Besides, Claire liked to run her mouth anyway. She would probably slip up and tell her if Lorna remained silent.

To Lorna's disappointment, Claire didn't make a slip. She purchased her cheesecake and went back to Family and Children Services, leaving Lorna to her curiosity.

The door to the shop blew open when two heavyset women stormed in.

"Afternoon, Miss Lorna," one of them greeted.

Lorna responded, "Hello, ladies. What can I get for y'all today?"

They wanted two slices of the white chocolate cheesecake. Lorna cut thick slices, set them on translucent paper, and folded it carefully.

"Isn't that Brittany Spencer over at the bus stop?" one woman asked her companion.

Lorna's ears perked up.

"Yeah . . . *that's her,*" the other women responded.

Her friend gave her a puzzled look. "Why you say it like that?"

"'Cause I don't care too much for her. Girl, Brittany think she all that. She get a check and food stamps, but she think she so much better than the rest of us."

"She like that?"

"Uh-huh. Don't get me wrong . . . I feel bad for what she got to deal with, but don't go round acting like you so much better. Least my kids got a chance of living a long time. She don't know if her boy gon' see tomorrow. I'd be there for her if she weren't so stuck-up."

"I heard he has leukemia."

Lorna dropped the knife she'd been holding. The loud clanking sound drew the customers' attention to her.

"You all right over there, Miss Lorna?"

"I'm fine," she answered, picking up the knife and moving it out of her way. "Your order's ready, ladies."

The two women picked up their slices and carried them over to one of the tables near the window, where they sat down.

"How he get leukemia?"

"I don't know. Might be something in Brittany's family or in Trader's family. You know he her lil' boy's daddy?"

"Yeah . . . I knew that."

The two women continued to discuss Brittany, but Lorna was no longer listening. It was hard to digest the fact that the little boy with the bald head and dimpled cheeks was fighting such a deadly disease.

Lorna felt the urge to make up for how she'd treated Brittany. She decided to make a special birthday cake for the little boy and prayed it wouldn't be his last. Just last year, a very good friend of hers had lost a daughter to the same dreadful disease.

She also knew of a person in her church who'd testified that God healed them of the disease. Lorna had heard that after being in remission for seven years or more, a person could be considered cured. She said a silent prayer for Brittany's son.

When Lorna got home that night, she walked into her kitchen and went to work, measuring out flour and sugar.

After the cake was done and Lorna was in the midst of icing the layers, it occurred to her that she didn't have a clue where Brittany lived. She picked up the phone to leave a message for Claire at her office, but she changed her mind. Claire would never give out Brittany's address. She would lose her job, for sure.

Lorna had another thought. She could give the birthday cake to Claire, who would make sure Brittany got it.

The next day Lorna left the shop at four-thirty and went to Family and Children Services to see Claire and drop off her gift.

Inside the building, she paused at the information desk, saying, "I'd like to see Claire Johnson, please."

The woman checked her directory. "She's on the third floor. Room 301."

Lorna navigated to the elevators and pressed the Up button.

A few seconds later, she was joined by another woman with two children in tow.

The group rode up to the third floor and got off.

Lorna followed them to the caseworkers' suite of rooms and stood in line for the sign-in sheet.

When it was her turn, Lorna said, "I'm here to

speak with Claire Johnson." In a louder voice, she added, "I'm a friend of hers and I have something to give her." She didn't want anyone there getting the wrong impression about her.

"I knew I recognized you. You're the lady from Nana's Bakery."

Lorna nodded. "I'm the owner," she announced proudly.

"Just have a seat. I'll let Claire know that you're here."

Lorna found an empty chair and sat down. She'd never been inside the building before and felt uncomfortable.

She glanced around.

It seemed like everyone was watching her. A couple of people started whispering.

Surely they can't believe that I'm here because I need food stamps? I don't need any help.

Lorna breathed a sigh of relief when Claire came to get her.

They headed to her office.

"Claire, I need you to do me a favor," Lorna told the caseworker as soon as she was seated. She quickly went over her idea.

"I can't believe you're doing this for Brittany and Kendall. This is so sweet," Claire stated. "That little boy is going to love it, Lorna. Kendall loves himself some trucks."

"I thought he might. The last time I saw him he had trucks on his shorts, trucks on his socks and a truck in each hand."

Claire laughed. "I'll call Brittany and let her know the cake is here. Thank you so much for doing this, Lorna. You have a heart of gold."

"Could you give her this note, too? I just want the child to know that I'm thinking of them."

When Lorna walked out of the building, she spotted Walter standing beside her car.

"You're not stalking me, are you?" she asked.

"I was on my way to the shop when I saw you turn in here. I figured I'd wait for you to come out of the building. You applying to accept food stamps?"

Chewing on her bottom lip, Lorna shook her head no. "I told you I would never consider accepting them. You don't listen." She unlocked the door to her car. "Well, I need to be on my way."

"Have dinner with me."

Lorna glanced up at Walter. "Why?"

"So we can talk. We really need to sit down and have a long talk. About us and our relationship. I was wrong to not tell you I was seeing Jasminah when we first started dating. But you've got to understand—I didn't know where things would go with us. When we started getting closer, I ended it with her. *That's the truth*."

"We're friends, Walter. Let's just leave it at that."

"I want more and I believe you do, too. Otherwise, you wouldn't be acting this way."

Walter was never one to skirt around the truth. He was right. Lorna wanted more from Walter. "Where do you want to go?"

"Let's go to our favorite restaurant. The one on Linden Avenue."

"I'll follow you in my car."

Why am I doing this?

Lorna knew the answer. Because she still held onto a shred of hope that she and Walter would end up together.

"I didn't know you were so jealous," Walter whispered while they waited to be seated at a table.

"I didn't know I had a reason to be," Lorna countered. "I actually never considered you were seeing anyone else."

"Jasminah and I could never have what we have, Lorna. She's young and materialistic. It's all about the dollar for her."

"Then why did you go out with her?" Lorna wanted to know.

"Because she made me feel good about myself. She stroked my ego. But it didn't take me long to figure out what she was really after."

They were led to their table by the maître d'.

The waiter arrived shortly thereafter, greeting them and taking their drink order.

"How much did she get you for?"

Walter laughed. "An apartment full of furniture."

Smiling, Lorna said, "I never knew you were so easy."

Their waiter returned with two glasses of sweet tea, sat them on the table, then pulled out a pad to write down their food choices.

"I'll have the shrimp scampi," Lorna stated. "With a baked potato, sour cream and butter only."

"I'll take the tilapia special, and I want the rice pilaf instead of a baked potato."

"Lorna, what's on your mind?" Walter inquired after the waiter walked away. "You look so sad."

"There's a little boy diagnosed with leukemia. I told you about his mother—she was the one asking about the EBT payment. If I'd known at the time just how serious the situation was, I would've worked something out with her."

"I'm sorry to hear that. It bothers me when kids suffer from these terrible diseases."

Lorna agreed. "It seems so unfair. His birthday is coming up soon."

"Are you making a cake for him?"

"I already did," she confirmed, "and gave it to the caseworker. I felt like I needed to do something nice for him."

"I'm sure she appreciated it."

"I feel bad over the way I treated her."

The food arrived.

Lorna sampled her shrimp scampi while Walter sliced off a piece of his tilapia, sticking it in his mouth.

"We need to talk about us," Walter announced after taking a sip of his tea.

Lorna nodded and sat back in her chair, bracing herself for his next words.

"Honey, I'm real sorry over the way I handled things between us. I never meant to disrespect you or hurt you in any way. And I want you to know that I have been faithful to you for a little more than a year. That's the truth."

"I know we never really talked about dating exclusively. I just assumed it was understood," Lorna responded. She ate the last of her shrimp and pasta dish.

"I'm very serious about you, Lorna. I love what we have and I don't want it to end. I hope you feel the same way."

"I do. But what about Jasminah? What are you going to tell her?"

"I've already told her on more than one occasion that we can only be friends. She knows."

"Uh-huh . . . ," Lorna muttered. She added more pepper to her baked potato. "If she knows, why did she call you the other night?"

Shrugging, Walter answered, "I don't know.

Maybe she thought that after some time passed, I'd be willing to resume our relationship."

"You aren't?"

"I only want you, Lorna. Is that clear enough?"

Later, once Lorna was home alone, she danced through her house. Maybe all was not lost where Walter was concerned. He'd finally made a commitment to her, and she was thrilled.

He would make a wonderful husband. They had a great deal in common. They both enjoyed old movies, long walks in the park and romantic dinners by candlelight. Lorna loved the way Walter serenaded her with love songs. He wasn't that great a singer, but she cherished his efforts. Walter was the type of man she'd always dreamed of. She wanted to live the rest of her life married to Walter, and if she played her cards right, she would have him.

Chapter Five

Ten days had passed since Lorna had given Claire the birthday cake, and it was becoming clear to her that she would most likely never hear from Brittany.

"Oh well . . . I tried," she mumbled to herself. Lorna looked up and saw Kevin standing in the doorway of the kitchen.

"You have a visitor," he announced.

Assuming it was Walter, Lorna paused long enough to check herself out in the bathroom mirror before walking to the front of the store.

But instead of Walter, Brittany waited for her dressed in a pair of tight denim jeans and a pink T-shirt.

Brittany stared sullenly at her, her chin assuming a defiant tilt. "Mrs. Hamilton . . . ," she began.

"It's miss," Lorna quickly corrected, hating the sound of it herself. It made her feel like an old maid. "I'm not married."

"Kendall loved the birthday cake," Brittany blurted. "Thanks for doing that." She reached inside her purse. "I want you to know that I can pay for it now. I have a little cash—"

"Didn't you read my note?" Lorna questioned. "I meant what I said. It was my present to Kendall."

"He bought a truck with the gift card you sent." Brittany gave a tiny smile. "My boy loves trucks. Keeps saying he's gonna be a truck driver like his daddy was." Her smile disappeared. "I don't want him to be anything like his daddy."

"Brittany, I know we got off on the wrong foot and I'm real sorry about that."

Shrugging, Brittany responded, "It's okay. I don't dwell too much on the past. Don't do no good."

"I agree."

"Well, that's all I came to say. I need to be going. Gotta get back to my son."

"Thanks for dropping by," Lorna commented. "I'm glad Kendall liked his cake."

Brittany hesitated a moment. "Can I ask you a question?"

"Sure. What is it?"

"Why are you being so nice all of a sudden . . ." Brittany's voice trailed off as the answer came to mind. "You *know*, don't you? You know that my son has leukemia. That's what this is all about." Sudden anger lit her eyes. "How did you find out? Did Miss Johnson tell you?"

"Claire didn't tell me anything. I overheard two women here in the shop talking about it."

"Look lady, I don't need your pity," Brittany snapped. "I'm outta here."

"Wait," Lorna called out.

Brittany stopped at the door. "What now?"

Lorna walked up to her. "Look, I don't pity you. That is not what this is about. A friend of mine lost a child to leukemia. I know how hard it can be and I guess I just wanted to do something nice for your son."

"You don't have to worry about Kendall. My son is gonna be all right. God has been with him all this time and He's not leaving him. I know it like I know my own name." She wiped away a tear.

"I didn't mean to upset you."

"I'm all right."

"You sure?"

"Really, I'm okay," she insisted. "I gotta go."

Lorna watched the young woman leave her shop and pause a moment outside to secure her braids in a ponytail before crossing the street.

Doris walked out of the kitchen. "Did she like the birthday cake?"

"Yes," Lorna answered. "I'm glad."

Doris's stomach growled, prompting Lorna to ask, "Do you eat ham and pepper jack cheese? I'm trying something new today."

Laughing, Doris replied, "You know I'm not real picky when it comes to food."

Lorna had baked some hoagie rolls with grated parmesan cheese on top, and she wanted to try it with a new sandwich combination.

Carrying a tray laden with two sodas and two sandwiches, Lorna came around the counter ten minutes later.

She sat down across from Doris. "We'd better hurry up. The lunch crowd will be blowing in soon."

Doris bit into her sandwich. After chewing and swallowing, she said, "Mmmm . . . this is so good. What did you put on it?"

"It's a new spicy mustard I found."

"It's delicious. You make sandwiches like Goldberg's Deli used to do. To be honest, I think this is better."

"I miss having them across the street. Now people are going up toward State Street where all the restaurants are."

"Somebody should open up another sandwich shop." Doris took a sip of her soda. "When they do, I hope it's a good one. Goldberg's had some real good subs."

Lorna noted a couple of familiar faces walking up to the bakery doors and announced, "It's lunchtime. Maya and Anita are here."

Doris laughed. "It must be Wednesday. They come in here every Wednesday for coffee and cream cheese danish."

"They call it cheat day. It's the one day they stray from their diets."

"I need to find a diet to cheat on," Doris responded with a chuckle as she and Lorna got back to work.

"I can't believe I'm running into you again."

Lorna turned around to find Brittany standing behind her. Kendall waved from the stroller.

"I came here to pick up some fresh catfish for dinner."

"Me, too. Pickett's got the freshest seafood in town." Brittany bent down. "Kendall, this is the nice lady that made your birthday cake. What do you tell her?"

"Thank you," he murmured.

"You're quite welcome." Lorna's heart did a tiny flip when he awarded her a big smile. "Kendall, I have to tell you. You're a very handsome little boy."

He giggled.

Lorna was handed her order. She turned to Brittany. "It's nice seeing you again, Brittany."

"You too, Miss Hamilton."

It was Brittany's turn to place her order.

Lorna eyed Brittany's soft lavender sundress with the cap sleeves. It complimented her curves but didn't give away too much. The dress looked as if it had been made for Brittany.

"You look very nice today," Lorna complimented. "I love your dress."

"I made it," Brittany stated. "Thank you."

"Really? I've always wanted to sew but never had time to learn."

"It's not hard at all. You have to be patient and good at following instructions. Just like with baking I'm sure."

Lorna played with Kendall while Brittany paid for her order.

They walked outside together.

"I hope I'm not being too personal, but how old are you?" Lorna asked after they walked out of the store.

"Twenty-one. Why?"

Lorna assessed her. "I didn't think you were that old. You look a lot younger."

Brittany met her gaze. "How old are you, Miss Hamilton?"

"Girl, I'm forty-two."

"I didn't think you were that old either. You look like you're in your thirties."

Smiling, Lorna said, "Thanks for that. I needed to hear a kind word today."

"I've had days like that," Brittany confessed.

Lorna thought back to the way she'd initially treated Brittany.

"I wasn't talking about you, Miss Hamilton."

Lorna glanced down at Kendall.

Brittany followed her gaze. "He's not a problem for me. As long as I got breath in my body, I'ma take care of him. And we do just fine, don't we, sweetie?"

Kendall nodded.

"Do you have any family around here to help you?"

Brittany shook her head. "I lost my daddy when I was about Kendall's age. My mom . . . she's an alcoholic." Her eyes met Lorna's. "I learned early on that in order to survive in this world I needed to keep my eyes on God and stay on the lookout for signs of light. If you don't, the darkness in our lives will consume us."

"Humph. I'd never thought of it that way."

"That's what keeps me going."

Lorna and Brittany said good-bye and went their separate ways. It occurred to Lorna after the fact that perhaps she should've offered Brittany and Kendall a ride.

Brittany wouldn't have accepted, Lorna decided. She was a proud young woman. This girl wasn't looking for a free ride.

Chapter Six

Dark clouds hung over Woodlake, dimming what had been a bright sunny day.

Lorna hoped the rain would hold off until she closed the shop and was at home. She didn't enjoy being out in bad weather.

She heard the door open and looked up.

"We just stopped in to say hello," Brittany stated.

Lorna came from around the counter. "Well, I'm glad you did. Hello, Kendall. How are you today?"

"Fine," he replied sweetly.

"Can I give him a cookie?" Lorna whispered.

Brittany hesitated a moment before nodding.

"I have something for you," Lorna told the little boy. "Do you like oatmeal and raisin cookies?"

Kendall nodded.

Lorna went behind the counter, put on plastic gloves and picked up a cookie.

She gave it to Kendall.

"Thank you," he mumbled between bites.

"You're welcome. Brittany, would you like one?"

"No, thanks. I'm okay. I can pay you for the cookie."

"It's my treat."

It began to rain.

Brittany glanced out the door. "We need to go. The bus should be coming soon."

"It's starting to rain harder," Lorna observed. "Maybe you two should just stay in here."

"Hopefully we'll be home before it gets too bad. I don't want Kendall getting sick." Brittany pushed the stroller toward the door.

"I'm leaving here soon. I can give you and Kendall a ride home. That way you don't have to risk him getting all wet. It won't do any good for you to get sick either."

After a moment, Brittany asked, "Are you sure this isn't taking you out of your way? I live in Madison Square Apartments."

"I don't live too far from there." Lorna headed

toward the back of the shop. "Let me get my purse and then we can leave."

Before long, they were in the car.

Lorna and Brittany made small talk on the short drive to Madison Square Apartments, located ten miles from the neighborhood of grand homes where Lorna lived.

"Thanks for the ride," Brittany said when Lorna pulled into the narrow parking lot. "I live right over there," she said, pointing to apartment fifty-two.

"What's your name?" Kendall asked from the backseat.

"You forgot my name?"

He giggled.

Smiling, Lorna replied, "My name is Miss Lorna."

"Miss Lo . . . na," he repeated slowly.

"C'mon, Kendall. We don't want to keep Miss Hamilton out in this weather."

"Her name is Miss Lo . . . na."

Lorna climbed out of the car to help Brittany with the stroller.

"I can do it," Brittany stated. "You don't need to get all wet."

"A little water don't scare me," Lorna countered. "You go on and take Kendall inside. You don't want him to get sick. I'll bring in the stroller."

Inside the apartment, Brittany's sparsely furnished living room was painted a dull beige color. A huge picture of Jesus hung above a worn, pea-green sofa.

"Thanks again."

"You're welcome, Brittany."

Kendall walked over to Lorna and wrapped his thin arms around her legs, hugging her.

"Aw, honey . . . ," Lorna murmured. "You are such a sweetheart."

"He likes you," Brittany stated. "He don't just take to people like that."

"Well, I like him, too." Lorna gave him a wink before heading to the door. "You and Kendall have a good evening. Stay dry."

"You too, Miss Hamilton."

Lorna had a date with Walter later that evening, so she rushed home to get ready.

Lorna met Walter at the restaurant promptly at eight. He greeted her with a kiss.

After they were seated, Walter inquired, "How was your day?"

She gave him a brief recap. "I saw Brittany and her son today. Remember the girl I told you about with the sick son? Well, they stopped by the shop to see me."

"That was nice of her."

"I thought so, too. That little Kendall is just the sweetest little boy. He gave me a hug when I dropped them home earlier."

"Does she have any help? What about her family?"

"I don't think she has much family around here. Her father is dead and she mentioned an alcoholic mother. I don't know about Kendall's daddy, but I'm pretty sure he's not in the picture."

After they ordered their food, Lorna said, "I really think I was wrong about her. Brittany seems like she's focused. Kendall is her priority, which is the way it should be. She's very proud, and doesn't want to accept help from anyone."

Chuckling, Walter stated, "She sounds a lot like you."

"What do you mean by that?"

"Honey, you'd die if you had to come to someone for help. It's just not in your nature. I think independence in a woman is great, but you take it to the extreme."

"Walter . . . just because I insisted on changing my own flat tire—"

"I'm not just talking about that, but yeah . . . you don't need to change tires when I'm around. Honey, I want to spoil you. I want to pamper you."

"You do all those things, Walter. But I need you to understand that it's important to me to be able to take care of myself. For whatever reason, you may not always be here. My life has to go on."

Chapter Seven

"*Your little friend is here,*" Doris announced when she strode into the kitchen.

"Who?" Lorna wanted to know. She was in the middle of decorating an anniversary cake with lavender and green flowers.

"Kendall."

"Oh my goodness," Lorna said. "What a pleasant surprise." She walked to the front of the store, where she found Brittany sitting at one of the tables with Kendall. "Hey you two," she greeted.

Kendall got up to hug Lorna. She picked him up and sat down with him in her lap.

"He wanted to come say hello. I couldn't get him to the bus stop without coming inside."

Lorna smiled at Brittany. "It's always good to see you and this little handsome fellow."

"We just left the doctor's office."

Lorna looked down at Kendall. "Did you have a good visit with your doctor?"

Kendall shook his head.

"Even though he doesn't like doctors, he was a good sport. I guess he's seen so many."

"I don't like doctors either," Lorna confessed. "But I think I know something that will make you feel better." She glanced over at Brittany, who nodded.

"What is it?" Kendall queried with a big smile.

"Oatmeal raisin cookies."

"Yeah . . ."

Lorna put Kendall down and led him by the hand to the counter, where she gave him a cookie.

"Thank you," he whispered before taking a bite.

While Kendall ate his cookie, Lorna quietly observed Brittany. She looked exhausted. There were dark circles under her eyes, and she looked like she was having trouble keeping them open.

Brittany caught Lorna watching her. "Is something wrong?"

Lorna shook her head. She picked up one of her business cards and wrote down her home number and handed it to Brittany. "Just in case you want to talk."

Brittany silently looked at the card before accepting it. Lorna suspected she would never do anything with it.

"Can I go to your house?" Kendall asked, breaking the silence.

"Sweetie, don't do that," Brittany cautioned. "You've got manners."

"Dear, it's okay," Lorna assured her.

"No, it's not. You don't go putting me on the spot like that. Kendall knows better." Brittany picked up her purse. "We need to try and catch this next bus. The five-fifteen bus is usually crowded."

Lorna's heart fell when Kendall started to cry.

"I don't want to leave."

"Don't start, Kendall. We have to go home. I need to cook dinner for us." Her voice softened. "I'm making spaghetti."

"You gon' put cheese on it?"

Brittany gave her son a big smile. "If you want me to I will."

"Yeah."

Kendall wouldn't leave without giving Lorna a big hug. She waved them off and watched them until they walked across the street to the bus stop.

She'd found a friend in the small boy. Lorna

wondered if Brittany would be offended if she bought another truck for Kendall.

I can always return it if she won't let him keep it, she decided.

Three weeks passed before Lorna saw Brittany and Kendall again. She was driving along Fitzpatrick Street when she glimpsed them getting off the bus, a block away from their apartment.

Lorna pulled over and rolled down the window. "I have something for Kendall. I can bring it by your apartment later if it's okay with you."

Brittany glanced down at her son, then over at Lorna. "Sure."

"I'll stop by around two."

"Okay."

"You coming to my house?" Kendall asked, his voice filled with excitement.

"Yes, I am," Lorna answered. "I have something for you, but I'm not gonna stay long."

"You coming now?"

"Not right now. I'll come by later." After a moment, Lorna inquired, "I can drop y'all off. I'm going right by the apartment."

"We can walk. It's just one block."

Lorna didn't push. She rolled up her window and drove off.

Two hours later, she was back on Fitzpatrick and

turning into the parking lot of Madison Square Apartments.

Lorna climbed out of her car, walked up to Brittany's apartment, and knocked on the door.

"Hey," Brittany greeted and let her inside.

Lorna noticed she'd changed from the dress she'd had on earlier into a pair of jeans and a T-shirt.

"We were coming home from church when you saw us," Brittany explained, as if she could read Lorna's thoughts. She strode over to a Formica dining table with two chairs, leaning on one for support. "Kendall, come here, baby," she called.

Lorna sat down on the pea-green sofa. It squealed in protest.

"I hope you don't mind my buying him this truck."

"It's fine. Thank you," Brittany muttered.

Kendall ran into the room. "I was in the bathroom. I had to pee."

"Kendall . . ."

Lorna laughed.

She and Kendall embraced. Then she handed him the gift bag containing the truck. "This is for you."

He jumped up and down in excitement, his joy pleasing Lorna. It thrilled her to have given him a small measure of happiness.

Even Brittany seemed affected by his delight. "Miss Hamilton, thank you so much. He's been wanting that truck for a while. You've made my son very happy."

"I'm glad."

"Miss Lo . . . na. You gon' stay and eat with us? My mama made some mac'roni and cheese. She made some chicken. I love chicken and she made some bread."

Lorna didn't know what to say. Kendall's simple invitation touched her heart. "I wish I could, but I've already made plans with someone. Maybe next time. Okay?"

Kendall looked disappointed.

"There's enough food, Miss Hamilton."

"I really do have plans." Lorna stood up. "But I don't have any for next Sunday. How about you and Kendall coming to my house for dinner?"

Shaking her head, Brittany muttered, "You don't have to do that."

"I'm serious. I'd like you and Kendall to come over."

"Kendall has to have a treatment this week. I'll have to wait and see how he's feeling by then. I still have your number."

"Fair enough."

Brittany and Kendall both escorted Lorna to the door and said their good-byes.

Brittany glanced around. "Miss Hamilton, you have a real nice house."

"Thank you, Brittany."

"I plan to one day have a small house of my own. I want to put some color on the walls—I love color. Just can't put any on. I appreciate my apartment, but I don't wanna rent forever."

"Have you considered Habitat for Humanity?" Lorna inquired from where she was standing in the kitchen. Brittany and Kendall were seated in the family room, watching television.

"Right now I wouldn't qualify," Brittany responded. "You have to have a steady income for at least a year. I haven't been able to work because of Kendall's treatments and doctor visits. This last year has been trying for my little man."

"He's such a happy little boy."

Brittany nodded. "I love that about him. Life is meant to be enjoyed . . . I want Kendall to enjoy and experience everything his life has to offer." She got up and crossed the room, taking a seat at the breakfast bar. "He deserves that."

Lorna nodded in agreement. "When did you find out that he had leukemia?"

"It was about this time last year when he started feeling bad. He was losing weight and passing out. I took him to the doctor and they tested him for everything. When they told me it was leukemia, I just about fell out the chair. I couldn't believe it."

"I can imagine," Lorna murmured while stirring the pot of collard greens.

"Those words will never leave my head. They were the scariest words I'd ever heard. But I didn't have time to fall apart. Kendall was put in the hospital and I was given papers, books . . . all this stuff I had no clue how to comprehend." Brittany gave a tiny smile. "Kendall never complained, though. Not even when his medaport was placed so he could begin chemo. He kept his beautiful smile no matter how ill the treatments made him."

Lorna removed the baked ham from the oven. Taking off the mitts, she said, "He's a very special boy. And smart. I was listening to him earlier reading his book."

"He is," Brittany confirmed. "He's memorized that story, but he's trying to read. My little man wants to learn, so I'm working with him. Kendall is God's gift to me, and I'm not taking that for granted."

"You're very wise for your age."

"Miss Hamilton, you make me sound like I'm unique or something." Brittany took a breath. "I'm not."

"I don't hear a lot of women your age talking like you," Lorna admitted. "They usually just talk about partying, getting some drug dealer to take care of them and buying designer labels."

Shrugging, Brittany stated, "I don't care about

those things. There are a lot more people that think like me."

"Not as many as you may think, I'm afraid."

"Miss Hamilton, you shouldn't be so judgmental. I'm sure a smart lady like you has heard of the saying 'You can't judge a book by its cover.'"

Lorna didn't respond.

"I have this friend—she's been trying to find a job for almost three years now. She's been on a few temp jobs, but they never hire her permanent. All she wants is to take care of her four children and get off public assistance."

"They have the same daddy?" Lorna questioned.

"No." Pulling her braids up into a ponytail, Brittany leveled her gaze on Lorna. "What's that got to do with anything? *They're hers*."

"I can't believe she can't find a job."

"Miss Hamilton, when was the last time you had to look for a job?"

"I've never had a problem getting one."

"I bet you went to college and you have a degree, don't you?"

"Yeah . . . but—"

Brittany cut her off, saying, "Miss Hamilton, we don't live in a big city. There aren't that many jobs out there for girls with GEDs or high school diplomas. Especially jobs that pay any real money."

Lorna considered Brittany's words. She hadn't really considered the fact that there might not be any jobs available. She remembered Walter saying something similar in the past.

Lorna led Brittany and Kendall to the dining room table. After saying grace, they all sat down to eat.

"I love ham," Kendall announced.

Brittany and Lorna chuckled.

"I love your kitchen," Brittany said while cutting a piece of her meat. "This whole house is nice . . . and big."

"I love having space. I wanted a huge gourmet kitchen because I love to cook—especially when it comes to baking."

"Is that why you opened the bakery?"

Lorna nodded.

"I'd planned on becoming a lawyer," Brittany announced. "I got pregnant in high school, though, and that changed some things for me. I always planned on going to college, no matter what. You might find it hard to believe, but Miss Hamilton, I'm not a dumb person."

Lorna recalled Claire telling her that Brittany had given up on college to take care of Kendall. "I . . ."

"I know what most people think about women on welfare. Like them, you probably think we're lazy, uneducated, just want free handouts and live to cheat the system." Brittany's gaze met hers. "Miss Hamilton, we're not all like that."

Lorna didn't respond. Everything Brittany was saying—Lorna believed.

"Even though I'm not on some job collecting a paycheck, I work harder and longer than most executives in their offices. Taking care of Kendall and getting him back and forth to the doctors; cleaning, laundry, and cooking . . . I barely have time to breathe. I don't know about you, but to me, this is not the lap of luxury."

"There are women who are lazy and uneducated on public assistance, Brittany. Surely, you can't deny that."

"Yes, you're probably correct. But you have to remember that sometimes things happen beyond our control that can land you in the system." Brittany took a sip of water. "Take my life, for example. Just two years ago, I worked in a hair salon as a stylist. I hated doing hair, but I knew it was only temporary. You see, I was planning to go off to Howard University in the fall." Brittany stole a peek at her son, who was seated on the floor of the family room watching a Disney movie. "Right before we were supposed to leave, Kendall was diagnosed with leukemia."

"Were you licensed?"

"Yes, ma'am. I started cosmetology school before

I graduated high school. I'd had a baby and I wanted to be able to take care of him without going on public assistance, so I figured that was the way to go. I hated it, but it was a job. *I did what I had to do*."

Lorna listened.

"I didn't want to be on welfare and I was determined to fight it. My focus changed when Kendall was diagnosed. My whole world changed. I just thank God for allowing me to be healthy enough to take care of my son."

"I've heard you mention God a few times."

Brittany nodded. "God is my strength, Miss Hamilton. He is that sign of light in my life. When Kendall's feeling up to it, we go to church. I can't say we go every Sunday, but I read my Bible."

Lorna never imagined a young girl like Brittany could be so spiritual. "It sounds like you and God are close."

"We are," Brittany acknowledged. "At least that's what I'm striving for. There are times in our lives when things just go from bad to worse. I need to be able to handle that. You know what I mean?"

Lorna nodded. She liked Brittany. The young woman was not at all what she'd imagined. Instead, she was a brave, spiritual, and intelligent twenty-one-year-old who adored her son—a son who might not grow up to be a man.

"Kendall's still on chemo but hopefully after December, he won't have to have any more."

"I'll keep him in my prayers."

A tiny voice cut into their conversation.

"Mommy, I'm tired. I wanna lay down."

Lorna rose to her feet. "Sweetie, you can lay right over here on this couch. I'll get you a pillow and a blanket."

"Can I watch cartoons?"

"If your mother says it's okay." Lorna stole a peek at Brittany, who nodded.

A few minutes later, Lorna had Kendall settled comfortably in front of the television.

She and Brittany finished dinner.

Afterward, they joined Kendall in the family room.

Kendall pointed to a picture on the fireplace and asked, "That your mama?"

"That's my grandmother. I called her Nana." Lorna lapsed into one of her favorite memories. "She and I used to make chocolate chip muffins every Saturday morning. When Nana wasn't looking, I would sneak some of the chocolate chips because I loved them."

"I like choc'late chip too," Kendall chimed in. "Mama makes me choc'late chip pancakes sometimes."

"I love those too."

Lorna could feel the heat of Brittany's gaze on her. She looked up. "I'm so glad y'all could have dinner with me."

Brittany smiled. "We enjoyed everything, Miss Hamilton." Glancing over at the clock on the wall, she added, "We don't want to wear out our welcome so we're gonna leave. Kendall, sweetie, let's get ready to go."

The little boy groaned.

"You're more than welcome to come back for a visit," Lorna assured him.

"Can we come back tomorrow?" Kendall asked, sparking laughter from both Lorna and Brittany.

"Thanks for dinner," Brittany said before she and Kendall walked out of the house.

Lorna offered to drive them home, but Brittany insisted on taking the bus, saying it was only five stops away.

Shortly after they left, the doorbell sounded, surprising Lorna. She wasn't expecting anyone.

Her lips turned upward when she found that Walter was her visitor.

"Walter Reynolds, I didn't know you were coming by this evening. I thought you were having dinner with your daughter."

"She blew me off for some boy."

He looked so hurt that Lorna wrapped her arms around him. "This will probably not be the last time something like that happens. You know?"

"I know. I just never thought it would happen to me."

Lorna spent the evening trying to make Walter feel better.

Chapter Eight

Hey Miss H. . . ."

Lorna looked up from her paperwork. A smile trembled on her lips when she spotted Kendall and Brittany. Over the course of three months, she and Brittany had grown close enough for the girl to stop addressing her so formally. "What y'all doing here?"

"We came to see you. Kendall's been asking about you all day long. We made cookies last night and he wanted to share."

"I made them for you," Kendall announced, a proud expression on his face.

"Well, aren't you just a sweetie." Lorna strode from around the counter, taking the plate of cookies

Brittany held out to her. She removed the foil, picked up a cookie and bit into it.

"Mmm . . . these are good," Lorna complimented. "You made this from scratch?"

Brittany nodded. "Yes, ma'am. We sure did. I make everything from scratch—even my yeast rolls. I'm just not real good with cakes."

"Mommy's cakes look funny all the time." He broke into laughter.

"You don't have to rub it in," Brittany chided with a chuckle. "You know you wrong."

Lorna ate another cookie. "These are really delicious. What did you put in them? Honey?"

"Yeah." Pointing at Lorna's hair, Brittany said, "Miss H. You have some pretty hair. You should wear it in a style. You always got that bun in the back."

"It is in a style . . . I got it pinned up."

"Is it all one length?"

Lorna nodded.

"Have you ever considered layering it?" Brittany inquired. "I think you'd look great with layers."

"Let me think about it," Lorna murmured. "I've been playing around with the idea of getting it cut. Would you do it for me if I decide to get it done?"

"I don't do hair anymore, but for you I'll make an exception." Brittany reached inside her purse. "I have mine in braids mostly, but this is what it looks like when I used to take time to do it."

She handed Lorna a photo.

It was a picture of Brittany and Kendall when he was a baby. From the looks of it, he was a happy and healthy infant. "You used to do your own hair?"

Brittany nodded. "Yes, ma'am. I can't afford to get it done. I gave up manicures and pedicures, too. I do my own stuff. Sometimes I make a little extra money doing some of the girls' nails around the apartment complex." She turned up her nose. "I don't mess with feet, though. They got to go somewhere else with that."

Lorna let out a small laugh.

A customer entered the bakery.

"I'll be right back," Lorna said in a low voice before moving to assist the woman.

When Lorna returned a few minutes later, she asked, "Would you mind cutting my hair for me?"

Brittany gasped in surprise. "You sure you want me to do it?"

"You're a hairdresser, aren't you?"

"Yes, ma'am. But you haven't seen my work."

"Your hair looks nice in the picture. I trust you."

"Uh . . . I think I'll buy a wig and cut that first. You can try it on and see if you like the style before we go cutting off your hair. I don't want you going into shock or anything."

Lorna burst into laughter. "I won't go into shock."

"Has your hair ever been cut?"

"No. Not really—just trimmed."

"Let's get a wig first," Brittany suggested. "I'm not sure you're ready for something like this. It might be too drastic for you. I had a woman faint on me one time after I cut all her hair off like she asked me to do."

Lorna placed a hand to her hair. "I need a change. I want a new look. Something that'll knock Walter's socks off."

"So what do you think?" Brittany asked, holding up the wig.

Lorna had picked up Kendall and Brittany and brought them over to her house. Lorna and Brittany were in the bathroom, and Kendall was sitting in the family room watching cartoons.

"It looks nice."

"Try it on."

Lorna sat down at her vanity with the wig. She studied it for a moment before placing it on her head. She turned her head to the left, then the right, surveying herself in the mirror.

"So, do you like it? I think you look good."

"I love it," Lorna murmured. She fingered the soft curls. "It makes me look kind of sexy, don't you think?"

"Sure does."

"You did a wonderful job with this wig, Brittany."

"Thanks. It's not what I want to spend the rest of my life doing, but I thought it would be a good job to get me through college. I really want to be a lawyer. I'm not giving up on my dream."

"Good for you. I'm glad to hear that. You shouldn't ever give up on dreams." Lorna removed the wig from her head. "So, you ready to cut mine just like this? I love the style. My hair won't hold curls, but maybe with layers, it will."

Lorna removed the pins from her hair, allowing it to flow around her face and shoulders. She ran her fingers through the dark tresses and said, "I'm ready. Let's do it."

When Brittany finished an hour later, she and Lorna stood together in the mirror. Soft, wispy curls fell around Lorna's face. She smiled at her reflection and shook her head to get a feel for the new cut.

Brittany moved away from the mirror. "So tell me, do you like your hair?"

Grinning, Lorna turned around to face Brittany. "I love it."

"Really?"

"Yes, Brittany. I really really love my hair. Thank you."

"You look beautiful." Brittany fell back into a nearby chair. "I used to fantasize that me and my mom would do things like this—hair and makeup." She folded her arms across her chest. "Stupid, huh?"

"No, sweetie. It's not stupid. Not at all. If I had a

daughter . . . I'd like to think she and I would do stuff like this."

"Miss H. . . ."

When she didn't finish, Lorna prompted, "What is it, Brittany?"

"Nothing." She cleared her throat. "I need to check on Kendall."

Brittany left Lorna wondering what she'd been about to say.

Walter did a double take when Lorna opened the front door the following evening.

"WOW," he exclaimed. "Baby, I love your hair. You look great."

"I don't know if I should be offended or flattered. You make it sound like I never looked this good before."

"That's not it at all. I just think you should wear your hair down more often. You look beautiful with it down."

Lorna smiled, pleased that Walter seemed to love her new look. She even felt more beautiful.

He took her by the hand and led her to his car.

"Where are we going?"

"Someplace special," was all he would tell her.

Curious, Lorna tried to coax Walter into giving her more information, but he refused.

"It's a surprise," he kept saying over and over again.

"This is an art gallery," Lorna observed when Walter pulled into a parking space and turned off the car. "Why are we here?"

"You'll see."

Walter escorted her inside. "I want you to meet this new artist. His name is Menlo."

"Menlo what?"

"He just goes by Menlo. There's a special painting I want you to see."

Curious, Lorna followed him.

Walter walked over to a portrait hanging near the gallery office.

She couldn't believe her eyes.

"This is a painting of the bakery," Lorna murmured after finding her voice. "When . . . how . . ." She couldn't seem to get the words out of her mouth.

"The artist is a friend of my daughter's, and as a special favor to me, he painted it. This is my gift to you, Lorna."

"Th-This beautiful painting is mine?" Lorna started to smile, pleased by the thought.

Walter nodded. "I know you've been looking for the perfect painting for the keeping room. So, what do you think?"

Grinning, Lorna whispered, "It's perfect, Walter. Absolutely perfect."

He gestured, getting the attention of a young man standing nearby. "I want you to meet the artist. Menlo, this is Lorna Hamilton, the lovely owner of Nana's Gourmet Bakery. Honey, this is Menlo."

"I love the painting, Menlo. You really captured the essence of Nana's. It's beautiful."

"Miss Hamilton, the honor is all mine. The bakery is one of my favorite haunts. I don't get downtown often, but when I do, I always stop in for the orange mango cheesecake."

"Menlo, I'd like to make a whole one up for you. Just let me know when you're coming downtown and I'll have it ready for you."

"Thank you, Miss Hamilton." He turned to Walter. "Will you be taking the painting with you tonight?"

"Yes. I'm sure this little lady is anxious to get it home."

"Walter, thank you so much. This means more to me than I can ever convey to you." Lorna wrapped her arms around him. "I love you."

"I love you, too. I'm glad you like the painting."

"I don't just *like* the painting, Walter. *I love it*."

Menlo had someone take down the painting.

"I love seeing you smile," Walter stated. "You and I have something special between us and we click. I like that."

"We make a great team," she responded.

Walter nodded. "We do. Yeah, I can see a bright future for us."

Lorna was still smiling when she returned home later that evening with her painting.

This was the first time Walter had brought up the subject of their having a future together. The idea of being his wife brought another smile to her lips.

Chapter Nine

You look great, Miss Lo . . . na," Kendall exclaimed when he and Brittany entered the bakery a couple of days later.

"Thank you, sweetie." Lorna planted a kiss on his forehead.

Brittany surveyed Lorna's face. "You do have a glow about you today." In a low voice, she added, "Must have something to do with Mr. Reynolds."

Lorna had introduced Walter to Brittany a little over a month ago. "Actually, it does," she confessed. Lorna told Brittany about the painting.

"That's so romantic," Brittany gushed.

"He's a wonderful man."

"You're in love with him." It was a statement.

"I am," Lorna confirmed. "And I think he's coming around to the idea of getting married again."

"Congratulations."

"Oh, no," Lorna blurted. "He hasn't asked me yet. He just kind of mentioned that he'd been thinking about us and that he could see spending his life with me. No proposal."

"I still think it's wonderful." A shadow of sadness crossed her face. "No man has ever mentioned marrying me."

"Brittany, you're still young, honey. Look at me—I'm forty-two years old and I've never been married or even close to it. Well, I take that back. I was engaged once, but he was a jerk so I don't really count it."

"I always wanted to be married before I had children," Brittany admitted. "I don't regret my son, though."

"Where is Kendall's father?"

Brittany made a face. "Incarcerated. He carried drugs across state lines for a drug dealer and got caught." She quickly added, "I didn't know anything about it. We weren't together then."

"How did you meet him?"

"He used to come to the high school to meet up with some of his boys. I thought he was cute and very cool. I was into bad boys back then." Brittany glanced down at her nails. "He used to pay me to do his manicures and then . . . things just changed between us. I thought we were in love—I was in love and he was just in lust. After being with him a couple of times, I found myself pregnant. He didn't want anything to do with me after I told him about the baby."

"You went through your pregnancy alone?"

Brittany nodded. "Pretty much. It was okay, though. I didn't want that fool around Kendall. I only want my son around good men. He needs positive role models, you know?"

Lorna nodded in agreement.

Brittany looked out the storefront window to the empty space across the street. "Someone needs to put a sandwich shop over there," she murmured. "They'd make a lot of money." Brittany checked her watch. "We need to get going. We'll see you later. I got an appointment with Miss Johnson."

"When is Kendall's next treatment?"

"Tomorrow."

"Nooo," Kendall groaned, sparking a smile from his mother.

"I know, baby. We have to do it. You know that. We want to make you all better."

"Don't like it . . ."

Soothing him, Brittany pushed the stroller toward the double doors.

Lorna called, "I'll come pick y'all up. That way you don't have to call a cab."

Brittany glanced over her shoulder. "Miss H. . . . I told you not to worry about that. We can get home."

"I want to do it," Lorna assured her. She knew that chemo made Kendall weak, and having to wait on a cab didn't make it any better for him.

The more she got to know Brittany, the more the young woman reminded Lorna of herself. Walter was right. They were both independent spirits. Lorna knew Brittany would never ask anything of her unless she desperately needed help.

Brittany and her son were becoming very dear to her—something she'd never expected to happen.

Brittany called Lorna in hysterics a week later.

"Miss H., can you come to the hospital? Kendall's not doing too well." Brittany's voice broke. "I n-need y-you."

"I'll be right there."

Brittany was in the hallway speaking to the doctor when Lorna arrived twenty minutes later.

Lorna waited a few feet away before joining Brittany when the doctor walked off. "How is Kendall?"

"The doctors haven't told me anything yet." Brittany wiped away her tears. She suddenly reached out and embraced Lorna, surprising her. "I'm so scared."

"He's gonna be fine," Lorna whispered. "We have to believe that."

"I can't l-lose my s-son. He's all I h-have."

Lorna closed her eyes and said a quick prayer.

An hour slowly ticked by, then another. While Brittany was speaking to one of the nurses, Lorna remembered she had a date with Walter. She made a mental note to call him. Right now, she didn't want to make a move without knowing what was wrong with Kendall.

Brittany couldn't sit still. She went back to see Kendall and sit with him for a while before returning to the waiting room. When the doctor arrived, she motioned for Lorna to join her.

"He has a staph infection," the doctor announced. "We're going to remove his medaport and give him some antibiotics. Hopefully, it should clear right up."

"He's so weak," Brittany stated.

"We're going to keep a close eye on him. Kendall's already getting two antibiotics in his system and I'm adding a third. I really think in a few days the infection will be gone."

When the doctor left, Brittany broke down in tears.

"It's all right," Lorna soothed. "I'm here now. It's all right now."

Composing herself, Brittany said, "Let's go inside. If Kendall's awake, he's gonna get upset if I'm not there. He's already mad because I let the doctor do all those things to him. He hates coming to the hospital."

Lorna nodded in understanding. She didn't like hospitals either.

"Kendall can't give up now. He's got to keep fighting." She gazed at her sleeping son, tears rolling down her cheeks. "I . . ."

Lorna embraced her. "He's gonna be fine. Kendall's a fighter, Brittany."

"I'm trying so hard to be strong . . ." She shook her head. "It's not always easy."

"I can only imagine." Lorna escorted Brittany over to a chair. "Sweetie, sit down. I don't want you passing out on me."

"I'm so tired."

"I know you are. Why don't you go home and let me stay with Kendall tonight?"

"Miss H., I can't leave my baby."

"Then at least try and get some sleep. I'll stay up while you rest."

"You sure you don't mind?"

"I wouldn't have offered if I didn't mean it."

Brittany glanced over at the reclining chair in the corner.

"Go ahead," Lorna urged. "Get some sleep."

"You'll wake me if Kendall needs me?"

"Of course."

Brittany slept for three hours.

"Feel better?" Lorna asked.

"Yes." Brittany jumped to her feet. "How's Kendall doing? Did he wake up?"

Shaking her head, Lorna replied, "He's sleeping

peacefully. The nurse was just in here to check on him. He's improving. The antibiotics are working."

"Thank you, Jesus," Brittany murmured. "I'm so grateful . . ."

Lorna glanced at the clock on the wall and remembered she was supposed to cancel with Walter. She rose to her feet. "I'm gonna go make a quick call, then I'll be right back."

"Okay."

Lorna walked to the nearest exit and stepped outside to use her cell phone.

Lorna placed a call to Doris first. "I won't be in tomorrow. Could you see if Charlotte can come in tomorrow morning? If she can't, I know Kevin won't mind. He doesn't have class on Wednesdays."

Lorna's second call was to Walter. He answered on the second ring. "Hey babe, where are you?"

"At the hospital with Brittany."

"Everything okay?"

"It is now," Lorna responded. "Sorry about tonight. I know you really wanted to see that movie."

"We can do it another night. Want me to come out there?"

"You don't have to. Kendall's gonna be fine. He has a staph infection but the doctors are giving him antibiotics. He should feel up to his old self in a few days."

"Then it's not the disease progressing?"

"No, it's not. Thank the Lord . . ."

"I'll keep him in my prayers."

"You do that," Lorna encouraged. "I'll give you a call later."

She knew Walter cared just as much about Brittany and Kendall as she did, which is why it didn't surprise her when he showed up forty-five minutes later.

They stayed at the hospital with Brittany until one of the nurses forced them to leave.

Five days later, Kendall was able to leave the hospital.

Lorna prepared a couple of casseroles for Brittany so that she didn't have to worry about cooking. She and Walter took them over one evening after she closed the bakery.

Brittany embraced her. "Miss H. . . . you didn't have to go through all this trouble. Thank you, though. I appreciate it."

Lorna heard Kendall call out for her and headed to his bedroom. She was totally unprepared for the narrow room—it was just big enough for the bed and dresser. Posters of Michael Jordan, Shaq and Kobe flanked the otherwise bare walls.

Kendall looked so tiny in the twin bed beneath a blue-and-white sports-themed comforter. Lorna planted a kiss on his forehead. "Hey, handsome."

"I knew you were here. I heard your voice. Will you tell me a story about Nana?"

Lorna laughed. "You like hearing about my nana, huh? She woulda loved a little sweetie like you."

Walter joined her a few minutes later.

Lorna began her tale of Nana and the Easter Bunny at the mall.

"See what you started," Brittany said as she entered the bedroom carrying a tray of food.

"I don't mind telling him about Nana. I wish y'all could've met her. She was something else."

Walter and Lorna stayed until Kendall fell asleep. Brittany walked them to the door. "Thanks for the food and for coming by to see us. Kendall and I appreciate it."

"It was our pleasure," Lorna and Walter said in unison.

Lorna wished she'd been blessed with a daughter like Brittany. For one so young, she was a devoted mother. She'd been dealt a serious blow, but she fought back with faith and optimism.

Brittany was an inspiration to Lorna.

Chapter Ten

Lorna and Brittany took Kendall on a picnic the Saturday before Labor Day to celebrate his coming home from the hospital the week before.

"I love coming here." Brittany fell back on the blanket.

"This is one of my favorite places, too. I used to bring my grandmother out here." Lorna poured a cup of lemonade and handed it to Kendall. "Here you are, sweetie."

Brittany pulled out a sandwich and offered a portion of it to her son.

"That looks good," Lorna complimented. "Did you make it?"

Brittany nodded. "Yes, ma'am. I sure did." She gave Lorna the other half. "Here, try it."

Lorna bit into the sandwich. "Mmmm . . . this is delicious."

Brittany had placed layers of ham, salami, pepperoni, onion, green pepper, tomatoes, lettuce, Swiss cheese and Italian salad dressing on a French roll.

"I hated when Goldberg's Deli closed down," Lorna said when the sandwich was gone. "I miss the Italian panini. The mortadella, salami, capicolla and provolone . . . mmmm . . . with that basil mayo . . ."

"Why don't you open a sandwich shop?" Brittany suggested. "You make great sandwiches, and then with the bakery across the street . . . Miss H., you can make a lot of money between the two shops. You'd own that corner. I think it'd be a smart business move."

Lorna handed Kendall one of his toys as she considered Brittany's suggestion.

"Tell me something, Miss H. Why are you spending all this time with me and Kendall? What about your own family? Do you see them often?"

"I don't really have much family left to speak of," Lorna explained. "Not anybody close. I never really met my daddy's people. I just know they live somewhere in Toronto."

"Your dad was from Canada?"

Lorna nodded. "My aunt told me we lived in Toronto until my dad died. I was a year old when he was killed by a drunk driver. My mama and I moved to Philadelphia to live with my aunt. But then my mama got sick and she died when I was four."

"My dad died when I was three years old," Brittany interjected. "It didn't take long for my mom to remarry. I hated Leon. He wasn't too nice to me and when I told my mom, she did nothing. Just said I had to obey him."

"He didn't . . ."

Brittany shook her head. "Oh no. I woulda kilt the man. No, it weren't none of that. He was just mean as all get-out, but he never touched me."

"Were you and your mother close?"

"Not really. She was more concerned about Leon and what he was doing. My mom was always running up in some other woman's face about him. She loved that man to death. I don't know why. When he left her, she started drinking and she's never stopped. Now she's a full-time alkie."

"I'm so sorry, Brittany."

"Don't be. It's not your fault." Shrugging, she added, "I don't want to waste my time talking about her. Kendall and I got enough on our own to deal with. We don't need her problems, too."

Lorna changed the subject by asking, "How did Kendall's checkup go yesterday?"

"The blood counts all came back just fine. We have to go again in November. It's nice waiting two months in between appointments."

Lorna loved the way Brittany was able to find a sign of light out of something as simple as doctor appointments.

Brittany finished off her sandwich. She pulled out a bag of potato chips and opened them.

"I can't eat another bite," Lorna declared. "That sandwich was filling."

"Kendall ate half of mine, so I'm still hungry."

"There's still another one in the basket."

"These chips should hold me okay. I don't think I could eat a whole half, and I don't want to waste it. I can take it home with me and eat it later."

On the way back to Brittany's house, the subject of opening a sandwich shop came up again.

"I'm telling you, Miss H. . . . you should really think about getting that space and opening up a sandwich shop of your own. You'd make a lot of money."

"I'm gonna really think about it. You may be on to something."

Lorna mulled over Brittany's suggestion for the rest of the evening after arriving back at her own house. She'd been thinking about opening up a second bakery, but the idea of a sandwich shop . . .

She decided to discuss it with Walter. She valued his opinion and trusted him. He would help her make the decision. She decided to drop by his house to talk about it.

"Brittany suggested I open another sandwich shop where Goldberg's was. What do you think?"

"It's a good idea. I was actually thinking about something like that myself."

"Why don't we do it together?" Lorna suggested. "We could be equal partners."

"You know . . . I'd like that. In fact, I was thinking along the lines of equal partnership when I called you earlier."

"I'm not following you."

"Lorna, I think it's time we talked seriously about marriage."

Her mouth dropped open in surprise.

Walter laughed. "Don't look so shocked, honey."

"Well, I am. I didn't think you were really thinking about getting married—especially now."

"Lorna, I love you and I'd like to spend the rest of my life with you. I know you can't have kids and I have to be honest—I'm not interested in raising any more. I want to spend the rest of our lives traveling and just enjoying each other."

"This sounds nice, Walter. It really does, but I am committed to helping Brittany and Kendall. They are a big part of my life now. I'm not gonna walk away from them. Too many people have already done that."

"I understand that. Hey, I know Brittany is like a daughter to you now and it doesn't bother me at all. I like the girl and her son. I don't mind playing the part of grandfather to Kendall."

"So is this it?" Lorna asked. "Are you proposing to me?"

"I hope I don't have to get down on my knees or anything. You know if I get down there, I might not be able to get back up."

Laughing, Lorna shook her head.

"Woman, are you gonna marry me or not?"

Folding her arms across her chest, Lorna replied, "You better think of a better way to phrase that question, Walter. I'm not desperate, you know."

Chuckling, Walter pulled out a small black velvet box and opened it to reveal a gorgeous emerald-cut diamond engagement ring. "Lorna, honey, will you do me the honor of becoming my wife?"

"Yes," she whispered. "I would love to be your wife."

He slipped the ring on her finger, then pulled her into his arms and kissed her.

Later, at Lorna's house, Walter brought up the subject of marriage again.

"I was thinking we could go down to the courthouse and get married. Instead of some big fancy ceremony, we could just have a real nice reception. What do you think?"

Appalled at the suggestion, Lorna said, "I don't

intend to get married at some courthouse. I've been waiting too long for my wedding day for something so . . . so tawdry."

"You want a big wedding?" Beads of perspiration popped out on his forehead as he pulled out his checkbook.

Laughing, Lorna replied, "Walter, you can put the checkbook away. I don't need nothing big. We can have a small wedding in the backyard at the house."

"I can just wear a suit?"

"Yeah. It's not gonna be something formal. I'm gonna throw on a nice dress—nothing long. We can just invite family and close friends."

"I like that idea. How soon can you plan everything?"

"You sound like you're ready to get married. How does two weeks sound?"

"Like long enough."

Lorna burst into laughter. "You're ready to move out of that town house of yours?"

He nodded. "I'm gonna give away most of the stuff I have—none of it looks as nice as yours."

"Walter, you own a furniture store. Your town house is decorated beautifully, so what are you talking about?"

"I was thinking Brittany could use a lot of it. That couch of hers has seen its last days."

"Yeah," Lorna agreed. "She told me all of her furniture was secondhand. Brittany is such a sweet person. She's appreciative of everything."

"That's why I don't mind giving her my furniture. The girl deserves a break in life."

Chapter Eleven

"*Walter and I are getting married,*" Lorna announced when she arrived at Brittany's apartment.

The two women embraced.

"*Congratulations*. I knew it was gonna happen. I told you. . . ."

"I didn't think he was ready, though." Lorna hugged herself and turned in a circle. "I'm getting married!" Turning around to face Brittany, she continued, "I'm getting married in two weeks."

"*Two weeks*. So soon?"

Lorna nodded. "I need you to help me plan my wedding. It's not gonna be anything big. Just a simple ceremony in my backyard."

Lorna sat down on the ugly pea-green sofa, resisting the urge to tell Brittany about Walter's plan of giving her his furniture. Lorna wanted him to have the pleasure of telling her himself.

Brittany pulled out a pen and small notebook from her purse, then sat down beside Lorna. "Just tell me what you want me to do."

"I'm thinking we could use handmade paper for the invitations, something with pressed flower petals and a velum overlay."

"Sounds like you've already got this wedding planned."

"I've dreamed of my wedding day a long time." Smiling, Lorna added, "I've had years to perfect it."

"So what else do we need? Are you gonna need any ribbon for the invitations?"

"Yeah. Putting ribbon around the invitations is a good touch. We'll need solid tablecloths and vintage overlays for the tables. We can have buffet-style catering with large clear glass jugs of lemonade, punch and sweet tea in keeping with the tone of the wedding."

She waited for Brittany to finish writing her notes before continuing. "We can rent a trellis and decorate it with ivy, Spanish moss and fresh flowers. After the wedding, we can place the cake table underneath it. What do you think?"

"I think it all sounds very romantic. If I ever get

married, I want you to plan my wedding. Now, what about your dress?"

"I have to go out and look for one. What about you? Do you have a dress for the wedding? I'd like for you to be my maid of honor."

Brittany's brows rose a fraction. "You want *me* to be in your wedding? Are you serious?"

"Yes, I am. It would mean a lot to me."

"As a wedding gift to you, Miss H., I'd love to make your dress for you. We could find a pattern for the dress or you can give me a picture."

"You make some beautiful clothes. I think you missed your calling as a designer. Let's see, I want something romantic and kind of old-fashioned. My house is Victorian, and I want the wedding theme to match the house since we're getting married there."

"I can come up with a nice dress for you. Trust me, Miss H. I won't let you down. I want your wedding to be everything you've ever dreamed."

"With you helping me, I know it will."

Surrounded by close friends in the backyard of her house, Lorna became Mrs. Walter Reynolds shortly after five-thirty on the first Saturday in October.

Garbed in the dress Brittany had designed for her, Lorna had never felt so beautiful in her life. Her dress featured delicate layers of chiffon cascading downward to an asymmetrical hemline. The bodice had spaghetti straps that tied at the shoulders, while the back had delicate crisscross ribbon cords, giving the dress an authentic vintage look.

Brittany had even styled Lorna's hair reminiscent of the '30s. And she'd outdone herself on her own dress, which featured an embroidered tulle lace overlay on a satin chemise sheath with a round neckline and three-quarter-length sheer lace embroidered sleeves.

To give it a more vintage look, Lorna had suggested that Brittany give it an antique lace scalloped hemline.

Lorna glanced around the backyard, making sure their guests were comfortable. They'd used soft pink chair covers and tied them with a white sash. Before each sash was tied, Brittany had placed a single flower bud in each knot.

Coffee was served in vintage teacups and saucers from local flea market finds. Pleased with her choices, Lorna relaxed and prepared to enjoy the celebration.

Today was her day. The ceremony was perfect—just as Lorna had always dreamed.

She was Walter's wife, and now his children were also her children. Brittany and Kendall were an extension of that family. All she'd ever really wanted was family, so Lorna couldn't complain. God had blessed her with all she'd asked for, and she was humbled by that fact.

"Walter and I made a decision," Lorna announced a couple of days after returning from her honeymoon in Cancun, Mexico. "We're going to open the sandwich shop across the street."

"That's great news! North Main is the busiest street downtown, and with all the businesses around the area, y'all are gonna make a lot of money."

"You know, Brittany . . . I've been praying about something. I really misjudged you when we first met. I never realized that beneath all the gold bangles, the braids, long nails, there was a bright, ambitious young woman just trying to make a way for herself and her son."

Brittany gave a tiny smile.

"You're trying so hard and I want to help you. Years ago, I put away money for my future children's education. I had no idea at the time that I would never be a mother."

Brittany held up her hand. "Miss H. . . ."

"Let me finish." When Brittany nodded, Lorna continued, "I have a friend who's a retired nurse. She's willing to stay with Kendall in the evenings while you attend class in the fall."

Shaking her head, Brittany said, "I can't let you

do this. You should keep your money. You've worked hard for it."

"You can't stop me, Brittany. I believe in you and I know one day you're gonna be a wonderful lawyer. Look at it this way, I'm investing in your future."

Tears streamed down Brittany's face.

"There's one other thing. I'd like for you to help me out in the sandwich shop from time to time. Your hours won't interfere with your studies or Kendall's doctor appointments. I promise."

"I don't believe this . . . this has been my prayer for such a long time . . . I just needed a chance to go to college . . ." Brittany shook her head. "Miss H., thank you so much."

"I thought everything was fine with me because I was successful, but I didn't even realize that I was drowning in my own darkness. I didn't know it until I met you. You're my light, illuminating the path for my life. Thank you so much for that."

"Miss H., you're the closest thing to a mother for me. Would you mind if Kendall and I called you Auntie?"

Tears in her eyes, Lorna smiled. This was as close to having a daughter as she would come. Brittany and Kendall filled the empty void in her life. "It would be an honor," she replied, swiping at her eyes. "Okay," she murmured. "No more crying."

"Thank you so much, Miss H. . . . I mean Auntie." Brittany paused and took a deep breath before continuing. "Auntie, there are a lot of women out there like me. Single mothers doing the best they can with what they have. All they need is a chance. You've given me a wonderful opportunity, and I was thinking that maybe you could help other women too by giving them jobs. You could use some more help in the bakery, and now with the sandwich shop, you're gonna need employees."

Lorna smiled. "I like that idea. I'll talk to some of the caseworkers. Maybe they could give me referrals."

Brittany nodded. "They'll have an idea which of their clients are serious about finding work."

Lorna nodded. "When I talk to Claire, I'll find out if social services can come up with a program and invite the surrounding businesses to participate."

"I'm so excited. It's a blessing to know that there are still some phenomenal people in the world. People who still care about others. Auntie, you didn't have to do any of this for me. When you sent me out of your bakery that day, you didn't have to look back, but you did."

Lorna picked up her glass and took a sip of lemonade. "There was always something about you, Brittany. It wasn't just Kendall's illness that drew me to you. And it was no accident the day you came into the shop. We were meant to meet and become the people we are today. You were supposed to change my way of thinking. You've opened my eyes, Brittany. I see things in a much different way now. And I'm gonna do something about it. I'm gonna give some of these girls a chance. Men too."

Brittany grinned. "I know you're gonna bless everyone that is fortunate enough to know you. Anyone looking for signs of light only has to meet you."

Touched beyond words, Lorna could only smile.

Faith Will Overcome

ReShonda Tate Billingsley

Chapter One

You's a tramp. Grandma Pearl's words rang loudly in Faith Logan's head. It's as if her overly religious grandmother were sitting right in the motel room spewing the words herself.

Faith stared at the balding, brown-skinned man who looked like he was seven months' pregnant. The sight of him actually made her stomach turn. *So why are you laid up in this seedy motel room with him then?* Grandma Pearl's voice seemed to say. It was a question Faith couldn't answer.

Faith felt a lump begin to form in her throat as she took in her surroundings. The spring rain was beating softly on the roof, creating what should have been a cozy atmosphere. But there was nothing cozy about the dingy yellow walls, dirty carpet, and stale-smelling motel room. They were in a motel because he didn't want to go to her place—"someone might see" them. But why hadn't she at least made him take her to the Hyatt or something? She worked as a maid in a seedy motel just like this one. She definitely didn't want to spend her day off in one.

Faith bit down on her bottom lip as she watched her latest liaison get dressed. She always started out trying to act lackadaisical about what she was doing, but it never ended that way. By the time the guy was gathering up his clothes to go, she felt like the worthless piece of crap Grandma Pearl always said she was.

"Umphhh, Sweet Thang. Big Daddy got you crying." The fat man chuckled as he reached down to caress her cheek. She scooted back, not even aware that she was indeed crying. "Yep," he gloated as he stuck out his chest and rubbed his belly. "Big Daddy does that to women. It just comes with the territory."

Faith wanted to scream at him to stop referring to himself in the third person. She'd been hoping this time would be different. Even though he was overweight, unattractive, and did nothing for her, he was a powerful man, and being with him would make people stop thinking she was a tramp. Faith brushed her golden-colored curls out of her face and forced herself to smile.

"I thought you said we were gonna hang out, maybe go catch a movie or something," Faith said softly.

"Nope, Big Daddy gots to go. The old lady will be home from church soon, and Big Daddy don't want to hear her mouth." He slipped his arm into his wrinkled, dingy white dress shirt.

Faith felt her frustration mount. One minute he was telling her how unhappily married he was, and how he was going to leave his wife so he and Faith could start building a life together. The next, he was trying to rush home.

"I'm starting to feel like this relationship is headed nowhere," Faith groaned.

"Look, would you stop nagging me?" he said as he sucked in his stomach and tried to button his pants.

Faith debated responding, then decided against it because she simply did not feel like arguing. How could she let herself be fooled again by a man's empty promises? Faith tried to shake off the melancholy thoughts creeping through her mind. Although she envisioned a decent, stable life with him, deep down she knew being with him wasn't what she wanted.

Still, she couldn't understand how she kept ending up in these situations. She was a beautiful woman. Men told her so almost every day. They loved her smooth caramel-colored skin, five-eight frame and 38-26-36 measurements. Although she'd never gone to college, she had graduated high school with a B average and considered herself pretty intelligent. She'd had plans to get out of her small hometown of Beaumont, Texas, where success was not something most people strived for. It was her dream to move an hour up the road to Houston. She'd promised herself she'd be gone by her twenty-fourth birthday, but that had come and gone five months ago and she was still in Beaumont. Her time was coming, though, but for right now she was working at a flea-trap motel in order to save enough money to go to beauty school when she finally did move to Houston. Her dream was to one day have her own beauty shop, maybe even her own line of beauty products. Those dreams were much too big for Beaumont, and she thought this man understood that. In fact, he had promised to move to Houston with her and help her open her own business.

Between her ambition and good looks, Faith couldn't for the life of her understand why she couldn't find a meaningful relationship.

"You keep making all of these promises, telling me you are goin' to leave your wife because she doesn't make you happy," Faith reminded him. Even though she wasn't remotely attracted to the deacon standing before her, she yearned to be a part of something bigger than herself. A normal relationship. Even if it was with fat, snobby Deacon Eli Wright.

"What's that you say?" he responded.

Faith slumped back against the headboard and crossed her arms. "Never mind."

"You need to stop talking all that nonsense about us being together. You know all that stuff I said wasn't nothing but pillow talk. I'm a happily married man."

Faith lowered her head in shame. "So what are you doing here then, Mr. Happily Married?" she mumbled.

Deacon Wright frowned before breaking out into a big smile again. "'Cuz you the best this side of the Mississippi." He laughed as he headed to the door. "Plus, Big Daddy knows you'll give it to me anytime I want it."

Chapter Two

Jasmine Davis moved the black Wet 'n Wild eyeliner pencil across the edge of her top lip. After doing the same to her bottom lip, she filled in her lips with vibrant red lipstick before blowing herself a kiss in the mirror.

"Would you hurry up?" Faith moaned to her best friend of fifteen years. She was still in a foul mood over Deacon Wright's comments yesterday. Each time she thought about how she had allowed herself to be so blind to his ways, she became more and more angry. Faith had thought that agreeing to a blind date with a friend of Jasmine's boyfriend might be the way to get her mind off Deacon Wright, but now she wasn't so sure. Faith had even tried to back out when she'd first arrived at Jasmine's apartment, but Jasmine had done her usual begging and pleading and, like always, had managed to convince Faith to give in.

Faith glanced around Jasmine's small, cluttered bedroom. Jasmine was the master at getting men to give her things—like the fifty-two-inch TV, queen sleigh bed and matching dresser, and the plethora of knickknacks that adorned her apartment. Faith told her friend constantly that she needed a bigger place than the small one-bedroom apartment, but Jasmine wouldn't move because she knew it was only "a matter of time" before she hit pay dirt with a Prince Charming who was going to whisk her off to some fifteen-thousand-square-foot mansion.

"How much longer are you going to take?" Faith asked. She was starting to get an uneasy feeling in the pit of her stomach.

"You can't rush perfection," Jasmine replied as she fluffed out her braids, then brushed her hands down her neon green mini-mini skirt. She also wore a black backless halter top that, although it looked a size too small, still flattered her size eight body. She turned around and surveyed her backside in the full-length mirror.

"Does my booty look too big in this skirt?"

"Yes."

"Good," Jasmine laughed. "Let's go."

Faith shook her head at her friend and followed her out of the apartment and downstairs to the waiting souped-up Monte Carlo. The two men inside didn't bother getting out to greet them.

"Fool, ya'll gon' open the door or what?" Jasmine snapped as she stood in front of the car with her hands planted firmly on her hips.

The driver, Jasmine's on-again, off-again boyfriend Tyrone, flicked his Swisher Sweet out of the window and smiled seductively. "Depends."

"Look," Jasmine said, "we do have our own transpo, so don't act like you doing us any favors." Jasmine wiggled her neck in true sista-girl fashion, her braids flying side to side.

"Girl, you know I'm just messing with you. Get in." Tyrone stepped out of the car and pushed his seat up so Jasmine could climb in the back. Jasmine shot him a mean look.

"I know you don't think I'm getting in the back. Make that trifling friend of yours get in the backseat."

Tyrone's friend, a burly, big-necked man named Truck, shot Jasmine the finger.

"You wish you could, you big ape-looking—"

"Chill," Tyrone cut Jasmine off. Faith stood outside the car groaning, wondering why she'd ever let Jasmine talk her into going on a blind date with somebody who took pride in calling himself Truck.

"You betta act like you know," Jasmine quipped.

Tyrone leaned into the car. "Truck, man, get in the back and let my lady sit up front."

Truck rolled his eyes but still didn't say anything as he stepped out of the car and moved to the backseat.

Jasmine smiled at Faith. "See, that's what I'm talking about," she said, holding the seat forward for Faith to get in the back. "You got to make these fools respect you."

Faith looked at her friend. As much as she loved Jasmine the girl was almost laughable. Respect? Jasmine didn't mind sleeping with anything moving, as long as he had money in the bank and could pay her bills. Jasmine might be a crazy gold digger, but they'd been friends since before either of them even had interest in boys. Jasmine had been the one to fight off everyone at school who'd bad-mouthed Faith's mother. Faith knew that no matter what, Jasmine had her back.

Faith sighed as she climbed in next to Truck. He didn't even look her way. He just sat like he was mad about having to ride in the back.

"Ummm, how are you? I'm Faith," she finally said after it became evident that Truck wasn't going to talk to her.

"What up?"

Faith forced a smile and sat back as Tyrone started the car and took off.

"It looks like it's gonna rain," Faith said after more silence.

Truck looked at her like she was crazy.

She fidgeted before asking, "So, how do you know Tyrone?"

"That's my boy. We did time together," Truck replied nonchalantly.

Oh, great, Faith thought. Jasmine had conveniently left out the fact that Truck was an ex-con. That was probably because Jasmine didn't think hanging out with criminals was any big deal. But for Faith, convicts were an immediate turnoff. *Jasmine owes me big for this one,* Faith thought.

They pulled into the civic center, where they were going to see rapper/producer Kanye West perform. Faith pulled Jasmine aside when the men went to get the tickets.

"Why didn't you tell me he was an ex-con?"

"You didn't ask," Jasmine shrugged.

"Come on, girl. I mean, I know I was only coming along 'cause you begged me to, but I at least thought maybe you'd set me up with somebody with potential. How you gon' do me like that? You know I don't want nobody who's been to jail."

Jasmine rolled her eyes. "Oh, I keep forgetting you a ho with morals."

Faith looked at Jasmine in shock. "I can't believe you just said that."

"What? Called you a ho?"

"Yes."

"So? What's the big deal? I'm one, too. The only difference is you a free ho. I'm an expensive one." Jasmine flashed a cheesy grin. "You go out looking for love and happiness and all that other bs. I'm looking to use what I got to get what I can."

Faith stared at her friend in disbelief. Grandma Pearl used to always say you are a reflection of the company you keep. Maybe Grandma Pearl was right.

Jasmine gently pushed Faith's shoulder. "What you doin', gettin' all sensitive on me? You know I'm your girl. I'm just messing with you. Dang."

"Whatever." Faith hated giving Grandma Pearl any credit, but how would Faith ever better her life hanging around people like Jasmine?

Tyrone and Truck returned with the tickets, and Faith put Jasmine's comments to the back of her mind as they walked into the civic center.

Faith was surprised that she actually managed to enjoy the concert.

Afterward, they headed to a local lake and parked. Tyrone said they were just going to sit and shoot the breeze, but as soon as they parked, Tyrone and Jasmine commenced making out in the front seat. Without saying a word, Truck, who had said little to Faith all night, began removing his shirt.

"Excuse me. What are you doing?" Faith asked.

"What does it look like?" he replied as he continued to pull his shirt over his head. Faith almost gagged at the sight of his massive, hairy chest.

"I'm sorry, but this ain't even that kind of party."

Truck looked at her like she had lost her mind. "You for real?"

"Are you? I'm not doing anything with you."

"Ain't this a trip?" He reached up and hit Tyrone in the arm. "Say, man, I thought you said if I bought these tickets, she'd be down for whatever."

Tyrone came up for air, looking thoroughly agitated that Truck seemed to be disrupting his groove.

"Come on, Faith, don't be like that," Tyrone moaned.

"Y'all are out of your minds," Faith said.

"Jasmine, talk to your girl." Tyrone sat back in the seat, clearly frustrated.

Jasmine turned around and leaned toward the backseat. "Let me holla at you outside."

Faith shot Truck a nasty look, then climbed out of the backseat. She wasn't out of the car before Jasmine turned on her. "Dang, Faith, we just having a good time. Didn't you have fun at the concert?"

"Yes, but not enough to sleep with Atilla the Hun in the backseat of a Monte Carlo," Faith replied.

"Why are you trippin'?"

"No, Jasmine, why are *you* trippin'? I'm not doin' anything with him."

Jasmine sighed in frustration. "I don't get you. Why you try to get picky about who you sleep with? You laid all up in a motel with that fat, nasty deacon, but you got a problem with Truck. He ain't the cutest thing, but he better than Deacon Wright."

"Jasmine, Eli and I had a relationship that was headed places." Faith looked away. "I mean, at least I thought it was."

"Don't be stupid all your life, Faith. The deacon only wanted what Truck wants. And at least Truck came up off some Kanye West tickets. What you get out the deal with Eli?"

Faith stared at her friend. The older she got, the more she wondered how she and Jasmine remained friends. Jasmine saw them as one and the same, but Faith didn't sleep with just anyone. She reserved herself for men she thought she'd have a future with. It wasn't her fault that most of the guys she dated were full of it and didn't turn out to be what she'd expected. But the one thing she did know was that she didn't see any future with Truck and therefore he wouldn't be seeing any part of her body.

Just then Truck rolled his window down. "Look here, either you get back in this car and come up out that dress, or somebody need to give me my fifty dollars back for them tickets," he said.

Faith looked back and forth between Truck and Jasmine with disgust. She reached in her little coin purse, pulled out a twenty-dollar bill—all the money she had until payday—and flung it at Truck. "Get the rest from Tyrone!"

Faith spun around and walked off, not caring that she had at least a thirty-minute walk home. That was a small price to pay for that very expensive lesson: no more blind dates with Jasmine.

Chapter Three

It had been a long day. Faith had worked a full nine hours cleaning rooms at the motel, and she was worn out. But today was the second Sunday, the day she usually went to check on Grandma Pearl. She was always scared that the one day she didn't go by there, they'd find her grandmother dead inside or something and Faith would never be able to forgive herself.

Faith stood at the entrance to Grandma Pearl's weathered-down one-story house. The place had definitely seen better days. The yellow paint was chipped in several places, displaying rotten wood. The porch looked like it was about to cave in, and the screen door was barely hanging on.

Growing up, this place had been like her own private hell. Grandma Pearl was a Bible-toting, verse-spouting, overzealous disciplinarian, and she'd made every day of Faith's childhood miserable.

Despite Grandma Pearl's ways, Faith felt an obligation to make sure she was okay. After all, the woman had raised her since she was a baby, ever since her mother, Vera, decided she didn't like motherhood and took off. And since Faith's father had died before she was even born, it had just been her and Grandma Pearl for most of her life. Faith had moved out the day she'd graduated high school and only came back twice a month to check on Grandma Pearl.

Faith drew in a deep breath before lightly knocking on the door.

"What you want?" Grandma Pearl called out from the kitchen.

Faith leaned in and peered through the screen door. "Grandma, it's me, Faith. Can I come in?"

Grandma Pearl peeped her head around the corner of the kitchen, then leaned into the hallway to get a better look at Faith. She was clad in her signature blue housecoat with two large pockets in the front and slip-on tattered house shoes. Her long white hair was plaited in two ponytails that hung on her shoulders. "Wait. Let me get my holy oil."

Faith stood patiently as Grandma Pearl disappeared in a back room then returned with a small bottle. Faith had never known whether what was in the bottle was actually holy or not, but Grandma Pearl sure believed it was.

Faith watched as her grandmother sprinkled oil throughout the living room, across the sofa and into the air.

"Come on in, gal," Grandma Pearl said after she was done.

Faith inhaled deeply. Part of her wondered if she was a glutton for punishment for even coming over there. She jumped as Grandma Pearl dashed some oil in her face.

"Blood of Jesus, blood of Jesus, save her tainted soul," Grandma Pearl muttered.

Faith bit her bottom lip, wiped her face and continued into the living room.

"Grandma, I've asked you not to do that."

"Do what? Ask the Lord to save your soul? I'm trying to keep you from eternal damnation. You know you's a violated woman—many, many times. Everybody knows it. Just like your mama. Lord, I just don't know where I went wrong." Grandma Pearl dropped to her knees, raising her hands to the sky, the bottle of holy oil still clutched in one hand, her tattered King James Bible in the other. "Precious Lawd, king of kings, prince of peace, giver of all givers, healer of the sick, judger of all nations. Where did I go wrong? Save this sinning granddaughter of mine. Ain't no man gon' want her, but help her, Lawd. Cleanse her soul. She's soiled, but

I know you can cleanse her! You's an all-knowing God. You brought Mary Magdalene from the pits of hell, I know you can do the same for my grandbaby!"

Faith plopped down on the sofa. She should be used to this by now. She couldn't step foot in Grandma Pearl's home without having to go through this whole holy ritual. Faith picked the latest issue of the *National Enquirer* off Grandma Pearl's coffee table and started flipping through the pages. Grandma Pearl would continue the ritual for another ten minutes, then she'd go on like everything was normal.

Sure enough, ten minutes later, Grandma Pearl rose. "So you want some tea cakes? I got some fresh brewed tea."

Faith had spent her life being berated by her grandmother. She used to pray that her mother, Vera, would come to the rescue. But whenever Vera did come for a rare visit, she never stayed for more than a day, and she always left without taking her only daughter with her. Faith stared at the picture of her mother on top of Grandma Pearl's piano. Vera was standing outside of Faith Memorial Missionary Baptist Church, Grandma Pearl's home church of more than forty years, and the place where Faith had gotten her name. That had been Vera's way of trying to make amends with Grandma Pearl. It hadn't worked.

Faith picked up the photo and examined it for the thousandth time. Vera had to be no more than twelve in the picture. She wore white lace gloves and a frilly lace dress. She had a small Bible clutched tightly in her hand. Faith chuckled at the sight. That was a far cry from the Vera she knew. In fact, as far as Faith knew, her mother hadn't been anywhere near a Bible since that day. But Faith surmised that this was how Grandma Pearl wanted to remember her only daughter; it was the only photograph of Vera on display in the whole house.

Faith's mind flashed back to the last time she remembered taking a picture with her mother. It was for the junior prom. Faith had been so excited when her mother had returned to town to help her get ready for the special day. Vera had helped Faith take up the dress Grandma Pearl had made for her, even cutting a little of the fabric near the cleavage so the dress wouldn't look so frumpy. It was one of the few motherly acts Vera had ever performed.

As Grandma Pearl made her way back from the kitchen, Faith wondered what had ever happened to that picture. Grandma Pearl walked in and set a tray of tea cakes down on the coffee table. She handed Faith a cup of tea and a saucer of tea cakes, then sat in the rocking chair across from Faith.

"So, you ready to be saved?" Grandma Pearl asked, her expression serious.

"Grandma, please don't start." Faith sighed as she took a bite of Grandma Pearl's infamous tea cake. "I just came to check on you, that's all. How have you been doing?"

"Umphh, I'm cloaked in the blood of Jesus so I'm just fine, which is more than I can say for you."

Faith tried to ignore her grandmother's religious preachings and make other small talk, but after ten more minutes of hearing how she was facing eternal damnation, Faith was fed up. She didn't know why she'd thought she could have a civilized conversation with her holy-rollin' grandmother in the first place.

"Well, I gotta run." Faith threw her half-eaten tea cake back on the tray.

"You can run but you can't hide." Grandma Pearl continued rocking back and forth.

Faith got up and headed toward the door. She was mad that she'd wasted her time—time that she could've been at home asleep. "Bye, Grandma."

"The Lord is watching you even when you think he ain't."

Faith let the screen door slam on the sound of Grandma Pearl's voice. She headed home, where she should've gone in the first place.

Chapter Four

Faith scratched off the number on her weekly grand lottery ticket. She bought those tickets faithfully, sure that one day she'd get lucky. She'd already planned how she was going to spend her thousand dollars a week when she won: developing her beauty shop and getting the heck out of Beaumont.

Faith groaned when she wiped off the last number and saw that she didn't match a single number. She tossed the ticket in the garbage can outside the convenience store where she was standing. Faith had just dropped her car off at the auto repair shop next door to get her transmission fixed. She'd popped in the store to get her lottery ticket as she'd waited for Jasmine to come pick her up.

"Hey, pretty lady. Your husband let you out of the house?"

Faith turned toward the deep baritone voice. She immediately smiled when she took in the Morris Chestnut look-alike. He stood over six-feet-five-inches tall. His bald head glistened in the sun, and he had a mesmerizing smile that curved up on one end. Two men, equally good-looking, stood next to him. They were all wearing red, white and blue warm-ups.

Faith smiled. "I don't have a husband," she said softly.

"Music to my ears," the man replied. "I'm Xavier."

Faith blushed. "I'm Faith."

"Halleluluhah," one of the men responded.

Faith ignored him and kept her attention focused on Xavier. Then it dawned on her who he was. "Oh, wow. You're Xavier Manning from Lamar University. The star basketball player."

Xavier stroked his chin. "The one and only. These are my teammates." He pointed to the two guys standing behind him. They waved.

Faith beamed. Jasmine would die if she knew Faith was standing there talking to Xavier Manning. He was the star of the local university's basketball team and slated to be a first-round draft pick. Faith didn't follow sports, but everyone within a fifty-mile radius of Beaumont knew who he was. Jasmine, who watched Xavier play on the local television station all the time, had vowed that she would get him at some point. But here he was, standing in front of Faith.

"You sure are beautiful, Miss Faith."

"Thank you." Faith shifted her weight, grateful that she had slipped on her form-fitting jeans and not the sweatpants she'd initially put on.

"Do you usually stand outside of convenience stores by yourself?" Xavier asked.

"No, I was waiting on my friend."

"Male or female?" Xavier asked.

"Female. And here she comes." Faith pointed toward Jasmine's car as she navigated into the parking lot. Jasmine rolled her window down and was about to say something to Faith when she recognized Xavier. She threw the car in park and jumped out.

"Good God Almighty," Jasmine said, slamming her car door. "I know this is not that fine Xavier Manning standing here before me!"

Faith watched as Xavier lost his smile. In fact, he seemed turned off by Jasmine's loud demeanor.

"What's up?" Xavier said. His friends stood off to the back like they were used to being ignored.

"I know what I want to be up," Jasmine responded coyly. "Faith, girl, you holding out on me? I didn't know you knew X-Man."

"The name is Xavier," he snapped.

Jasmine ran her finger across his chest. "I know,

but X-Man is what I call you when I'm watching you do your thing on the court. Ain't it cute?"

"Hello, Jasmine," Faith interrupted. "I just met Xavier and his friends here."

Jasmine never removed her gaze. She just kept staring at Xavier and licking her lips.

"Jasmine!" Faith said, embarrassed by her friend's actions.

"Wha— Oh, my bad." Jasmine giggled.

"Are you ready to go?" Faith actually would have loved to stay and talk to Xavier, but now that Jasmine was all over him, that was out the window. Besides, she didn't want to stay there and watch Jasmine make any more of a fool out of herself than she had already.

"Xavier, it was nice to meet you." Faith turned to the other two guys. "And you too. But we gotta run." She grabbed Jasmine's hand and pulled her toward the car.

"Wait," Xavier said. "I'd love to call you sometime."

"I thought you'd never ask," Jasmine said, breaking free of Faith's grip. "Gimme your hand, I'll write my number on it."

Xavier looked at her like she was crazy. "I was talking to Faith."

Jasmine's eyes grew wide, and Faith's mouth dropped open. While Faith could hold her own, guys always gravitated toward Jasmine whenever the two girls were together.

Faith looked from Xavier to Jasmine. Of course she wanted to give him her number, but she and Jasmine had a cardinal rule. Never mess with a man someone else is interested in.

Jasmine shrugged. "Go on, girl. He looks a little slow for me anyway."

Xavier ignored Jasmine's snide remark as he reached in his pocket, pulled out a pen and piece of paper, and wrote Faith's number down.

Faith found herself waiting anxiously by the phone for the next two days. Even when she had to go to work, she raced home and checked her answering machine. Her heart dropped every time it came up empty.

Faith had actually given up on expecting a call from Xavier when she picked up her ringing telephone on the third day. She had prepared to disguise her voice in case it was a bill collector.

"Hal-lo," Faith said, sounding like an old woman.

"Ummmm, may I speak to Faith?"

"Who may I tell her is calling?" Faith hated that she had to disguise her voice, but with her car note two months behind and her only credit card past due, she didn't feel like being harassed by bill collectors.

"It's Xavier."

Faith almost dropped the phone. "Ummm, hold on, please," she said, still sounding like an old woman.

Faith held the phone close to her chest as she

closed her eyes and tried to figure out her next move. She took a deep breath, then called out, "Thank you, Maria. That's all I need for today." She moved the phone to her ear. "Hello."

"Hey you, it's Xavier, from the other day."

"Oh, hi Xavier." Faith tried her best to keep her cool.

"You have a personal answering service or something?" he joked.

"Nah, that was the cleaning lady. She comes once a week and I had her answer my phone because I was on the balcony." Faith hated to start off lying, but what else was she supposed to tell him?

"Ohhh, a cleaning lady? You're big-time, huh?"

"Not hardly," Faith laughed.

The two of them eased into a gentle conversation. Although much of it centered on Xavier and his basketball career, he was still great to talk to.

"Well, I have to go," Xavier finally said. "But when will I get a chance to see you again?"

"When do you want to see me again?" Faith asked.

"How's tomorrow?"

Faith didn't want to seem too eager. Besides, she had to work, and if she called in for a day off, her supervisor Barbara Ann would hit the roof. "I have to work tomorrow, but Sunday's good."

"Coach is making the team go to church on Sunday. He does it once a month. Trust me, we hate going, but if we don't go, Coach got this stupid rule that we can't play."

Faith bit down on her bottom lip. As much as she wanted to see him, she just didn't know about going to church.

"Tell you what," Xavier continued when she didn't respond. "Why don't you come to the church—that way we can just hook up afterward?"

Faith hesitated before speaking. "I guess so. Where is it?"

"It's at Faith Memorial over on Fifteenth Street."

Faith shook her head. Out of all the churches in town, he would be going there. "I know where that church is," Faith sighed. "How about I just meet you after service out front."

"Sounds like a plan. And Faith," he said.

"Yes?" His voice was intoxicating.

"I can't wait to see you."

"Me either." Faith placed the phone back on the cradle and plopped down on her sofa with a huge smile across her face.

Chapter Five

The roaring sounds of the choir billowed from the double doors of the Faith Memorial Missionary Baptist Church. Faith stood at the entrance, mesmerized, like something was willing her to go in. It was just after eleven. She knew Grandma Pearl was inside, positioned in her standard spot in the front pew. Only death could keep her grandmother away from church on Sunday morning.

"If anybody needs to be moving quickly inside, it would be you," a hoarse-sounding voice snapped at Faith. Faith turned to find herself face-to-face with Sister Wilma Wright, Deacon Wright's wife. Faith fought back a groan. The woman had made her life miserable back when she had attended church. Sister Wilma was a self-appointed overseer of the church and condemner of all sinners. She was part of the reason Faith had vowed never to set foot in Faith Memorial again. Faith wondered if her hatred for Wilma was part of the reason she gave crusty old Deacon Wright the time of day.

"How are you today, Sister Wilma?" Faith managed a smile.

"Blessed and highly favored," Sister Wilma said snidely. "I'm sure you can't say the same. Came to be saved today, huh?"

Faith shifted nervously. If she had a dime for every time somebody tried to save her soul, she'd be a rich woman. "Actually, I was just passing by. I'm um . . . um . . . going to meet a friend just down the street."

Faith knew she couldn't go in now. Sister Wilma would be all up in her face throughout service.

"I'm sure it's a male friend, probably somebody's husband," Sister Wilma muttered. Faith wondered if she knew about her husband's infidelities, but Faith dismissed the thought. If she did, they'd both be dead. Sister Wilma would lose all her religion if she knew for sure that her husband was messing around with Faith. Besides, that was old news. Faith had promised herself that after that last time, Deacon Wright was history.

"When you gon' get tired of sinnin', chile?" Wilma asked as she shook her Bible in Faith's face.

Faith closed her eyes and rubbed her temples.

A deep, male voice answered. "That's the million-dollar question—for all of us."

Both Sister Wilma and Faith turned toward the tall, handsome man who had stepped right into their conversation. "I remember my grandmother telling me no one sin is greater than the next," he said as he walked toward the women. "So it seems to me like we are all sinners in one way or another."

Sister Wilma frowned. "And you would be?"

The man extended his hand, his bright smile contagious. "I'm Ida Williams's grandson. Just moved here from San Diego. My name is Darius Winston Williams the second."

"Well, Darius Winston Williams the second, did your grandmother tell you being the town floozy was okay, too?" Sister Wilma snarled without looking at Faith.

Darius laughed, unfazed by Wilma's nastiness. "Naw, but she said it was no worse than lying, or stealing, or being a mean, evil old bat to people." He turned and smiled at Faith. "May I have the pleasure of escorting you inside?"

Faith felt butterflies in her stomach. No one had ever come to her defense like that. "Ummm, thank you, but I'm not going in. I was, ummm, just passing through," she said.

"Yeah, she don't go to church. Ain't been to church since the second coming."

Darius ignored Sister Wilma. "That's a shame. But you have yourself a good day." He nodded toward Faith before turning to Sister Wilma. "Ms. . . . you have a good day, too." With that he made his way up the stairs and into the church.

"Why is he waltzing in here all late anyway? Who does he think he is, trying to talk to me about sinning?" Sister Wilma griped. Faith stared after Darius, a small smile across her face.

"Just a shame! A shame befo' God!" Sister Wilma chastised.

Faith snapped out of her zone, kicking herself for allowing thoughts of Darius to invade her mind with Sister Wilma standing right there.

"I see the lust in yo' eyes. You just a harlot! A jezebel! You need to march right in that church and up to the front, drop to your knees and ask the Lord to have mercy on your soul!"

Faith took a deep breath. Although she thought she was immune to all the hateful comments, they still hurt deep down inside. She flung her hair out of her face and held her head up high.

"Sister Wilma, you have a blessed day." Faith stepped around Sister Wilma and started across the street. She would just wait on Xavier at the park across from the church.

"Your poor grandma. Such a good woman. It's a shame she got to deal with this. I'm gonna pray for you! You just evil! You probably gonna sleep with that Darius before the day is over!"

Faith stopped in her tracks and swung around. She thought about not responding, but she was fed up with the Sister Wrights of the world.

"That's a great idea. What time does church let out? I may just have to come back and do exactly that."

Sister Wilma gasped as Faith turned back around and sashayed on to her destination.

Faith flashed a smile at Xavier as he quickly made his way out of the church. Somehow, she knew he would be one of the first ones out.

"Hey, beautiful. I didn't see you inside," he said as he leaned in to hug her.

"I was, umm, sitting in the back." There she went lying again. Faith promised herself that was her last major lie. She wanted to start off on the right foot with Xavier; she had a good feeling about him.

"Okay, let's get out of here and go get something to eat." He waved to his teammates, then grabbed Faith's hand. "I don't do church, and I thought I was going to lose my mind waiting for the service to end."

Faith laughed as she followed Xavier down the street to a soul food restaurant.

"I hope this is okay with you," he said as he opened the door for her to go in. "I've never eaten here, but Coach said they got some bomb food."

"It's fine," Faith replied. She wanted to tell him they could go eat three-week-old hot dogs out of a cart and that would be just fine with her.

They slid into a booth, and Faith struggled again to contain her excitement. Xavier looked handsome in a mock turtleneck and Polo khakis.

Faith took note as Xavier's eyes made their way down to her double Ds. She was used to that. It was usually the first thing men noticed about her. Her mother had told her her breasts could be her meal ticket if she learned to jiggle them just right.

"They sure are looking good this afternoon," Xavier said as he eased back into his seat.

"Excuse me?"

Xavier laughed. "I meant *you* sure are looking good this afternoon."

Faith blushed. "Thank you." Despite his compliment about her breasts, he seemed genuinely happy to be with her.

"So, Miss Faith, tell me again what you do."

Faith smiled. During their first conversation, he had talked about himself so much that they'd never gotten around to her.

"Umm . . . I . . . work for a hotel chain," Faith replied, telling herself she wasn't totally lying.

"Really? Which one?"

Faith toyed with her menu. How in the world could she tell him that she was a maid at a sleazy motel? She couldn't tell him that. After all, he was a big-time college star; he wouldn't want a future with someone who cleaned nasty motel rooms, even if it was a means to an end.

"You know, Xavier, I'm more interested in talking about you," Faith said.

Xavier leaned back and grinned, like he had no problem talking about himself.

"So I guess you've seen me play?"

"I've never actually been to a game, but I have seen you on TV. You're one of the best players around. Everybody knows that."

"Right, right," Xavier nodded.

The waitress appeared, and Faith and Xavier both ordered smothered pork chops and rice. For the next twenty minutes they talked about everything under the sun, but no matter what direction their conversation went in, it usually made its way back to Xavier's basketball career. He planned on going pro next year, his senior year. And from what Faith had heard about him, he had a pretty good chance of making it. An NBA player's wife. Faith smiled at the prospect. She knew she was getting ahead of herself, but there was something about Xavier. They connected. She wanted to get to know more about him, and although his eyes kept making their way down her chest, she was sure he felt the same way.

"Let's get out of here," Xavier said as he tossed a twenty-dollar bill on the table.

Faith smiled. He still wanted to spend time with her. Maybe they could go take a walk in the park. It had been a long time since she had done anything romantic. It was usually wham, bam, thank you ma'am.

Xavier extended his hand to help Faith out of her seat. She exhaled as she took his hand, shivers running up her spine. Could it actually be possible? Had she finally found something real? She wanted that chance. Sure, he probably had women throwing themselves at him left and right. But Faith was positive that given the chance, she could turn him into a one-woman man.

Xavier made small talk as they walked down the street. Faith didn't know where they were headed and didn't care. All she knew was the wonderful feeling she had inside. They'd only gone a few steps when Xavier stopped walking.

"Hey, babe, I need to run in here a minute."

Faith tried to keep her heart from dropping. "A motel? You need to run into a motel?"

"Yeah. Umm, I'm staying here overnight because the air went out in the athletic apartment complex."

Faith shot him an incredulous look.

"What?" he asked.

"I guess you need me to go in with you?"

Xavier slyly grinned and squeezed her hand tightly. "That would be nice."

Faith jerked her hand away. "You don't have to run game," she snapped. "A motel?"

"I'm not running game, baby. It's just that you're so fine. I just want you right here, right now."

As Faith stared at Xavier Grandma Pearl's words rang in her ears. *How you ever gon' get somebody to marry you if you give it up on the first date?*

"Xavier, I like you. A lot. But I was hoping we could take it slow."

"Look, Faith. I like you a lot, too. But I'm grown and you're grown, so I don't see what the big deal is. I just want to show you how much I'm feeling you."

Faith inhaled. *No, no, no,* she kept telling herself. She quickly replayed her past relationships. She'd felt pressured into sex too early in all of them. And she'd given in each time, even though her head had told her it had been the wrong thing to do. But she'd never listened, and she'd always followed her heart. This time had to be different. She wanted to be with Xavier, and the only way to make that happen was to make him wait.

"I'm sorry. I just can't."

Xavier let out a long sigh. "You know what, Faith? Don't even worry about it. I don't have to beg nobody to sleep with me. I told you I was feeling you and I want to get to know you better. If that isn't good enough for you, then so be it. I'll holla at you later."

Faith watched as Xavier spun around and started to walk off. Her one chance at happiness was about to slip through her fingers, and for what? Because she wanted to wait to sleep with him? And why was she doing that, because society said so? Because of some lopsided value system that applauded men who slept around, yet degraded women who did the same thing?

Faith wanted desperately to call him back, but if she wanted this one to be different, she'd have to start off differently. And that meant she would just have to take her chances that she was doing the right thing by waiting.

As Faith watched Xavier stomp off back toward the church, she couldn't help but feel that maybe waiting wasn't the right thing.

Chapter Six

Faith eyed the clock on the dingy wall with the peeling paint. Only fifteen more minutes to quitting time. She sighed heavily. Those fifteen minutes might as well be fifteen hours. That's how ready she was to go. Her date with Xavier had been weighing heavily on her mind. She hadn't heard from him in a week, and she wondered if her decision to stand her ground and not sleep with him was the reason why. It seemed like no matter what she did, she couldn't keep a guy. If she slept with him too soon, he didn't call. If she didn't sleep with him at all, he still didn't call. It seemed like a lose-lose situation to her.

Watching her dreams with Xavier go up in smoke

had put Faith in a foul mood, and work was the last place she wanted to be.

Faith hated her job at the Super 8. The run-down motel looked like it needed to be condemned. The sign outside the building was lopsided, hanging on by one wire. The pool was a nasty green and had all kinds of debris floating in it. And the rooms themselves had a foul, musty smell. Faith would scrub and scrub, but no matter what she did, she couldn't get rid of that musty smell.

Not only did Faith hate her job but she also hated cleaning up after other folks, period. But it was a paycheck—had been for the last two years—and it allowed her to keep her four-hundred-square-foot efficiency apartment. There wasn't much to her tiny place, but it was hers, and for Faith, that alone was worth its weight in gold.

"Did you make sure the linens were pulled tightly on the corners of that bed?"

Faith glared at her supervisor, who seemed to have magically appeared out of nowhere and was standing outside the last room on Faith's cleaning route. Faith couldn't stand the woman; not only was she a mean old bat but she also represented everything Faith hoped to never become—an overweight, bitter woman who took pride in talking about all she could have achieved in life if she had just been able to get out of Beaumont. Working around Barbara Ann gave

Faith the incentive she needed to save her money so she could follow her dreams.

"Yes, Barbara Ann. The linen is pulled tightly."

"Let me check for myself," Barbara Ann muttered. "I swear I have to go behind you all like you don't know how to do your jobs." She set her clipboard on the cart and pushed her way into the room.

She leaned in and began inspecting the bed. "See, this is exactly what I'm talking about!" she said, throwing back the covers on the bed. "Look how this sheet is all scrunched up." She began smoothing out the bedsheet. "Oh, my God! These sheets aren't even clean! Look at that!" She pointed to a stain in the middle of the sheet.

Faith cringed. Granted, she hadn't changed the sheets like she was supposed to—she just wanted to get out of there—but she had at least tried to glance at the sheets to make sure they were clean.

"Just disgusting!" Barbara Ann snapped as she snatched the sheet off the bed. "What would our customers say if they saw this?"

Faith wanted to say, What do customers expect from a motel that rents by the hour? But she knew she was already in trouble, so she kept her mouth shut. As much as she hated her job, losing it meant she'd have to move back in with Grandma Pearl. And she'd rather die than do that.

Barbara Ann flung the sheet at Faith. It landed on

her head and covered her face. "Take that downstairs to the laundry right now!"

Faith held her breath to keep from smelling the stained sheet as she pulled it off her head. "Yes, ma'am." She turned and scurried down the steps.

"You need to be fired!" Barbara Ann called out after her.

Faith felt the tears welling up inside. She hated her life. How had she been reduced to this? A tiny apartment, a two-bit, meaningless job and a string of good times, at least good for the men, because it was seldom good for Faith. Every relationship she'd hoped would turn into something meaningful had left her feeling worthless.

Faith had only had one real boyfriend, and that had been in the twelfth grade. His name was William. He'd been new to town, and his father had been a deacon at the church. Faith had been head over heels in love with him. They had never even had sex, because he'd said he was saving himself for marriage. She had thought that was so noble. William was the only guy who'd ever loved her for her, but that had all changed when he'd found out she hadn't been the virgin she had claimed to be, and that she'd slept with two different guys on the basketball team. He'd said he'd never be able to look at her the same again. He hadn't even cared that Faith had thought she was in love with both of those guys and it had turned out they'd both been using her. William hadn't even heard her out; he'd walked out of her life just like that. Faith had been heartbroken. But eventually, she'd picked up the pieces and moved on.

Faith stuffed the soiled sheet into the oversized washing machine in the motel's washroom.

When she was little, Faith used to dream of being a pediatrician. Grandma Pearl had quickly shot that dream down, telling Faith she would never amount to anything because "that's just your destiny."

At first, Faith had tried to fight it and make something out of herself. She'd studied hard and had been determined to get a scholarship to go to college with William. But after he'd dumped her, she'd decided maybe Grandma Pearl was right—being a worthless harlot was her destiny.

Faith started the washing machine and was turning to leave when she heard giggling coming from the back of the washroom. She followed the voice outside, where she noticed a couple leaning against the wall.

"Sweetheart, you are the cure for what ails me. And while you only asked for twenty, here's another ten for doing such a good job." Faith stood in stunned disbelief as she watched the tall, gray-haired man hand the woman some money.

The woman giggled again, took the money and stuffed it in her bra. She pulled down her leopard miniskirt, flung her long blonde wig, and replied, "Anytime, handsome, anytime."

The man pinched her on the behind before walking off with a look of total satisfaction.

Faith's heart sank as she stepped toward her mother.

"Vera?" Faith's voice was shaky. Her mother turned toward her and grinned widely.

"Baby doll! What's cooking?" Vera exclaimed. Her eyes were droopy, but they seemed to light up at the sight of Faith.

Faith surveyed her mother. She looked a mess. In addition to the outlandish outfit, one breast sat higher than the other. "Vera, where have you been? What are you doing here?"

"Whoa, slow your roll, baby doll." She dug in her purse and took out a package of Benson & Hedges, tapped the pack and pulled out a cigarette. She fumbled in her purse again and pulled out a lighter that had a picture of a naked woman on it. She lit her cigarette. "Whew," she said after taking a long drag on the nicotine stick. "I needed that." She slowly exhaled the smoke. "That old man could go."

Faith felt her stomach turn. "Vera, are you out here turning tricks?" Grandma Pearl was always calling Vera a whore, but Faith had never known she meant that literally.

"Doin' what I gotta do, baby. Livin' ain't cheap," Vera said, taking another puff of the cigarette.

Faith shook her head in disgust. "You didn't even make him get a room?"

"Oh, don't go getting all prude on me. I had enough of that crap from your grandma. Speaking of which, how is the old biddy?"

"The same."

"You still staying with her? If you are, I can't see how."

"Actually, I got my own place a long time ago."

Vera's eyes lit up. "For real? Look here, maybe you can let your mama crash at your place for a little while. I been staying here and there since I got back in town last week." Vera swayed from side to side.

Faith leaned in a little closer and stared into her mother's eyes. "Vera, are you drunk?"

"I only had a little . . ." Vera suddenly stopped talking as something above Faith's shoulder caught her eye. Faith turned around and saw a trucker inserting his key in the room upstairs. Vera flashed a flirtatious smile when he glanced their way.

The man smiled back, his eyes lingering on Vera's scantily clad body. He opened his door and tossed his bag inside before turning and making his way down to where Faith and Vera were standing.

"My, my, my," the man said, eyeing Faith's

uniform. "What's a brother got to do to get some room service around here?"

Faith prepared to tell him the Super 8 didn't offer room service, but Vera cut her off.

"Depends on how much a brother's willing to pay," Vera said seductively.

"I'm feeling generous today. Thirty dollars for one hour."

"Make it fifty and you have a deal."

Faith's mouth fell open. "Vera, what are you doing?"

Vera gently caressed the man's arm. "Look here, hulk. You go on up, get comfortable and I'll be up in a minute. I just need to holler at my daughter here for a minute."

Faith watched the man walk off. "Vera, why are you doing this?" she finally asked as she leaned in to sniff Vera. "And are you drunk?"

"Oh, good grief, Faith. You ain't no little girl. And from what I hear you ain't no saint your dang self, so don't judge me. I had that my whole life and I ain't about to have it from someone I brought into this world. I am who I am." Vera stuck her chest out and smoothed down her skirt. "I'm who my evil Mama predicted I would be. And you know what? I'm okay with that. If you ain't, then you best keep movin' because I ain't gon' change."

Faith fought back the lump forming in her throat. "Don't you want better?"

Vera laughed. "Better? Better than what? What, you want me to move back to Mama's and let her splash some holy oil on me so she can cure me of my sinful ways? Been there, done that."

"You can find happiness," Faith said as her thoughts went back to Xavier. She was still hopeful that things would work out.

"Girl, don't be no fool. A man don't want nothing but one thing from a woman. And you'd be a fool if you didn't get something in return."

Faith was not about to listen to Vera when it came to men. Vera had never been married, and the closest she'd ever come to a serious relationship had been with Faith's father, who had died in a car accident when Vera was six months pregnant.

Vera didn't seem fazed by Faith's disgust. She reached in her purse, pulled out a piece of paper and a pen, and scribbled something on it. "Here's my number. Call me sometime." She blew Faith a kiss. "Gotta run. Got bizness to take care of."

Faith stood frozen and stunned. It had been seven years since she'd seen her mother. She'd envisioned a reunion with her mother many, many times. Only in her dreams it had never been like this.

Chapter Seven

It had taken nearly two weeks, but Xavier had finally called. He hadn't acted like anything was wrong. Faith had silently praised herself. Her holding out had worked.

In the past week alone, they had gone out on two dates, once to the movies and another time to watch a basketball game in a nearby town.

Faith felt confident that this was the relationship she'd waited for all her life. She felt so comfortable around him, and when he started talking about taking their relationship to the next level, she felt her guard dropping.

Xavier gently ran his fingers over Faith's hair as

they lay on the sofa in his off-campus apartment. "Girl, do you have any idea how fine you are?" he asked.

Faith smiled and closed her eyes. What would her grandmother say when she came home with a man like Xavier on her arm? All those hypocrites at church would fall over themselves because she'd managed to snag a prize like Xavier.

"You know I don't want to pressure you, but how long do you plan to make me wait?" He softly stroked her hair. "We've been talking for almost four weeks now, and I'm not used to waiting, you know."

Faith didn't know if the entire past month counted, since she'd gone two weeks without talking to him, but looking into his eyes, it didn't seem to matter anymore. He made her feel good, and she wanted to make him happy.

"I don't want you to wait anymore, Xavier."

"Are you saying what I think you're saying?" He smiled mischievously.

Faith slowly nodded as she began unbuttoning her top. She sighed as he took her hand and led her into the bedroom.

The memory of last night was still on Faith's mind when Xavier called her and asked her to meet him at the Marriott hotel ballroom for a party put together by some fraternity members at Lamar. Being in this atmosphere made her regret not going to college, but

Xavier was making her feel so at ease. Though plenty of girls vied for Xavier's attention, he only had eyes for Faith.

Faith was on cloud nine. Making love to Xavier hadn't been anything spectacular, but the fact that she'd finally been doing it with someone who cared about her had made it much more special.

"You enjoying yourself?" Xavier leaned down to whisper into her ear.

Faith nodded. She could hardly hear him with the sounds of 50 Cent blaring out of the loudspeaker positioned directly across from her.

"You want another drink?" he asked, holding up his glass.

Faith shook her head. She didn't know what this concoction was he'd given her, but she was on her third glass. It tasted like regular Kool-Aid, but it was definitely spiked with something because she felt herself wobbling.

"You all right?" he asked.

"Yeah, what's in this drink?"

"It's called trash can punch. Just Kool-Aid and Everclear."

Faith knew she wasn't drunk, but the drink was definitely making her head hurt.

"Let's get out of here. This music is too loud. Some of the players have a suite upstairs for a private party with some of the recruits."

He grabbed Faith's hand and led her out. She shook off the dizziness and smiled at the scowls of the women watching her as they passed.

A few minutes later they were inside a lavish suite. Smoke filled the room. There were a couple of guys sitting on a sofa watching ESPN. Another guy stood in a corner looking like he was desperately trying to mack on a young-looking girl. Outkast blared from the sound system, while a few people danced in the middle of the floor. Almost everyone had a glass in their hands.

Faith didn't know if this was how college after-parties went since she had never been to one, but the whole atmosphere made her uneasy.

"Hold on, I'll be right back." Xavier motioned for Faith to take a seat at the bar. He made a couple of rounds speaking to people, including a group of guys who kept looking her way. She nervously bobbed her head to the music until Xavier came back.

"Baby, I need you to do me a favor," he said. "You know I can't stand the thought of sharing you with anyone, but the school is really trying to recruit this boy"—he paused and pointed toward a tall, lanky guy standing in the kitchen area—"and I think some time with you will be just what he needs to convince him to come to Lamar." Xavier wrapped one of her curls around his finger.

Faith looked confused. What could she possibly say to convince him to go to a school she knew hardly anything about?

"What do you want me to say?" she asked.

"Just wing it." Xavier grabbed her hand and pulled her off the bar stool. He motioned for the guy to follow him into one of the bedrooms attached to the suite.

Faith eyed the boy. He looked like he had stepped straight off the farm. His butter-colored complexion was in need of a good tan and his short Afro looked like it hadn't been combed in weeks. He wore baggy pants with one leg tucked in his sock and a Sean John pullover. He looked like he was trying real hard to be cool.

Faith's gaze made its way to Xavier.

"Faith, this is Henry from Alabama."

Faith tried to smile, but her smile quickly faded when she saw the other two tall boys ease in the room behind Xavier. He turned toward both of them. "And this is Brandon and JeCarious. They're some of the best ballplayers in the country and they're thinking about coming to Lamar." He turned toward Faith with a huge grin on his face. "We're hoping you can help convince them that Lamar is the place for them."

Faith's mouth dropped open as it dawned on her what Xavier was asking.

"Xavier . . . ," Faith stammered. "What's going on?"

"What does it look like? I need you to hook my boys up." All three guys licked their lips hungrily.

Faith shook her head in shock. "You must have me confused," she said.

Xavier frowned. "What's the big deal?"

"You've lost your mind, that's what the big deal is." Faith didn't mean to snap at Xavier, but she was appalled that he would try to do her like that.

"Yo, can y'all step outside? I need to holla at Faith real quick."

The boys grumbled before heading out.

Xavier spun toward her. "How you gon' try and front me in front of those kids?"

"That's just it. They're kids," Faith pleaded.

"That's just a figure of speech. All of 'em are eighteen, so they're considered adults."

"But there's three of them . . ."

"And?"

"Xavier, don't, please. I can't do this. I won't do this." She gently placed her hand on his arm.

Xavier glared at her. "You know what, I don't have time for this." He snatched his arm away and began walking toward the door. Faith ran after him.

"Why would you ask me to do something like that? I thought you cared about me." She asked the question just as he pulled the door open.

Xavier spun toward her. "Care about you? Are you on drugs?"

Faith felt her heart drop. Why had she fooled herself into thinking things would be different with Xavier?

"I . . . I thought I meant something to you."

Xavier's look softened. "Faith, I was feeling you, I really was. Because you sho' know how to make a man feel like a man, but let's keep it real. I know all about you. Everybody does. I can't take you home to my mama. I mean, I wouldn't even want nobody to know I was with you other than for a roll in the hay."

Faith was shocked. She'd heard some pretty vile things in her lifetime, compliments of Grandma Pearl, but Xavier's words were like daggers in her heart.

Before Faith could respond, the three boys stepped up behind Xavier. By this time the whole room had gotten quiet, and the recruits were staring at Xavier and Faith.

"Yo, man, we gon' do this or what?" one of them asked.

Xavier looked toward Faith. "So, what's up? You gon' let my boys have a little Faith?"

Faith stood with a look of stunned disbelief on her face. On top of everything he had just said, he still expected her to sleep with the recruits. She wanted to curse him out, scream at him, scratch his eyes out. But everything he'd said had been true, and at least he'd been man enough to say it to her face.

Faith's eyes filled with defeat as she lowered her head.

"Man, forget this skeezer," Xavier said, flicking Faith off. The three boys looked disappointed as Xavier stomped over to the door and held it open. They shook their heads as Faith slowly walked by.

"Dang, she was fine, too," one of them muttered.

It took everything in Faith's power not to burst into tears. She held her head high and walked out of the party, flinching as Xavier slammed the door behind her.

Chapter Eight

Faith stood outside the Marriott on the pay phone. She was kicking herself right about now. She didn't know why she'd called Jasmine, who was going on a mile a minute.

"I knew he wasn't no good when I saw him. He looks like a low-down dirty dog," Jasmine snapped.

Faith sniffled. "Just come get me, okay? I rode here with him. I just want to get home."

"I told you to leave him alone after he didn't call you back the first time. Everything that glitters ain't gold." Jasmine huffed, then let out a loud breath. "I'm on my way."

Fifteen minutes later Faith was sitting in the

passenger side of Jasmine's Z328. She had tuned out her friend and was reflecting on how she'd ended up in this situation—again.

Faith snapped out of her thoughts when she realized they were pulling into The Daiquiri Factory, one of the city's hot spots for hanging out. "What are you doing?"

"What does it look like?" Jasmine replied as she swung into a parking space near the front door.

"I told you I just want to go home. I'm in no mood to hang out."

"You need a Hurricane Daiquiri to help you get over your troubles."

"Jasmine, I want to go home," Faith sternly said.

"I'm not hearing you," Jasmine replied as she turned off the ignition and checked her makeup in the rearview mirror. She flashed a smile at Faith. "Come on, just for a little while. It'll make you feel better."

Faith contemplated walking home, but she was a good twenty minutes by car. She could call a cab, but she doubted that the eleven bucks in her pocket would get her far.

Faith groaned and silently cursed Jasmine. But she knew her friend. It would be useless to protest. The sooner she got out and went inside, the sooner she could leave and go home.

"Fine. But I ain't staying here all night," Faith snarled.

"That's my girl," Jasmine said as Faith jumped out of the car.

Faith rolled her eyes and followed her friend inside. They had been inside less than five minutes when Faith spotted Xavier walking in. He was laughing like nothing was wrong. Just the sight of him made her sick.

"What are you staring at?" Jasmine said as she followed Faith's gaze. "Oh, no, he ain't coming in here acting like everything's fine. I'm about to give him a piece of my mind."

Faith grabbed Jasmine's arm. "No, let's just go."

"Uh-uh. We were here first. He needs to leave." Faith lowered her head as she noticed Xavier look her way and point. She wanted to cry when she saw he was walking toward them, a smirk across his face.

"Dang, if you wanted to party, we coulda stayed in the room," Xavier said.

Faith didn't reply, but Jasmine didn't hesitate.

"What the hell you want? Sorry, no good, trifling—"

"Hey, beautiful."

His niceness must have caught Jasmine by surprise, because she was speechless for a moment. She seemed to catch herself from falling into his trance. "Don't play nice with me. Faith told me what you did tonight."

Xavier shrugged, then turned toward his friends

and let out a laugh. "We were just trying to have a good time. And Faith here is the good-time queen."

Faith felt herself losing it. A rage came over her and the next thing she knew she had pounced out of her seat and onto Xavier, clawing at his face before anyone knew what was going on.

"You bastard!" she screamed.

Faith didn't know all the people who were grabbing her, pulling her off him. All she knew was the punch he landed to her left jaw, which caused blood to trickle out of her mouth and sent her flying to the floor.

"You hit her! You sorry piece of—" Jasmine screamed as she struggled to help Faith up off the floor.

"She jumped me!" Xavier yelled back as he rubbed his face.

Jasmine grabbed a napkin and put it up to Faith's bleeding mouth. "Are you all right?"

"No! No! Just leave me alone. All of you." Faith pulled herself up. "I told you I didn't want to come here!" Faith bolted toward the door and ran right into a group of men heading in.

"Hey, you," Darius said, the smile leaving his face when he noticed her tears and the blood dripping from her mouth. "Wha . . . What's going on?"

Faith immediately recognized the man from

church. But right now she couldn't think of anything but getting out of the bar. She ignored him, racing past him and out the door.

Faith was stomping down the street by the time Darius caught up with her. "Hey, wait up. Are you okay?"

Faith ignored him and kept walking. He reached out and grabbed her arm. "Faith, isn't it? Are you all right?"

Faith stopped and turned to him. "Look, no disrespect, but can you please leave me alone?"

"I'm sorry, I can't do that."

She looked down at his hand still firmly grasped around her arm. "Let me go and leave me alone. Please."

Darius's eyes narrowed, but he released her arm. "You're bleeding pretty bad," he said, pointing to her mouth. "Are you sure you don't want me to call an ambulance?"

"No."

"Well, where are you going?"

Faith looked down the deserted street. It was almost two in the morning. She didn't know where she was going. The buses had stopped running a long time ago, and she still didn't have enough money for cab fare.

Darius could see her confusion. "Look, let me take

you home. I'm not a serial killer or anything. I just don't think it's smart for you to be on the streets this late by yourself."

Faith sighed and crossed her arms. How did she always end up at the mercy of some man? She looked away.

"Come on, just let me run back and get my car. It'll only take a minute and you'll be resting in the comfort of your home in no time," Darius pleaded.

Faith rubbed her jaw. She was ready to get home. "Fine. I live on Twenty-third and Pecan." Faith trailed Darius back to the parking lot, saying little along the way.

Once they got into his car, she sighed, closed her eyes, and sank down in the passenger seat. She imagined she had to look a mess. Her head was throbbing, and the blood had stained her white tank top.

Darius, thankfully, didn't ask any more questions, and they took much of the twenty-minute journey in silence. After Faith guided Darius to her apartment complex, he pulled up in front.

Darius placed his hand on her arm as she was getting out of the car. "Are you sure you're going to be okay?" he asked.

Faith swallowed and tried desperately not to cry.

"You want to tell me what happened?" he asked.

Faith didn't respond.

"You know what, how about you tell me when

you're ready?" He pulled out a piece of paper and wrote down his number. "You call me if you need anything, okay?"

Faith forced a smile as she took the paper. As soon as she walked into her apartment building, she tossed the paper in the trash. After this madness with Xavier, she was through with men, especially cute ones like Darius Winston Williams II.

Chapter Nine

Faith admired Darius as he sifted through a box of envelopes. She couldn't believe she was sitting in this man's living room. But she had been touched when he'd called her last Sunday to make sure she was okay. Especially because he'd gone through so much trouble to get her number. He'd convinced Jasmine to give him the number after he'd gone back to The Daiquiri Factory to pick up his friends.

Faith didn't know whether to be mad at the fact that Jasmine had given him the number or the fact that she'd still been hanging out long after Faith had left.

Faith shook off thoughts of Jasmine as she watched Darius make his way around his apartment. He had just moved in over the weekend, so boxes were still everywhere. He was going through one now, trying to find his credit card.

"I'm sorry," he mumbled as he pulled stuff out of a box. "They just sent me my renewal card, and I remember putting the envelope in one of these boxes."

"That's okay. Take your time," Faith said.

Faith knew she had sworn off men less than a week ago, but after Darius's initial call, they'd talked every day thereafter, one time as long as three hours. She'd enjoyed their conversations because he never seemed to be macking. They just talked like old friends. He was a very spiritual person, often making religious references, but it wasn't to the point of being overbearing.

They'd gotten off the phone last night with the agreement to go to dinner. Tonight they'd been on their way to the restaurant when he'd told her he'd left his credit card in his apartment. Faith's whole attitude had changed. She'd just known he would ask her to come upstairs, and the next thing she'd know he'd be trying to get her into bed.

She'd made up her mind that she was going to demand that he take her home, but before she'd been able to say anything, he'd pulled up in front of his apartment and told her she could wait in the car while he went to retrieve his card.

Faith had waited almost fifteen minutes. She'd

finally gotten out and come in to see what had been taking him so long. He mumbled an apology and continued to tear open box after box.

Faith glanced around the spacious apartment some more. She was impressed with the layout. She noticed a stack of CDs on the bar and walked over and picked one up. She started reading the back. "You like jazz?" she asked.

"Found it!" Darius said. "I was getting worried." He turned toward Faith. "Oh, I'm sorry, what'd you say?"

"I said, do you like jazz?"

"Yeah, that's Kirk Whalum, one of my favorites. What about you, you like jazz?"

Faith shrugged, a faint smile across her face. "Not really, I'm more of a hip-hop person myself. I would've thought you to be more of a gospel guy."

Darius laughed and sat down on the bar stool next to Faith. "And why is that?"

"I don't know, you seem so wholesome."

"Please." Darius laughed. "I think people just have a hard time accepting black men who are confident in their Christianity."

"So you're a Christian?"

"You're not?"

Faith thought about it. Sure, she loved God and all, but with the life she lived, she didn't even feel right talking about Him.

"Just because you don't always walk with God

doesn't mean you can't accept Him into your heart. While God wants us to be righteous, He knows we aren't perfect but He loves us just the same."

Faith stared at Darius. He seemed so strong and confident. "How are you so strong and unwavering in your faith?"

This time it was Darius who shrugged. "I don't know. I guess I just know that good or bad, God will work it out. He may not work it out when you want him to, but trust me, it'll happen."

Faith took in his words. The last thing she'd expected when she'd come up here was to be sitting up talking about religion. Not once had he questioned why she seemed so pessimistic about religion, nor did he condemn her.

"I don't cast stones," he said as if he were reading her thoughts. "I guess I'm what you call a new-school Christian. I understand that Christians don't always walk a righteous path."

Faith toyed with the strap on her sash. "I wish my grandmother would take a lesson or two from you."

The next thing Faith knew she had made herself comfortable on Darius's couch and was opening up to Darius about her life with her grandmother. Before she knew it, they'd put on a bunch of jazz CDs and ordered a pizza.

Faith finally shared with him what had happened at The Daiquiri Factory.

"So I guess you think I shouldn't have hit him?"

"You shoulda knocked the crap out of him. And I wish I had been there. I would've beat his behind myself."

Faith grinned as she sized up Darius. Although Xavier was taller, Darius looked like he could give Xavier a run for his money.

Faith's smile slowly faded as she noticed the look of pity on Darius's face. Suddenly she regretted opening up to him so much.

"Darius, I know I've made some stupid decisions and you probably think I'm some kind of slut, but I'm not." She looked away.

Darius reached out and gently guided Faith's chin back toward him. "Faith, I don't think you're a slut. I think you are a beautiful young woman who has been searching for love in all the wrong places. Let me be clear. The only thing I want from you is your friendship."

Faith didn't know how to take that. Of course she didn't want the man jumping her bones, but she would've liked for him to find her attractive. Darius must've sensed her confusion.

"Faith, it seems like you're used to a certain type of man. That's not me," he continued. "As beautiful as you are, I wouldn't want to be with you, even make love to you . . . because in just the short time I've known you, and please don't take offense to this, but I can tell you don't love yourself."

Faith looked taken aback. "What is that supposed to mean?"

Darius took her hand. "From what you've told me, I can tell you're not happy with your life. But in order to change that, you have to pray. After that you have to get rid of or tackle the negative forces in your life. Then, you have to love yourself. When you learn to love yourself, you'll realize that what you have is special and should be reserved for only that special man."

So that was it. He didn't want to be with her because of her reputation.

"I could do like all the other men in your life have done and just sleep with you and move on. But I'm not about that," he continued.

"Oh, I get it. You a holy roller or something?" Faith retorted, trying to use sarcasm to mask her pain.

Darius chuckled. "While I believe in God, I'm far from a holy roller. Remember, when you bumped into me the other night I was going into The Daiquiri Factory to get my drink on. Believe me, I've done my share of sinning. But there is something special inside of you and if I'm going to love anything, that's what I'm going to love."

Faith stared at Darius in disbelief. "What kind of game are you running?"

"Not running any games. Not a holy roller. Not gay. And not even a virgin. I just try to live right. And

I guess I'm just one of the few men left out there who doesn't need sex to validate my manhood."

"What man doesn't need sex?"

"I didn't say I don't need it. I said I don't need it to validate my manhood."

"It's because of what I told you about me getting around, isn't it?" Faith regretted opening up to him now. During one of their many phone conversations she'd told him how she'd gotten around and how unhappy she was with her life. She had surprised herself at the way she'd opened up. Vera used to say never tell a man all your business. This must be why, Faith thought.

"No, like I told you, I'm no saint and I've been around myself."

"What's your story then?" Faith asked.

"I don't have one."

"I learned a long time ago that if it looks too good to be true, it probably is," Faith said skeptically.

Darius let out a hearty laugh. "Too good to be true? I'm far from that. I leave my clothes in the middle of the floor. I chew with my mouth open and," he leaned in, "sometimes I pass gas and don't say excuse me."

"Ewwww." Faith playfully pushed Darius. Just that quick, he had knocked down her guard and put her at ease again. "Seriously, I don't understand you," Faith said. "You are so handsome, and I'm sure you can have any woman you want."

"I can? Well then, why isn't Halle Berry here yet?"

Faith stared at Darius, enamored by everything about him. She leaned in and gave him a gentle hug. "She doesn't know about you yet. That's the only thing I can think of." Faith eyed the clock as she pulled herself from his embrace. "Wow, I didn't realize it was that late. I better get going."

Darius stretched. "I'm sorry we didn't get to go out. May I have a rain check for next Friday?"

Faith smiled as she stood up. "You sure may." As she walked toward the door, she waited on Darius to make a move, sure that sooner or later it was coming. It didn't. Instead Darius walked her out to her car.

"I had a really great time," Faith murmured as she lingered at her car door. Part of her wanted him to kiss her good night, but the other part felt like she'd found a friend and she needed to keep it that way.

Darius must have felt the same way, because he opened the door and motioned for her to get in. She did, and he waved before walking back toward his apartment.

Chapter Ten

So let me get this straight. You up in this man's apartment. You got the Kirk Whalum goin', although for the life of me I can't understand why anyone would listen to that crap. He should've been bumping that new Jay-Z slow cut. Anyway, y'all got the atmosphere working, talking and all. And he doesn't try anything?" Jasmine made herself comfortable on Faith's sofa as she flipped through *Vibe* magazine. Faith had tried to act mad when Jasmine had shown up at her doorstep the following evening, but Jasmine was the type that wouldn't let you stay mad at her for long. She'd wear you down until you forgave her for whatever it was she'd done. The bad part was she was always doing something that needed to be forgiven.

"That's what I said," Faith replied.

"That Negro is gay," Jasmine said.

"Whatever."

"Don't whatever me. Whatever his boyfriend."

"Jasmine, shut up. Darius is not gay. He told me he wants me to learn to love myself before we are intimate."

Jasmine threw the magazine on the table. "Oh snap, he ain't gay, he's runnin' game. He wants you to think he's all sensitive and stuff. Go on Darius. I ain't mad at him. I ain't seen no game like that in a long time."

Faith rolled her eyes as she made her way into the kitchen and began cleaning up and placing dishes in the sink. "No, he's just helping me see some things more clearly."

Jasmine followed her into the kitchen and leaned up against the wall. "Things like what?"

"About myself. Darius says if I truly loved myself I wouldn't give my body up so freely."

"And? You grown. Ain't nothing wrong with getting your freak on." Jasmine acted like she couldn't fathom what Faith was saying.

Faith didn't look at her friend. She knew Jasmine wouldn't understand. "Besides, it's just morally wrong, a sin."

Jasmine stared at Faith, a stunned look across her face. "Oh my God. Your grandmother has finally gotten to you."

"No, Darius said—"

"Who the hell is this Darius? He sounds like Jim Jones to me, corrupting your mind and stuff." Jasmine started pacing back and forth. "Faith, you are so naive. You let anybody tell you anything. This man, who you barely know, comes along and runs this major game to make you think he's all sweet, saved and stuff, and you're ready to go get baptized all over again."

Faith shook her head as she wiped down her counter. She threw the towel in the sink, then turned to Jasmine. "I am not naive. I admit I've done some dumb things when it comes to guys, but maybe there is something to what Darius is saying."

Jasmine groaned before throwing up her hands. "All this crazy talk is making my head hurt. Let's go to the club."

Faith sighed. Jasmine hadn't heard anything she'd said. Yep, it was time for a change. And that meant getting rid of the negative forces in her life. First on the list, Jasmine.

Chapter Eleven

It's just a matter of time. Faith couldn't help but let the negative thoughts creep up in her mind. After all, she and Darius had been going strong for almost three weeks now. They saw each other every day, even when she had to work. And what made their relationship so special was that they were friends, nothing more. Even though she sometimes longed for something more, she couldn't help but relish their friendship.

Faith was nervous as she surveyed her reflection in the sun-visor's mirror. Her makeup was modest. She looked down at her outfit. Her ankle-length skirt and sweater tank top set were achieving the conservative look she was going for, but she still couldn't help but be uneasy.

Faith couldn't believe she was actually going to church. Darius sat patiently in the driver's seat. They were in the parking lot of Mt. Sinai Baptist Church. Darius's cousin was preaching his first sermon there this morning. Faith had been flattered when Darius had asked her to attend. But when she'd found out his grandmother was going to be there, her nerves had shot up.

Ida Williams was a faithful member of Faith Memorial. And while she'd never given Faith a hard time growing up, she did associate with all those other women who did, including Wilma Wright.

"You think we can make it in before service ends?" Darius asked.

"Sorry. I'm just a little nervous."

"You'll be fine. You're with me and I'll make sure of it." Darius squeezed her hand and gave her a comforting smile. She returned his smile before getting out of the car and following him inside.

"So, did you enjoy service?" Darius asked as he led Faith outside of the church.

"It was nice. I really enjoyed it. Your cousin is an awesome preacher. It's just a matter of time before he gets his own church." Faith was surprised that she'd actually gotten into the service. She had pretty much written off all churches because she couldn't stand the hypocrisy. She'd never considered that maybe it was just Faith Memorial she didn't like.

"Yeah, Lester has a natural talent. Can you believe he's been an insurance adjuster for eight years? He's only been preaching a couple of months, but rumor is he's going to get his own church in Houston soon."

"Wow, maybe when I move to Houston, I can visit his church," Faith said.

"Maybe *we* can," Darius said with a sly smile.

"Well, if it isn't my handsome grandson." Both Darius and Faith turned toward a tall, elderly woman walking their way.

"Hey, Grandma Ida. I saw you up on the front row." Darius leaned in and kissed his grandmother on the cheek. "You know I don't like front rows," he joked.

"That's the best place to receive the word," Mrs. Ida said. She looked regal in a navy blue skirt, white blouse and pearls. Her salt-and-pepper hair was swept up in a French twist.

"Grandma, you know Faith," Darius said, pushing Faith toward her.

"Well, hello, Faith. It's so nice to see you again. It's been a long time."

Faith tried to keep her gaze steady, but her stomach was in knots. She didn't know why she was so nervous. "Hello, Mrs. Ida. It's good to see you, too."

Ida gave Faith a warm smile. "Why don't you two

come join me for dinner? I cooked chicken and dressing before I left. So all I have to do is warm it up and we'll be good to go," she said. She didn't wait for Darius and Faith to give her an answer. "So, I'll see you two back at the house." With that, she turned and walked off.

Dinner? Faith didn't know if she could sit through a whole afternoon with Darius's grandmother.

"Why are you looking so hesitant?" Darius asked.

"You have to ask?" Faith softly said. She smiled as Darius took her hand. She felt her nerves melting away. Darius had a way of making everything seem as if it were going to be all right.

"My grandmother is really a sweet person," Darius said soothingly.

"Yeah, that's before her beloved grandson brought home the town pariah."

Darius squeezed Faith's hand. "Would you stop it? Grandma may be a bit protective, but there's nothing you can't handle."

Faith tried to return the reassuring smile he was flashing her way. "If you say so."

Fifteen minutes later they were sitting at the breakfast table inside Mrs. Ida's home.

"So, we finally get to spend time together. I've heard a lot about you."

Faith wanted to bolt out the door.

"And yes, it's all pretty much been bad." Mrs. Ida

reached out and took Faith's hand. "But I'm my own judge of character, so I will decide for myself whether the stuff I heard is true or just a gross exaggeration, as I'm sure you know how my sisters in Christ can do it." Mrs. Ida giggled, and Faith felt her nerves easing.

Darius stood in back of his grandmother, a look of confidence across his face. She turned toward him.

"Now, Darius, why don't you go in the den and watch that fool-ball on TV and let Faith and I chat."

Darius looked like he was about to protest, then decided against it. "Okay. Faith, I'm right in the back if you need me."

"And what, pray tell, would she need you for?" Mrs. Ida asked.

Darius smiled at his grandmother as she shooed him away. Mrs. Ida stood, walked over to the teakettle, filled it with water, and began brewing some tea. Faith watched her while she worked. She was humming some hymn and seemed so content.

"So, did you know that I know your grandmother well?" Mrs. Ida said as she handed Faith a cup of tea and sat down across from her at the kitchen table.

"Yes, ma'am."

"We're not friends or anything, but we both have been members of Faith Memorial for a long time." Faith couldn't help but notice the way Mrs. Ida's tone shifted when she spoke of Grandma Pearl. "Yep, Pearl and I have a history." Mrs. Ida shook her head. Faith wanted to press for more details but decided against it. Mrs. Ida quickly changed the subject anyway.

"I haven't seen you around Faith Memorial in a while. Tell me, why did you stop coming to church?"

Faith wanted to tell her the truth—that she thought the people in the church were just a bunch of hypocrites. She wanted to tell Mrs. Ida how she felt that the peace and comfort most people claimed to find in church had never made its way into her heart. But she didn't want to insult Mrs. Ida, who appeared to be a God-fearing woman.

"I guess I just wasn't being fulfilled," Faith managed to say.

Mrs. Ida nodded without commenting. Her look was one of compassion, and she gave Faith a smile that seemed to say "let me know when you're ready to talk."

"Darius told me he met you outside of the church," Mrs. Ida said.

"Yes, ma'am, but I . . . I wasn't on my way in. Just kind of passing by," Faith responded. "He kinda came to my aid when Sister Wright was giving me a hard time."

"Don't take it personal. She gives everyone a hard time." Mrs. Ida laughed before her expression turned serious. "You know my grandson means the world to me."

"Yes, ma'am. I can see that."

"His mother is my only child and he's my only grandson. Kind of like you, I suppose. But I'm just going to be honest with you. If I had my way, he'd find himself a woman who is a lot more, shall I say, suitable for him."

Faith didn't know what to say. She thought they'd been getting along, but she guessed Mrs. Ida's true feelings were about to come out. Mrs. Ida didn't give her time to respond.

"But the one thing I won't do is condemn you for whatever it is you have or have not done," she continued. "And what matters above all else is the light I see in my baby's eyes when he talks about you. To me, that's all that matters. Besides, I was a bit wild in my day, so I say let he who is without sin cast the first stone."

Faith smiled wistfully. "I wish you could get my grandmother to see that."

The hard look returned to Mrs. Ida's face. "Sometimes those who preach the loudest are the biggest sinners of us all. Just remember, things aren't always what they seem with Pearl Logan."

Faith wanted to press her for more, but Darius reappeared in the doorway.

"How are my two favorite ladies?"

Mrs. Ida's expression immediately softened. "Getting along fine, just fine." She patted Faith's hand.

Faith smiled. Now she could see where Darius got his warm spirit.

Chapter Twelve

I could get used to this, Faith thought. She and Darius were at the Southeast Texas State Fair. She felt like a kid again, they were having so much fun.

They'd spent almost every day of the last four weeks together, and Faith was trying to avoid planning, wishing, hoping for anything more than just friendship. She wanted to just take it one day at a time. But she was really starting to get worried. They hadn't so much as caressed each other. He didn't hesitate to show her affection; she just wasn't used to being this involved with someone and not being intimate.

"Hey, baby girl!" Faith heard a familiar voice call out as she and Darius stood in line for a funnel cake.

Faith turned and groaned at the sight of her mother, clad in her signature leopard-skin skirt, this time in orange. She also had on a black skintight top and three-inch heels. Faith had assumed her mother had left town again, since she hadn't heard from her in over a month. "Vera, what's goin' on?"

"Umphh, and who might this be?" Vera asked as she strutted over toward the couple. Her eyes were scanning Darius.

"This is my friend, Darius. Darius, this is my mother, Vera."

Darius shook Vera's hand. "Pleased to meet you, Miss Vera."

Vera giggled. "Ohhhh, cute and he got him some manners."

Faith turned up her nose. The smell of liquor permeated Vera's clothes, and her eyes were bloodshot red. It was obvious she was drunk. "Vera, what are you doing out here?" Not only was Faith embarrassed, but she was also anxious to get her mother to move on. Things were going good with her and Darius, and she didn't want him to get turned off by her mother's wild ways.

"What, you think the fair is only for you young folks? I'm out here with Deacon Wright."

Faith felt herself getting nauseated.

Vera leaned in close to Faith's ear. "Girl, you know he said his wife ain't gave him none in six years. I told him he's practically a virgin again. He just laughed and said how I was the best this side of the Mississippi. He's a porker, but ain't nothing I can't work with." She laughed.

Faith was repulsed. Of course, Vera had no way of knowing she'd been with Deacon Wright, but the thought was repulsive nonetheless. Darius was trying to act like he wasn't listening, but she knew he could hear everything.

"Okay, Vera. We'll see you later." Faith blew off the funnel cake. She just wanted to get away from her mother. Watching her mother drunk, loud and looking like she had just stepped off a corner tore at Faith's heart.

Vera ignored her and kept talking. "Mama would have a heart attack if she knew I was with her precious Deacon Wright."

"Bye, Vera." Faith grabbed Darius's hand and pulled him out of line. He didn't question her sudden desire to leave.

"Wait, you ain't gon' stick around and say hi to the Deacon? He ought to be out the toilet any minute now. He been in there twenty minutes already. I told him about eating all them dang turkey legs and fried pickles." Vera slapped her leg as she laughed.

Faith felt like she wanted to cry. Maybe it was better when Vera wasn't around. That way she could always create an image of how her mother was, and not be subject to witnessing the real thing. "No, we gotta go," Faith said.

"It was nice to meet you, Miss Vera." Darius gave a meek wave.

"You too, darling," Vera replied.

Faith shook her head at her mother. Just as they were leaving, she heard her mother call out, "Wait! Here comes the deacon." Vera turned and frantically waved toward the men's restroom. As soon as she turned her back, Faith pulled Darius's hand even harder and darted off.

"Your mother's quite a character." Faith and Darius were sitting on his balcony after a full day at the fair. The night was clear, and they had been stargazing for nearly an hour. Faith had hoped to escape any conversation about her mother, but she'd figured that sooner or later Darius would bring it up.

"Yeah, she's something else," Faith replied, a melancholy look across her face.

"You want to tell me what's wrong? You've seemed down ever since we got back from the fair."

Faith leaned back in the patio chair. "You saw my mother. And even though you were trying to act like you didn't, I'm sure you heard her, too."

Darius flashed a wicked grin. "Well, I did kinda hear her talking about getting her groove on with the deacon."

Faith rolled her eyes. "That's exactly what I'm talking about. If you came from a family like that, you'd be down too."

"Oh, what's the big deal? I have some characters in my family, too."

"Whatever. Your grandmother is the epitome of class."

Darius lowered his voice and gazed out over the balcony. "Yes, but my mother was schizophrenic. Nobody knows that. It's the family secret. Grandma Ida had her sent to a mental hospital in San Diego, which is how I ended up there. I went to college to be near her. When she died, I moved back home to Beaumont," Darius said. "So you see, we definitely aren't perfect."

"I'm sorry. I had no idea."

"Why would you?"

They sat in silence for a few more minutes before Faith spoke again.

"At least your mother had an excuse. She had a real disease. My mother doesn't have an excuse. She gets drunk just to get drunk. Just like my grandmother doesn't have an excuse for being so evil. That's just the way they are," Faith said.

Darius took her hand. "Faith, alcoholism is a disease as well. Maybe if you could help her get to the root of her problems, she could conquer it."

"Help her? I need help myself." Faith lowered her head. "You just don't understand what it was like for me." Her voice softened. "My mother was known as the town tramp. Kids at school used to tease me about how she was sleeping with so-and-so's daddy, or breaking up somebody's home. My best friend in the fifth grade stopped speaking to me because Vera messed with her father and caused her parents to get a divorce. She was in and out of my life all the time. And when she was in, all I ever wanted was her love, for her to be a normal mother. But that never happened. And my grandmother, she seemed to take all her anger at my mother out on me."

Darius listened intently, gently rubbing Faith's back as she talked.

"I don't know why I'm telling you all of this." Faith didn't want to burden Darius with her drama, especially because she was fearful that it might drive him away, but he was just so easy to talk to.

"It helps sometimes to tell someone," Darius replied.

"You know, I've never talked about my mother. Not to Jasmine, not to any of the men I've been with. And surely not to my grandmother. I actually tried to talk to her, but she's so busy spouting prayers, she never listens to me."

"Why do you think your mother is the way she is?"

Faith shrugged. "I don't know. I think she is just wild, like my grandmother claimed." Faith wanted to say if she could answer that, maybe she'd understand why she was out there herself. "And the sad part is I feel like I'm following in her footsteps," Faith continued.

"You don't have to."

"I never wanted to."

"Maybe if you understood your mother and her motivations, it would better help you deal with your issues," Darius suggested. "Have you tried sitting down with your mother and grandmother and talking about everything?" Darius asked.

Faith thought about it. Maybe he had a point. "What would I say? 'Mama, why are you such a loose woman? Why do you drink so much? Grandma, why are you such an evil witch?'" Faith forced a laugh. "Nope, don't think so."

"How about you try?"

Faith shot him an "are you serious" look. The expression on his face told her that he was.

"I never thought about that. Plus, Vera is never in town long enough."

"She's here now. Do you know how to get in touch with her?"

Faith nodded. "She gave me her cell phone number."

Darius reached over, grabbed his cordless phone and handed it to Faith. She hesitated before taking it.

"I can't believe I'm doing this," she said as she punched in Vera's cell phone number.

Vera answered on the second ring.

"Ummm, Vera?"

"Yeah, who's this?"

Faith looked at Darius, who gave her a reassuring nod before walking inside the apartment to give her some privacy.

"It's me, Faith."

"Hey, baby girl." Vera sounded groggy, almost like she had been crying.

"Are you okay?" Faith asked.

"Ummm-hmmm. Just lying around."

"Where are you?"

"Staying at a friend's place."

Faith contemplated asking more questions but decided she didn't know if she wanted to hear the answers, so she left it alone.

"I . . . I just wanted to check on you. Are you still with the deacon?"

"Naw, he gave me some mumbo jumbo about having to get home to his wife." Faith could have sworn she heard pain in her mother's voice.

"I'm sorry, Vera."

"Don't even worry about it, baby girl. I told you men ain't no good." Vera sniffed.

"Are you sure you're okay? I mean, you were, I mean, you were a little wired earlier," Faith said.

"Naw, baby. I'm sobering up. Just got a lot of stuff on my mind. That's all."

"Well, I won't hold you. I was . . . um . . . I was

just wondering if you can meet me at Grandma Pearl's tomorrow?"

Vera seemed to perk up. "What? You want to meet where?"

"At Grandma Pearl's."

Vera was silent.

"I just think it's time for us to sit down and get some things out in the open. You know, deal with some issues."

Vera still didn't say anything, but Faith could tell she was contemplating the idea.

"I haven't asked you for much in life. But I'm asking you to do this for me. Please," Faith said.

Vera slowly exhaled. "Fine. It's time for me to face the old bat anyway."

Faith felt a sense of relief. "Thank you, Vera. You need me to come pick you up?"

"Yeah, meet me outside of Luby's at two o'clock."

"Luby's, the restaurant off I-10?"

"Yeah, I got a little part-time gig there."

Faith was speechless. She'd never known her mother to work. "Okay, I'll see you then."

Faith replaced the phone in the cradle and motioned for Darius to come back out on the balcony.

"We're meeting tomorrow at my grandmother's," Faith said as he stepped outside. "I hope I'm doing the right thing."

Darius sat down next to her. "You said yourself

you have some issues. The first step in dealing with them is facing your demons, finding out why things are the way they are."

"How did you get so wise?"

Darius laughed. "Wise, me? Yeah, right. I just see a beautiful woman who I am falling so in love with, and who I just want to be happy."

Faith's eyes grew wide. "What did you just say?"

Darius lifted Faith's chin. "I said I'm falling in love with you and I want you, us, to be happy."

Faith felt her eyes begin to pool with tears. But for the first time since she could remember, she cried happy tears.

Chapter Thirteen

Faith knew her mother was regretting the decision to come. She could see it all in her face. It was the first time the three of them had been together in years. When they arrived at Grandma Pearl's house, she hadn't even hugged her daughter. As soon as she'd seen Vera, she dropped to the floor in prayer.

That's where she was right now, kneeling in the middle of the living room floor, her hands clutched together, her eyes squeezed shut.

"And Lord, bless my house because these two sinners are surrounded by the devil. Keep your shield of armor around my home. Oh merciful Holy Father, hear my prayer. In Jesus' name, amen."

Vera was sitting on the sofa across from Faith, snickering and twiddling with her purse strap. Faith sat across from her, wondering what was so funny.

"You finished, Mama?" Vera asked.

Grandma Pearl grabbed onto the side of her rocking chair and pulled her hefty frame off the floor. "I ain't never finished praying for you. Ain't enough praying in this world for you."

Vera stretched her legs and put her feet on the coffee table. "That's right, Mama, because God don't save sinners like me."

Grandma Pearl shook her head. "And look at what you have on. Just shameful. Looking like the devil's wife."

Vera brushed her pink tiger-print skirt and pushed her breasts up. "I'll have you know I've been told I look quite good."

"The serpent told Eve the apple was good and the whole world's been shot to hell ever since," Grandma Pearl snapped.

"Would you two stop it?" Faith interjected. "That's not what we came here for."

Vera dropped her feet off the table and turned toward Faith, obviously exasperated. "What did we come here for, Faith?"

"I been asking myself that question since the two of you showed up on my doorstep," Grandma Pearl snarled as she plopped down in her rocking chair.

"I wanted us to talk," Faith said.

"We need to be praying, that's what we need to be doing." Grandma Pearl closed her eyes and bowed her head. "Precious Lord, we come before you today—"

Faith cut her off. "Grandma, please."

Grandma Pearl snapped her head up and opened her eyes. "Don't 'please' me. Ain't nothing left for y'all but prayer. I don't know how I raised some harlots. Lord knows yo' daddy, God rest his soul, and me tried our best. But I think the devil just had ahold of you both since birth."

Vera jumped up, throwing her hands up in exasperation. "Mama, save that crap! First of all, he wasn't my daddy."

Grandma Pearl's look turned ferocious. "He was the only daddy you ever knew," she said through clenched teeth.

Vera glared back at her. "I would have rather stayed fatherless."

"I will not have you stand in my house and talk ill of your father."

Vera stood defiantly in front of Grandma Pearl. "Let's shoot straight, Mama. My father is some rapist who you want to pretend didn't exist."

Grandma Pearl's mouth dropped open. "Don't you dare."

"Don't I dare what, Mama? Don't tell Faith how

you went down to the juke joint, got wasted and left with some man who raped you? Don't tell Faith that her mother is the product of that rape? Or don't tell her how noble Daddy was in forgiving you for going out? How he was sterile and couldn't have kids of his own, yet he still stood by your side as you birthed a baby he couldn't stand to look at? All my life I reminded him of that rape, of the man who violated his precious Pearl. I reminded him of your indiscretion. And he hated the ground I walked on until the day he died." Vera was crying now. Faith couldn't recall ever seeing her mother shed tears.

"Or do you not want me to tell Faith how his rage led to him doing the exact same thing to me?" Vera continued.

Faith was unprepared for the slap Grandma Pearl administered across Vera's face.

"Don't you start with those lies again." Grandma Pearl's voice was shaking.

Vera seemed unfazed by the slap. If anything, it seemed to empower her. "Or what? You'll put me out again? You'll turn your back on me again? Well, it's time the world knew your precious, beloved husband raped your only child and you did nothing about it."

"You jezebel! Nothing like that ever happened!" Grandma Pearl hissed.

"The doctor told you. He told you I'd been raped."

Although tears were flowing freely down Vera's face, her voice remained strong.

"You always were loose." Grandma Pearl shook her head. "You gave yourself to one of them nappy-headed boys, then you tried to blame it on your father."

"He's not my father!" Vera screamed.

"You're a whore! A drunken, lying whore!"

"You made me that way!" Vera took a deep breath, obviously trying to calm herself down.

"Don't you dare blame me for your sinful ways. I never put a bottle to your mouth or made you lay down in bed with one of your many men." Grandma Pearl seemed as if she was trying her best not to cry. The whole scene was surreal to Faith.

"I don't blame you." Vera stepped in closer to her mother. "But I'm just living up to your expectations. Do you know when I started drinking? When I became so loose, as you say? At fifteen, after your husband raped me and you put me out when I told you about it. I turned to men and liquor for comfort. At fifteen! I was a virgin before that. Did you know that, Mother? Your husband took my virginity, my sanctity, and you. And I hope he's rotting in hell."

Vera snatched her purse up and stomped out of the house.

Faith sat on the sofa in stunned disbelief. She considered running after Vera, but she was too shocked to move. "Grandma, is what she said true?"

"Of course not." Grandma Pearl was shaking. "It's just lies. She's a lying whore."

"Grandma . . ."

Grandma Pearl wearily sat back down in her rocker. "And you're just like her. Get out. Get out of my house."

"Grandma, please let's talk about this," Faith pleaded.

"Get out of my house. Why did you bring her here? Leave, and may God have mercy on your soul." Grandma Pearl picked up her Bible, opened it and began reading. Faith knew her grandmother. This conversation was over.

Faith sighed in exasperation as she made her way out to the car. She looked around for Vera and saw her off in the distance, stomping up the street. Faith jumped in her car and caught up with Vera, who had a look of fury etched across her face.

"Vera, get in."

"Faith, leave me alone, okay?" Vera's mascara was running down her face.

"Vera, please."

Vera stopped and sighed before stepping in the car. They rode in silence for several minutes before Faith finally spoke. "What just happened back there?"

"The truth."

"Was it really?"

Vera nodded as she wiped her face with the back

of her hand. "She still won't admit it. The doctor told her I was raped and she still wouldn't believe it. She wouldn't even ask Daddy anything about it. She called me everything but a child of God, then she threw me out in the streets. So the streets became my life. The sad part is she acts so self-righteous, but she is the biggest harlot of us all."

"Do you think it was her fault she got raped?" Faith didn't know why she was defending her grandmother. She was just having a hard time making sense of all of this.

"No, she didn't deserve to get raped, but if she didn't have her wild behind down in the juke joint in the first place it wouldn't have happened. Besides, it wasn't like it was the first time she had stepped out on her husband. In fact, she almost got herself killed messing around with someone's husband."

Faith almost lost control of the car. "What!" she said as she swerved back into her lane. "Grandma Pearl messing with someone's husband?"

"Yep, some classy lady from the church. I think her name was something Williams."

"Oh my God. Ida Williams?"

"Yeah, you know her?"

Faith gripped the steering wheel. That was the source of tension for Mrs. Ida. "Wow. That's Darius's grandmother."

Vera let out a small chuckle. "Small world. Yep, Mrs. Ida tried to strangle Mama when she caught her with her husband. Told Daddy and everything, but he was so blindly in love that he forgave her. Then Mama wants to act all holier than thou."

Faith navigated her Ford Escort onto the highway. She was at a loss for words. She wondered if Darius knew. This was all just too much. They rode in silence for a while before Vera said with conviction, "Baby girl, don't be like me or your grandmother. I've been fighting an inner battle all my life, and to be honest, I've kind of given up on myself. But you still have a chance. Don't let Mama do to you what she did to me. Shoot, don't even let me play any role in bringing you down. You're strong, beautiful and you can make something of yourself. You're so much better than me. Don't follow in my footsteps."

Faith stared at her mother, who still had tears on her face. It hurt Faith's heart to see her mother in such pain. No, they had never had the ideal relationship, but Faith could now tell Vera was struggling with her own demons. Faith took her mother's hand and gently squeezed it as Vera looked out the passenger window.

"Baby, I'm not an alcoholic," Vera said. "I only really drink when I come here. I have to dull the pain, make the memories go away. They do, but they always come back."

Faith felt sorry for her mother. If this was the burden she'd carried all her life, no wonder Vera was the way she was.

Faith took a deep breath. When Darius had convinced her to deal with her issues, never in a million years had she thought they'd be this deep.

Chapter Fourteen

Faith couldn't help but smile as she gathered up the dirty linen. Even a morning of dealing with her bossy supervisor couldn't ruin her mood. After she'd dropped her mother off, Faith had gone straight to Darius's apartment.

After she'd filled him in on everything, including the part about his grandmother, he'd held her well into the night. Their cuddling had turned passionate, and Faith had been sure they would take things to the next level. But Darius had shocked her even more by saying he still didn't want to make love to her. He'd said that was something he wanted to reserve for their wedding night. Faith had almost had a heart attack.

While it wasn't quite a proposal, it was the closest she had ever come—at least where the man actually meant it. Faith relished the fact that Darius was falling in love with her and not her body. But even more important, he'd helped her deal with issues that would help her learn to love herself. She still had some issues to work through, but Darius had Faith finally wanting to respect herself, and that made her feel good.

Faith smiled as she thought of how they'd fallen asleep in each other's arms. He'd gotten up early and cooked her breakfast before she'd headed out. She'd come to work in a good mood, and nothing could ruin that.

Faith knocked on the door of the first room on her route. "Housekeeping."

Faith heard playful banter. "I'll come back," she called out. She was just about to turn and leave when she heard a familiar voice say, "Boy, you better get back over here."

Faith leaned in closer to the door. She heard a male voice mumbling something before the woman broke out in more giggles. Faith knew she should've just kept going on her route, but curiosity won out. She tapped on the door again. "Jasmine, is that you?" She paused a few seconds. "Jasmine, stop playing. I know that's you, girl."

Faith heard the giggling die down, then a lot of scuffling before Jasmine, clad only in one of the motel's raggedy bath towels, cracked open the door. "What's up, Faith?"

"What's up with you?" Faith peered over Jasmine's shoulder. The uneasy look on her best friend's face was raising Faith's antennae. "Who you got in there?"

Jasmine looked flustered. "I thought you were off on Mondays."

"Normally I am, but I'm working for someone today." Faith stood on her toes, trying to peek in the room. "Who's in there?"

Jasmine refused to move from the door. "Look, Faith, let me get with you later, a'ight? I'm kinda handling some business right now."

"Girl, you are something else. I know that ain't Tyrone, because he wouldn't be caught dead up in this sleazy place. But you handle your business then." Faith was just about to turn when she noticed the black Jeep Cherokee out of the corner of her eye. It was parked right in front of the motel room, the personalized plates leaving no doubt about who was in the room.

"Is Xavier in there with you?" Faith asked, stunned.

Jasmine shifted her gaze away from Faith.

"I don't believe you! You know how much he hurt me and you're laid up in the motel *where I work* with him?"

"Calm down." Jasmine lowered her voice. "It ain't even like that."

"What's it like then, Jasmine?"

Jasmine sighed heavily, then ran her fingers through her blonde braids.

"Did you come here just to hurt me? Both of y'all have apartments, why would you come here?" Faith searched Jasmine's face for answers.

Jasmine shifted her weight and leaned against the door. She couldn't look Faith in the eye. "We didn't want folks all up in our business. And I told you, I didn't think you would be here."

Faith just stared at her friend. "I thought you were my girl."

Jasmine sucked her teeth and rolled her eyes. "Oh, so now you wanna act like we all close and stuff. You ain't even been around lately. Every time I ask you to go to the club, you blow me off. Plus, you got Prince Charming. Darius," Jasmine continued. "So why you worried about what I'm doing or who I'm doing it with?"

Xavier reached over Jasmine's shoulder and pulled the door open. "Y'all talking about me?" he asked with a mischievous grin.

Faith was just about to say something when she noticed the tall, lanky man behind Darius slipping on his pants. She shook her head in disgust.

"So I guess she did for you what I wouldn't?"

"I guess so," Xavier snidely replied.

"You know what, you both are low down and deserve each other."

"Why you actin' like he meant something to you?" Jasmine cried.

"He didn't, you did." Faith spun off, leaving her cart behind her. She was surprised that the tears didn't come. Jasmine's betrayal stung, but it was as if a revelation had come over Faith. If ever there was a sign that it was time to let Jasmine go, this was it.

Faith clocked out, not caring if she got in trouble for leaving early. She debated going over to Darius's apartment and actually started heading that way. But something inside her made her turn around. As sweet as Darius was, maybe it was time Faith stopped running to him for comfort and found her own comfort within.

Faith passed Parkdale Mall and navigated her way onto I-10. How did she keep ending up in dysfunctional relationships? From her family, to Jasmine, to all the men in her life, why couldn't she have a normal, healthy relationship?

"Darius is normal," she muttered to herself. "So then maybe it's me, maybe I'm the dysfunctional one."

"How can I be good for someone when I'm no good for myself?" Faith needed time to clear her head. She needed to figure out how to get her life back on track. She'd been so consumed with finding a good relationship that she'd never thought about working on herself. Faith didn't realize she was talking out loud to herself until she noticed the trucker driving next to her looking at her like she was crazy.

Faith smiled and waved before focusing back on the road.

Before she knew it, Faith found herself on the outskirts of Houston. She drove to the southwest side, to an area she knew well. It was a small shopping complex that she had visited many times. It was the place where she hoped to one day open her beauty salon.

Faith parked, got out and sat on the hood of her car to think about her dreams. She'd been using money as an excuse, but Faith realized that deep down, she had been hoping she'd find the man of her dreams and they'd come to Houston together. Now that she'd finally found him—at least she thought she had—why was she suddenly ready to move to Houston, with or without him?

"What sense does that make?" Faith mumbled. She shook her head as she slid down off her car. She'd made up her mind; it was time to move on. She was going back to Beaumont to close some doors, then she was making the move she should've made a long time ago.

Now, she just had to figure out where Darius fit in her new plan.

Chapter Fifteen

Faith prayed all the way back to Beaumont and, once she finally got back home, throughout the night. Darius blew up her phone trying to get in touch with her. She didn't want to talk to him because she wanted to make sure she was making the right decision. She called him first thing in the morning and told him that she wanted to see him because they needed to talk. They made plans to meet, and Faith had every intention of telling him that as much as she cared about him, she had to leave. It was time she stepped out on faith and moved to Houston to follow her dreams. She finally felt strong enough. And Darius had helped her find that strength. That's why it saddened her to have to leave him.

Faith would deal with Darius later today. Right now, she was ready to face her demons. She'd decided it was part of her closure process. She picked up the phone and punched in Jasmine's number.

"Faith, what's up?" Jasmine answered, obviously looking at the caller ID. "I'm glad you called. Look, I'm sorry about yesterday. I just got caught up. You know how slick Xavier is and all. We were just having a little fun. It didn't mean anything, really. As soon as you left, I told him that was it."

Faith wasn't in the mood to hear any excuses. She wasn't about to let Jasmine talk her way out of this. "Jasmine, that's the sad part. You threw away our friendship over a man who didn't mean anything."

"Come on, Faith. What's the big deal? You know how I do."

"I do, Jasmine, and that's part of the problem."

"What is that supposed to mean?"

"It means that I have always known how you were and I made excuses."

Jasmine got offended. "So you think you're better than somebody now?" Jasmine snapped. "Bring your behind over here and say that to my face."

Faith exhaled as she shook her head in frustration. "Jasmine, I'm not trying to fight you."

"That's because you know I will kick your a—"

Faith interrupted her tirade. "I called to tell you I'm moving on and we need to just end our friendship now. Thank you for being there for me all those years, but we're two different people now, going in two different directions."

"I don't believe you, Faith. You gon' throw nearly twenty years of friendship away over some dude? I thought we were deeper than that," Jasmine protested.

"Jasmine, this isn't just about Xavier."

"Then what is it about? That preacher got you ready to join a cult or something? I can't stand him, coming in here messing with your mind and stuff."

"He's not a preacher, although he is a man of God. And he isn't messing with my mind, except getting me to see that I deserve to live better than I have been living."

"Whatever, Faith. When he sleeps with you, then dumps you, don't come crawling back to me, begging me to be your friend again."

Faith laughed. Jasmine was something else. "You know what, Jasmine? That is something you don't ever have to worry about. Take care of yourself." With that, Faith placed the phone back in its cradle. She felt good and needed to head to the next demon on her list—Grandma Pearl. But that was a conversation she needed to have face-to-face.

Thirty minutes later, Faith was standing on Grandma Pearl's front porch.

"Who is it?" Grandma Pearl snapped after Faith banged on the front screen door.

"It's Faith."

"It's unlocked," Grandma Pearl called out. "But wait before you come in. I have to get my holy oil." Faith didn't wait, instead pulling open the screen door and making her way inside.

Faith watched her grandmother. She looked unusually frail as she walked toward Faith, the oil positioned to pour in her hands. Faith gently grabbed her grandmother's arm. "No, Grandma. Do not do that," Faith said sternly.

Grandma Pearl looked taken aback and was about to say something when Faith cut her off. "No more oil, water, or whatever that is. No more, ever again."

"Don't you dare—"

"Grandma, I don't mean to be disrespectful, but sit down."

Grandma Pearl gasped. "I'm going to pray, that's what I'm gonna do."

"No! No praying. No oil. Just sit your old behind down and listen for a change, dangit!"

Grandma Pearl clutched her chest, her eyes wide. "How dare you get blasphemous in my house."

"Grandma, I said 'dangit.' That is not a curse word. Now sit down and let me say what I came to say. After I'm done, I'll never darken your doorstep again." Faith didn't know where she was getting the strength to stand up to her grandmother, but she knew this was long overdue.

Grandma Pearl sat down. Faith sat next to her and looked her grandmother in the eye. "I need to know if what Vera said is true."

"I told you don't believe nothing that lying floozy of a mother of yours says."

"Stop lying to me and to yourself. What made my mother into a floozy? Was it your not believing that she'd been raped?"

"I refuse to answer that foolishness." Grandma Pearl stood and began busying herself stacking the magazines on the coffee table.

Faith could no longer contain her frustration. "You stand there so self-righteous, condemning me, condemning my mother. You made me hate her and myself because I was just like her. But the more I'm seeing, it's not my mother I'm like, it's you."

Grandma Pearl raised her hand to slap Faith, but the look on Faith's face stopped her in her tracks. She lowered her hand and glared at her granddaughter.

Faith pursed her lips. "You think hitting me hurts any more than what you've done all these years? That one little slap is nothing compared to the scalding hot baths you made me take as you tried to wash away my sins. Or the thrashings with anything in sight because I remotely showed interest in boys. None of that compares to the pain you caused me inside.

"I think you know what happened to my mother. Just like I know all about you. How you got caught with Mrs. Ida's husband. How you weren't always the saint you pretend to be. You try to bury yourself in that Bible as a cover-up. Always praying for someone else." Faith turned to leave. There was no getting through to her grandmother. Never had been, never would be. "As you sit here and wither away a lonely, old bitter woman, you need to pray for yourself. Repent for not saving your child. Ask for forgiveness for being the biggest sinner of us all."

With that, Faith walked out of her grandmother's house for what she felt was surely the last time.

Chapter Sixteen

Four Months Later

The sun beat down on Faith's back. But with the exception of the beads of sweat forming on her forehead, Faith barely noticed. Faith soaked in the rays as she sat on a bench outside the church. She needed a few minutes to just meditate before she went inside.

Faith ran her fingers lightly over the cover of the small Bible that sat in her lap. Could she really find peace in these pages? Could she ever develop the faith that seemed to keep Darius at peace? A calm came over her that told her she could.

"Hi, baby girl. You look beautiful."

Faith looked up at Vera and smiled.

"Hey there. So do you, but that skirt," Faith chuckled as she motioned toward her mother's red zebra-skinned miniskirt. "Do you have one of those in every color?"

Vera laughed. "You know how I do it." She wiggled her hips. Vera's blouse was actually pretty conservative, so Faith figured she wouldn't give her a hard time about the miniskirt.

"Why are you sitting out here alone?" Vera looked around. "Shouldn't you be inside?"

"I just wanted to sit here and get my head together. You know, get mentally prepared."

"Girl, it's gonna take more than some mental stuff. Just take your mama's advice and keep you a man on the side."

"Vera," Faith groaned.

Vera shrugged. "Okay, but don't say I didn't warn you," she joked. Her expression turned serious. "I'm just messing with you, baby girl." She rubbed Faith's cheek. "It looks like you got you a good man. Don't listen to me. I ain't ever been married before. Probably never will be. So you go inside that church, you marry that man, and you keep God at the center of your marriage and you'll be all right."

"What? You're giving me some spiritual advice?"

"And? God speaks to heathens too. We just don't

listen most of the time." Vera flashed a comforting smile, then reached out and hugged Faith tightly. "I'm sorry, but I'm not staying," Vera softly said as she released Faith from her embrace.

"Huh? But I want you to stay."

Vera shook her head. "No can do. My time here is done. Going on two months without a drink—cold turkey." Vera triumphantly waved her fists. "You were my inspiration, baby."

"I'm happy for you. So, are you giving up the men, too?" Faith smiled.

"Come on now. It's only so much torture a girl can take. Letting the liquor go is hard enough," Vera chuckled.

"I'm proud of you, you know that?" Faith said.

"Shoot, I'm the one who's proud. You really got yourself together."

"You're not doing so bad yourself. I heard you got a promotion at Luby's, so I don't understand why you're leaving."

"It's time. Besides, me and the work thing just don't get along." Vera sat down on the bench next to her daughter. "No, seriously, I guess we all had some demons to deal with, and facing mine helped give me the strength to get my act together."

"I'm happy to hear that." Faith scooted in closer to her mother. She knew neither of them had spoken to Grandma Pearl in months. Maybe it was better that way, because once they'd let her go, they'd both seemed able to move on with their lives.

"Well, I'd love to sit out here in the one-hundred-degree sun with you all day, but you need to get moving," Vera said.

"Please stay." Faith looked longingly at her mother.

"I'm leaving, but not for good this time. I'll be back, but I'm only coming to visit you in Houston. I'm done with Beaumont. You're still going, right?"

"In two weeks. Darius has already found a job there."

Vera shook her head. "I can't believe you got him to go with you."

Faith smiled as she thought about how eager Darius had been to make the move. "I think he's more excited than me. He said we could live in Alaska as long as we're together. But I'm really hoping to have my own business in a few years. I'm just going to work in a salon there until I save enough money to start my own."

"That's my girl. You'll do it." Vera stood up. "I'm sorry, I have to run. I want to get out of here before those Faith Memorial folks start rolling in."

"Vera, it's an intimate wedding, we probably invited thirty people, and those are all people Mrs. Ida wanted here. We could've just gone to the courthouse, but Mrs. Ida acted like she would die when we even suggested it."

"Umphh. Is your grandmother coming?"

"I doubt it. I haven't talked to her, and I heard she's keeping pretty much to herself." Faith expected a smart comment from Vera, but instead Vera just turned her head. Faith couldn't help but notice the sad expression on her face. Vera seemed to shake off whatever was bothering her and turned back to Faith.

"I wanted to give you something." Faith laughed as Vera reached in her bra and pulled out a small folded-up napkin. She unfolded the napkin and removed a small locket.

"Your grandma Pearl gave this to me when I was only twelve years old. I've kept it all these years because it is the only good memory I have." She handed it to Faith. "I want you to have it. It's your something old."

Faith reached out and took the locket. She opened it up. Inside was a picture of Vera as a baby. On the other side was a baby picture of Faith.

"I put your picture in there the day I left Beaumont. I know you didn't think so, but you were always in my heart."

Faith stared at the locket and didn't realize she was crying until the tears dropped into her hands.

"Come on now. You gon' mess up your beautiful

makeup. Remember, no matter what, I love you," Vera said.

"I love you, too, Mama," Faith replied somberly.

Vera smiled warmly. "Mama. You haven't called me that since you were a little girl. That means a lot. Now stop before you have me crying, too." She wiped Faith's tears. "Darius is a smart man. He's going to make you very happy. I want you to be happy so I can live through you. I'm sorry I won't be inside the church as you tie the knot, but you're inside here." She pointed to her heart, before leaning in and kissing Faith on the cheek. "Now go marry your man."

Faith hugged her mother tightly one more time before Vera stood to walk off.

Vera blew Faith a kiss, then got into a waiting car with a man Faith didn't recognize. Faith could only smile. Her mother would never change, at least when it came to men. But Faith could. She had. And couldn't be happier.

Four hours later, Mrs. Darius Winston Williams II lay across the bed in the Westin Hotel's honeymoon suite. She felt on cloud nine as she squirmed in the plush, heavenly bed.

Faith watched as her husband made his way to her bed. Yes, their relationship had progressed quickly. They'd been together less than a year. But Faith had no doubt that this was right.

She felt a wholeness as Darius slid in bed next to her and took her in his arms. He had held true to his convictions, and they had not made love. Tonight would be their first time. Faith had only heard about stuff like this in the movies. Never in a million years had she thought that she would be living it. She was nervous, excited, and feeling a mixture of emotions. But most of all, she felt happy because she was finally about to give herself to a man—the right way.

Maybelline
J. D. Mason

Nate's Place

"Hey, sugah," Nate Walker said, then smiled and kissed her tenderly on her cheek. Olivia Phillips doubted he even knew her name, but "sugah" was certainly a nice alternative, and it was the greeting he gave her every time he saw her at his club, or at the bank where she worked when he came in to make his weekly deposits.

"Hey, Nate," she replied as she squeezed his hands in hers. His gentle, bedroom eyes twinkled at her in the dimly lit bar. He was a little older than Olivia. The hints of gray sprinkled around his temples and in his goatee told her that. And he was a handsome man, medium brown skin, short salt-and-pepper hair. She guessed him to be five-ten, maybe six feet, but barely, with an average build, and a bit of a belly that only added to his charm and character.

"Got your table ready for you, darlin'." He held her hand and led her to the small table in the corner of the room, clouded in shadow and just left of the stage. He pulled out her chair for her to sit down. "Mrs. Walker will be with you shortly," he said softly in her ear. He had the kind of voice that turned a woman's knees to jelly, low and smooth, erupting from deep underneath the ground, through the bottoms of his feet, and eventually past his lips. It was a voice that commanded patience and provoked anticipation, because he sounded so good.

"Thanks, Nate."

Nate greeted a few more customers, and then finally made himself at home at the piano on the small stage in the center of the room. A nameless melody emanating from his fingers fluttered through the room, soothing all manner of savage beast brave enough to step inside and be slain by the magic sword that was his piano. Nate fell into a trance of his own doing, losing himself in the glory days of his illustrious career as a jazz musician, clouded by too many drugs, too much money, and too many women to recall. He'd long since disappeared from the spotlight of the music world, choosing to settle down in this small Oklahoma town, on this particular corner of the city, inside his own establishment—Nate's Place. It seemed an appropriate enough name, and it summed up everything it was and wasn't in those two little words. To anybody passing by, it was an odd little hole-in-the-wall on a corner that didn't seem to suit it. But to Olivia and everyone else who frequented the place, it was a haven, and a sanctuary from the debris of nine to fives, lovers' quarrels, and disappointments. Nate never seemed to lock his doors, earnestly welcoming patrons with a warm, inviting smile and a cold beer.

Mrs. Walker. It was the only name she'd ever heard the woman called. Even Nate, her husband, never called her by any other name. Tall, statuesque, and beautiful, she glided across the room and over to Olivia's table, looking more like an apparition than a cocktail waitress. Years younger than her husband, she was slender, but with the kind of ample behind that left men standing knee deep in a puddle of their own drool. Her shoulder-length hair was pulled off her face and pinned up in back. Full, pretty lips parted into a lovely smile by the time she reached Olivia. "Here you go, sweetie." She set Olivia's drink down on the table. "The usual."

Olivia smiled. "One of these days, I'm going to surprise you and order something different."

Mrs. Walker frowned. "Oh, don't do that. There's something comfortable about you regulars, like family. And if any of you ever changed, it would break my heart." She glided back across the bar and disappeared behind a door. Longing male gazes fixed themselves on that door, anxiously awaiting Mrs. Walker's return. Men used to look at Olivia that way. A long time ago. A very long time ago.

Nate hunched over his instrument, slowly shaking his head from side to side, a cigarette dangling from the corner of his mouth. His eyes were shut tight as he tapped his foot evenly to the rhythmic beat playing in his head. The rest of the band just watched him play, awed by the power of this one man. Physically, he was in that room with the rest of them, but his spirit had left a long time ago.

The sound of outside crept in from the open door when Q walked in. He stood there for a moment, scanning the room until he spotted her. Quinton Bradford was his name, but most people just called him Q. Olivia's heart raced at the sight of him, and she sat up straight in her seat and waived her hand to make sure he'd seen her. How long had it been? Nearly a year since the last time she'd seen him, and so much had happened. Her life had changed. She'd changed. Had he? Lord, she hoped not. Please, let him be the same man he was back then. Let him still love her the way he had back then.

"Sorry I'm late," he said, out of breath, sitting down next to her. "Had to stay a few minutes late after school . . . the team was . . . well," he shrugged. Q was a high school gym teacher and football coach.

"That's fine," she said, trying not to sound too anxious. "I just got here myself."

Q looked like perfection. He looked like the image she would draw from her imagination of what perfect should look like on a man. Tall—six-two, dark, smooth skin, bald, mustache drawn thinly over his lip, and those eyes. He'd always been able to make her weak with those eyes, rich, marble brown eyes that bore a hole into her if he stared too long. She'd missed him more than she'd realized, and she fought the urge to lunge into his lap and smother him with a million kisses. There'd been no kisses between them the last time they'd been together. Just angry words, tears, and bitterness, all coming from her.

Mrs. Walker appeared out of nowhere. "What can I get you?"

"A beer is fine," he said. "Thanks."

There was an awkwardness between them that didn't used to be there. There had been a time when he'd been her best friend, when talking to Q had come naturally and easily and there had been nothing she hadn't been able to say to him. Likewise for him. But that had been before breast cancer. It had changed Olivia in ways she'd never imagined any single thing could. And she'd turned on him, her man, like a rabid dog, for no other reason than the fact that he'd been there.

"How've you been?" she asked, nervously, for lack of anything better to say.

"You asked me that earlier, on the phone." He made no attempt to hide his indifference. She'd have preferred hatred over indifference. "I'm good," he nodded. "You?"

She tried to make a joke of it. "You asked me that over the phone too." Q showed no sign of emotion. "I've missed you." She blurted out the words because they'd been burning the tip of her tongue since he'd walked through that door, and even before that, since she'd gathered up the courage to call him two days earlier.

Q stared at the stage, watching Nate work magic that only Nate knew how to make. "Is it gone?" He turned to her. "The cancer?"

"It's never really gone, Q. I'm in remission. Hopefully, I'll stay in remission."

Mrs. Walker returned with his beer, and Q paid the tab for both drinks.

"You didn't have to do that," Olivia said to him. "I've got money. I can pay for my drink."

Frustration showed on his face. "Oh, here we go."

"What?" She looked perplexed.

"I paid for the drinks because I wanted to, Olivia. It's not about who's got money and who's—"

Her independence was getting in the way again. It was the tension between them that grew into all kinds of debates at any given hour or place. He was a giver. It was just his nature. She was not a taker, and that was her nature. She'd always been fierce in her independence, her I-can-do-it-by-myself stance, because it was easier than depending on someone else, and having them let her down. She'd learned the lesson young, when her father had left without a trace and her mother had dropped her off at a neighbor's, kissed her good-bye and never bothered coming back. It was what she knew, her way of making the best out of a bad situation that happened to be her life. And sometimes, she sensed that he hated her for it.

"I'm sorry. Old habits die hard sometimes."

"Why'd you want to see me, Olivia?" he asked frankly.

"I told you. I missed you, Q." She swallowed the trembling in her voice. "I just needed to see you."

He took a long gulp of his beer and sat quietly for a minute. "A year ago," he started to say in a low voice, "you told me to get the hell out of your place, your business, and your life."

"I know."

"I begged you to let me stay," he said as tears glistened in his eyes.

"Q—"

"I tried, Olivia. I tried to be there for you, and to see you through this thing."

"I know you did," she said, desperately trying to explain. "But I was so messed up over this. I was so messed up . . . you have no idea."

"You're right. I have no idea. But the harder I pushed to be there for you, the harder you pushed back."

"I'm sorry, Q." Olivia felt tears burning her eyes too. "I was so wrong and so selfish, and—" She reached out to him, but he pulled away. "Q?"

"Whatever it took, Olivia. Whatever you needed, I wanted to be there for you. I tried. I tried my hardest."

"I was sick. I didn't know how to handle it, Q. I didn't know what else to do."

"What do you want? Why did you ask me to come here?" The expression on his face confirmed Olivia's worst fear—that Q was no longer that gentle, caring, giving man she'd fallen in love with. But then, she'd changed, so why shouldn't he?

She sat back and sipped on her drink. "I just hoped—" She felt so pitiful. "I still love you. I never stopped."

He shook his head and stared at her. "You have no idea what it is to love somebody, Olivia. It was always about you in this relationship, even before the cancer. It was always about what you wanted, when and how you wanted, and I jumped through hoops for you like a trained dog working a circus."

"That's not true," she said sadly, knowing deep down that he was right. "I never meant to make you feel like that."

"I don't think you know how to make me feel any other way. I'm happy you're better," he said with finality as he pushed back from the table and finished the last of his beer. "Six months ago I waited, hoping you'd call me and tell me you wanted me as much as I wanted you."

I do. She wanted so badly to tell him.

"But," he shrugged, "I'm over it, Olivia. I'm over you. Finally."

She watched him leave, and she ached when the door closed behind him. The pain she felt was the same kind of pain she felt when she realized she was alone in this world, and that all she ever had was herself. Olivia pushed away the memories of all the terrible things she'd said to Q, and all the terrible ways she'd treated him, blaming it on the illness when in fact the illness had just been a license to hurt someone she loved before they could hurt her. He was just protecting himself. That's all it was, and she couldn't blame him for that.

"I'm so sorry, Q. I really am," she muttered to

herself. She finished the last of her drink, then got up to leave. Nate was still lost in the space of his music, and Mrs. Walker was still serving drinks. She took one last look around before leaving. She sure was going to miss this place, she thought woefully. Nate nodded in her direction. *Good-bye.* He seemed to sense it too.

My Soul to Take

Q was nothing more than a last-ditch effort to find some meaning to her life. That's all he was. In retrospect, that's probably all he'd ever been. Olivia stood naked in front of the mirror in her bedroom, staring unemotionally at the place where her right breast should've been. There was nothing there now but an ugly scar in an empty space, and she marveled at the irony. She was just like that scar, and her life had always been empty.

She'd been fine back in the day, though. She recalled a time when she'd worn her blouses cut low in the front, her ample cleavage pushed up and out. Her hair had always been so thick and long, and she'd worn it bone straight and parted to one side. Chemo had taken every last bit of it out, and it was just starting to grow back, short and natural. Another chaotic mess that was just a part of who she was. Doctors prided themselves on saving her life, as if taking a breast were as simple as removing a hangnail.

Be glad we caught it when we did.

Many women have mastectomies and go on to live full and rich lives, Olivia.

But it wasn't about losing a breast. That was just another symptom of everything wrong with her. Olivia didn't know how to love, or to be loved. She'd wandered aimlessly through life, hungry for it, with no idea of what it should look, feel, smell, or taste like—until she'd lost Q, that is. And by the time she'd come to her senses and recognized it for what it was, she'd blown it. The only person in the world to accept her whole self, to be patient enough to hang around longer than an orgasm, to want to save her from everything, including herself, had been the one person she'd bent over backward to push away.

"Baby, I know this is hard on you." Q looked as desperate as she felt. He'd been calling and knocking on her door, and calling some more, until finally she let him in long enough to cuss him out.

"You don't know a damn thing! You don't know what

this feels like! You don't know what I'm going through, so don't try and pretend like you do!"

"Olivia! Why can't you let me be there for you? Why can't you just—"

Chemo had had her thoughts and stomach twisted. It had left her sense of reason tied in knots. Cutting off her breast had cut away at her humanity and deep into her soul, leaving behind a gaping wound too deep to heal because it had become infected with the hopelessness and sadness from the rest of her life.

"Because I don't need you! How many times—how many ways do I have to say it?" She wanted to hurt him, to run him off, to make him see that she really wasn't the catch he'd been so convinced she was. "How dumb can you be? How stupid, Q? And I don't need no fool in my life, chasing after me like some stray dog, right now! I don't want you in my life, in my business, or in my damn house! So get the hell out!"

He looked wounded when he left, but he made a promise to her before she slammed the door behind him. "You need me! When are you going to see that? I'm not giving up on you, on us, Olivia. I swear I—"

He'd called. She'd never answered. He'd come by. She hadn't opened the door. He'd even come to her job once, but she'd had the security guard escort him to the door. And then, he'd stopped. He'd just stopped, and the deafening sound of loneliness had begun to ring in her ears, giving her terrible headaches sometimes. That void he'd left inside her throbbed like the pain after her surgery, and it never went away.

If she'd seen the old Q rise up in his eyes tonight, she'd have had hope. If she'd heard that familiar tenderness in his voice tonight, she'd have looked forward to tomorrow. But that man was gone, and left in his place was another kind of man, one who wasn't about to let her harm him again.

Swallowing a bottle of sleeping pills isn't as traumatic as they make it look on television. The scene with the sobbing heroine, trembling as she writes her suicide note, swallowing one pill at a time, washing each one down with a sip from a clear, clean glass of water is all Hollywood. There is no background music adding to the tension of the scene in real life. Pills are swallowed by the handfuls, not one at a time, and there is no need to write a note, because who in the hell would she address it to? And the hero isn't standing right outside the door, ready to burst in just before she dozes off into eternal slumber.

Olivia wanted to die. No, she just didn't want to live. Too many disappointments, too many failed dreams, too much heartache, and one breast short of being the ideal woman made that whole living thing seem so overrated.

She lay naked in bed, staring up at the ceiling, then decided against the whole naked thing and got up to put on a T-shirt and some clean panties for when they finally found her body. It was pretty easy, actually, and she wondered why she hadn't thought of it before. Maybe because she'd thought it might hurt, or maybe because she'd thought she still had a chance to . . . to amount to something, to achieve something, to be more than nothing.

The sun was going down. No, wait. The sun set a long time ago. Olivia's eyes grew heavy, and she wondered why she struggled so hard to keep them open. The bed felt like quicksand, and her body began to sink down into the mattress billowing up around her, swallowing her in one massive gulp. That morbid little child's prayer crept into her thoughts, and Olivia whispered the words with heavy lips and a thick tongue:

Now I lay me
. . . to sleep
I pray . . . Lord
My . . . soul . . . my soul . . . to

Finally . . . some peace. It enveloped her and wrapped itself around her like a warm blanket, and Olivia gave in to the battle she'd been fighting with herself her whole life.

"What's her name?"

"On the count of three. One . . . two . . . three!"

"Olivia! Olivia Phillips!"

Light mixed with dark.

Life with—death.

"Olivia? Can you hear me? Open your eyes. Olivia?"

People pulling . . . tugging. Ripping. Pushing. Poking. Pressing. Light shining as bright as the sun, without the warmth.

"Olivia! Open your eyes for me!"

"Do we know what she took?"

"The date on the prescription is recent. I'm guessing she probably took all of them."

"She's not breathing!"

Waves and oceans. Heaviness. Weightlessness. Floating.

"Pressure's dropping! We're losing her!"

"Get that cart over here! Stat!"

"Charging! Clear!"

"Again!"

Breathless and light and warm. So warm . . . Yes. Home.

"Clear!"

"Doctors didn't save your life just so you could take it, Olivia." Dr. Lacy was a counselor who'd been assigned to Olivia during her observation period. She was too smug and condescending for Olivia's taste, her punishment from God for trying to kill herself and failing. Yeah. God had a sense of humor like that.

"I told you. It was an accident," Olivia said

indifferently, the same way she'd been saying it for the last three days.

"You swallowed twenty sleeping pills *accidentally*?" The good doctor's frustration was showing.

"Yes," Olivia said, emphatically.

"It always is," Dr. Lacy said arrogantly, scribbling something on a pad of paper. "Suicide isn't the answer. It never is."

Then what is the answer? Olivia waited for the woman to answer her unasked question, but she didn't, probably because she didn't have an answer.

"And that mastectomy wasn't the end of your life, Olivia. It was a new beginning. In time, maybe you'll see that." She got up from behind her desk, sat down next to Olivia, and handed her the note.

"I'm recommending antidepressants. They'll help, Olivia. Promise me you'll take them?"

"Sure." Olivia never flinched. "But it was an accident."

Pieces of a Dream

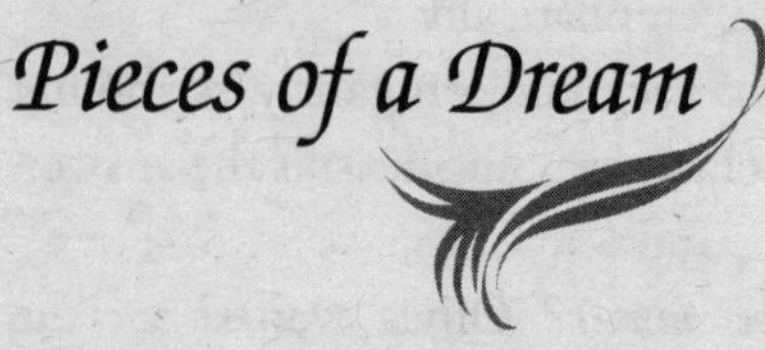

Maybelline braced herself in one corner of the compact elevator, cracking her gum and holding on tight to the rails. If there was one thing she hated more than elevators, it was riding in elevators, and cracking her gum helped to calm her nerves.

The elevator stopped and Maybelline smiled in welcome. It was her all right. That pretty girl who was carried out of here in an ambulance not too long ago. Maybelline's eyes lit up at the sight of her stepping into the elevator of their apartment building. She started to speak, but something told her that that girl was in no mood for idle chitchat. Something about her just screamed, "Leave me the hell alone!" So Maybelline cracked her gum even louder and kept her hellos to herself.

The woman stood with her back to Maybelline, staring up at the lighted numbers above the elevator door, watching them add one to each other. She wore a short natural, and Maybelline still loved naturals, even though black folks hardly ever wore them the way they used to back when she was coming up. Maybelline peered over the top rim of her glasses and leaned forward just enough, trying to see the kind of hair that was on that girl's head. She had a good grade—sort of. Naturals looked best when the hair was good and nappy. Hers was working all right.

Maybelline had the gift of discerning spirits. This one wasn't happy. That was easy enough to see in her hunched shoulders and the dark circles Maybelline had seen before the woman had turned her back to her on that elevator. And she smelled sad too. Oh, yes. Sadness had a scent to it, and no matter how hard you tried, you couldn't wash it off. It could only be cleansed with joy, but of course, sad people didn't too often have joy to bathe in, which was why they were sad, which was why they smelled the way they did.

What she wore couldn't have helped her spirits any. The young woman had on a dull gray blazer with matching skirt, and black flat shoes. Maybelline would've expected a woman her age to be wearing some high heels. Those sexy kind that made the muscles flex in a woman's calves. The kind she used to wear before she got fat. Although, fat or not, a woman could still look sexy in a pair of high-heeled shoes, but Maybelline's feet were bad too. And some lipstick wouldn't have hurt her any. Lipstick always made a woman feel better. Maybelline never left home without hers.

"Nice weather we're having," she blurted out, hoping to bait the girl into some conversation. But she just nodded a bit and faked a smile.

Maybelline wasn't offended, though. A nod and fake smile was the best that poor woman could do right now, so, no. She wasn't the least bit offended.

"Have a nice evening," Maybelline called out to her as she stepped off the elevator onto her floor. Maybelline smiled. She always did like the hard ones.

Olivia threw her keys on the coffee table and put her purse down on the couch. She'd been back to work a little over a week now, like nothing had ever happened. All anyone at the bank knew was that she had been ill. That's all they needed to know. And actually, no one seemed to have even realized she was gone.

"Haven't seen you around in awhile, girl. Where you been?"

"How was your trip? By the way . . . where'd you go?"

They didn't care, just like she didn't care, which was all good, as far as Olivia was concerned. She found a can of soup in the cupboard and a wine cooler in the refrigerator. Dinner.

While the soup cooked, she checked her answering machine—no one had called. She flipped through her mail—bills, bills, and look . . . more bills. Olivia poured hot soup into a bowl and took her meal into the living room, where she sat down on the couch, propped her feet up on the table, then turned on the television. She needed the noise to keep her thoughts at bay. She needed the visuals to keep her own memories from creeping to the forefront of her mind. That weird woman flashed in her mind, though. The one on the elevator popping her gum like crazy and drowning in all those bright colors she could never seem to match up right. Today she'd had on lime green polyester slacks, two sizes too small, and a floral patterned smock that had every color known to man in it. Olivia chuckled. The woman looked like a cartoon character, with those big, square glasses that filled her whole face. She wore a bad wig with blond hair hanging down her back. A dull gold tooth twinkled in the front of her mouth, and her bright red lipstick made her lips look like someone had punched her in them. Oh, and that perfume! Damn! Was she dipped in that bottle or what? It was so strong, Olivia grew nauseous just thinking about it. She shook her head and flipped through the channels until she found her favorite lawyer show. Olivia finished her soup, got comfortable on the sofa, and eventually dozed off.

"You're sinking, Olivia. Can't you feel yourself sinking?"

The voice was a man's voice, a familiar voice. It was Q's voice. Olivia struggled to open her eyes, but she couldn't. She struggled to lift her arms, move her head, to say something, anything, but she was paralyzed. Cold—it started at the tips of her toes, then gradually crept up her feet to her ankles.

"What are you going to do now?" he asked and hesitated, waiting for her to answer, but Olivia couldn't move her lips. He laughed. It was Q's laugh, hearty and robust, genuine. "Remember that time we went rollerblading? It was your first time. Remember? You told me you didn't need me. Now, why would you say something like that to me?" Her eyes were closed, but she saw his face and the sadness in his eyes.

I need you now, Q! she wanted to scream at the top of her lungs, but the words wouldn't come. Olivia felt powerless as the cold traveled farther up her legs to her calves, her thighs.

"You stumbled about a hundred times," he continued talking, telling the story of the first time they went rollerblading. "And all I wanted to do was catch you before you fell and hurt yourself. Do you remember what you did when I reached out to you, Olivia?" Again, he waited for her to answer, but she couldn't. "You swatted my hands away and screamed, 'I don't need your help!' Do you remember, Olivia? Tell me. Tell me you remember."

Olivia shivered, as the cold traveled up her hips to her waist. *I need you now! Please! I need you now!* She tried to reply, but still her lips wouldn't move.

"Sometimes, we ignore precious things, taking them for granted until it's too late. Love is a precious thing, Olivia. Life is precious and when you drift too far away from either, if you're not careful, you may not get any second chances."

Olivia struggled to open her eyes. They fluttered, capturing glimpses of light flickering across the room. The cold was on her chest now, and she found it harder to breathe. The weight of it threatened to suffocate her, and Olivia gasped desperately for air.

"Take my hand, Olivia," he said, reassuringly. "This could be the last chance you have. It could be the last chance I give you."

She wanted to reach for his hand, but her arms were pinned to her sides. Olivia felt her shoulder bucking against the backrest of the couch, as she wrestled with herself for the strength to reach out and take his hand. This time she wouldn't turn him away. She wouldn't deny his love, and she would hang on to him for as long as he let her.

"Take it now, Olivia. Before it's too late. I promise, I won't let you down, sweetheart."

She struggled harder to wake up, to reach out, to hold him. Why couldn't she move? Why couldn't she find the strength to break the spell of the cold, now squeezing her neck, choking and strangling her? Oh, dear God! She really didn't want to die.

Knock! Knock! Knock!

Olivia bolted up from where she lay sleeping, awakened by the sound. She drank in air, clutched her hand to her throat, and tried to make sense of her surroundings. It was just a dream, she surmised. A dream.

Olivia stumbled over to the door to answer it.

"Who is it?" she asked through the door.

"It's Maybelline. Your neighbor," a woman's voice answered.

Olivia cracked open the door, shocked to see the colorful little elevator woman standing in the hallway, holding a steaming pie between two oven-mitted hands, grinning from ear to ear, showing off that gold tooth of hers.

"I hope I didn't disturb you," she said apologetically. Olivia just stared at her. "But I made too much pie filling again and ended up with a whole 'nother pie

I shouldn't eat." She laughed. "I thought you might be so kind as to take it off my hands for me. It's sweet potato," she said, pushing the pie toward Olivia. "If I keep it in the house, I'll just eat it, and Lawd knows I don't need no more pie."

She wanted the woman to go away. And no, she didn't want her pie, but her eyes begged her to take it. "I really don't eat . . ."

The woman frowned. "Oh, please. I tried to give it to Mr. Sully, next door, but he said he's allergic to sweet potatoes. And it's a good pie." She grinned again, and her eyes twinkled. "My great-grandmomma's recipe. I just made too much is all. Really, I shouldn't be eating it anyway. My doctor's put me on a diet." She whispered it like her doctor might be listening. "But sometimes I can't resist, and sweet potato pie is my favorite."

If Olivia took the woman's pie, then the woman would go away. Olivia figured she was making this whole thing way too hard. She'd take the pie, pour it down the garbage disposal, and tell the woman later on that she didn't care for it. Olivia opened the door wider and reluctantly accepted the woman's gift. "Thank you," she said quietly. "How much—"

The woman waved her hand in the air. "Oh, it ain't no charge. It's just a pie," she said nonchalantly. "And besides, you doing me a favor by taking it." The woman started to walk away, and said over her shoulder, "Oh, and don't worry 'bout the pie tin. I'll be back for it in a few days." She pushed the button to the elevator and disappeared into it less than a minute later. Olivia had never known that elevator to come that quickly.

She closed and locked the door, then went into the kitchen to get rid of that weird woman's pie. And then the strangest thought came to her. How did the woman know where Olivia lived?

Maybelline

Tell me there's a smile waiting for me behind that lovely frown of yours, and I'll die a happy man."

Sometimes, Nate's lines were too smooth for his own good. Of course, Olivia couldn't help herself, and she smiled as he'd asked.

He sat down next to her and smiled back. "All right," he said, sounding relieved. "I'm cool now."

He wore black tonight. Nate looked good in black, especially expensive black. The crisp, white shirt underneath his blazer added to his classic appeal.

"How you doing, Nate?" Olivia tried her hardest

not to blush around this married man. Mrs. Walker knew what she had in him, and chances were she kept a closer eye on him than she let on.

"Good as new and shining like a brand-new dime," he winked. "What about you? You feeling all right, sugah?"

His deep voice washed over her like a warm shower. "I'm doing all right." She tried to sound convincing, but she could see in his face that he didn't quite believe her. "Really," she said, more convincingly. "I am."

"Got a new singer starting a set at nine. You staying?"

She looked at her watch. It wasn't even eight yet. "No," she frowned. "I have to get up early in the morning for work."

He started to protest, but then Mrs. Walker made her way over to the table. She gave her husband a sly look. "You over here starting something, Nathaniel?" she cooed as she looked at Olivia and winked playfully.

He laughed. "Now, you know me better than that, Mrs. Walker." Nate stood up and kissed her cheek. "Of course I am." He turned to Olivia before leaving the table. "You should stay and listen. She's pretty good."

Nate disappeared through the door behind the bar. Mrs. Walker turned her attention back to Olivia.

"These Walker men will take your breath away if you ain't careful, girl." Mrs. Walker chuckled. "You want another one?"

Olivia shook her head. "No, thanks. I'm leaving in a minute."

Mrs. Walker smiled. "Early night, huh?"

"Yeah. Very early."

Olivia scraped out the last of the sweet potato pie that strange woman had dropped off with her the other night. She'd had every intention of throwing it out, but it had never made it to the garbage disposal. Olivia had happened to take a small bite just before the dumping ceremony, and she'd nearly fainted at how good it had tasted. It could've just been a good pie; then again, she could've just been sick of living off chicken noodle soup. Whatever the case, she'd been eating that pie breakfast, lunch, and dinner for the last two days.

". . . don't worry 'bout the pie tin. I'll be back for it in a few days."

She cringed at the thought of seeing that woman again. Her pie was the bomb, but her company left a lot to be desired. Olivia washed out the tin, then decided that the best way to avoid her was to beat her to the punch. She dialed the super's number to ask him what the odd woman's apartment number was.

"Hello?" the super asked. Mr. Palmer had to have been at least seventy, maybe seventy-five, and he'd been living in that building for decades.

"Mr. Palmer. This is Olivia Phillips in 5C."

"Who?" he said loudly. "Who's this?"

"Olivia Phillips. 5C."

"Yes?"

She was frustrated already, and she'd been on the phone with the man less than a minute. "I need to find an apartment number." Olivia realized she was talking loud too.

"A what?"

"An apartment number? There's a lady who lives here who—"

"Who?"

Frustration got the best of her. He couldn't hear. And she didn't even remember the woman's name, for crying out loud. "Maylene. She's new to the building and her name is Maylene, or something like that. I just need to know what apartment she lives in."

"May who? She live here?"

"I don't know. I'm asking you. Older lady, about my height, big glasses."

"Naw. Naw. Don't know who you talking 'bout. You sure you got the right number? Cause I don't know no Mays."

Just then, a knock came at the door, and Olivia knew instinctively that it was her. She could almost see the glow of bright colors shining into her living room, and practically smell that loud perfume of hers filtering in through the cracks into her apartment.

Without even saying good-bye, she hung up on Mr. Palmer. *The Twilight Zone* came to mind. "Who is it?" she asked hesitantly, anticipating the sound of her voice.

"It's Maybelline! Your neighbor!"

Olivia braced herself before answering the door. After all, she couldn't very well eat that woman's delicious pie and still be rude to her. She forced a smile and held the pie tin in her hand, ready to say her thank yous and shove the pie tin in the other woman's face before the conversation went any further. But Maybelline was too quick for her.

"Girl, I did it again," she chuckled and brushed past Olivia and into the living room, leaving Olivia standing with her mouth gaping open in the doorway. "I hope you like pecan."

The strong scent of Maybelline's perfume pushed Olivia back and temporarily clouded her vision. A blur of color with a large, black Afro wig made its way into her kitchen and began rummaging through cabinets and drawers until it found what it was looking for. Gradually, Olivia's vision began to clear in time to see Maybelline cutting into a pecan pie and carefully putting two slices onto two small plates.

Maybelline looked over at her and grinned.

"C'mon," she said, all too enthusiastically. "It tastes better when it's warm. Smells good, don't it?"

How would she know? All she could smell was some of the strongest cologne known to man or woman. Olivia wasn't sure if she was high from that drink she'd had earlier down at Nate's, or if it was Maybelline's perfume.

"I know you ain't gonna stand there all night with the door open," Maybelline said as she sat down on the sofa with both plates, and filled her mouth with a forkful of pie. Her eyes rolled in her head. "Mmmmm . . . girl, if you don't come on, I'm gonna eat this whole thing all by myself."

Finally Olivia closed the door. Her first instinct was to be rude and tell the woman that she hadn't been invited in and that she had no business taking liberties and making herself so at home. But then Maybelline's friendly eyes glistened at her. "Did you like the sweet potato pie I gave you?"

Olivia sort of nodded.

"Then I know you gonna like this one too. Between the two," she said, taking another bite, "I don't know which one is my favorite. You tell me which one you like better."

Apprehensively, Olivia sat beside Maybelline and took a bite. The pie melted in her mouth. "Mmmm . . ." was all she could say. It was as good as, if not better than, the other pie she'd eaten, and Olivia hurried and took another bite before she'd finished the last.

Maybelline laughed. "Good enough to make you wanna slap somebody, ain't it?"

Olivia nodded enthusiastically. "It's delicious," she said, with her mouth full. She hurried from her seat and went over to the refrigerator, pulled out a carton of milk, and filled two glasses.

She set one down in front of Maybelline. "It's lactose free," she said between bites.

Maybelline laughed again. "Pie is good for the soul, and lactose-free milk is good for everything else."

This time, Olivia laughed too.

"I keep eating all these pies, I'm going to get . . ." Olivia looked sheepishly at Maybelline, who was finishing her second slice. "I mean . . ."

"You mean fat." Maybelline wiped her mouth, then glared at Olivia. "Fat like me?"

"No, that's not what I meant. I just meant that—"

"I'll have you know," Maybelline started smugly, "that I am not fat."

Olivia suddenly felt bad. This nice old woman had been kind enough to feed her some of the best pies she'd ever tasted in her life, and she'd been inconsiderate enough to say something rude.

"I am full figured."

Olivia nearly choked on her food.

Maybelline smiled. "And I look good and I love

me some pies and you could stand to have some meat on them bones of yours anyway, cause you too damn skinny in the first place." Both women shook with laughter. "Go to the gym or something if you got a problem with getting fat," Maybelline insisted. "Go jogging." She said the word like it was from another language, slowly pronouncing each syllable between laughs so that it sounded like *jog-gin-g*.

Olivia couldn't remember the last time she'd laughed. She couldn't remember the last time she'd forgotten to be depressed and feel worthless, or like her life didn't matter. But for just a few minutes that evening, she did forget, and she felt like a weight lifted up off her shoulders.

Maybelline left Olivia the last of the pie. As she walked down the hall to the elevator, she yelled back over her shoulder, "Don't worry about the tin. I'll pick it up in a few days."

Q *dialed all but the last* digit of Olivia's phone number, then hung up. Olivia stirred him up again, and he resented her for it. It was late, and a gym teacher had no business staying that late after school. He grabbed his gym bag, got up and turned out the light, and closed his office door behind him. He nodded goodnight to the school custodian sweeping the gymnasium floor.

The drive home was uneventful. Q pulled into the driveway of his small house and sat there for a minute, hoping Olivia would fade from his thoughts like a dream. But she was stubborn. She was good and deep into his system and refused to let him go. He'd almost kicked the habit that was her. He'd almost learned to live without her. But seeing her the other night . . . it had messed him up again, and now he was stuck back at the beginning of trying to let her go.

From the beginning, she'd been stubborn and hard to get to know. She was fine, though, which is why he'd persisted. Q's thoughts drifted back to the way they used to be before cancer had messed up her head. As fine as she'd been, she'd never taken her looks too seriously. She was a natural beauty, never having to work too hard at it. Every inch of her just seemed to fall perfectly into place, and all she had to do was stand there and be beautiful.

Her hair had been longer then, down past her shoulders, and she'd worn it staight. He used to tease her about that mile-long mane on her head, and then he'd run his fingers through it, losing himself in the softness. Olivia's bright eyes used to shine and twinkle like stars, and he never grew tired of gazing into them. And her smile; it had caught him off guard the first time he'd seen it, and he'd stumbled, literally, at the sight of it. Her body was perfectly proportioned, balanced, curving effortlessly into itself. He couldn't have dreamed her if he'd tried.

For the most part, everything between them had been cool, except when it had come to her independence. Q had come up the old-fashioned way. Born and raised in Tulsa, he'd been taught that real men took care of things. It didn't matter what it was, a real man stepped up to the challenge, planted his feet, and dug in for whatever came his way. She'd called it a caveman mentality, but he'd known that deep down it was what she'd needed. He'd known that she'd been fending for herself most of her life and that she'd been afraid to trust him like that. Afraid that he would have let her down like her parents had let her down, like everyone she'd ever loved had let her down.

He hated coming home sometimes. Q hated being alone. His folks claimed he was just too picky and could get a wife if he wanted one. Maybe they were right, he thought, turning on the kitchen light and opening the door to the refrigerator. He pulled out a bowl of spaghetti and smelled it, then stuck the bowl in the microwave to heat it up.

If all he wanted was just a woman to curl up next to, he could've found someone a long time ago. Q wanted his partner, his soul mate, and until she'd become ill, he'd been convinced Olivia was it.

She'd crumbled into his arms when she'd first told him. She'd shrunk and curled up next to him, begging him not to let her go, and to stay with her. *"No matter what, Q . . . stay with me."*

He'd promised he would, and he'd meant it too. But then he'd made the mistake of leaving her alone to sort things out the way Olivia always sorted things out, and just as quickly, she'd changed on him, turning back into that armor-wearing warrior who didn't need him anymore.

"I can handle it on my own! I don't need you to help me!" It was the way she'd said it that had hurt. She'd said it like she'd really meant it. Like she really hadn't needed him. No matter how hard he'd tried to get her to see otherwise, she'd added one more brick to that wall she'd built around herself and closed him out completely.

The spaghetti wasn't that good. He'd made it, and he was never good at making spaghetti. Q finished the entire bowl, took a shower, brushed his teeth, then crawled into bed to watch the news. He missed the nights when she'd slept next to him. He missed the way she'd draped her arm across him while they'd slept. Hell, he just missed her.

She reached out to you, man, he thought to himself, remembering the other night at that bar. Proud women like Olivia didn't reach out to anybody, and when they did, the last thing they needed was to have it thrown back in their face. She'd reached out to him. *". . . I still love you. I never stopped."*

Had she really said that to him, or had he just been wishing she would? He'd waited nearly a year for the sound of her voice telling him she loved him. He'd counted the days, weeks, months, and finally, when she did say it, it was his pride that got in the way, not hers.

Q bolted up in bed and reached for the phone. She needed him. She'd told him as much. Now the ball was in his court.

"Olivia?" He breathed a sigh of relief at the sound of her voice. "It's me. We need to talk."

Till U Come Back to Me

It was the best thing to happen to her in a long time. He was the best thing to happen to her in a long time, and Olivia wasn't about to blow this rare and appreciated second chance. She rushed into her building, glancing at her watch. Q would be by in less than half an hour, so she had to hurry and shower and change and . . . *"We need to talk,"* was all he'd said. Not make up or make love. Just talk. She stood at the elevator of her apartment trying to calm herself. When the doors finally opened, she saw Maybelline standing inside with a basket full of neatly folded laundry.

"Well, hello," Maybelline said, popping her gum. Again, that perfume of hers was treacherous, but Olivia had grown to like the woman, so she forgave her.

"Hi, Maybelline," Olivia said, relieved she'd remembered her name. She smiled. "How are you today?"

Maybelline looked astonished. "Well, apparently, not as good as you. I see we wearing joy today." Maybelline wrinkled her nose. "Looks good on you, darlin'."

Olivia couldn't help but laugh. Maybelline wasn't so bad. Loud colors, bad wigs, gum popping, overwhelmingly strong perfume—she was a nice woman who made delicious pies and always had something nice to say.

"Thank you." Olivia felt like telling someone her good news. She felt like it was time to peel back the layers of her defenses and finally start to open up. What better way to prepare herself for Q? "A friend of mine is on his way over," she said enthusiastically. "Someone I really care about."

Maybelline gently reached out and touched Olivia on the arm. "Then he must be a good friend, because I can see how happy he makes you—it's all in your eyes, girl."

Olivia blushed. "It is?"

"You've heard what they say about the eyes being the windows to the soul. Yours are shining crystal clear, dear."

Hope swelled inside Olivia for the first time in a long time as she stared back into her new friend's eyes. "He's very special to me," she said, almost whispering.

"Yes." Maybelline stopped popping her gum. "I can see that."

The elevator stopped on the fifth floor, where Olivia lived. She stepped off and turned and waved good-bye to Maybelline one last time before hurrying off to her apartment.

She didn't need to shower, but she did anyway. And she didn't need to slip into something more attractive, but she did anyway. Olivia wore her tangerine terry lounge set. She'd had it hanging up in her closet for ages. She'd bought it before her mastectomy and had avoided wearing it because it was cut so low in the front. There was no way she could get away with wearing it without her scar showing, so she put a white tank top underneath, which covered it up nicely. Q had never seen her naked after her surgery. He'd always loved her body, her breasts, and now, half of her was missing. How would he respond to that? Come to think of it, how would she respond to it if and when he ever did see her?

"Just be glad we caught it in time," her doctor had told her when Olivia had seen what they'd done to her body. "It was the only alternative, Olivia. The only way we could save your life."

They'd saved it, all right, and butchered her in the process. But tonight wasn't the night to be thinking like that. Olivia picked out her hair and applied eyeliner and mascara to her eyes. She dabbed a little concealer underneath them to hide the dark circles, then applied a light coat of clear lip gloss to her lips.

Anticipation filled her small apartment tonight. Q had been everything to her, and she hadn't realized it until it had been too late. Hope was an emotion she had turned her back on and almost forgotten what it looked like. But there it was, staring back at her from her reflection, and she smiled. Maybelline was right. That good feeling did look good on her.

A knock came at the front door. Olivia glanced at the clock in her bedroom that read seven o'clock. Q was right on time. Her heart raced and she took deep breaths to calm herself down, fighting back the myriad of negative thoughts threatening to keep her from answering the door.

What if he's still angry?

What if he doesn't want to get back together?

What if he's found someone else?

What if he needs a woman with two breasts instead of just one?

She defiantly stepped over each and every one of her fears and finally made her way to the door, slowly opening it to Q standing on the other side.

He had flowers. He held them out to her when

she answered the door, and Olivia couldn't help but laugh at the gesture. "Thank you."

"Corny, huh?" he asked, stepping inside.

She nodded. "Yep. But in a good way." Their eyes met, and it was as if they'd never lost sight of each other.

Q had promised himself to take it slow, and he held back the urge to pull her into his arms. Olivia always was the skittish type, and any sudden movement could send her into a defensive frenzy. It was irritating, yes, but for some strange reason, he kind of dug that about her.

"Please . . ." She gestured for him to sit on the sofa. She went into the kitchen to put the flowers in water. "Would you like something to drink? I have wine, soda, beer."

"You hate beer," he said, surprised.

She came back into the room, handed him a bottle, then took her seat across from him in the chair. "I know. But I bought it for you."

Q smiled. "My favorite kind," he said, looking at the label. "You remembered."

"Of course I did. Two years together, you think I'd forget something like that?"

"Two long years," he teased.

She threw a pillow at him. "That's not funny." But it was. He always did know how to make her laugh, especially at herself.

There was silence between them, but it wasn't

uncomfortable. They were savoring the experience of being together again with no malice or pain.

He spoke first. "I don't want to rush this."

Olivia nodded, reassured by his tone of voice and by what he didn't say.

"We need to be patient with each other, and careful, because I can hurt too, Olivia, just like you can."

"I know," she said, quickly regretting every terrible word she'd ever said to him. "I know, Q."

"I can't take losing you again, baby." He swallowed the lump swelling in his throat. "I love you, and—I can't seem to stop, no matter how hard I try."

Tears pooled in her eyes. The good kind. The relieved kind. "I love you," she said quietly. "And can't live without you either."

Q put down his beer, came over to her, and knelt down in front of her. She recalled every line of his handsome face, and Olivia knew he was all she needed in the world.

"It'll be like starting over from scratch, only better," he reassured her, gazing into her eyes. A tear escaped down her cheek and he wiped it away with his thumb. "We know our mistakes ahead of time." Q smiled. "That's the best thing about second chances."

She nodded, then wrapped both arms around his neck, resting them on his broad shoulders, holding on tight. "I'll do better this time, Q," she sobbed. "I promise."

"We'll both do better, Olivia." Q kissed her hands, and then lay his head down in her lap. Neither of them said another word, until it was time for him to leave.

Olivia wanted him to stay. He wanted to stay, but now was not the time.

When Love Calls

He told her that they needed to take it slow. But slow was hard to do when she was this happy. A song played over and over again in her head, an omen, or confirmation that things were moving in the right direction.

> *When love calls*
> *You'd better answer*

Love was calling loud and clear, and Olivia wasn't about to ignore it this time. Q was too damn important to her happiness, her survival. She'd spent so much energy keeping people from getting too close, but he'd found a way in, and it felt good having him close.

"What time you getting home tonight?" he asked over the phone. Olivia wasn't supposed to get personal calls at work, but technically, work didn't start for another three minutes.

"The usual. Around six-thirty," she answered in a low voice. "Why?"

"Why? Cause I wanna see you, that's why. Is that all right with you?" He tried to sound offended, but she knew he really wasn't.

"That's always all right with me."

"Wanna go grab a bite to eat?"

Her smile lit up her face. "The Greek place?"

He sighed, knowing full well that was her favorite restaurant. "Yes, the Greek place."

"I'll be ready."

Mrs. Walker walked in as soon as the doors to the bank were unlocked, and she made her way over to Olivia's counter. "Hey, girl," she greeted Olivia. As usual, the woman looked radiant, even in sweatpants and a T-shirt. "I'm here to make the weekly deposit."

A large diamond shimmered on her ring finger, and for the first time, Olivia dared to imagine what that must feel like. "What happened to Mr. Walker? He's usually the one up in here bright and early."

Mrs. Walker frowned. "He's out of town until tomorrow."

"Miss him?"

Mrs. Walker laughed. "Yeah," she sounded a bit condescending. "I miss him."

She handed a large brown leather satchel filled with money and a deposit slip to Olivia.

"How long have you been married?" Olivia asked. She and Mrs. Walker had never talked beyond what she wanted to drink.

She closed her eyes and thought for a moment. "Four years," she smiled. "Four lovely and long years."

"Lovely and long?" Olivia laughed. "What's that mean?"

"Well, marriage is cool. I mean, I love my man. But it's not easy. Just because you fall in love doesn't mean the work is done. In fact, it's just starting, and marriage ain't no joke, girl. You have to work at it every day, just like you work at your job. Most people don't think about it, though."

"They think love is all there is?"

"Yeah. And it is, but it isn't. Know what I mean?"

"Sort of," Olivia shrugged.

"I mean, yeah, love is great. It's cool, and I dig being in love. But there's more to making a marriage work than love. I mean, cause sometimes he might say or do some things that don't make him all that loveable," she laughed. "Just like I might do some things. But if you're committed to each other, you have to be willing to work through them anyway, even when you ain't so in love."

"Makes sense," Olivia nodded.

Mrs. Walker studied her for a moment. "You got somebody?"

Olivia shrugged. "I'm working on it."

"But you ain't never been married?"

She shook her head. "No." Not yet, she wanted to add, but it was too soon.

Mrs. Walker smiled. "I'll have to be sure to mention that to Nate, then."

With that, she turned to leave. "Ciao, girl." She waved back at Olivia on her way out.

At dinner, Olivia was the first to speak.

"One minute you feel like you're going to live forever." She hesitated. "The next . . . you realize that all of a sudden, tomorrow isn't guaranteed and there's absolutely nothing you can do about it."

"Tomorrow's never been promised, Olivia."

"Until I was diagnosed with cancer, Q, I never really gave much thought to dying," she shrugged. "There was just living and the constant struggle to do it better than anyone who'd ever hurt me expected me to."

He laughed. "Miss I-Can-Do-It-All-By-Myself."

"That was me." she stared longingly into his eyes. "The old me." Olivia paused as the waitress came by to take their order.

Q ordered the same thing every time they went to that restaurant—the panfried trout with Greek potatoes, dinner salad, and raspberry iced tea. Olivia opted for the traditional Greek salad with chicken, dolmades on the side, warm pita bread, and diet soda.

"It was hard after the surgery." Olivia traced small circles on the tablecloth with her finger while she spoke. Opening up was hard but necessary if she wanted him to understand what her life had been like without him. Q still cared for her, that much was obvious. But his eyes were filled with apprehension and a need to know why she'd acted the way she had when she'd been diagnosed with cancer. "I couldn't stand to look at myself, or to face anybody, Q. Because I didn't feel like me anymore. There was so much going on, recovering from the mastectomy, then chemo, and my whole body seemed to be my own worst enemy. It was like a war, and I had to fight it, and I had to fight it by myself because no one else could."

"That might be true, but I would've liked to have been in your corner, baby. Sort of like Dundee was to Ali," he chuckled.

"Who?" she asked, dumbfounded.

He shook his head. Olivia wasn't the sports buff he was. "Never mind. The point is, I know I couldn't have fought the battle for you, but I could've been there to support you while you did."

"All I knew was how to go it alone, baby. That's the way I'd always done it. When things got tough in my life, then I had to get tougher and just face it head-on."

He reached his hand across the table and took hold of hers. "That's not how it has to be, Olivia. Not when you have somebody who loves you."

She smiled. "It took not having you in my life for me to learn that. And I'm still learning it, but the difference between now and back then is—I want to learn it." She stared deeply into his eyes. "I don't want to spend the rest of my life alone, Q. And I certainly don't want to spend the rest of my life without you."

He seemed as relieved to hear it as she was to finally say it.

After dinner, they strolled back to his car, Olivia's arm looped in his. "Remember the first time you asked me out?"

He looked surprised. "I asked *you* out? Naw!" he shook his head. "You asked *me* out."

"You're right. I could tell you wanted to ask me out but didn't have the guts to do it. You looked scared."

"Baby, I wasn't scared," he smirked. "I was just playing hard to get. And it worked too. You asked me out, just like I planned."

Olivia laughed. "Believe what you want. Whatever makes you feel better."

They got to his car and he held the door open for her. "You make me feel better."

She hesitated before getting in. Olivia stood on her toes and kissed him tenderly on the lips. "I certainly hope so," she whispered.

Olivia rode the elevator up to her apartment, but she could just as well have flown. She was in love again, and better yet, she was loved. Q was the answer she'd been searching for her whole life, and now he was back and she was ready to hang on for dear life if she had to.

She'd barely put down her purse when a knock came on her door.

"Maybelline?" Olivia asked, surprised to see her standing there.

Maybelline looked sheepish. "Hello, dear," she tried smiling. "Sorry to bother you so late."

"That's fine." The woman looked concerned about something. "Come in." Olivia stepped aside to let her in.

"I ain't staying long. It's just, well—I hadn't seen you in a while, and I wanted to make sure you were all right."

It was an odd concern to Olivia, since she and Maybelline had only recently become acquainted. "I'm fine."

The old woman seemed relieved. "Oh, good. I'm so glad to hear that."

"Am I missing something? Why would you think I wasn't all right?"

Maybelline looked caught off guard by the question. She wrung her hands nervously. "It's just that my timing's off sometimes. I just didn't want to be too late." She hurried back toward the door.

"Too late?" Olivia was more confused than ever. "For what, Maybelline?"

Maybelline had a desperate look in her eyes, like she'd forgotten something she was supposed to remember. "Nothing, child," she said irritably. "I just . . . I fall behind sometimes. I get busy making my pies, or eating 'em, and I fall behind. And sometimes, I miss . . ." She stared sadly at Olivia. Tears filled the rims of her eyes. "You remind me so much of somebody I used to know," she said remorsefully.

Olivia was starting to become worried. Maybelline could be sick, or have Alzheimer's disease or something. Maybe she was just crazy.

Maybelline put her hand to her cheek and looked at Olivia. "Lord, I just don't want to be too late this time. I don't know what I'd do if . . ." She seemed to sense that she was scaring Olivia and quickly composed herself. "It's late," she said, apologetically, opening the door to leave. "And I'm just standing here rambling, going on and on about stuff that don't make no sense." She turned to Olivia one last time. "I'm making custard pie this weekend. Can I bring you one down?" She smiled, her eyes twinkling behind her big glasses. "It's mighty good."

Olivia tried to smile too. "Sure. That sounds great, Maybelline. Goodnight."

Maybelline waved as she left, and Olivia slowly closed the door behind her. Her behavior had been odd, and sad. Sad for no reason. Olivia shrugged off her visit and decided to go to bed. Maybelline was a strange old woman, lonely maybe, and, by all accounts, harmless. But Olivia would have to keep her distance. The last thing she needed or wanted was to be saddled with a crazy woman who had a tendency to lose sight of reality. She was sweet, but she sure was out there.

Close to You

Dinner was delicious. Miss Olivia claimed she didn't like to cook, but she could put her foot in it when she wanted. He'd rented some movies, and the two of them snuggled together on the sofa like old times. She wedged into that spot in his arms made just for her, and fit perfectly. Olivia was just hard to resist and hard not to miss. Q felt complete again, whole and satisfied.

"I love this part," she muttered, more to herself than to him. Olivia was as much of a sci-fi buff as he was, transfixed by the action unfolding on-screen and caught up in the fantasy of *The Matrix*. But he was caught up in the fantasy of her.

He'd been the one to insist they take things slowly, but for him that was like asking a drowning man to breathe under water. They'd been seeing each other for nearly two weeks now, and when he wasn't with her, he wanted to be, and when he was with her, he wanted to touch her, make love to her the way he used to, slow . . . slower, taking his time, dreading the moment it was over.

She was wary, though. Even though she wouldn't come out and admit it, he could see it in her eyes every time he reached out to her. Olivia was guarded, afraid of what he might think seeing her naked. Admittedly, he was skittish too. After all, they hadn't been together since before she'd had the surgery, and frankly, he had no idea what to expect.

It was a hurdle both of them needed to cross. Putting it off wasn't doing either one of them any good, and he'd made up his mind that tonight was going to have to be the night. The two of them were going to have to face her apprehensions and doubts together so that they could finally move forward in their relationship. As much as he loved watching *The Matrix*, he couldn't wait for it to end.

"Olivia," he said in a low, seductive voice.

Olivia grunted. "Huh?"

He gently pried the remote control from her

hand, turned off the television, and placed the remote on the back of the sofa.

"What?" She tried her best to sound irritable, but it was so hard with him holding her like that. She sat up and looked into his eyes. Immediately, she knew what was on his mind, and a dreadful feeling washed over her.

He smiled, put his hand under her chin, and coaxed her lips to his.

She tasted even better than he'd remembered. She tasted better than he'd dreamed. How in the world could the two of them ever survive without each other? Of course, they'd been fools for even trying.

"Q," she pulled away, reluctant to look in his eyes. "I'm not sure I'm ready for this. I need time."

"To do what?" he asked gently, and smiled. "Waiting won't get us anywhere, Olivia. It's just going to prolong the inevitable—you know it, and so do I."

"But I look so different," her voice trembled. For the first time since he'd known her, she looked so fragile, so vulnerable, making him want her even more. "I'm not the same."

He smiled. "I know."

"You don't know. You have no idea." Olivia was beginning to panic. She started to get up from the couch, but he held on to her. Not this time. He made up his mind. She couldn't run from him this time.

"Give me more credit than that," he said, holding

on firmly to her waist. "Olivia, if we don't do this . . . if we don't do it now, then when?"

Olivia searched herself for an answer. "I don't know," she said quietly.

He wanted her to trust him, to trust them and the power of everything they meant to each other. He wanted her to throw all that defensiveness to the wind and just let him be the man in her world and let him take care of her.

"I want to make love to you, baby," he murmured as he pulled her hand to his lips and kissed it. "I want to love you the way I used to." Q looked at her and smiled. "The way you love for me to."

The mischievous twinkle in his eyes brought a smile to her lips. "Oh, you wanna do it like that, do you?"

"Yeah—I wanna do it like that."

Sex with Q was incredible. Just thinking about the way it used to be between them made her flush and warm all over. It had been more than a year since they'd made love. "Remember the last time?" She caught herself smiling.

He laughed. "Yeah. I remember. You wanted to be blindfolded."

"And tied up too," she hurried to add.

"You chickened out on that one, boo."

"I did," Olivia chuckled. "But I had every intention of going through with it, at first."

Q shook his head. "I knew you wouldn't let me do it."

"The blindfold was nice, though. At least that was something."

"That was something," he said as he stared into her eyes. "But you don't have to be that brave tonight, love."

Her expression turned serious. "No, Q. I have to be more brave tonight. I could take off or put on a blindfold, but this"—she looked down at her chest—"this I can't do too much about."

"I love you, Olivia. I love you just like you are, honey, and nothing's going to change that. And I want to prove that to you, but you have to trust me and know that I would never hurt you. I would never turn my back on you, no matter what."

The look in her eyes softened.

"I'm not like those other people in your life, Olivia. I never have been. And I never will be. If you need me, baby, I'm here. I'm right here." He pulled her down onto his lap, then kissed her passionately, feeling her relax and melt in his arms.

She felt so right against him, close to him, and safe in his arms. Q's life hadn't been the same without Olivia in it, and holding her like this, kissing her like this, reminded him of how empty he'd been since she'd been gone.

"I love you so much, baby," he whispered between

kisses. "More than I ever thought it was possible to love any woman."

Olivia lightly stroked his face and hugged him close to her. Finally, he was back. Her man was back where he belonged, and Olivia decided at that moment that no matter what it took, she'd do whatever she needed to do to make sure he stayed right here where he belonged . . . with her.

Q's kisses became more heated and passionate, and he carefully lay her back down on the sofa. "I want to make love, Olivia. Please? Let me make love to you, baby."

The apprehension in her eyes was hard to miss. Even without her saying it, Q understood that she had reservations. He had them too, but now was not the time to give in to them. "It'll be all right, Olivia," he reassured her, stroking her hair. "I promise."

This was it, his opportunity to prove her wrong and to show her that all of her worries and fears were unfounded. That her faith in him was warranted and guarded with his heart and soul. Q wouldn't let her down now or ever.

"Go slow?" she asked, looking sweet and beautiful. She gathered her courage and put her faith in Q's love for her.

"I'm in no hurry, baby." He smiled down at her. "We've got all night and a whole lifetime to get there. So, yes. I'll go slowly."

Olivia looked into his eyes and remembered all those things she loved so much about him. Q was the calm in her storm. He always had been. He was the reason in her irrational world. He was everything she'd grown up without and missed so much. She closed her eyes and let Q do the kinds of things he did best: make love, be love, and give love.

Q kissed the side of her neck. He slid one hand under her shirt to her bare waist and gasped at how soft she still was. He hadn't been with any other woman since Olivia, because he hadn't wanted anyone but her. It took every ounce of conviction he had to ward off the urge to rush to this prize he'd been dreaming of since they'd split up. But he'd made a promise not to hurry, and he planned on keeping that promise if it killed him.

His hand gradually moved up under her shirt, higher, and he felt her recoil underneath him. Q stopped and whispered, "Trust me, Olivia. I won't hurt you, baby."

Of course he wouldn't. Olivia wasn't worried about him hurting her. She pushed away all the terrible images in her head, of that terrible scar on her chest, and of all the ugly things she'd thought of herself since the operation. Now was not the time.

Relax, Olivia, she told herself. *It's Q, and it's all right*.

Q cupped her breast and sighed. It was still Olivia.

Olivia buried her face in the crook of his neck.

He pulled back a little, then rested his head against her chest and listened to her heart beating. Nothing had changed. She was still the same woman he'd fallen in love with years ago and would love until the day he died.

Then Q turned his head and pulled down her shirt, exposing . . .

He tried not to stare, but he couldn't help himself. Of course she'd told him about the mastectomy. And he knew what to expect. Q froze, realizing in that instant how close Olivia had come to dying.

"What is it?" she asked, hesitantly.

He tried to smile. "Nothing, baby. I just . . ."

Olivia's eyes filled with remorse. "It's still me, Q."

"I know," he said, softly, then kissed her scarred chest. But something wasn't right. Something inside him just wasn't right.

"It's all right," he said, desperately. He loved this woman. So how come he couldn't . . .

Q sat up, trying to make sense of what was happening. "We just need time, Olivia," he said, trying to convince himself more than her. "That's all. It's just going to take time."

Olivia sat up too, disgusted with herself for believing that anyone could look past what was left of her, to be able to love what was left of her. "For what, Q? It's not like it's going to grow back."

"No. No, I . . ." Q had never choked before in his life until now. He'd never lost his levelheadedness, his cool, his sense of logic and reason. He'd never been scared before. Not like this. He didn't even understand what he was afraid of. But he could see in her, and feel in himself, that he'd turned the corner the wrong way, and there was little hope for recovery. And then he sealed the deal, blurting out the most ridiculous question. "Can't you get implants or something?"

The look she gave him sent an icy chill up his spine, and he knew with certainty that there was no fixing this. "You need to leave," she said, indifferently.

The Forest for the Trees

Deep down, she knew he'd done the best he could. Q wanted to be her hero and had come to her rescue, but he just hadn't been able to come through and ultimately failed them both.

Olivia called in sick to work. It wasn't a lie. She was sick—sick of sticking her chin out, only to get punched again and again. People were just people. And everybody had their limitations. Her strong man had his, and she'd seen it for the first time last night. He'd seen it too, and he'd looked more disappointed than she had. She almost felt sorry for him. Almost.

She didn't eat breakfast. Olivia saw no need for food. But she drank all morning, rum and Coke, her favorite. She halfway expected to be sick, drinking this mess on an empty stomach, but that didn't happen. She was good and drunk, though. Stumbling around her small apartment from room to room in her pajamas, thinking and drinking and paying homage to the kind of life she'd always wanted, and to the kind of woman she'd always wished to be.

They should've named her Pitiful when she was born. Pitiful Phillips, because that's all she'd ever been. And her future didn't look so bright that she'd ever be anything else, either. She cried between drinks and thoughts and memories.

Olivia sat curled up on the sofa, trying to remember a time when she'd felt like it was worth being alive and waking up another day. But she could hardly remember a time like that. She used to believe she'd given up on the idea of killing herself, especially after the last time. That wasn't it, though. She hadn't given it up. She'd just put it away for a little while, long enough to try something else instead. But she'd always kept it close for safekeeping, because she'd always known that ultimately, it was all she had.

Sleeping pills were cool, and she searched all the cabinets and drawers, hoping she'd been smart enough to stash a bottle somewhere for backup. She remembered the euphoric feeling of drifting off into death, like sliding down in a warm tub, sleeping and sinking, and disappearing.

Jack Daniel's sloshed around in her glass and spilled down the front of her pajamas. Olivia laughed. "It's all good," she slurred. "It's all good."

Razor blades. She hurried into the bathroom, rummaging through her medicine cabinet. That whole wrist-slashing thing never had appealed to her, but the fact that she was drunk gave her all sorts of courage, and yes, she could do it if she could find some razor blades. Olivia found a pink disposable shaver with two thin blades embedded in plastic. "Damn!" She took a comb and tried desperately to force the blades from the plastic handle, but she poked herself in the cheek trying.

"Ouch!" She threw the comb and razor across the room, then crumbled to the floor, sobbing. "I can't do anything right," she hiccupped.

"Whatcha call yourself trying to do, sweetheart?"

Maybelline stood in the bathroom doorway with her hands on her hips, looking absolutely appalled.

"Who the hell let you in?" Olivia tried to stand, using the sink for leverage, but she slipped and fell back down to the floor. "You didn't knock!"

"Course I did," Maybelline said convincingly. "How come you didn't answer?" She reached down and helped Olivia to her feet.

"Cause you didn't knock."

Maybelline held Olivia by the arm, trying to help her into the bedroom, but Olivia jerked away.

"I lost my . . ." She stumbled around the house, ultimately ending up back in the bathroom until she found it. "You want one?" she slurred as she held up her glass to Maybelline, who smiled. "What's so funny?"

"I'm just so happy to see you," she said, laughing. "Last time, I was almost too late, but . . . I'm happy to see you, baby."

Olivia plopped down on the couch, then started to cry. "I'm not a baby, Maybelline."

"Oh, now hush!" Maybelline sat down next to her. "I meant that figuratively, not literally. Ain't no reason to cry."

"Who let you in?"

"You did. Don't you remember?"

Olivia thought for a moment. "Oh . . . yeah. Well, what are you doing here?"

"I've come to make sure you didn't do anything silly."

"Everything I do is silly," Olivia said harshly. "I'm a silly woman, Maybelline."

Maybelline stared lovingly at her. "You certainly are, child. But you can't help yourself. You only doing what you know to do."

"What are you talking about?" Maybelline was getting on her nerves, and she was beginning to wonder why she'd let that old woman in her apartment in the first place.

"Killing yourself is a silly thing to do." Maybelline patted Olivia on the thigh. "You should've figured that out the last time."

Olivia stared at the woman, stunned. "How would you know about that?" she asked bluntly. "Maybe it's not so silly. Maybe it's the only thing that makes sense." Tears blurred her eyes again.

"Oh, what do you know?" Maybelline asked irritably.

"I know!" Olivia nodded her head and pointed her finger hard on her chest. "Believe me, Maybelline. I know more than you ever will!"

Maybelline leaned close to Olivia. "And what is it you think you know, girl?"

Olivia's bottom lip quivered. Sadness swelled in her neck and threatened to strangle her. "I know everything! I know my momma left me on the neighbor's porch because she didn't want me! And daddy left because he didn't want either one of us." The floodgates opened, and she cried uncontrollably. "And nobody ever stays or keeps their promises! Nobody is strong enough, or big enough, or tough enough, Maybelline . . . to be with me! I know that he said he loves me, but he can't! Not the way I am now! Not like this!" All of a sudden, Olivia lifted her shirt long enough for Maybelline to see the scar left behind by her mastectomy. "Nobody's going to want me like this! I know that too!"

She bolted up from the couch and went over to the kitchen to fill up her glass again. Maybelline sat motionless, with her hands folded in her lap, watching her. "Is that all you got?" she asked, nonchalantly.

Olivia took a long sip and wiped her mouth with the back of her hand. "What?" She dried her cheeks with the collar of her shirt.

Maybelline slowly stood to her feet. "Your daddy left cause he was sorry," she blurted out. "Your momma left cause she was sorrier. You just happen to get caught in between two sorry-ass people who didn't deserve a pet roach, let alone a little girl. And you right. People ain't always so strong or big or tough, child, but that don't mean they can't be there for you when you need 'em. We all lean on each other. And you need to ask yourself something too." Maybelline pointed a crooked finger at her. "When's the last time you been big and strong for somebody when they had a need?" Maybelline rolled her eyes and crossed her arms over her ample bosom. "And as for that titty of yours, or that titty you used to have . . . it's a titty, girl. That's all it is, and all it ever was. And there's way more to being a woman than to have a set of those! If you don't know that by now, then you are one of the dumbest broads I know!"

Olivia's chin dropped.

"You need to thank God that's all you lost. You can see, walk, talk, hear, got a strong heart, you ain't got AIDS, you can work, run, jump, and live, child! While you sitting over here whining about all the things you ain't got, you missing out on a world of good things you do have, and you ought to be ashamed of yourself for being so selfish!"

"I'm not selfish," Olivia said meekly.

"Sure you are! Always have been, but that's neither here nor there." Maybelline picked up the bottle of Jack Daniel's off Olivia's kitchen counter, capped it, and started walking toward the door. "Get something in your stomach before you get sick," she demanded, her wide hips swishing violently back and forth. "And pull yourself together, girl! God don't keep saving your life for nothing! You ain't but thirty-seven years old, got plenty of time left here in this world, and if you come out of that pity party long enough, you might find you something good in it. Sitting up here worried over some man," she muttered loud enough for Olivia to hear. "If you stop being so stubborn and hardheaded, you might just see that what you been looking for been there the whole time." She opened the front door and turned to Olivia one last time before leaving. "Whatever you want, sugah, whatever you need, just say the word, and it's all yours cause you deserve absolutely all of it." Maybelline smiled one last radiant smile, then closed the door behind her.

Olivia stood motionless for what seemed like hours but was actually only a few minutes. Maybelline came like she went. She was there one minute, and then just . . . gone, and the only evidence that she'd even been there at all was that terrible scent of her perfume saturating the entire room and filling Olivia's nostrils.

Olivia hurried to the bathroom, bent over the toilet, and . . .

"Olivia," Q said somberly into her answering machine. He'd been calling most of the day, but she wouldn't answer the phone. This time, he decided to leave a message. She sat up in bed and listened. "I'm sorry. I don't know what happened. I don't know why I acted the way I did. But I am sorry. I just think I need some time, that's all. Time to . . . to . . . I don't know. It was a shock, and I didn't handle it too well. But it wasn't you, Olivia. It was me, and all I can say is that I am sorry."

She turned off the lamp on the nightstand and clutched her spare pillow to her chest. Her alarm was set for her to get up in the morning to get to work on time. Maybe afterward, she'd stop off and treat herself to an Indian taco at the little shack down the street from work and stop off at DSW to pick up those boots she'd been thinking about getting.

From the Rain

I'm not saying I can't get past it," Q reasoned, as they sat in the restaurant, facing each other across a table. He'd been calling all week, and finally she'd agreed to see him again. "I overreacted, Olivia. I expected . . . hell, I don't know what I expected, but I thought I could handle it."

She wasn't angry or even hurt anymore. Olivia stared at him, watching him wage some kind of war inside himself over something he couldn't help. But she saw no reason to come to his rescue, because as far as she was concerned, there was nothing to rescue him from.

"I need to know," he said intently, leaning forward. "What are the chances of it coming back?"

Olivia looked at him and shook her head.

"It could come back, couldn't it?" he cried out. "And then what?" Cancer had taken away part of her. Could it come back and take away the rest? And then what? What would he do if he had to watch it eat away at her one precious piece at a time?

"I don't know if it'll come back, Q," she said calmly. "I try not to spend too much time dwelling on it."

"But what if it does?"

"And what if it doesn't?" Olivia was surprised at her stance on the subject. It sounded almost optimistic. "What if I stay in remission for the rest of my life, and I end up one boob less than the standard issue?" She almost laughed. Q's expression was stern. "That doesn't change who I am. There's way more to being a woman than a set of breasts." She'd heard that before, or dreamed it. No, Maybelline. She'd said it. Hadn't she?

"I know that. I know you probably think I'm shallow, but . . ."

"I think you're human, Q. That's it. And you can't help how you feel."

He reached across the table and took hold of her hand. "I want to make this work, baby. I don't want to lose you over something like this."

She squeezed his hand and smiled. "Something like this . . . is who I am, Q." He looked so wounded. "And accepting me means accepting the total package or none of it. Sometimes, life doesn't turn out the way we want it to, but that doesn't mean it's wrong."

"What's it mean, then?"

"That we have to adjust accordingly, and move forward in it anyway, and hope that whatever comes our way, we can find a way to get through, get over, around." She laughed. "I don't know the answers. But I'm still here for a reason, and believe me, if it were left up to me, I wouldn't be sitting here with you now. There has to be a reason for that. Someone up there," she glanced upwards, "keeps saving my life. And I can't help but to wonder why."

Olivia walked six blocks from the restaurant where she'd left Q sitting and thinking, to her apartment building. Maybe they could work it out, she thought sanguinely. Or maybe they never would. Maybe cancer would come back to claim her other breast or even her life. Then again, maybe it would never come back. Olivia had spent a lifetime blaming the world for all the suffering she'd endured. Q had had an unfair disadvantage from the beginning. He was damned if he did, and damned if he didn't. She'd wanted someone to love her with everything, and when he had, she'd pushed him away, because she'd been so afraid of needing that. And once he was gone, she'd realized she'd needed him after all. It had never dawned on her that he might have needs too. She'd never stepped up to ask him, "Q. What do you need from me?"

Right now, he needed time. She could give him that. He needed room to see that theirs had been a one-sided relationship, with him doing all the giving and Olivia, all the taking. That's not the way love was supposed to be. The concept of love was really not so cut-and-dried as she'd always believed. She'd spent too much time looking for it on the outside, when the place she really needed to look first was inside that lopsided chest of hers.

God don't keep saving your life for nothing.

Maybelline left her with plenty of food for thought with those words. It was the kind of revelation that played like a scratched record in her head over and over again until it finally settled into her soul. There was a bigger picture that Olivia needed to see, despite all of the disappointments in her life. What that picture was, exactly, she didn't know. But gut instinct told her that if she managed to stick it out long enough, maybe one of these days she'd finally get it and then laugh at herself because whatever "it" was had been right in front of her face all along.

Monday nights were bad nights for business. But Nate didn't mind. Monday nights in the club were his nights to rest, like Sunday was for God. He sat at his piano, tinkering on the keys, chuckling at the analogy. The club was technically closed, but the doors weren't locked. He couldn't bring himself to lock the doors in case someone might wander in, needing someplace to sit and listen.

Years ago, people had paid a lot of money to hear him play. Too much money, but he'd taken it. He'd drunk up most of it, gotten high on the rest, and doled out fistfuls of it to women whose names he couldn't even remember.

He'd had no choice but to quit that game. Quit it or die before he was ready. The message had come loud and clear one night when he'd been attacked in an alley behind a club he'd been playing in in Chicago.

He'd been too high to defend himself, so he'd stumbled and crawled on all fours next to the rats and cockroaches and garbage while a mugger had stuck a knife into him half a dozen times. Eventually, he'd quit crawling, the crook had searched his pockets, taken his money, and left him for dead. Twenty-eight stitches and a revelation was what he'd woken up to in that hospital. Nate had been killing himself. Slowly. Foolishly. And so he'd quit and retired here, in this little piece of business that wasn't much of anything. And he'd never been happier.

The door opened slowly and she walked in, looking like the answer to his prayers. He couldn't help himself and smiled. She stood there for a minute, scanning the room, then spotted him at the piano. She came closer and stopped.

"Are you closed?" she smiled. Lord, why'd she have to go and do that? Nate had been in love a million times in his life, but never as sweetly as he was with her. And yet she didn't even seem to notice. It was a bittersweet realization worthy of a song.

"Not for you," he continued playing.

She looked around nervously and shrugged. "Where is everybody?"

"We're right here," he nodded.

She laughed. Lord, why'd she have to go and do that? "I mean, everybody else."

Love at first sight was the only kind of love that was true. He'd learned that years ago, before the drugs and booze. Too many people discounted it, because they were afraid of it. She was afraid of it too, he guessed. But Nate never had been. It was the only kind of love he trusted, untainted and unbridled.

The first time he'd seen her, she'd come into the club wearing that dull gray suit she chose to hide inside of, afraid of her own beauty and maybe even herself. She'd been sad, lonely, distant. He would've reached for her then, but a voice inside had told him, *Now's not the time, man.* Nate had listened and respected that voice, because it was the same one that kept him sober and sane. And so, he'd waited.

"I should leave," she said, turning to walk back out the door that had delivered her to him.

Now, his voice said, *is the time, man.*

Nate suddenly stopped playing. "Don't you dare," he told her, and she stopped. He stood up and walked past her to the bar. "What can I get you to drink, darlin'?"

"No, really, Nate," she sounded nervous. "I don't want to be any trouble. I can leave."

"The usual?" he ignored her.

She smiled. "A Coke?"

He filled a glass with ice and Coke, walked back over to where she was standing, and handed it to her.

"How much do I owe you?" she smiled.

"We're even," was all he said. He gently took hold of her elbow, led her to his piano, and sat her down on the bench, next to him. Nate played. This time, though, he played for her, to impress her. Like the male peacock struts around for the female peacock, he strutted his stuff on the keys, hoping she'd hear that this melody was for her.

"That's beautiful," she said. "Is it an original piece?"

He nodded, and smiled.

She closed her eyes, and sighed. "I love it." And then, she just listened.

Nate was a flirt, and harmless. Olivia let herself get caught up in the serenity of the moment. She'd heard him playing from outside and stopped in on a whim, expecting the usual crowd, but he'd been alone. There had been something magical about seeing him under that single light, playing, looking so handsome, and at ease.

Her eyes were closed when suddenly he stopped playing and the warmth of his lips pressed tenderly against hers. She opened her eyes and looked into his.

"What are you doing, Nate?" She swallowed hard.

Nate shrugged, then started playing again. "Kissing."

"But—why?" Olivia was stunned. What in the world was he thinking, kissing her when he had a perfectly good wife to be kissing on, probably close by, too.

He laughed. "Cause I felt like it."

Her astonishment quickly began to turn to anger at the audacity of this pompous man, thinking it was cool to kiss her simply because he felt like it.

"You didn't dig it?" he stopped playing and asked.

"No!" she blurted out. "I mean, whether I dug it or not isn't the point."

He grinned. "So, you did dig it?"

"No, I didn't," she said firmly.

"Why not?" he asked, looking genuinely perplexed. But it was an act she wasn't buying.

"Don't play dumb."

He shrugged. "Who's playing?" Then he laughed out loud.

"What about Mrs. Walker?" she asked, appalled.

Nate frowned. "Mrs. Walker?"

"Your wife, Nate!"

Nate stared at her for a moment, then threw his head back and laughed loud enough to echo through the whole place. "My wife?"

"Your wife, fool!"

It took him a minute to catch his breath, but finally he did. And when he did, he stopped and stared at the most beautiful woman he'd ever seen in his life. "Mrs. Walker," he started slowly, "isn't my wife, darlin'."

Olivia was stunned. Either he was lying or she really wasn't his wife, and Olivia was lost. "She's not your wife?"

He shook his head.

She hesitated and then asked innocently, "Your daughter?"

He raised his eyebrows. "Damn. I look that old?"

She shrugged.

"No, baby. She's not my daughter either. She's my sister-in-law, married to my brother Rosco. Plays horn here on Friday nights." His eyes twinkled. "So if you want me, darlin', I'm free as the wind and all yours."

Olivia stared at her reflection in the full-length mirror on the back of her bedroom door. Nate had invited her to dinner.

"Wear your prettiest dress," he'd told her.

Her first thought had been to say no, but for some reason, she hadn't. Her second thought had been to call him up and tell him she'd caught some mysterious virus at the last minute, but—she hadn't. Finally, she'd considered just plain standing him up, but here she was, wearing her prettiest dress (that she'd spent all day shopping for), trying not to look terrified about the evening.

Why am I going through with this? she couldn't help asking herself. For all she knew, he would trip out on her the same way Q had the last time they'd been together. But wait. Who said it was even going to go there with Nate? No. Nate was a friend, a nice man. A friend. And she was just having dinner tonight with her friend. So what he happened to be good-looking, and a man, romantic, and sexy? So what?

There was a spark in her that she'd never felt before in her life. And all it had taken to put it there had been rejection by an old flame, half a bottle of Jack Daniel's, and a good cussing out by some crazy, old, pie-baking woman who wore too much perfume, popped her gum like crazy and had no idea what the word *coordinate* meant. Speaking of Maybelline, she hadn't seen her in a while, which was odd. Seemed like for a while there, she'd seen her nearly every day, and strangely enough, Olivia sort of missed her. She'd been meaning to go down to Mr. Palmer's anyway to ask him which apartment she lived in. If she made it through tonight in one piece, she'd go down tomorrow and ask him.

Olivia finished putting on her lipstick just in time. The doorbell rang and she answered it, expecting to see Nate standing there. But instead, a white man with brilliant blue eyes stood in her doorway, dressed in black from head to toe.

"Ms.," he said, smiling, taking off his hat. "Your car is waiting."

Olivia sat alone in the back of a black stretch limo, grinning from ear to ear. She was tempted to roll down the windows and shout something ridiculous from the car, like, "Hey everybody! It's me! Olivia Phillips and this is my limo!" but that would be too ghetto, so she opted to just savor the moment privately. She had no idea where she was going tonight, or in life for that matter, but for the moment it didn't even matter, because for now nothing bad in this world could reach high enough to touch her.

They drove to the other side of town and finally stopped in front of the Bourbon Street Café. The chauffeur came to the back of the car, opened her door, and held out his hand to help her out.

Olivia fumbled with her purse, thinking the least she could do was tip the man, but he held up his hand. "It's been taken care of, ma'am." He smiled, then escorted her to the door and held it open for her.

The Bourbon Street Café was usually packed to capacity on Saturday nights, but not this particular Saturday night. The place looked deserted at first, but then she saw the maître d' walking in her direction. "May I take your wrap, miss?"

Olivia handed him her shawl and followed him

past the bar to the restaurant, which was completely empty. She felt a little odd sitting there alone, and confused as to why the place was so empty, and why Nate wasn't there.

"Could I possibly bring you something to drink, madam?"

"Um . . ." Olivia decided against her usual rum and Coke. The thought alone made her nauseous. "White wine spritzer . . . no! A Coke, please?"

He disappeared to get her drink. The lights dimmed, and Nate and the rest of his band, including Mrs. Walker, came out onto the stage. He turned to her, bowed deeply, then blew her an invisible kiss from his fingertips. Nate found his home at the piano, the rest of the band settled in, and Mrs. Walker took her place behind the mic.

For the next thirty minutes, Olivia was privy to every song that made Nate Walker the legend he still was. He played as if he'd never walked away from the world that made him famous. Mrs. Walker filled in the lyrics with a surprisingly lovely voice, and Olivia clapped between each song, forgetting all about the fact that she was the only one in the audience. He sounded so good, and she wished he'd play all night.

At the end of his last song, he made his way over to the table. Mrs. Walker and her husband, Rosco, followed. "So you really thought me and Nate were married?" She laughed.

"I really did."

"Girl, please." She looked at Nate, then leaned close to Rosco and kissed him seductively on the lips. "Nate ain't even my type," she purred. "Is he, baby?"

Rosco looked at Nate and laughed. "Hell, naw!" Then he took his woman to the back of the room, finding their own corner to snuggle up in.

Nate took her hand in his and kissed it. "You look lovely, darlin'."

"I didn't expect all this," she blushed. "The limo, this place, you . . . the performance. Nate, it's all so wonderful."

"I'm a little rusty, but I think I did all right. It's not over, though." That deep voice of his sent shivers up her spine. "We still got to eat," he laughed.

Dinner was delicious—calamari royal, crab cakes, voodoo pork, Caribbean tilapia, and for dessert, the best crème brulée she'd ever tasted.

"I gave up drinking ten years ago," he confessed. "Been sober ever since."

"So, you don't find owning and working in a nightclub tempting? Seems like teasing yourself to me."

He shook his head. "No. I don't need it. Don't miss it either. So, if you want to partake," he nodded toward the bar, "by all means . . ."

"Oh . . . no, I'm fine. I'm trying to cut back too."

"How come you're not married?" He caught her off guard with his question. Nate's eyes twinkled at her surprised expression.

"Me?"

"You."

She shrugged. "I don't know. Maybe I'm not planning on getting married. Maybe I think marriage is overrated."

"Marriage is."

"What?"

"Overrated. I've done it a couple of times, and people make way too much of it."

"How many times?" she asked, apprehensively.

Nate expertly changed the subject. "You're a beautiful woman, darlin'."

"Do you even know my name, Nate?"

He shook his head. "No. What is it?"

She laughed. "I knew it! Were you ever going to ask?"

He looked a bit embarrassed. "I suppose I—I would've gotten around to it, eventually."

"When?"

"Definitely before the wedding."

"I thought you said marriage was overrated."

"It is. Except when you and I get hitched. Then, I have a feeling it'll be worth it."

"We're not getting married."

"We will. When you're ready. . . . What's your name?"

She looked offended. "How come you never asked before?"

"I'm asking now, darlin'. What's your name?"

"I shouldn't tell you."

"How am I going to propose properly if I don't know your name?"

She laughed. "Oh, you got jokes."

"Fine, sugah. But don't be mad when I drop down on one knee, hold a ring out in front of me and pop the question, 'Will you marry me—'"

"Sugah! Darlin'! Honey!"

"Pick one, and that's the one I'll use."

She didn't tell him her name and eventually, Nate stopped asking. But Olivia didn't mind. Sugah suited her just fine, especially on a night like this.

After dinner they danced slow in the middle of the floor as music played softly in the background. Olivia felt even better than he'd imagined she would in his arms, her warm, petite frame fitting perfectly with his, smelling like springtime.

One by one, the members of his band left, and eventually, Mr. and Mrs. Rosco Walker left too, leaving Nate and Olivia alone in the restaurant. Soon, the waiter, chef, and even the maître d' left too.

"They trust us here alone?" she asked, surprised.

"They should. I own the place," he said, smiling.

She laughed. "Really?"

"I didn't blow all my money on drugs, sex, and rock and roll, darlin'," he winked.

Olivia loved the way he held her. Nate had outdone himself tonight, and no matter what else happened, she would remember it forever.

"What's on your mind, darlin'?" he asked out of the blue.

She looked up at him, touched that he noticed. "I'm having the time of my life," she said softly. "Thank you for this, Nate."

"It doesn't have to end, sugah. I'd rather it didn't."

She'd rather it didn't either, but Olivia knew better. She wasn't ready to take that next step. Nate was virtually a stranger, but even if he wasn't, she wasn't ready to put herself on the line like that again. Q's reaction had left another kind of scar altogether. Nate's reaction might split her in two.

She leaned in and kissed him this time. If things were different, if she were different, less marred and wounded, she might take the chance to believe in the kind of love he offered. But she wasn't different and she wasn't quite ready to believe either. "It's getting late. I need to get home."

"Yours, or mine?" he grinned.

"Me to mine. You to yours."

"I understand. It's too soon. You hardly know me, and I can respect that. In fact, I dig that."

"That's part of it."

"What's the other part?"

"I'd rather not say." It wasn't the right time or place. Olivia was enjoying her evening and didn't want anything to mar it.

"I wish you would. It's one step closer to us getting to know each other and one step closer to my proposal."

There was no other way to say it but to blurt it out. There was no nice way to put it. Telling him would only ruin the rest of their night and would serve no purpose whatsoever in the end.

"I see something in your eyes, love," he spoke softly. "I see a darkness that shouldn't be there, and I wonder what it is. That's all."

"They shouldn't be so dark now," she said with a smile. "Because I'm happy."

"But not completely, sugah. And that's where I come in." He spun her around in a dramatic circle to the chorus of the music. It was like something out of a movie, Olivia thought, laughing. He was Fred, she was Ginger, and the whole world was in Technicolor.

"I've got some sad stories," she said, staring into his handsome face.

"And some happy ones?"

She nodded, hesitantly. "I suppose. A few."

"And even more than that, if I have anything to do with it."

Nate said too many lovely things, in this lovely space, spinning her around to this lovely music, and all of a sudden, Olivia felt herself become overwhelmed with sadness. It would've been nice to hold on to a night like this forever, and to fall faith first into his feigned plan for a proposal. It would've been nice to finally find someone who loved her for all her shortcomings, insecurities, and fears. But it wasn't as simple as that. Nate's romantic self was as idealistic as she wanted to be, and he needed the truth to set him free from whatever fantasy he was living in.

"I've had cancer, Nate," she said abruptly.

The dancing stopped, but the music kept playing.

She felt like Cinderella at the ball, and the clock was well on its way to striking midnight. That long black pumpkin outside would disappear in a flash soon, and she'd be back in her old shoddy skin in a minute.

"I've had a breast removed." She swallowed hard. The look on his face was like stone. Nate just stared expressionless at her, unblinking. The damage had been done, or at least started, and this fantasy was over. She stepped back, reached into her bra, and pulled out the gelled prosthetic, waving it in his face.

"You still want to get married?" She tried to laugh, but tears came instead, and Olivia turned quickly to leave. What was she thinking? He'd never had to know, and the night could've just ended. She could've moved and never set foot in his club again. It could've just been a cool night, but she'd had to go ahead and ruin it. All she wanted to do was run as fast and as far away as she could—and vanish.

Nate caught up with her before she made it to the door. "Hold up!"

"Let go!" She struggled to get free.

He dragged her back to the bar, put his hands around her waist, and lifted her up to sit on it. Nate took the prosthetic from her hand and looked at it. "Are they both fake?" he asked, shocked.

Olivia cried. "No! Just this one." She pointed to the flat section on her chest. She squirmed at the way he was staring, then snatched her prosthetic back and covered it up with her hands in her lap. "I'm so embarrassed," she cried, defeated.

"Well you should be." He glared at her. "You can't just go whipping that thing out at people like that, girl! You'll scare the hell out of folks doing that."

"Well, you asked!"

"I didn't ask you to throw your tit around, Olivia."

He'd said her name. "You know my name?" she sniffed.

"Of course I know your name. Olivia Phillips. A man should know the name of the woman he loves. Wouldn't you agree?"

"Love?"

"Trying to," he said in frustration.

"Why? How?"

He put his hand up to stop her questions. "Give me a minute, sugah. I need a minute to take all this in."

Nate pulled the fake breast from her lap and looked at it, then he gave it back to her, and looked at her.

"You all right otherwise?"

Olivia nodded. "I'm fine."

Tentatively, he reached for her blouse. Olivia grabbed his hands. "What are you doing?" she asked, surprised.

He stared intently into her eyes. "Looking."

Olivia conceeded and slowly he unbuttoned the front of her blouse. Olivia watched him, surprised at herself that she didn't try harder to stop him. One side of her bra lay flat against her chest. He gently lifted up the bottom of it and ran his long fingers lightly over what he could see of the scar. She watched him, amazed that he didn't flinch, or cringe, or run away screaming. Nate studied it like he was a surgeon, and when he finished, he closed the front of her blouse and carefully buttoned it back up. He took her fake breast and held it out in front of him.

"Next time you pull this thing out like that, I'm going to take it and throw it across the room."

Sweet Potato Pie

"*Who is it?" Mr. Palmer* yelled loudly through his door. Olivia figured he'd forgotten to put in his hearing aid again, which is the reason he usually talked so loud.

"It's Olivia Phillips, Mr. Palmer," she yelled back, holding her rent check in her hand, ready to shove it at him as soon as he opened the door because she knew he'd ask for it, even though it wasn't late.

"You got my . . ."

Olivia smiled. "Here you go," she said sweetly. He

took it and was just about to close the door, when Olivia blurted, "Mr. Palmer?"

That man had to be at least eighty, she surmised from looking at him. Maybe closer to a hundred was more like it. "What?" he asked rudely.

"Can you tell me which apartment Maybelline lives in? I think her last name is Brown."

He shook his head. "Naw."

"Naw . . . Brown's not her last name? Or naw . . . you can't tell me her apartment number?"

"Ain't no Maybelline in this building."

Again, he started to close the door in her face, but Olivia stopped him. Surely his old self was mistaken. Mr. Palmer's problem was that he stayed locked up in that apartment all day, counting his money and devising new and improved ways to be mean and rude to his tenants.

"She's about my height, big glasses, gold tooth?" He stared at her blankly. "Wears bright colors, way too much perfume, and cracks her gum all the time. Oh, and bad wigs," she laughed, making gestures with her hands.

Mr. Palmer was speechless.

"You've had to have seen her, Mr. Palmer. She's pretty hard to miss."

Mr. Palmer's memory certainly wasn't what it used to be, but there was no way he could ever forget

Maybelline Brown, even if he tried. All the color flushed from his face. "Maybelline Brown died thirty years ago, gal," he said coldly. "Whatchu tryin' to do to me?" For a moment, he looked like he was going to charge her, raising his cane up off the floor.

"Nothing! Nothing, I . . . I think you must be confused." The old man looked stunned. He was old and his memory was obviously playing tricks on him. She felt ill all of a sudden. "Mr. Palmer, surely you must be mistaken. Maybelline Brown, she lives in this building. I've seen her in the elevator, and—she's been to my apartment."

"She dead! You hear me! She been dead, gal!"

"Maybelline Brown?" Maybelline wasn't dead. The woman had been in her home. They'd talked and laughed and eaten some of the best pies Olivia had ever tasted.

"I called her Bell." His eyes started to water. "She liked to be called Bell, or May, but never . . ."

"Maybel," Olivia whispered, finishing his sentence. "You can call me May, or call me Bell, but don't ever call me Maybel. I had an uncle once who had a cow name Maybel."

His eyes grew wide with fear. "Don't play with me! Don't you mess with me like that!"

"I'm not, Mr. Palmer," Olivia said, panicked. Her thoughts jumbled in her head, turning flips over each other. Maybelline had been in that elevator.

She'd been in Olivia's apartment, she'd talked to the woman, touched her.

"Back in '75." Mr. Palmer stared at Olivia. His hands trembled. "I was the super then too, but I lived on the third floor in B. Maybelline lived down the hall. She was my wife's friend, but sometimes, she talked too much, and too loud. She wore that loud-smelling perfume all the time, and painted her lips red."

Olivia stared back, shocked at what she was hearing. "She made pies?" she asked, softly.

"Tried to. Made some awful pies, always trying to get everybody to eat 'em but we wouldn't. Not after that first one. Sweet potato." Olivia shivered.

But she'd seen her. She'd tasted Maybelline's delicious pies, and loved them.

Mr. Palmer probably didn't even realize he was crying, but he was. His expression went blank, and he stared past Olivia to the wall behind her, like he was seeing something that was no longer there.

"She just up and died one day," his voice cracked. "Fool gal didn't even want to tell nobody she was sick! Walked around like everything was fine when we all knew it wasn't."

"Why?" Olivia's eyes watered too. "Why would she do that?"

"'Cause she was proud. Didn't want nobody to know she had cancer. Back in them days, they couldn't find it fast as they do now sometimes. It got away from her, and I went to get my rent from her one day. . . ." His bottom lip quivered.

Riding up in the elevator, Olivia tried to catch her breath. Mr. Palmer was an old man, and chances were his recollection of the past was warped, if not just flat-out wrong. Maybelline was a living, breathing woman. Olivia's apartment still smelled of her perfume. Her mouth still watered at the thought of one of her pies.

. . . I just didn't want to be too late . . .

Too late? No!

Maybelline had cancer . . .

No! No! No! Olivia fought back her panic. That old man was crazy. He was crazy, because even on this elevator, she could smell that woman's perfume. How could she be dead? Maybelline Brown was as real as she was. And she'd saved Olivia's life, just by being her friend, and bringing her pies, and . . .

. . . I just didn't want to be too late . . .

Maybelline had told Olivia she'd learned from Mr. Palmer that Olivia had been ill. A question suddenly came to mind. Who'd called the ambulance the night she'd tried to kill herself? The second time she'd gotten pissy drunk, rummaged through her house for more pills, even razor blades . . . and Maybelline had shown up.

Olivia had been under some kind of crazy spell,

maybe lost in a dream, or maybe . . . maybe she was dead after all. Maybe the ambulance had never come and she'd never had to meet with Dr. Lacy, and she'd never woken up.

Finally, the elevator stopped on her floor, and Olivia stumbled off. She grabbed hold of the skin on her arm and pinched herself hard, expecting to wake up, or come to her senses or something. But it just hurt real bad. That's all.

Inside her apartment, she locked the door behind her. Goose bumps swelled on her skin, as she inhaled the savory aroma of Maybelline's sweet potato pie. She was crazy! That's all it was. She'd lost her mind, probably gotten brain damage from those pills and she was just insane.

The phone rang, startling her, and Olivia stared at it momentarily, trying to decipher if it was really ringing, or if she was just dreaming it was ringing. Finally, she decided to answer it.

"Hello?"

"Hey, darlin'," the sound of Nate's voice was like taking a deep breath. "You doin' all right?"

No Nate, she wanted to say. *I'm crazy, insane, and I'm not going to be able to see you anymore.*

"I'm fine."

"We still on for tonight? And don't say no, cause that's my least favorite word in the whole English language, especially coming from you," he chuckled.

Olivia felt physically ill and sat down on the couch to keep from falling to the floor in case she passed out. "What do you want to do?"

"Well, you know what I want to do, but since that ain't happening, I'm leaving it up to you. Whatever you want, sugah, whatever you need, just say the word, and I'm all yours."

Déjà vu, she thought, smiling. Or was it? Her thoughts drifted back to the last time she'd seen Maybelline. What was it she'd said before she'd left?

Whatever you want, sugah, whatever you need, just say the word, and it's all yours.

"You there?" he asked.

"Yes. I'm here." Olivia was just about to make up an excuse to get off the phone when suddenly she noticed a steaming sweet potato pie on her kitchen table with a card addressed to her next to it. "Can you hold on a second, Nate?" she asked absentmindedly.

"Yeah, sugah. I'll be here." Olivia put the phone down and went over to the table.

On the card was the recipe for the pie and a message scrawled in pink ink.

Took me a lifetime to learn to make a good pie.
It won't have to take you nearly as long.
You got what you need, darlin', a little faith, a good man, and a sweet potato pie.

Olivia took a nice long whiff of Maybelline's magical pie and realized an angel had made it. She hurried back to the phone where Nate was still waiting. "Nate? Why don't you just come over here tonight, and I'll make you dinner."

"Sounds good, darlin'." He seemed to be smiling.

"Oh, and do you like sweet potato pie?"

"Mmmm . . . It's my absolute favorite."

Survival Instincts

Sandra Kitt

Chapter One

The sudden and violent rattling of the door made Lynette Hayes jump.

The noise came from the employee and delivery entrance not far from her office, and the commotion drew her attention away from her study of the ledger pages in front of her. She'd heard the same rattling during the day as curious passersby had tested the lock's effectiveness, trying to get in. But at night the sound was thunderous and frightening.

"Mr. Benjamin?" Lynn called out to her elderly volunteer, and the only other person who might still be inside the building.

There was no answer except for the rattling of the door once again. And then all was quiet.

The library where she was manager was officially closed for the evening. With the air conditioner already turned off, the outside May heat had turned the interior of the two-storied building into a virtual oven. Coupled with the empty silence, the stifling air filling all the space around her made Lynn feel as if she were suffocating. She'd long ago trained herself to remember, if not to grin and bear it, that it could be worse. And sometimes it was.

She began reading down the columns of numbers on the last page of her budget, trying to figure out where she could borrow from Peter to pay Paul. What service or program could be cut at her branch in order to save resources for the purchase of new books, and even more desperately needed computer terminals and databases. What staff would she have to reduce to part-time hours in order to prevent a deficit at the end of the fiscal year?

"Miss Lynn? You still here? I thought I heard the door close just now."

"In my office, Mr. Benjamin," she called out.

Lynn put the budget sheet aside and used a calculator to add up the numbers. The resulting figure made her clench her teeth in frustration. A band of tension stretched between her temples, the start of a headache.

At least she'd managed to keep the library open for business.

She heard shuffling footsteps outside her office, and a minute later a rail-thin, elderly man stood hesitantly in the doorway, his gaunt face shadowed by the brim of his baseball cap. Lynn looked up and smiled kindly at Harold Benjamin, her warm gaze silently thanking him for his presence and devotion. Her gratitude was all she had to offer.

"I thought I just heard *you* leave," Lynn said.

"On my way now. It's late, ma'am. You need to go on home," Mr. Benjamin admonished.

"In a minute. I'm almost finished."

"I know they don't pay you 'nough to stay 'round here ten hours a day."

She ignored the tired derisiveness in his raspy voice, even though his intent was protective. "I get paid by the work that gets done, not the hours I keep."

Mr. Benjamin shook his head. "Damn shame. You a smart lady, Miss Lynn. How come you don't get yourself a better job than this?" He lifted his arms wearily to indicate the old and drab surroundings. "How come they put all the black Lib*er*ians in the po' neighborhoods? You should be downtown in one of them big places."

"I like it here," Lynn said simply.

Mr. Benjamin sighed, sounding every bit as ancient as he looked, with his clean but worn clothes, bent shoulders, and rheumy eyes. "Don't understand why. Ain't nothin' 'round here but a bunch of lazy, good for nothin' . . ."

"Did I forget to turn off the computers in the main room?" Lynn carefully interrupted, frowning.

"No, ma'am. They off. I seen you do it."

"Oh, good. Go home, Mr. Benjamin. You must be tired. I've told you before you don't have to stay the whole day."

"Well . . . I don't like leavin' you alone. It gets kind of spooky 'round here at night."

Lynn chuckled. "I'm not afraid. I'm getting ready to leave myself, but don't wait for me," Lynn said.

She gathered the budget sheets and slipped them into a folder on her desk. She could finish her review and report in the morning. Lynn was aware that the elderly gentleman watched as she expertly worked her keyboard. He was steadfast in his refusal to let her show him basic computer skills, huffily muttering that he'd gotten through life without that crazy machine and he didn't need to know how to use one now. She closed the files on her desktop PC and turned off the power.

"Done," Lynn announced for his sake.

"Well then, I guess I'll say goodnight." Mr. Benjamin gave her a vague wave and nod.

"Will you be coming in tomorrow?" Lynn asked rhetorically.

"Yes, ma'am. Ain't got nothin' else to do . . ." his voice trailed off.

"Then I'll see you in the morning. Goodnight."

Mr. Benjamin turned away, shuffling down the corridor to the side exit. "You be careful now, Miss Lynn. Home safe," his voice drifted back to her.

In another minute Lynn heard the solid slamming of the door as it closed and automatically locked behind him. The door had a crash bar ensuring that once anyone passed through, they could not gain reentry.

Lynn began the last of her nightly routine, gathering all her personal things together and placing them into her oversized shoulder bag. She absently plucked at the fabric of her linen blouse, fanning it back and forth against the slight dampness of her skin. She swept her hands back over her short, wavy hair and brought her hands forward again to fluff up the lightly curled strands, blindly fingering them into shape.

Leaving her small office, Lynn hit the light switch. Immediately the last sector of the first floor of the small branch library was plunged into darkness, except for the exit and emergency lights placed over certain doors and in the hallways. She'd only taken a few steps when her desk phone rang. For a second Lynn thought to ignore it, but there were any number of people who might need to reach her. Her own mother came to mind. She returned to the darkened office and reached blindly for the phone.

"Lynn Hayes."

"I knew you'd still be there. Girl, with the kind of hours you put in you could have stayed here at Graphic Central."

"Hey, Jo. They don't need me at Graphic Central. What's up? I was actually on my way out the door . . ."

Lynn stopped, suddenly detecting an unusual sound that was only amplified in the empty building.

"Just called to let you know Hillary Rosen got canned," JoAnn Benton drawled on the other end of the line.

Lynn listened to the account of what had happened. She no longer had a vested interest in her former employer or coworker, so JoAnn's gleeful report was interesting but not titillating.

"That's too bad. She's an excellent research librarian. She saved the company a lot of money and mistakes a couple of years ago."

"Yeah, over your *almost* dead body. She was conniving and I never trusted her. Turns out I was right. You hire her into an important position and then she uses it to bring you down. I say, 'turn around is fair play.' Some people are starting to realize that she may have planned that whole loss of data incident that you got blamed for that cost the company a big account, and got you fired."

"I wasn't fired, JoAnn. I quit."

"Same thing," JoAnn said dryly.

"I guess they're going on a hunt to replace Hillary."

"They didn't have to go very far. I'm supposed to meet with the head of research and development, and some of the account executives day after tomorrow. I think they're going to offer me the job," JoAnn said, her voice conspiratorial. "That will make me the youngest library director they've ever had."

"Good for you."

"If it happens we'll still be shorthanded. I know I can do the job, but you are a hard act to follow, Lynn. You were a great director. I think they should hire you back."

"I'd wait before congratulating yourself. You know how management is. They make lots of promises but don't always come through. And I'm not interested in coming back."

"You know you're crazy, working in that godforsaken hellhole when you could be here where things are happening."

"I wouldn't say my library is godforsaken, but it is a challenge. And the people in this community need the resources the library provides."

"Whatever," JoAnn murmured, losing interest. "Listen, the other reason why I'm calling is because I have passes to attend a premiere. We got the account to do advertising for three indie films, one of which opens this Friday. The screening is tomorrow."

"I can't commit right now. Let me get back to you, okay?"

"You got a date?" JoAnn asked, somewhat incredulous.

Lynn had to laugh. "Right. The last time I went out with a man was when I accompanied an electrician to the basement to check out the circuit breakers."

"Well, let me know as soon as you can. Otherwise I have someone else in mind."

"Who is he?" Lynn smiled.

It was JoAnn's turn to laugh. "Talk to you later." And she hung up.

Lynn fumbled in the dark to replace the receiver. She again headed for the exit. Suddenly, the closed-in interior of the empty building did seem eerie, as Mr. Benjamin suggested. There was the musky smell of books, dust and old wooden furniture. Lynn adjusted the shoulder strap of her bag and wiped away the moisture pooling on her forehead and chin from the heat. At Graphic Central, her last place of employment, not only would the air conditioner still have been on but also she would have been sent home by car service because of the late hour. Lynn recalled the brightly lit offices of Graphic Central, with its modern setting and state-of-the-art equipment, the employee perks and general atmosphere of prosperity.

For another moment Lynn considered her role at the other company. She'd been a manager, dealing with the fast-paced and demanding responsibilities inherent in the field of advertising. While she felt sadness that she was no longer there, she didn't regret the choices she'd made, or been forced into, in the last several years. *"How the mighty have fallen,"* she thought in amusement, but without rancor, as she pushed her way through the exit door and stepped into the late May night.

Lynn was immediately assailed with the smell of garbage carelessly deposited around or on top of already filled cans at the end of the alley, waiting for a morning sanitation pickup. She forced herself to ignore the pungent odors as she walked toward the street. She could hear, not more than 100 feet away on the main street, traffic and the faint voices of people talking, arguing, laughing. For no particular reason, Lynn glanced over her shoulder to see that three teenaged boys were loitering in the shadowed depths of the alley, smoking and laughing among themselves. She noticed that the safety lights on either side of the library exit were out again. As she faced forward and continued walking, she made a mental note to call about the lights in the morning.

Her thoughts drifted back to the conversation with JoAnn. JoAnn's news of a possible new position was in direct contrast to her own very real concerns,

Lynn thought. Could she, for instance, present a case to the downtown administration to increase her operating budget? Could she at least persuade them to let her fund-raise on her own? How much trouble would she face if it became known that she accepted local patrons as volunteers to supplement her paid staff? What if she was offered a job somewhere else? Would she take it? Should she have her mother, in remission from non-Hodgkin's lymphoma, finally move in with her?

Was Morris's son two or three years old, now?

She heard the soft pounding of sneakered feet hurrying behind her and automatically moved aside to make room for the fast-approaching teens to pass. Lynn gasped in shock when she was grabbed and stopped, and quickly surrounded. Her immediate reaction of annoyance turned to wariness when she saw that the two teens standing directly in front of her had pulled up their too-big Phat Farm T-shirts until their faces were hidden in the neck openings. Only their eyes were visible.

"What you got?" one boy challenged. "Better not say *nothin'*, bitch."

"Hurry up, man! Take her purse and let's get outta here," said the teen behind her.

Lynn felt his hot breath on her hair. He was nervous, panting, trying to pull her bag from her shoulder.

"Take it," Lynn said calmly, raising her arms to make it easier to remove. Her heart thundered in her chest. She felt something round, cold, and hard in her neck. She closed her eyes briefly, swallowing.

Oh, my God . . .

It was a gun.

"Better not say *nothin'*. Take her earrings. They real," said the one with the gun.

She reached at once to take the gold hoops from her pierced ears. The boy with the gun snatched them from her hand. She stared toward the street, hoping to see someone come by. It didn't help that the building right next to the library was officially deserted and boarded up, although a number of people were known to be squatting there. The three teens closed in around her, invading her space, cutting off any escape.

The tallest teen hovering over Lynn grabbed her bag from the boy behind her, turned it upside down and emptied the contents onto the ground at her feet.

"What you do that for, man? Take everything!"

"Where's the wallet . . . ," the leader muttered, kicking through Lynn's things on the ground.

"Let's go, let's *go,*" urged the boy behind her.

He was sweating profusely from his nervousness, soaking through the back of Lynn's blouse. She suddenly heard the voices of two women and watched as their shadows advanced along the sidewalk. The tall, skinny leader of the three abruptly clamped his hand roughly over Lynn's mouth, laughing as he thwarted her plan to call for help. The two ladies passed by, not even aware of the presence of four people within the close quarters of the alley.

Lynn felt her heart starting to race. Despite her rising panic, she tried to give the outward appearance of calm. The boy removed his hand from her mouth. Silently, she began to pray.

"Man! She smell good," the gunman sniffed. "We gittin' it?" he asked his buddy, who had taken what he wanted from the shoulder bag and left the rest on the ground.

"Naw, forget it, man. That ain't the deal," the one behind Lynn complained.

"Shut up, Ju Ju," said the leader, stuffing his booty into the side thigh pockets of his jeans.

"*You* shut up!" the gunman warned him.

The shift from simple mugging to possibly something far more distressing made Lynn's mouth go dry. She struggled for something to say to stop them but knew it would be a mistake to plead.

She looked at the leader but couldn't see his features. She tried to focus on his eyes and hold his attention. "You have everything. Just let me go."

"Not everything," cackled the gunman. "Common. Let's do it. Back there, back there."

He pointed to the deeper recess of the alley then grabbed hold of the front of Lynn's blouse and began pushing her backward.

"I ain't up for this, man. We said we was just

going to get her money. We got it. Let's *go!*" the third boy hissed urgently over her head.

Lynn listened to him, her attention distracted by his voice and his attempts to reason with his friends. She learned his body and size, and tried to construct an image of him as someone who was threatening, but somehow familiar. It was more than his voice or his body type. It was the name the other boy had called him that rang a bell in Lynn's memory. She realized that maybe she knew about him by way of a family member. But she was sure she'd seen him.

Lynn was pushed again, and her attention shifted away from the boy behind her to thoughts of her own safety, and survival.

The gunman grabbed her breast roughly and squeezed. Lynn gasped again and resisted the urge to push him away.

"Oh, man," the gunman hissed. "I want some of this. Won't take me long. You in?" he asked the leader.

"Common, man," moaned the boy holding her.

"Yeah, I'm in."

With that Lynn felt herself, inexorably, being forced back into the alley. She stiffened her body and planted her feet, her growing fear making her light-headed. Her breathing became shallow.

"Don't." Lynn raised her voice. A hand covered her mouth again. This time she reached for it, tried to pry the fingers away.

"What do you mean, no?" the first teen got in her face, his forehead almost touching hers as he intimidated her with his aggressiveness. "I should let my boy here pop you right now."

The gunman, pushing the cold muzzle of the gun into her skin, objected. "*Hell,* no. Not 'til I get me some."

The boy behind Lynn suddenly stepped back and released her.

"I'm out. I ain't doin' this."

The hand over her mouth blocked her nose. She couldn't breathe. Lynn mumbled, fighting to pull the hand away now, just to get air. She felt a sharp blow against the side of her head, stunning her into silence. She was losing sight of the street. The hand covering her face was dirty and smelled of old food and oil and sweat.

Trying to hold her and move at the same time, one of the boys stumbled, falling back into the overflowing garbage can. The can lid fell off and clanked to the ground.

The leader cursed at the resounding noise.

The gunman, unable to sidestep the top, inadvertently kicked it across the narrow passage, and it banged into the wall of the library. They cursed, blamed each other, raised their voices, losing control in the dark.

Lynn struggled in earnest, but it was an unfair

match from the start. The third teen stood to the side watching, ambivalent about being a part of what his buddies had in mind.

"We're gonna get *caught.*"

"Hey! Is everything okay back there?"

The boys instantly quieted down, but Lynn tried to scream from deep in her throat. The sound was an agonizing moan from behind the hand clamped to her mouth and nose.

"We hangin', man. Everything's cool."

"Yeah," the gunman cackled. "We cool."

The third youth stood silently to the side, no longer objecting, but not giving his friends up, either.

Lynn blinked in relief as the stranger stepped into the alley. He stood peering into the dark at the odd gathering. She tried to move but wasn't even sure he could see her.

"She hanging with you, too?" he asked, pointing to Lynn.

"Fuck off, man. Ain't none of yo' business."

"I think you better let the lady go."

"Say, *what?*"

"I said it looks like you're holding her against her will. Let her go, and it ends right now."

His voice was firm. No nonsense. Fearless.

With that, the third teen, the one who'd been holding Lynn, suddenly broke and began running. Confusion took over when the other two hesitated.

"I said, *let her go!*" The stranger's voice boomed and filled the alley.

Lynn gasped when she was suddenly released and shoved aside by the skinny leader. He and the gunman seemed unsure what to do now that the stranger's appearance and interference was forcing them to make a decision. They scrambled to get past Lynn and escape.

She had been pushed so hard she fell to the ground, landing hard on her hands and knees. Momentarily stunned by the pain, Lynn couldn't see what was going on. She glanced up to see the stranger running toward her.

The gunman, about to disappear through another door in the alley, stopped, pivoted, and pointed the gun . . .

And fired. *Pop!*

Lynn uttered a cry, putting up her arms defensively. But she felt no sudden impact or pain. She hadn't been hit. She heard a grunt and turned to the stranger behind her. He stopped in his tracks. Lynn stared in shock as he crossed his arms over his stomach and crumbled forward, falling to the ground.

Chapter Two

He wasn't dead.

Lynn stared in disbelief at the fallen man. His legs worked as he struggled to raise himself, only to fall back.

People were now gathering at the opening of the alley, gawking at her and the man on the ground. "Who got shot?" they shouted back and forth. A window cautiously opened in the deserted building, and occupants who had no business being there peered over the sill to the scene below. But no one came any closer or offered help.

The noise, a confusing mix of voices, car horns, and inappropriate laughter, finally penetrated Lynn's mind. Focused on the man on the ground, she tentatively crouched down, bending over his body. She could see blood on his hand and shirt. A small pool of it was seeping from under his left side. He glanced at her then, and she saw equal surprise in his dark eyes. His face writhed in pain. Lynn shook off her stupor and took action.

She looked for her purse and saw it several feet away. She hurried to pick it up and quickly searched the contents that had been spilled on the ground. Her cell phone was gone. She returned to the wounded man. Realizing what she needed, he indicated the holder on his belt. Lynn pulled the phone free. She dialed 911, and in a voice that sounded surprisingly calm and clear, she asked for assistance. She looked at the man on the ground, who lay with his eyes closed. His breathing was shallow.

"I need help. A man's been shot . . . yes, he's alive, but I can't tell how badly he's hurt. Please hurry. I don't know where he was hit . . . no, the gunman is gone . . . I'm a witness. Yes, I'll wait."

Lynn checked on him again. He was watching her through half-closed eyes. After giving her location to the dispatcher, she ended the call. There was nothing else for her to do but stay next to the wounded man. And wait. And pray.

She tentatively placed a hand on his shoulder. He half opened his eyes and gazed at her.

"I'm so sorry," she said, her voice a mix of deep regret and helplessness.

He lay staring at her, but he said nothing. Pain etched his features, his jaw muscles tightening reflexively.

Lynn's mind cleared, and she realized that she was sitting on the ground with a bleeding man, surrounded by curious onlookers. And that's all they did. It was almost as if an unexpected show had suddenly been staged for their benefit. A hot late-night drama complete with gunplay. They were the audience. She and the wounded man were players, there to entertain them in a tense scene that could still end in death.

She was oddly aware of the night, of the weird sensation that something profound had just happened, had *almost* happened to her. But she felt detached, like an observer. If the man had not interrupted the three teens, she might have been dragged behind the building and raped. When they were done they might have left her there, discarded but alive. Or, maybe not.

She glanced around at the onlookers who stood on the fringe, curious but without emotion. The crowd included any number of very young children, who should have been home in bed, but who stared wide-eyed and gaping at her and the stranger.

"I'm . . . losing a lot . . . of blood," he suddenly croaked.

Lynn squeezed his shoulder. "Please, hold on."

He winced in pain.

Nearby someone shouted out, "Here come the cops."

There was no siren, only several short warning blasts of the squad car alert horn, clearing a path through the crowd.

Suddenly the alley filled with cops, and an EMS crew and ambulance. Lynn and the stranger were separated as he was surrounded by the emergency team. When she indicated that her injuries were superficial, she was placed in a squad car and questioned by several officers.

It all felt surreal to Lynn. One moment she was leaving work and heading home to have a late dinner. In the next instant, she had become part of a melodrama with enough tension and action for a made-for-TV movie. And now that it was all over, she was also aware of how close she'd come to a bad ending. She could have become a statistic. The thought made her breathless and light-headed.

She should have left the library earlier. Or stayed a little later and finished her letter. She gazed at the wounded man. What if this stranger had not stopped and questioned what was going on in the alley?

The police kept asking for a description of the three assailants, but all Lynn could tell the officers was that they were teenagers, maybe sixteen or seventeen. All three had been dressed alike in the signature attire of urban hip-hop. The jeans, wide-legged and several sizes too big. The white T-shirts, loose and full and down to the knees, and ultraclean sneakers. There had been nothing to distinguish one from the other except for the teen who had drawn the line on what he'd been willing to do.

Over the shoulder of the officer questioning her, Lynn watched as her rescuer was placed on a collapsible gurney and loaded into an ambulance.

"Is he going to be all right?" she asked.

"We'll know as soon as we get him to the hospital," one officer responded noncommittally. He beckoned to her and gestured to the ambulance. "You can get in next to him, ma'am. There's room."

"But I'm not hurt," Lynn objected.

"We can't tell for sure," the officer said. "There's blood all over you."

Lynn looked down. Her white linen blouse had bloodstains on the front. Her pant legs were torn at the knees, revealing abrasions and scraped skin. The palms of her hands were the same. Only now did she recognize the stinging sensation of surface injuries.

"I'm okay. Please see after . . . him," she said, nodding toward the open door of the ambulance. "I just want to go home."

"Sorry, ma'am. You'll have to come along. We're going to take you both to the hospital, have the doctors check you over, make sure everything's okay. You can give the rest of your statement there."

She had no choice.

Another officer approached, holding out her shoulder bag. "This yours? Someone in the crowd picked up your stuff. Better take a look. See what's missing. We'll add it to the report."

She silently accepted the bag, holding it gingerly, as if it had become something foreign. It was a permanent reminder of the terrible evening and what had occurred in the alley next to the library. But Lynn just as quickly overcame her aversion. It was only a bag. The things that had been taken, her wallet and cell phone, could be replaced and were of no real value. She had survived a mugging. Her knees and hands would heal. She would move on, forgive, and forget.

Those were her options.

And yes, it could have been worse.

"This way, ma'am."

As Lynn was led to the ambulance, several people in the crowd called out to her.

"You comin' back tomorrow, Miss Hayes?"

"Where'd you get shot?"

"Yo, I know her. She run the liberry."

"Miss Hayes, can I keep my book for another week?"

Lynn didn't answer, her expression blank as she climbed into the ambulance. The lack of emotion and horror that the people of the neighborhood displayed used to astonish her, but now she understood their constraint as a defense mechanism. They were used to this. It happened all the time. Nothing changed. That's the way life was. Random. Surprising. She recognized some of the voices. She also knew that their odd remarks and questions, when decoded, showed a familiarity with her. And, in a way, showed concern.

The door slammed shut and locked behind her and the ambulance began to move. Lynn could hear the muffled voices of the crowd outside. Inside, the sounds of portable life-support equipment were beeping intermittently from sensors attached to the man who had been shot. The EMS worker was checking his blood pressure and pulse, quietly asking questions and speaking in reassuring tones, explaining everything that was being done. Lynn sat on a hard metal box, holding on for balance to a strap riveted to the wall of the ambulance.

The female EMS worker finally glanced at her, taking a quick, sharp assessment.

"You hurt anywhere?"

"I'm fine. Only scratches and bruises."

But Lynn was appalled at the amount of blood that stained the beige shirt the man was wearing, that colored his hands and arms. The shirt had been opened and there were monitoring devices attached to his chest, neck and arms. His breathing seemed normal.

"How's he doing?" she asked again, leaning forward to see his face through the clear plastic oxygen mask he wore.

"We'll know more when we get to the hospital," the EMS said evasively.

"I'm okay," he suddenly spoke up.

Lynn looked at him. He was awake and alert and responsive. His face was clear of the pain that had, just moments before, contorted his features. She listened to the rhythmic beating of his heart being measured by the machine.

She was also aware of the rising and falling of his chest. Aware of the black curlicues of hair sprinkled across the expanse. Lynn brought her gaze back to his face, but the image of someone else briefly superseded that of the injured man. Someone from the past who'd had such a profound effect on her life. She blinked, trying to separate the past from the present. Finally, Lynn focused on the man and a face that was square, the color of teak, with a mouth that was wide and well formed. His eyes seem to hold as much curiosity as hers.

He suddenly held up a hand. It was streaked and smeared with dried blood. Lynn didn't hesitate and put her hand in his as his fingers closed around hers, holding with a firmness that was surprising.

"Davis Manning," he said, his voice muffled by the mask.

"Lynette Hayes. Lynn," she added for no particular reason.

"Did they hurt you?" he asked pointedly.

"No," she shook her head. She made no attempt to pull her hand free.

"It looked to me like . . ."

"Try not to talk, Mr. Manning," the EMS worker interrupted. "We need to keep your pressure steady."

Lynn leaned forward. "Don't worry about me. I'll be fine."

Within minutes they arrived at the local hospital, pulling into the emergency parking port. Davis Manning was wheeled quickly inside and into a triage room. Lynn was helped out of the ambulance and she followed behind, accompanied by two police officers. Being in the emergency area brought home the seriousness of the incident. Medical personnel came running to attend to Davis's wound. Lynn felt herself being guided to another area, down a corridor and around a corner where she could neither hear nor see what was going on. She had no way of knowing, for the time being, if Davis Manning was alive, or dying.

A nurse treated her scratches and gave her a tetanus shot. She told Lynn to expect soreness for a few days, and perhaps a delayed reaction to the attack. And then it was the police's turn.

"Can you tell us what happened? What were you doing in the alley? Do you live in the neighborhood?"

Lynn tried to give her attention to the officers making out a preliminary report on the incident. It seemed like she answered the same questions over and over again, for at least another hour, until they were satisfied. They didn't promise that they'd catch the perpetrators. Chances were slim to none.

When the interrogation was done, one of the officers offered to have her driven home in a squad car. Lynn gratefully accepted and asked if they could give her a few minutes to take care of something. They agreed.

She found her way back to the triage area, but the treatment room where Davis Manning had been wheeled was empty. There was still evidence of his presence, however, in the bloody gauze swabs littering the floor. He *had* lost a lot of blood. Where was he now?

Lynn stopped a passing resident to question him.

"What happened to the man that came in, about an hour ago? His name is Davis Manning. He'd been shot."

The resident directed her to the supervising nurse. Lynn was told that Davis had been admitted for the night.

"How is he?" Lynn asked.

"He's stable," was the answer.

That told her nothing other than the fact that he was alive. She was also told that it was too late for visitors, and in any case the patient had been mildly sedated. Lynn politely accepted the response, but she'd already made up her mind that she couldn't just go home to pick up where she'd left off. She had to see for herself that Davis Manning was okay. She found the nearest visitors waiting room and used the phone to call the patient information desk. She was told Davis's ward and room number.

When Lynn got off the elevator, the ward was quiet and seemingly empty of hospital personnel. She had to pass the nurses' station to reach Davis's room. There was a lone male making notes on a patient chart and answering phones. He glanced up and saw her.

"Sorry. Visiting hours are over."

"I know, but I forgot something."

"What's the patient's name?"

Lynn gave the information. The young doctor adjusted his glasses and looked down a list of names taped to the edge of the counter. He glanced at her. "He was admitted less than two hours ago."

Caught in her white lie, Lynn was undeterred. "Can I see him for a few minutes? Please."

He already was shaking his head. "It's late, and the patient is probably asleep." He was about to turn away when he studied Lynn more closely, noting her torn pants, stained blouse and gauze-wrapped hands. "Are you family?"

"No, I'm not. But Mr. Manning saved my life."

Still skeptical, he pursed his lips.

She hastily dug through her purse to find her business card holder. Removing a card, Lynn wrote her information on the back and handed it to the night duty resident.

"You can ask the police, if you don't believe me."

He scanned the card briefly. "Five minutes."

Lynn murmured her thanks and went in search of the room. Stepping quietly inside, she immediately saw that the first patient was an elderly man, attached to a number of monitors as he slept. Beyond the curtain that divided the beds she found Davis Manning.

The soft night-light over the bed was still on, and it cast shadows over his face. He was in a reclining position, with an IV running into his right arm, and he appeared to be asleep. Standing next to the bed, Lynn silently watched him. He was younger than she'd thought he would be. Clean-shaven, fit, and obviously fearless, as she had witnessed herself.

Though she felt assured that Davis Manning was going to be all right, Lynn stayed, as if thinking something else had to happen. She briefly closed her eyes and silently wished that Davis would heal and be well, with no ill effects afterward from his gunshot wound. She prayed for his forgiveness for, even indirectly, being the cause of his getting hurt.

"You're not going to cry, are you?"

His voice broke into her thoughts, and Lynn saw

that he'd been watching her from beneath almost closed eyelids.

"I didn't mean to wake you. I'm not supposed to be here."

"Me, either," he said.

It took a second for Lynn to realize that he was making a joke. She grinned, uncertain and tentative.

"What are you doing here?"

"I wanted to make sure that . . ."

"I was still alive?"

"You weren't seriously hurt."

"I guess you could say I was lucky," he said sarcastically. "It's what they call a flesh wound. The bullet got me in the side but went right through. It didn't hit any major blood vessels or organs."

"Thank God," Lynn murmured fervently.

"What about you? Is that my blood or yours?" he asked, looking at the condition of her clothing.

She looked at her hands, glanced down at her blouse. "I don't know. I only have scratches. My knees are pretty badly scraped. I was lucky, too, thanks to you."

Davis's brow furrowed. "What the hell were you doing in that alley? Why were you even in that neighborhood? It's a bad place to be hanging out."

"I work there. I was on my way home when I got stopped by those boys."

"Work there?" he asked, astonished. "Doing what?"

"I manage the library."

"The library? Oh, yeah. I forgot there was one. I thought it was still closed."

"The city was supposed to make renovations but it never happened. We got them to reopen the library and—"

"But what are *you* doing there? What was up with those punks?"

Lynn ignored the derisiveness in his tone. "They mugged me. They wanted money and any valuables."

"That's not what I saw when I found you. Looked like they were ready to do a lot more to you. Why didn't you scream? Why didn't you fight like crazy to get away?"

"I thought if I gave them my purse I wouldn't get hurt and they'd let me go."

He looked skeptical. "That's dumb thinking, you know that? Look at you. You're attractive, and you're definitely not street. They could have taken you down with no problem. Were you planning on talking your way out of being raped?"

The blunt assessment of the situation brought Lynn right back to the scene outside the library and the moment of realization that she was going to be violated. Even now she couldn't say if she would have struggled to escape. And why not?

"It didn't happen, thanks to you. I just want to say—"

"I know, I know. How sorry you are that I was

the one who got shot. Well, let me tell you, I'm not too happy about it, either. When I heard voices in the alley I figured something was going down, and it wasn't good. You have to be careful around teens like that. They're up to no good and are going to end up dead or in jail. Be smarter next time."

Lynn listened to Davis's vehemence, to his anger, and felt it spread all over her. She felt humiliated by his observation, and that made her defensive.

"I hope there won't be a next time."

"Great. Would you feel the same way if I hadn't come along, and they'd taken more than your money?"

She stared at him. She actually hadn't allowed herself to think through to that real possibility. What would she have done?

"I know it's my fault you got shot. I can't tell you how sorry I am it happened. But I'm *very* grateful you came along when you did."

"Do me and yourself a favor. Don't be so kind and thoughtful next time. Think about staying safe. I almost didn't stop. I was at a meeting and on my way back to where I'd parked my car. Do you know any of the boys?"

Lynn let her gaze drop to his hand. He had been cleaned up. His hand was large and hairy on the back of the knuckles. It was balled into a fist. He was still angry. The distraction gave her a second or two to think.

"No, I don't."

"I gave a description to the cops, but I'm not going to hold my breath that they care or they'll do anything to catch the one who shot me. Sorry. I'm a little pissed off."

"I understand. You could have been killed. Thank God that didn't happen."

Lynn realized that Davis Manning stared at her with a combination of wrath and amusement. She found his reaction confusing.

"Let me tell you something. God had *nothing* to do with it."

Chapter Three

Hey, Miss Hayes. How you doin', honey?"

Lynn turned from the terminal, where she'd been helping a young mother navigate through an Internet site on inexpensive childcare facilities.

The woman who had spoken to Lynn, in her midfifties and overweight, was regarding her with concern. Lynn had not seen Mrs. Hopkins, a regular volunteer at the library who helped gather library materials at the end of the day, in two days.

"I'm doing fine, Mrs. Hopkins."

The woman nodded in relief. "I sure am glad to hear that. I'm sorry about what happened to you. You're a nice lady. Always trying to help folks around here."

Lynn gave quick instructions to the young woman at the terminal on how to continue. She then walked Mrs. Hopkins to a more private corner of the reading room.

"It's nice of you to say so. How's your daughter?"

Mrs. Hopkins shook her head. "I don't know. She checked herself out of that clinic again, but I haven't seen her. I was hoping she'd stay this time, get herself cleaned up. Her kids miss her," she added.

"Is there something I can do for you?" Lynn asked quietly.

Mrs. Hopkins seemed to hesitate. Finally, she shook her head. "I'll be all right. The daddy of one of my daughter's kids gives money when he can. I have my disability and city aid. The little ones are fine, but . . ." She suddenly thrust a folded newspaper toward Lynn. "Here. I saved this for you. It's about what happened."

Lynn accepted the paper. It was a day old and folded to an inside page. She'd been told there'd been a write-up about the incident, but she'd avoided the newspapers. It seemed voyeuristic to her, to have so many people read about it. "Thanks," she said, taking the paper.

"It don't say anything about those three boys. You see who did it?" Mrs. Hopkins asked.

Lynn was alert to the anxious question. She'd been expecting it. At least half a dozen times since that night, visitors to the library wanted to know if she'd recognized any of the three boys.

"I couldn't see their faces. Do you think they were from around here?" Lynn asked.

Mrs. Hopkins shrugged. "Maybe. Lots of these boys don't have enough to do around here. They won't stay in school, and they hang around the streets getting into trouble."

"I know. How's your grandson doing? What's his name again?"

Again, Mrs. Hopkins hesitated. "Shawn," she murmured, playing with a large cluster of keys in her hands.

"He used to come in sometimes after school. I don't think I've seen him lately," Lynn said.

The other woman shifted, hoisting her large bag onto her shoulder. "I don't know where he takes himself off to after school. Most of the time he don't even bother going. I can't make him do anything he don't want to. Shawn ain't a bad child, but I don't know what to do for him."

"I hope he's staying out of trouble," Lynn said.

"Yeah, I hope so, too." Mrs. Hopkins looked at Lynn, her eyes suddenly bright with excitement. "Miss Lynn, maybe you can help Shawn find some work for after school. Keep him from running in the street with his friends. I sure would appreciate that."

"Why don't you tell him to come see me? Maybe I can think of something."

Mrs. Hopkins murmured a halfhearted reply. She suddenly seemed in a hurry and said she had to go. Lynn watched her walk away, appearing a much older woman than Lynn knew her to be. Mr. Benjamin, who knew everybody in the neighborhood, had told her all about Shawn's grandmother. Lorraine Hopkins's youth, and maybe even her dreams, had been short-circuited by early pregnancies and now rearing her own grandchildren as their mother struggled with abusive relationships and alcoholism.

What chance did Shawn have when all the grown-ups he counted on were also lost and needed help?

Lynn returned to her office, thinking about how a woman like Lorraine Hopkins, who she knew had once worked as a professional medical technician, had fallen on hard times.

She unfolded the newspaper. There, in the metro section in bold text, was the headline REPORTER WOUNDED IN HOLDUP ATTEMPT.

The details in the story had been compiled from supposed eyewitness accounts and comments from Davis Manning himself. The focus of the story was not that she'd been accosted by three teens attempting to rape her but that Davis had been shot. Lynn was surprised to learn that he was a reporter and a thirteen-year veteran for another daily paper. He was thirty-eight. She also learned that he covered city hall, wrote occasional op-eds, and sat on the advisory board for a coalition of minority business owners. He had a ten-year-old daughter, but there was no mention of a wife.

The article did mention Lynn by name, and where she worked, but the mugging and attempted rape were secondary to the fact that a man had been shot. Lynn certainly didn't feel slighted. She'd not returned the calls from reporters requesting an interview. The memory of that night was still too new, too raw. She didn't want to review it or keep it alive.

Lynn read the article again. She would never have guessed Davis was a reporter. It seemed a contradiction, given his strong opinions and attitude the night he was shot. Then again, it was hard to be objective when someone was trying to kill you.

She glanced up and found Mr. Benjamin standing in her office doorway.

"What do you need, Mr. Benjamin?"

"Nothin' for me, Miss Lynn. Just checking if you okay. Did the police catch anybody yet?"

"I don't think a mugging is the kind of crime they're going to give much time to."

"They don't care 'cause it happened here in a black neighborhood. If this went on someplace white, they'd have them boys in jail 'fore you could take a deep breath. Least you didn't get hurt," Mr. Benjamin muttered, then calmed down. "Here. I brung this for you."

Lynn accepted the crumbled brown bag. "Thank you. What is it?" She opened the top and peered inside. There were two peaches in the bottom.

"I was passin' the Korean market, and I thought you'd like some fresh fruit."

Lynn smiled at the kindly man. "Thank you, Mr. Benjamin. That was so sweet of you."

"Yes, ma'am," he said, nodding shyly and turning away. He stopped and looked at her, his eyes watery and intense. "You ain't leavin', are you?"

"Leave? You mean, leave the library? Why would I?" Lynn asked him, genuinely curious.

"'Cause of what happened to you the other night. I knowed I should have stayed and left with you."

Lynn got up from her desk and joined him at the door. She placed her arm loosely around his bony shoulder. "What happened wasn't your fault. It's just one of those things. It could have been anyone, Mr. Benjamin. Don't worry, I'm not going anywhere."

"Well, I wouldn't blame you a bit if you did, but I'm sure glad to hear them hoodlums didn't scare you off. The good Lord was watchin' out for you."

Lynn smiled vacantly as the older man walked away. Had the good Lord been watching out for her? Then what about Davis Manning? Or those three boys? Or Mrs. Hopkins?

She sat at her desk and considered the letter on her screen. It was to the central office of the library system, requesting that they reconsider former plans to refurbish her branch. She emphasized the need for better security, given recent events. She reminded the administration that the branch was badly in need of better lighting, more modern and comfortable furniture, more computer terminals, more staff. The money for the work had been in the city budget long before her tenure, but the work itself had never been done. What had happened to the plans? Where was the money?

"Knock, knock!"

Lynn looked up at the woman filling her doorway. She was tall, with a slender elegance well suited to her thirty years and gregarious personality. Her hair was a bush of natural reddish locks grown out and unprocessed. The effect was stylish and becoming. For someone who looked more like an aspiring actress or dancer, it still struck Lynn as ironic that her friend and former coworker was a librarian.

"JoAnn, what are you doing here? Why didn't you tell me you were coming?"

"Hey, girl," JoAnn said, and walked around the desk to embrace Lynn. Then she stepped back and sat in the chair adjacent to Lynn's desk. Leaning over, she peered closely into Lynn's face. "You know I had to see for myself how you're doing."

Lynn grinned, holding up her hands and stretching out her legs to display her bruised knees.

"Why didn't you call me? I had to read all about it in the papers the next day, and field questions from people in the company."

"I didn't want to make a big deal of what happened," Lynn said calmly.

"Of course it had to be boyz from the hood who did this. I still think you're crazy for taking this job. You would have found another corporate position if you'd tried."

"It would have been more of the same thing, JoAnn. My job at Graphic Central wasn't about managing an efficient information center. It was about making sure the art directors and executives looked like they knew more than they did. When they make a presentation and don't have all the facts, they look like fools. Then it's my fault."

JoAnn grimaced. "It's a damn shame. You lost a good job."

"*This* is a good job. Just different."

JoAnn leaned forward and squinted again into Lynn's face. "You sure you're okay? You should have taken the rest of the week off. In fact, if I was you I'd sue the city for what happened."

"You know I'd never do that. What's the point?"

"Money," JoAnn said with a shrug. She reached and rattled a corner of the newspaper spread over Lynn's keyboard. "I read that. I guess this makes you famous."

"You know what? I just want to forget it. I don't get brownie points for being in the newspaper. I don't get a salary increase, and the lives of the people in this community don't get miraculously better. It just happened, JoAnn. I don't know why me."

"Well, calm down. I hear what you're saying. I guess this is like when you got let go from Graphic Central. And when your father suddenly died of a heart attack without any history of heart disease. Or when you had those miscarriages."

"Right," Lynn said quietly, nodding.

JoAnn sat back in her chair. "Maybe thems just the breaks. Maybe God has some great scheme in mind."

"I don't know. I'd be surprised if He does."

JoAnn arched a brow. "You mean, She."

They both laughed at the standoff.

"What did your mother say about what happened?" JoAnn asked.

"She was concerned, of course. But my mother is definitely one of those church ladies who puts everything in His, or Her, hands." JoAnn giggled. "She doesn't question anything much anymore since my father passed. She just accepts that it's God's will, whatever happens. It's not like she feels she can do anything about the good, the sad and the uglies in life. The Lord will provide, and all that."

"I take it that doesn't work for you?"

"I don't know. Maybe not all the time," Lynn said, pensive.

"Then you need to get back to church and pray on it."

Lynn didn't respond to JoAnn's suggestion. Instead, she changed the subject by asking about the movie premiere she'd missed.

It was a much easier topic to discuss than God.

JoAnn looked at her watch. "I told them at my office I wouldn't be back today. Can you get away a little early? Let's do something."

Lynn shook her head. "I really can't. I have to finish this letter. It's important."

"It's Friday. It's not going to get posted 'til tomorrow anyway. Let's go to a movie . . ."

"I don't think so."

". . . or have dinner someplace. There's a sale at Nordstrom, although I really shouldn't be spending money right now . . ."

"No, thanks. I'm not in the mood."

JoAnn didn't pursue the matter but settled into her seat and lowered her voice conspiratorially.

"You'll never guess who called me this morning."

"Who?" Lynn asked, mildly curious.

"Morris."

At the mention of her ex-husband's name there

was a constriction in Lynn's chest. She quickly recovered and relaxed after her initial surprise. JoAnn was waiting to see if there would be any other response, but Lynn only raised her brows at her friend's announcement.

"Really? What did he want?"

"To find out about you. He heard about what happened to you."

"Why didn't he call me himself?"

"Because you probably would have hung up on him *after* you cursed him out."

"I wouldn't have wasted my breath. Morris explained himself very well when he left me. He knew what he wanted . . . and he got it. I still don't understand why he bothered to call," Lynn said with a nonchalance that surprised her. It was liberating.

"Maybe he's still in love with you."

"Please. He leaves me and immediately marries someone else, remember?"

JoAnn pursed her lips and stared at her pedicured toes. "You said yourself he didn't cheat on you. Didn't he know his second wife from grad school or something like that?"

"Sorry, JoAnn, but that doesn't make me feel better. I'm supposed to be okay with my husband leaving me because I can't have children? He remarried pretty fast. It's like he had his second wife waiting in the wings as a backup. Who knows? Maybe he would have left me for her anyway."

"I thought it showed real class that he called to check on you."

Lynn forced herself to let go of a rising anger that was proof she still smarted from the humiliation of her ex-husband's action. But she didn't want to be angry. People change. Things happen. There's no one to blame. Which only made it worse. Fate at work again? Bad Karma?

"How's he doing?" Lynn asked, curiosity getting the best of her.

"Good. They recently moved to Atlanta. He has a new job at CNN."

Lynn glanced at JoAnn, who'd stopped to monitor her reaction. "What else?"

"His son is almost two. His wife is pregnant again."

Lynn silently nodded.

"He really was worried about you. He didn't even want me to tell you he'd called."

Lynn slowly smiled. "That's because he knew you would."

JoAnn chuckled. "He asked me how you happen to know Davis Manning. Turns out Davis was once offered a job in Atlanta but declined."

"The first time the man and I met was the night

of the attack. Believe me, I wished it had all been different."

"Me, too."

Lynn and JoAnn both turned to the masculine voice of Davis Manning as he joined them in the small office.

Chapter Four

Davis laughed at JoAnn's comments about her coworkers and the cutthroat business of advertising. She was a bright, attractive woman, no question, but he also couldn't help feeling like she was putting on a show of being charming and funny just for him.

Davis knew he might have taken the bait under almost any other circumstances. But he hadn't expected to meet someone like JoAnn here in the library, and he hadn't hung around just to flirt with her. This was a visit to see Lynn Hayes. It was all about the other night.

He quickly glanced down at the sheaf of papers

he held in one hand. He deftly folded them over and shoved them into his pant pocket.

"You sure don't look like a man who was shot just thirty-six hours ago," JoAnn said in a teasing, but admiring, voice.

Davis smiled. He liked JoAnn's confidence and openness. He liked her amazing hair. He just wasn't in the mood. "And you don't look like a librarian."

"Thank you," JoAnn postured.

"Neither does Lynn. Librarians certainly have changed from when I used to go to school."

JoAnn laughed again.

Despite the pleasant banter, Davis was glad when Lynn finally left her office and began her routine of closing down the branch facility for the night. He'd wanted to see for himself how she was doing since the night of the attack. He also knew that a different kind of curiosity about Lynn had drawn him back to the neighborhood. Meeting her friend, JoAnn, was a nice distraction, but it was Lynn he really wanted to see.

Davis was trying to be attentive to JoAnn, but he was more aware of Lynn's movement as she went about her routine. There was an elderly man who dutifully performed the tasks she gave him, and a number of kids hanging around, as well as a few adults, who also offered to do whatever Lynn wanted. He was pretty sure this was not the normal way libraries were run, but the patrons of this small, run-down branch seemed devoted and fond of the woman who managed it for their use.

He saw a young mother who'd been deeply involved in a romance novel reluctantly put the book down and put her toddler into his stroller. She gave the book to Lynn as she was leaving with the instruction that she'd return the next day to finish. He also noticed a stockily built teen, wearing an oversized baseball cap over his white do-rag, aimlessly leafing through sports magazines. Suddenly, the boy dropped the issue he was holding onto a study table and left the library as Lynn circulated around the reading room. Quickly the room emptied out.

JoAnn looked around, and then back to Davis.

"Looks like we're the last ones. I couldn't talk Lynn into going out with me tonight. Would you care to join me for drinks? We can continue our discussion. Get to know each other better."

Davis returned JoAnn's smile, flattered and intrigued. But he shook his head. "Maybe some other time." He'd arrived carrying a cane, and he tapped it lightly on the floor. "I'm still getting around slowly. Besides, I need to discuss something important with Lynn."

JoAnn stood up gracefully. "Oh, well. Can't say I didn't try. But I'm going to hold you to that 'some other time' promise."

Davis stood up as well. The lights were slowly being turned out around them. The older man glanced at him warily as he made his way around the room, straightening and pushing in chairs.

JoAnn was holding out her hand. He shook it, aware of very soft, feminine skin. He looked into her eyes. "It's been a pleasure."

"It sure has," JoAnn said.

Davis watched as she crossed the room, maneuvering around tables to reach Lynn, who was replacing magazines on a display rack. They conversed quietly for a moment. Lynn cast a glance briefly in his direction before the two women embraced and said goodnight to each other. JoAnn headed to the exit. At the door she turned and waved to him over her shoulder.

Davis turned back and found Lynn watching him. He openly returned her gaze. He felt an instant connection that caught him off guard.

It was the first time he'd been able to really look at Lynn without something or someone else being part of the scenario. Even the other night, when she'd made her way to his hospital room, he'd been in pain and mildly sedated, and not really aware of much about her. Now she began to make her way in his direction, and Davis took his time observing her.

Lynn was not as tall as he'd first remembered, but she wasn't really petite. She was certainly slender in build, but not thin like JoAnn. Her skin was fair, but on the tan side. Her hair was short and loosely curled, more like a spiked style that was cool and youthful looking. Today, she was wearing a khaki skirt. The breezy length showed off not only nice legs but also the evidence of injuries to her knees.

For whatever reason, Davis was glad that Lynn was not wearing sneakers or walking shoes. Instead, she wore a pair of fashionable low-heeled sandals, exposing small feet.

"How's it going?" Davis asked in opening, when she stood right in front of him.

"I'm doing all right. How about yourself?"

"Getting better."

He liked her demeanor. She seemed calm and friendly, but not effusive. Nor was she needlessly suspicious of his presence. If anything, Lynn gave the impression that nothing unusual had happened to her recently. In truth, that did annoy him a bit. How could she be so accepting of what happened?

Lynn pointed to his black lacquered cane, frowning. "What's that for?"

Davis lifted the cane and quickly twirled it through his fingers. "The doctors thought it would be a good idea for me to use one for a few days. It keeps my movements in check and reminds me that I'm still healing from a bullet wound. And . . . it keeps people from coming too close and bumping into me. That hurts."

She didn't respond directly to his attempt at humor. He glanced around.

"So, this is the library. It could use some fixing up."

"I'm hoping to do something about that." She looked up at him, puzzled. Suddenly, a look of concern came into her light brown eyes. "You're not going to sue, are you?"

Davis, surprised by the question, laughed out loud. "I probably could, but I wouldn't." He looked around. "I don't think you can afford it. I came to pick up my car."

"You want me to wait for you, Miss Lynn?"

Davis turned to the aged voice and the man who stood several feet away. Then he saw Lynn pick up two books from a nearby counter and approach the old man with them.

"You don't have to, Mr. Benjamin. I'm leaving in a few minutes. Here, I have something for you. I remembered you wanted these books, and they've been taken out of the catalog and circulation system."

"Why, thank you, Miss Lynn. I sure do want these. They got some beautiful pictures."

Davis had the feeling the old man was reluctant to leave Lynn alone with him, and his protectiveness surprised him. Mr. Benjamin cast a long, wary glance Davis's way as he said goodnight to Lynn. It was almost as if he was trying to remember what Davis looked like in case something else happened to the librarian. He murmured a last goodnight to Lynn and disappeared down a corridor. In a moment there was the sound of a door opening and shutting with a bang.

Lynn faced Davis again. "I'm getting ready to leave now. You said you came to get your car."

Davis pulled the folded papers from his pocket and held them up for Lynn to see. "Parking tickets. Six of them since I left my car parked two days ago."

"Oh, no," Lynn said, frowning.

He was glad to see she appreciated the unfairness of it.

"At least I wasn't towed or broken into, but I don't want to push my luck, so I came to drive it home. I didn't want to leave without stopping by. Can I give you a lift home?"

"You don't have to. I take the bus on the—"

"I'll wait here while you gather your things," Davis interrupted. He wasn't surprised she was going to turn his offer down.

He watched Lynn return to her office. In a moment the light was turned off and she came out again with her purse and a tote bag. She held something else, small and cylindrical, in her hand.

"This way out," Lynn pointed, heading toward the exit the older gentleman had used.

Outside the door, Davis could see at once that they were again in the alley of the attack. He quickly looked at Lynn for her reaction, but she seemed unaffected by the location. She didn't even bother to look behind her, as he did now, to make sure there was no one lurking in the deep shadows. He was stunned that this was apparently the only way for her to leave in the evening, and angered that she took it all in stride. As if she wasn't concerned for her own well-being.

Davis walked beside Lynn, his steps a bit slower and stiffer than his normal long-legged stride. He cursed under his breath, aware of the tender area on his left side where he'd been shot. If they were attacked now he'd be of limited use to Lynn and himself. He glanced down at her profile. She suddenly looked at him and held up her hand.

"Pepper spray," she said, showing the can.

Davis chuckled appreciatively. "Smart woman."

He walked them to his car, all the while very conscious of the surroundings and the number of people, including a lot of children, socializing on the street in front of row houses and storefront businesses. He was especially aware of the teenagers, his body alert and sensitive to the possibility of confrontation. Not so Lynn, who actually waved in a friendly manner to many of the people, until they came across a small cluster of boys, all about sixteen or seventeen, outside a convenience store. They stood around, casual and indifferent, sending out not-so-subtle signals of intimidation. Passersby were forced to either walk around them, or brave walking through the middle of the group.

Davis saw that Lynn was scanning the group of boys, and that she was going to walk through the gathering. He instinctively put his hand on her lower back to stay close. None of the boys moved, but he watched them closely, just in case.

Suddenly, Davis realized that Lynn had slowed her steps and was staring at one of the teens. He was slouched against the side of the building, looking off into space, as if trying to avoid eye contact with her. When Lynn stopped walking, Davis stopped with her, not sure what she was up to.

"You're Shawn," Lynn said to the boy.

"Who, me?" he asked.

Several of the other boys snickered. "Shawn," one said in derision. Two others began to repeat the name in a singsong way that Davis knew was an outright dis on the teen.

"I see you in the library sometimes," Lynn said comfortably. She paid no attention to the reaction around her.

The boy named Shawn only shrugged indifferently and looked away.

"I asked your grandmother about you just today. She said you were looking for a part-time job."

Davis felt himself grow increasingly wary of the boys, but when they started to laugh and make fun of Lynn's comment, he had no problem casting each of them a look that said clearly *Be careful, show some respect.*

"No I ain't," Shawn finally said, as if the idea were crazy.

In Davis's mind, the stocky teen also looked like he wished Lynn would go away and stop embarrassing him in front of his homies. He wondered himself why Lynn pursued the issue.

"If you change your mind, let me know. I think I can help you find something after school."

That did it.

"School!" went up a chorus of amused astonishment. The boys fell out in raucous laughter, carrying on at the idea.

Davis looked around the group. "Hey! Settle down. What's so funny about that?" he said in a deep, authoritative tone. It had only a marginal effect. They began sauntering away, bored with the encounter.

Shawn made no response at all to Lynn's offer, other than to walk away from her in brooding silence to join his friends.

"Yo! We ain't interested in no job, right, Ju Ju?"

The boys clamored in agreement. When he caught up to his friends, Shawn was greeted with several hands held high in the air, waiting for a slap and shake of solidarity from him.

"Let's go," Davis said to Lynn, trying to urge her forward. "So much for trying to do the right thing."

He unlocked his car and held the door as she got into the front passenger seat. There was another ticket on his windshield. Davis snatched it up, crumbling it in his fist. He uttered a curse of aggravation as he tossed his cane into the backseat and eased himself behind the wheel, wincing at the pain in his side. He tossed the crushed ticket aside and started the engine. He drove two blocks before saying anything.

"You showed a lot of brass for someone who only had a can of pepper spray," Davis commented dryly.

"They're just kids. A lot of talk and no action."

Davis shook his head. "I don't think any of them would have a problem with cussing you out or taking you down. You forget that boys like that bunch cornered you in an alley and mugged you."

She looked at him. "The boys the other night were worse. Definitely hard-core. They were mean and didn't care. I know that two of them would do anything. They shot you."

"What do you mean, *two* of them?" he asked. "There were three boys that night."

Lynn didn't answer him. Instead, she picked up the balled traffic ticket he'd dropped on the floor of his car and smoothed it out.

"You can add it to these," Davis instructed Lynn, angrily passing her all the summonses. "That's about three hundred dollars you're holding."

"At least you're not dead," Lynn said.

Davis chortled under his breath, shaking his head in disbelief. "Right. I guess that was meant to make me feel better."

"I'm just suggesting that you keep it in perspective, Davis. Balance it out. It could have been worse."

"All I can see is what I'd like to do to those street rats if I could get my hands on them," he said forcefully, unable to contain his annoyance. "You seem like a smart woman. If I were you I'd find a better job and get the hell out of that neighborhood. You saw those boys. Not one of them is going to amount to a thing. They're wasting their lives and making a lot of other people miserable."

"You don't understand," Lynn said, almost as forcefully. "You make it sound like every one of those boys are the same kind of boy. That everyone who lives in this community is a lowlife who can't do better, who doesn't even want to try."

"I guess you're right. I do see it that way."

Lynn glared at him. "You're a reporter. You're supposed to be objective. You're supposed to be able to see both sides of the story."

He turned his head and glared right back. "What about you? You telling me that if I hadn't come along and you were raped that you'd have forgiven them?"

"I would try," Lynn said, her voice sure and calm.

"Bull! I don't believe you. How can you even tell me that after you boast about having pepper spray to protect yourself? Am I missing something?"

"Yes," she said.

Davis suddenly slammed on his brakes and the car screeched to a halt, jerking them both forward against the constraint of the seat belts. Davis took a deep breath, realizing he'd almost run through a red light. Next to him Lynn sat staring out the windshield. He wanted to shake her. He wanted to get under her skin, get a rise out of her. It bothered him that she could stay in control while he felt bottled up with frustration and anger. He wanted to blame her, but he couldn't. He wanted revenge.

"You have a daughter," Lynn suddenly said. "The newspaper article I read today said so. How old is she again?"

"She's ten," Davis responded, focusing his attention on traffic as the light changed.

"Don't you want to teach her to be fair? Don't you want her to learn that people aren't all one way or another, and that things go wrong in everyone's life? Bad things can happen. Sometimes there's no one to blame."

"What I want her to learn," Davis began, "is to be careful of who she trusts. I want her to not take anything for granted."

"That's scaring her," Lynn said, appalled.

"I'm teaching her to protect herself." Davis let out a long breath, trying to dissipate his foul mood. "Look, I don't know where I'm going. Where do you live?" Lynn recited her address, and he set a direction for getting there.

They lapsed into silence, and Davis did nothing to ease the tension between them. He didn't need to be preached to. He also didn't want his flaws pointed out and held up for him to see. And he certainly didn't like that Lynn made him feel cold and judgmental. But then again, why should he care what she thought about him at all?

When he turned into her street, he noticed that it was quiet and residential. Very middle class, and a nice blend of limestone row houses and low-rise 1950s or '60s apartment buildings. The street was clean. What people he saw were not hanging out but out and about to run errands, or just arriving home from work. There were a few kids on bicycles under the watchful eye of an adult. Normal. Safe. This was more like it. This is what he was talking about.

Davis started to relax. He turned off the engine after double-parking in front of Lynn's house, one of the neat three-storied row houses.

"Nice."

"Thank you."

Davis felt the cool aloofness of her reply.

"You live here alone?"

She seemed to hesitate over her answer. "I have a tenant in the ground-floor apartment, but, yes. I live here alone."

"No husband?"

"No."

"Kids?"

"No."

Davis was surprised. He was tempted to ask why not, but it was none of his business. He glanced at her profile until she finally met his gaze.

"I owe you an apology. I shouldn't have gone at you like that before," Davis said quietly.

Lynn shrugged. "You're mad about what happened. I understand that."

Davis frowned, running his hand along the side of the steering wheel. "It's more than that."

"Why don't you write about it?"

"What?"

"You're a reporter. Write what it was like to face death."

"I cover city hall. Speeches and announcements. Sometimes I'll interview a council member or other official. It's dry stuff. It's not creative."

"I read that you do op-eds. Make it personal. Write about why you're so angry. Was it those teens, or something else?"

Davis stared at her. He grew warm with embarrassment, because it seemed as though Lynn Hayes had found his journals, read his private thoughts, and nailed it.

"I'll think about it," he muttered, opening his door to get out of the car. Then he stopped and turned back to her. "I have to ask you something. You religious or something?"

"Why are you asking me that?" she asked, puzzled.

"I'm hearing a lot of love thy neighbor, and forgive and forget in the way you talk. I'm just curious."

He watched as at first she seemed surprised, then thoughtful for a long moment, considering her answer.

"It's not about religion, Davis," she said softly, shaking her head. "I don't think I'm particularly religious at all, much to my mother's regret. And to be perfectly honest, I'm not even sure I believe in God."

Chapter Five

Lynette, did you read this piece in today's paper? It's by that reporter who tried to help you that night. Davis Manning. It's very interesting."

"I'll read it later."

Lynn, in the kitchen, went back to packing the leftover food from the dinner she and her mother, Alice, had shared. She had read everything else Davis had written in the last week and a half since the shooting. He had begun using his regular column, called Soul of the City, to write about crime in the black community, shiftless young black teens not interested in education, too many babies and not enough parenting.

To Lynn, Davis's articles were angry and accusatory. He pointed a finger and found fault. It's not that anything he said was wrong, but what he said was very one-sided. She wasn't interested in reading another indictment against poor people without any discussion about why poverty, and its effects, persist. She was hoping that Davis would learn from his experience what she'd learned from hers. Not to be so quick to judge.

"He's done this time line that shows how racism and prejudice, lack of opportunity and even some government programs have conspired to make getting ahead difficult and stressful for black men."

Lynn stopped what she was doing. "Really?"

"But then he writes, that's no excuse for not taking control and responsibility for one's life. Amen!"

Lynn thoughtfully considered her mother's synopsis of Davis's piece. The article her mother described didn't sound at all like the man Lynn had met and spoken to. She glanced up as her mother appeared in the doorway of the kitchen, carrying her empty cup and plate.

"Can I help with anything?"

"No, you can't," Lynn said emphatically. "Go sit down and relax. I'll take you back home when I'm done."

Her mother sighed. "Girl, all I do is relax. I'm starting to feel useless."

"You're still recovering from chemo, Mom," Lynn reminded her.

Her mother was deep in thought, staring into space. She was only an inch or so shorter, but Lynn had the impression that her mother had somehow shrunk in the past year or so. She'd lost weight. She'd stopped coloring her hair, but the natural gray, nicely salt and pepper, was striking and becoming.

Her mother was recovering from more than a life-threatening disease. Her husband had died unexpectedly of a heart attack eighteen months earlier. Her oldest child, her son, had been killed in a commuter accident on the way to work one morning five years ago. For a while it had seemed to Lynn that her mother would give up the fight to live, and she'd often said she was ready for God to take her.

Lynn had felt somewhat the same after losing her own job, her husband, two pregnancies, and then being warned that she might not ever have children. Her crises had not been life or death, and Lynn knew that in the cosmic scheme of things, she'd come off easy. But she had certainly wavered back and forth between praying for her mother's recovery and peace of mind, and her feelings of certainty that prayers didn't matter. Davis Manning had said as much after he'd been shot.

The earth had shifted beneath their feet. Nothing

was sure anymore. All bets were off. Life was filled with surprises. But sometimes, she still prayed.

"I'm going to finish the papers," Alice sighed again, heading for the living room.

The telephone rang and Lynn reached for the cordless on the counter. It was a police officer from the crime victim's unit.

"Sorry to call so late, but we have some good news. We're detaining three young teens we think may have been involved in your attack two weeks ago."

"How do you know?" Lynn asked quietly.

"One of them was in possession of your ATM card. Another had two cell phones. We traced one back to your service."

"What happens now?"

"We'd like you to come to the station for a lineup to see if you recognize one or all of the young men."

Lynn felt the tumult in her stomach. Not of excitement, but of ambivalence. The police were asking her to point *her* finger, identify three boys, and watch them being carted off to jail.

"What if I can't identify them?"

"We might have to let them go for lack of evidence and eyewitnesses. What they did is a little more serious than just mugging you. All three have previous records, so it's not like there aren't other victims out there. Please take the night to think it over.

Remember, it could have been worse. Call me in the morning, okay?"

Lynn hung up. *It could have been worse.* There it was again. She wandered into the living room.

"That was the police."

Alice peered closely at her daughter. "They caught those boys."

"Maybe. The police want me to try and identify several suspects they're holding."

"Oh, thank you, Jesus," Lynn's mother said quietly, eyes closed.

"If I do they'll probably go to jail."

"They should have thought of that before they went around trying to hurt hardworking, innocent people. Now they'll have a chance to rethink their lives. Jail could be a sobering experience," Alice stated.

"It could destroy them," Lynn suggested.

"Or it will build character. We all have choices, Lynn. It's about time those young men learned how to make better ones or pay the consequence."

Lynn said nothing. She knew her mother was right. But . . .

She avoided the subject for the rest of the evening, then took her mother back home. When she returned there was one message on her answering machine.

"Hi, it's Davis. I hope you don't mind that I called you at home. I got your phone number from a card you left at the hospital that night. It was on the back. I got a call from the police. They want me to come in to ID some suspects. I thought maybe you and I could go together. I'm not sure I understand how you feel about what happened, but I hope you agree those boys should be held accountable. Anyway, call me back."

She didn't.

Davis got off the elevator and headed toward the security desk. The guard had phoned his office a few minutes earlier and informed him that he had a visitor, a woman, who hadn't given her name but who'd told the guard he'd know who she was. When he reached the desk and saw JoAnn standing in the reception area, Davis could only stare at her, nonplussed. He was hoping to see someone else. Lynn.

He quickly recovered, showing genuine surprise and curiosity for the attractive woman who grinned prettily at him.

"Surprise," JoAnn said with a coquettish shrug.

"It sure is," Davis confessed, nonetheless greeting her amicably. "What brings you here?"

"You," she said. She held up a commercial food bag. "And lunch."

He chuckled, appreciating the gesture. "You took a chance, you know. I'm usually away from my desk most of the day."

"I was prepared. I called first and asked the right questions. I was told that because of a recent accident, you were staying mostly in the office."

"You should have been a reporter. Or a detective," Davis complimented her. He checked his watch. "I'm on a tight deadline, but okay. You're here. Where should we eat? I warn you, my office is a cubicle, and it's pretty messy."

"How about in front of the courthouse across the street? There are benches and trees."

Feeling swept along and not particularly liking the lack of control, Davis agreed. He phoned upstairs to his office and asked if there had been any calls for him in the last ten or fifteen minutes. Told no, Davis informed his assistant he was going to lunch and would be back in an hour. That last bit of information was as much for JoAnn's sake as for his staff.

The small pedestrian park outside the courthouse was mostly empty, and Davis directed them to a spot under the shade of several trees. JoAnn divided the contents of the bag between them—two sandwich wraps, containers of cole slaw, and lemonade.

After accepting that JoAnn had taken the bull by the horns and effectively wrestled him to stand still and pay attention, he did. She was funny, and sassy in a comfortable way. If the timing had been different, he certainly wouldn't have kicked her out of bed. But Davis was also pretty sure that JoAnn was not the kind of woman who was looking just to dilly-dally. And lately that was the most he'd had to offer.

Davis also noticed that she was not afraid to cut to the chase.

"Are you married?"

"My wife died about five years ago."

"I'm so sorry to hear that," JoAnn said.

Davis smiled to himself at the irony of her asking him to lunch without first knowing that about him. But who was he kidding? He understood that for some folks his having a wife would not necessarily have been a deal breaker.

"Any kids?"

"A daughter. She's ten."

"Do you want to get married again someday?"

Again Davis smiled to himself. He finished chewing the first half of his sandwich and wiped his mouth and hands. He shrugged. "I don't really think about it. But I haven't ruled it out," he told her honestly.

Armed with that little bit of hope, JoAnn set out to be charming and pretty much gave him the story of her life. But he had something else on his mind.

"How long have you known Lynn?"

"Oh, about six or seven years. She gave me my first professional full-time job after I got out of library school with my degree."

Davis found out not only what a supportive supervisor Lynn had been but also how she'd come to leave a position she'd apparently excelled at, due to the machinations of another employee. And, although JoAnn was discreet in her own way, he also learned about a failed marriage and the hint of other painful incidents that had changed Lynn from a corporate dynamo into a woman who had learned to turn the other cheek.

"What do you mean? Turn the other cheek?" Davis questioned her.

"Well . . . Lynn used to be one of those fast-track types. She had her life mapped out, all the *i*'s dotted and all the *t*'s crossed. She was very good at what she did but she wasn't cutthroat or anything like that. You know what I mean. Then all these things started going wrong. It changed her and changed her focus. It became about, I don't know, making peace with her plans falling apart and doing things that had meaning to her. Being grateful for what she had."

Davis frowned as he listened, trying to make sense of JoAnn's comments based on his own fledgling knowledge of Lynn.

"What sort of things went wrong?" he asked.

JoAnn hesitated and then shrugged. "I think you have to discuss that with Lynn. But she doesn't get as upset about day-to-day things going wrong. She's not manic, trying to be perfect and get everything right. She's pretty much chilled since leaving the old place. In some ways I like her better."

Davis had to think about that. Not knowing anything about Lynn's past, he only had the present, and the way she'd handled herself that one night, to judge her by. And he was already suspecting it was probably not a smart idea to judge Lynn out of hand.

JoAnn began to gather the debris from their lunch, and she deposited it into a nearby trash bin.

"I guess I should get back to my office," she said, facing him.

Davis stood smiling at her. "Thanks for lunch. It was a nice idea."

"Well, I thought it was worth a shot. But I get the feeling you're not interested."

Davis pursed his lips. Her honesty and lack of guile set him back. But he appreciated that she didn't want to play games any more than he did. "I've got a lot on my mind right now. I'm going through some changes . . ."

"And they don't include me. I'm okay with that. But if Lynn or what happened to you two has anything to do with it, take my advice and don't lead with your family jewels. That won't work with her."

Davis turned from pacing the entrance to the alley when he heard the side door open. Lynn exited the library. He watched her closely, but she didn't seem surprised to see him. As a matter of fact, Lynn shook her head and smiled at him as she got closer.

"We really have to stop meeting this way. In the alley, behind the building."

Davis burst out laughing. Her sense of humor always caught him off guard. He was always learning something new about her. She grinned at the response she'd gotten from him.

"Are the neighbors starting to wonder?"

"Oh, no. They're very in-your-face about it. When you didn't show up yesterday or the day before, I got asked if we'd had a fight."

Davis sobered. "I'm sorry. I didn't realize how it looked . . ."

"I think it's kind of sweet and funny. My patrons are a bit protective of me . . . and very nosy." He grinned. "You really don't have to keep picking me up after work, Davis. You can't keep me safe and, anyway, it's not your responsibility."

"That's not exactly what I had in mind," he told her. He had the satisfaction of seeing Lynn speechless as she stared at him. "I'm still taking you home, *after* I take you out to dinner."

With shyness that he found appealing, Lynn agreed without argument.

Davis wanted to take her someplace that not only had good food but also a relaxed atmosphere so they wouldn't be quickly rushed out the door to make room for the next diners. He knew of a quiet, uncrowded

Moroccan place a quarter of a mile from Lynn's home. She'd never eaten there.

They were sharing an appetizer when Davis looked pointedly at her. "You do realize that you have to try and make an ID, right?"

"Is that what dinner is all about?" she asked.

There was no rancor in the question, and Davis didn't pull any punches.

"I would have preferred to just have a nice dinner, but I have the feeling you're not thrilled about going to the precinct. I'd like to know why not."

"I think they should have a second chance."

Davis leaned across the table to hold her attention. "Dammit, woman! When do you start thinking about yourself and getting . . ."

"Even? Getting revenge?" she filled in.

"I was going to say closure, and knowing that those guys don't get to walk away scot-free. I don't understand your forgiving them."

"It's because the options are too ugly. Wanting revenge on three teenage boys would hurt me more. I don't want to hate them, or wish them a cruel punishment. I don't want to live my life angry and bitter. I already know what that can do. All I'm trying to do is find a way to live gracefully, in peace with myself and my conscience. That's all I have any control over."

Davis stared at Lynn, once again wanting to be

angry with her but stopped cold because he recognized what she was saying. It reminded him of his upbringing, and his grandmother's wisdom of forgiving and moving on. It made him uncomfortable because he was a long way from Lynn's kind of mind-set.

Dinner was served.

They began to eat in silence. Davis noticed that she didn't seem tense or even angry with him. He tried to attain the same composure. Lynn asked about his daughter and her summer plans once school was out in a few weeks. He had no trouble boasting about Taylor and her accomplishments as a budding gymnast and ballet student. They were being served coffee when Davis realized what Lynn had managed to do with one simple question about his daughter—divert his focus from her to Taylor. And make him stay in the moment, not the past. He was enjoying Lynn's company, her conversation. It was about real things. And she was having a calming effect on him.

He sipped his coffee thoughtfully, studying her over the rim.

"My wife was killed almost five years ago," he suddenly volunteered. He saw Lynn focus on him, silently waiting for him to continue. "It was a Friday night in October. She'd driven over to a local strip mall to get party supplies and stuff for Taylor's birthday party the next day. It should have taken, at most, forty-five minutes. After two hours I started wondering. She'd left her cell phone at home, so all I could do was wait.

"Another half hour and the doorbell rang. I answered and found two uniformed cops and a detective standing in front of me. I knew she was dead before they said one word."

"Oh, no," Lynn murmured, her entire face fixed with sympathy.

"It was a carjacking. Two teenage boys. My wife had just started the engine of the car when they pushed their way in and took over. Nobody knows why they didn't let her go if all they wanted was the car or her purse. They took her hostage. A few minutes later, going some forty or fifty miles an hour, they forced her out of the car. She died on the way to the hospital."

Lynn covered her mouth with her hand. Her gaze widened with shock. Davis saw her eyes were bright and watery with tears. She blinked to regain control.

Davis signaled for more coffee. When he'd started telling Lynn about his wife, his whole body had been as tight as a rod, and the anger he'd experienced when the police had visited had come again in full force, as it always did when he repeated the story. But in that moment, sitting opposite Lynn, he felt a lot less of that. It was as if a chronic pain had been lifted from his shoulders and the back of his neck. He felt purged. Most important, he realized that the loss of, and love for, his late wife had solidified into this one complete memory. He couldn't change the past, but he had those memories. And he had Taylor.

"If I'd died in that alley, my daughter would have been an orphan, Lynn. I think I owe it to her to make sure that doesn't happen to some other kid. I think I appreciate how you feel, but there's got to be a way to keep that and do what needs to be done."

Lynn kept her gaze down and then finally nodded. "I agree."

Davis sat back against the cushions of the banquette and reflected on how easy it was to confide in Lynn. What was it about her that allowed him to trust her with his deepest pain? Only now that he'd told her about his late wife did he realize he'd been grieving . . . angry . . . for too long. Davis gestured absently with his hand, searching for a way to express himself.

"I didn't hold God in very high esteem after what happened. Getting shot only confirmed my feelings, to be honest."

Lynn's response was warm with understanding. "I have my moments, too."

"Yeah, but you handle it better than I do."

"I don't think we should compare loss. No one can tell you when to stop mourning your wife, or when to forgive those responsible."

Davis nodded, pursing his mouth. "In other words, despite the foul play, the ball's in my court."

She chuckled. "That's one way to put it."

"You make it sound so easy," he murmured.

Davis drove her home, and again silence surrounded them during the short ride. He made no attempt to cut through it, and in truth he was reflective himself. There was a lot to process. He knew that he'd never forget Taylor's mother, but he had to let her go without being angry all the time about how his wife had died.

He walked Lynn to her door and declined coming in, as she was about to ask.

"I have to get home to my daughter. Her babysitter is already on overtime."

"Thanks for dinner." She hesitated. "Did they ever catch the two teens who—"

"Less than two hours later. They weren't smart enough to ditch the car, and there was a bulletin out for their arrest. They were both underage. They spent eighteen months in juvenile detention and another two years on probation. Their records are sealed and won't ever show what they did."

"It seems very unfair, doesn't it?" she murmured, almost to herself. Then she smiled warmly at him. "Thank you for sharing your personal story. It must still hurt."

Not as much as it used to, Davis thought to himself.

He liked the way Lynn always looked him right in the eyes. She was open and emotionally available in a self-assured way he didn't often see in women. He could sometimes see pain reflected in the depths of her eyes. But she never projected it. There was a natural grace about her that was appealing and he felt drawn to it, and to her. Almost as if Lynn herself was a way to salvation, or at least a chance at a new life.

Without thinking too much about it, Davis bent to kiss her cheek.

"Thank *you,*" he said.

Chapter Six

Lynn silently listened to the instructions from the two detectives who'd met her and Davis in the reception area of the precinct a half hour before. They'd been told how a lineup worked, and that the suspects on the other side of the window could not see them. She accepted the information and still felt a knot of anxiety in her stomach. Not because of what she had to do, but because of what she knew.

One of the officers explained that they would be taken in one at a time. They wanted to make sure that both she and Davis were making their decisions independent of each other. Lynn was personally glad. She didn't want anyone but the officers to witness what was going to happen. She didn't want Davis's tragedy, in particular, to influence her.

They took Davis first. As he stood to follow one of the officers into an adjacent room, he touched her shoulder in passing. Lynn hadn't expected the contact, but she unexpectedly drew comfort from it. In less than two minutes the two were back, the officer signaling it was her turn. Davis watched her leave.

The lights went out in the room. Beyond it was a stark space with height markings on the wall and a platform for the suspects to stand on. Eight young men lumbered out in varying degrees of indifference, all dressed more or less in the same urban attire. Lynn scanned their faces, her eyes darting back and forth down the line of teens.

"Take your time. We need you to be sure," the officer coached quietly behind her.

Lynn nodded. She took a deep breath and pointed to one stocky teen. It was Shawn.

She was taken back to the interrogation room, where Davis was still standing, waiting her return.

"You both agreed on the one suspect. We're going to put him with a detective and see if we can get a confession, or at least the names of his two accomplices."

"I'm not going to press charges," Lynn said in the middle of the officer's pronouncement.

"What?"

The response was said in unison by the officers and Davis. They all stared at her, dumbfounded.

"I can't press charges."

When all of the astonishment and disbelief had settled down, it was Davis who asked her why.

She spoke to him. "Because I know his grandmother. She volunteers for me at the library. She knows that Shawn has been brought into the police and I think she even knows why but doesn't want to face the possibility that his being held has anything to do with what happened to us that night."

"Ma'am, you're not helping by protecting his grandmother or the boy. That's like sweeping the whole thing under the carpet. It's out of sight, but still there. Know what I mean?"

"You don't understand," Lynn said calmly. "You can't sweep an entire community under the carpet, and that's been happening for years to the neighborhood where I work. Out of sight, out of mind. I think Shawn was involved that night out of desperation. He wants things his grandmother can't give him. His mother has been in and out of rehab since he was born."

"I hear you, Ms. Hayes, but letting him get away with what he did isn't going to change a thing. He could be dangerous."

"Shawn wasn't the shooter that night. As a matter of fact, he wanted to let me go after the three boys had taken my wallet and things. In his own way I think he tried to protect me."

"He committed a crime. He has to be held responsible for what he did," the second officer pitched in.

"But not in jail. There's got to be another way."

The officers were frustrated, but Lynn held her ground. Davis was watching closely, silently, and she in turn watched as his face went from stunned to thoughtful. While the two detectives conversed, trying to figure a way around the impasse, Davis leaned in to talk quietly with her.

"What do you have in mind?"

Lynn looked at him with gratitude reflected in her eyes. "An alternative. Another chance."

She watched as Davis got the officers' attention and suggested they listen to what she had to say. And they did. Skeptical at first, they finally conceded that in Shawn's case there might be a way of dealing with his crime. Another high-ranking officer was called in and Shawn's previous record was poured over. There was nothing violent, and it was all petty stuff to get money. In the end, the police agreed to help with Lynn's terms. And she agreed to theirs. But it wasn't that easy. A prosecutor from the DA's office would still have to be brought in and would have to agree to Lynn's plan. A family court judge might also have to get involved. Lynn was relieved, however, that the officers hadn't flat-out told her no.

Shawn was brought into the room, pouting and with swagger and attitude, but he wouldn't look any of them in the face. Davis sat next to Lynn, close enough so that she felt calm. Shawn slouched in the chair opposite them as if he couldn't care less. The officers left, but Lynn knew they were still being watched.

It was Davis who spoke first.

"Hey, Shawn. Remember me? I walked in on you and your friends that night in the alley. I was the one who got shot."

Shawn fleetingly lifted his gaze to look at Davis but shrugged indifferently. "I didn't do it."

"We know that," Lynn said. "But you were there. I recognized your voice. Your street name is Ju Ju. One of your friends called you that."

"They not my friends. Like, I just seen them around," he defended himself. "They was looking to score."

"Did you plan it?" Lynn asked.

Shawn shifted in his chair, gestured with his hand. "I said I know somebody who got money. I told them about you 'cause you work at the liberry. You have money."

"So you're saying you didn't count on the other two boys having a gun or getting rough with Ms. Hayes?" Davis said to clarify.

"Naw, man. That ain't the way it was 'posed to go down."

"Were you scared?" Lynn asked, her voice low and sympathetic.

Shawn shifted nervously again in the chair. "I wasn't scared, but . . ."

"You thought they were really going to attack me."

He silently nodded.

Lynn and Davis exchanged silent glances.

"I'm not going to have you arrested," Lynn announced. "I don't want them to put you in jail. I think it would do more harm than good, and it would break your grandmother's heart. She's trying to do her best, Shawn. You're old enough to know that and not make things harder for her or yourself."

There was not much reaction from Shawn, and he continued to stare down at the metal table between them.

"I agree with Ms. Hayes. I won't press charges, either."

That got his attention. He looked at Davis. "I can go? Just walk outta here?"

"Not exactly," Davis said dryly and turned to Lynn.

"The police might agree to let you go, but I have to be responsible for you. We're still trying to work something out."

Shawn looked skeptical. "How you gonna do that?"

"Like Ms. Hayes said, we're trying to work something out."

"In a way, Ms. Hayes is going to be your probation officer," Davis added.

Shawn sidled a glance at Lynn, confused but hopeful. "What?"

"You might get to go home to your grandmother's," Lynn told him. "You'll also have to go back to school. I think I can get you a part-time job at the library. I'll work it out. All you have to do is stay out of trouble. That's it."

"But you're not out of the woods yet. The police will be following what happens, Shawn. The first time you mess up, the deal is off and you come back here to face charges. Know what I'm saying?" Davis put it bluntly in terms Shawn would understand.

"Why you doing this?" Shawn asked Lynn, genuinely confused.

"I want something from you."

Shawn now looked totally disgusted. "I knew it. Y'all ain't gonna play me. I ain't sayin' *nothin*' 'bout that night."

"We're not asking you to," Davis tried to calm him. "But the cops are going to continue to question you until they get answers. And they will, sooner or later."

"Not from me, they ain't," Shawn shrugged. "So, what you gonna do now?"

The officers returned, explaining the offer to make sure Shawn understood he wasn't just walking out of there free. One officer then escorted Shawn out of the room, while the other officer turned to Lynn.

"I'll be honest with you, ma'am. I don't think this is going to work. Boys like Shawn don't change that easy, but we'll work with you. You keep in touch. The moment he acts up, give us a call."

"I won't have to," Lynn answered confidently as she and Davis got ready to leave.

"God bless you, lady," the officer said with admiration.

"I hope so," she said.

"I thought you didn't believe in God," Davis said.

They were in his car, and he was driving her back to the library to finish her workday. It had begun to rain outside, a late spring shower that left the air fragrant with the smell of wet leaves. Summer used to be her favorite time of the year, but Lynn had decided that spring was the best.

Everything was renewed in the spring.

She sighed deeply. "I said I don't know if I believe. But I think I know why you don't. It's because of your wife and how she died."

"That's part of it, but not all," Davis admitted. "Suffering doesn't make sense to me. The good and the innocent maimed or butchered or killed. Criminals not only getting over a lot of times, but doing well. People with power and money doing whatever it takes to gain more. Sure, I can find sociological reasons for all of the above. But I can't figure out where God comes into play. Teams pray to God before a game so they can win. But one team *is* going to lose. Is that God's work? I'm being simplistic, but my point is, who's in charge?"

"I don't know. I guess I believe it's mostly up to each of us. We're responsible for what we do," Lynn replied.

"That doesn't really answer my question," Davis said, glancing at her.

"I don't really have the answers any more than you do," Lynn reminded him. "Maybe God is just watching us. From a distance."

Davis frowned thoughtfully. "Sounds like a song."

"It is."

"Well, here's another one for you. 'God is man-made.'" He glanced briefly at her as he turned a corner. "That's from John Leonard, a New York journalist."

He'd reached the library and parked in front.

"I was raised to believe in a God," Lynn started. "My brother and I did the whole Sunday school thing when we were kids, but my parents never went to church very often. We almost never went as a family. The way I was taught, I remember being awed by God's power. But I never understood why he let terrible things happen. But I knew that if I was a good girl and did everything I was told to do, I had it made. My place in Heaven was a done deal." Davis grinned. "As an adult, however, I saw that doing what was right didn't guarantee anything. I worked hard to finish my degree, got a job that I loved. I married a man who was exciting and sharp and ambitious, too. Life was pretty good."

For a moment those years came rushing back to Lynn. Back then her beliefs had been affirmed by the goodness in her life. She recalled that feeling of satisfaction. It had been fleeting.

"Then my brother was killed in a multiple car crash on the way to work one morning. I took responsibility for a failed project at work and was forced to resign my position. I suffered two miscarriages and might never be able to have children, and my husband left. My father died of a sudden massive heart attack. My mother became seriously ill . . ." She felt Davis's hand lightly stroking her shoulder in comfort and understanding. "Everything came crashing down around my head. I became very suspicious of God and what was going on. How could these things happen? Where was justice?"

"That's pretty much how I feel right now," Davis put in. "That's why what you're doing for that kid made me wonder. Why let him get away with what he's done?"

"Because he doesn't get away with it, Davis. I believe that if Shawn continues doing wrong, he damages the person he could become. It kills his soul, and might get him killed. What he does with his life is a decision he has to make for himself, but Shawn might not be able to unless someone takes the time to show him that his life could be a lot better than it is."

"What has this to do with God?"

She shrugged. "Maybe nothing at all. Maybe everything. Nobody really knows what God intends, if there is a God. I don't have the answers any more than anyone else. Life, to me, seems pretty random. Anything can happen to anyone at any time for any reason, or no reason at all. Like that night in the alley, when you just happened to come by to stop what was going on. I try and make the best decisions I can, try not to hurt anyone, and try to forgive. All I have is my faith that if I'm loving and can forgive, if there is a God, then His work '. . . will be done on earth as it is in Heaven.'"

"I wish I had your faith," Davis murmured quietly.

"You have your own faith in your own way. That's all it takes," Lynn said simply. She moved to open the car door. "I better go. When it rains, the library fills up with schoolkids. It can get pretty crazy."

"One more thing. Do you by chance have my parking tickets? I'm going to get additional fines if I don't pay them soon."

"I already took care of them."

"You paid them? Wait a minute. I never expected that—"

"It seemed like the right thing to do. It was the least I could do, Davis." Lynn opened the car door.

He stopped her.

"Can I kiss you?"

"What?" she asked, not sure she'd heard right.

Davis looked embarrassed. "Not exactly a great follow-up to a discussion about God. Think He'll forgive me for muscling in?"

Lynn smiled, bemused. "I don't know. But I will."

Davis took a moment before actually doing so, letting his gaze wander over her features, as if he'd never quite seen her before. Lynn sat still through the examination, reasonably sure that Davis liked what he saw. When he kissed her, pressing his mouth to hers with a warm, gentle reverence, it was definitely a balm to her wounded heart.

Lynn stood so that she couldn't be seen observing the action in the open reading room. Several tables were occupied by young teens. They weren't there to do homework, and their restless antics were starting to get out of hand. She watched as an older and much bigger teen, his dress and body language familiar to them, stood over the kids and told them to shut up 'cause they were too loud.

Lynn winced. She was going to have to talk to

Shawn about the right way to handle his authority. Nevertheless, he was effective. The kids, intimidated, quieted down. School would let out in another week, and many of them would find other things to do. Staying in the library would lose its appeal. Despite the police officer's skepticism and Davis's warning to watch out for Shawn, Lynn felt he seemed to be taking his responsibility as library monitor to heart. But it hadn't been easy.

He hadn't shown up at all for the first day of the part-time job she'd arranged for him at the library. He'd arrived an hour late the next time he'd been due. She'd had to sit Shawn down and carefully explain the concept of being on time for work. Shawn's excuses had been typical of someone who'd never before been asked to be accountable. But Lynn thought he was not only settling down, he was also starting to like being in charge of the reading room when it was filled with neighborhood kids. Shawn had also not been shy about telling her the money he was getting was chump change, but Lynn had reminded him that at least he didn't risk going to jail by taking it.

Her phone rang, and she returned to her office to answer it. It was JoAnn.

"Haven't heard from you in a week. What's going on? Is that little hoodlum still working for you?"

"Shawn is doing fine. It's an adjustment for both of us, but he's really trying. He broke up a fight between two girls the other day in front of the library, and I think he was proud that the girls listened to him."

"Please be careful. He could still turn on you, you know."

"I'm betting he won't. His grandmother is so thrilled. Every time I see her she thanks me. And I think poor Mr. Benjamin is a little bent out of shape because Shawn is here. There's this rivalry going on between them. It's kind of funny."

"Glad you think so," JoAnn said dryly. "And how is Davis?"

"Davis? How come you're asking?"

"Well I certainly haven't heard from him lately."

Lately . . .

"I didn't know you had any contact with him," Lynn said smoothly.

"We had lunch together about two weeks ago."

Lynn felt a warning bell go off, but she resisted overreacting. "Really?"

"I guess he didn't tell you."

"I've seen him several times in the last week or so, but there's no reason why he should have told me."

"Are you interested in him?" JoAnn asked.

"What you really want to know is if Davis is showing any interest in me," Lynn stated clearly.

"Well?"

"If he hasn't called you that should be your answer."

"Just wanted to know where I stood. He's really

fine. You don't find many like him walking free and unattached." JoAnn chortled. "Not that having a wife or girlfriend would make a difference."

"I think Davis is clear that I can't be played that way," Lynn said. "He never mentioned that he had lunch with you, JoAnn. Maybe to him that's all it was."

JoAnn laughed. "You know, if you were a bitch or got on my nerves all the time I'd go after him. But you've always been fair and a really good friend. I don't want you to kick me to the curb over some man."

"Davis and I met in a really strange way. We're just getting to know each other, and we've bonded like survivors of a plane crash. We had that experience together. I do like him, but I don't know if anything else will develop."

"Girl, I think you do. I also called because I thought we could get together this Saturday and drive out to the mall. Big sale at Nordstrom. And do me a favor? Find out if Davis has any available friends."

As Davis approached the library he spotted Shawn sitting on the steps to the entrance, smoking a cigarette. His heart sank, and he slowed his steps to observe the teen. Shawn looked sullen as always, but also aimless. What had gone wrong? Had Lynn let him go? Had he quit? Had he been right after all about the boy's lack of discipline and unwillingness to get his act together?

Davis was still a half block away when he saw five adolescent boys approach the library, each carrying bags of food and drink from a local fast-food place. Shawn leaned forward to talk to them, stopping them in their tracks. The boys appeared to be listening. Davis slowed his steps so that he wouldn't be spotted by Shawn and the younger teens. He stopped completely as the boys spread themselves out on the steps and sat to eat their snack. Shawn flicked his cigarette butt out into the street and stood up. After some final parting words to the boys, he went back inside the library. Davis was surprised. Shawn had made sure the boys didn't come into the library bringing food that wasn't allowed. Score two for Lynn.

When Davis walked into the building, it was relatively quiet. There was a man dozing in a chair near the magazine display, surrounded by shopping bags filled with his possessions. A woman was studiously making notes near the reference section, and several girls with chairs pulled close together gossiped among themselves. Shawn was nowhere in sight. Davis also didn't see Lynn, who would normally be performing one function or another, or talking with a visitor. He continued on to her office. Shawn was just leaving, and they almost collided at the door.

Davis quickly recovered. "How's it going?" he asked.

If Shawn was surprised by the unexpected encounter, he didn't show it. "I'm cool." He sidestepped Davis and walked away.

Davis stuck his head into Lynn's office. She glanced up from the papers on her desk and looked at him, distracted.

"You okay? What's up with Shawn?"

"Everything's good. He just wanted to leave early today. I told him he could."

Davis looked at his watch. "It's only two o'clock. Isn't he supposed to stay 'til four?"

"I can't make him stay if he doesn't want to. He may really have had something legitimate he had to do. I didn't ask. I told him I'd see him tomorrow."

"You could threaten to put his a— put him in jail," Davis said, annoyed.

"I'm not going to threaten him, Davis. Shawn has to figure it out on his own. When he's here he's pretty good. But he gets bored, and I think some of his friends may be giving him a hard time about having a job."

"Lynn, if he's making more work for you or acting up, your experiment in saving the kid isn't worth it."

"Don't worry about me. I'm learning a lot about him. He hasn't had it easy, Davis. Except for his grandmother, all the adults in his life have abandoned him. Shawn's got issues."

"We all have issues," Davis groused. "What are you going to do?"

"About Shawn? Stick with him. I'm putting him in charge of setting up for a special children's program I've planned for next Saturday. What are you doing here? Don't you have a job or something?" she teased.

He calmed down, letting her change the subject. "I'm on my way to a press conference with the head of the teachers' union and the mayor. I stopped by to ask if I could take you to dinner tonight."

"No. You have to get home to your daughter."

"Taylor is included. I'd like you to meet her." He watched as Lynn processed his request and comment.

"You told your daughter about me?"

"You have a problem with that?"

"No, but what about Taylor?"

Davis pursed his lips. "I think she does. That's why I want you two to meet."

"Davis, maybe this isn't a good time."

"Scared?"

"Concerned."

"Same thing. I'll come back for you. Six okay?"

"Are you sure?"

"Aren't you?" he asked. He had the satisfaction

of seeing that she knew exactly what he was talking about.

"Okay. Six."

Lynn suspected that Davis was nervous. So was she. She recognized that her dating history, since her divorce, was pretty sad. She'd only said yes to a grand total of two dates. Her exile and celibacy had been entirely of her own making. She hadn't particularly wanted to be bothered. It was not lost on Lynn that Davis hadn't had to campaign long and hard to get her consent to meet his daughter. But that didn't mean she wasn't still skeptical and anxious, for more reasons than he'd ever know.

They talked on the drive to his house, fifteen miles from the center of town. Apartment buildings gave way to the outskirts of the city and the start of suburban communities with single-family homes, cul-de-sacs, and planned estates. By the time Davis pulled into the driveway of his split-level, she couldn't recall much of the conversation.

When he escorted her inside, they found the housekeeper in the kitchen. She told them that Taylor was in her room.

"I'll give you the dime tour later," Davis said. "Have a seat in the living room. I'll go get Taylor."

Lynn looked around. Davis's home was neat and

attractive. There were magazines and newspapers piled on the floor by the sofa and a laptop on the coffee table. A young girl's purse hung by a strap over the doorknob of a hall closet, and a pair of purple sneakers was next to an ottoman. There were framed photographs on a bookcase. Lynn immediately approached them, wanting to see if there was one of Davis's deceased wife. But there were voices from the staircase and no time to look.

Davis appeared first, and just behind him came a thin young girl with hair braided in cornrows pulled back into a ponytail, framing a heart-shaped face with doe eyes and a small, pointed chin. She was in her stocking feet, denim shorts and a yellow cami that covered her still flat chest.

"Taylor, this is Lynn Hayes. My daughter, Taylor."

Taylor stepped forward and held out her hand. Surprised by the grown-up gesture, Lynn quickly took the child's hand in hers. Lynn couldn't help staring at her. She was quite pretty.

"It's nice to meet you," Taylor said politely, in her soft voice.

"Me, too," Lynn said. "Thank you for letting me join you and your father for dinner."

"You're welcome. Would you like something to drink? We have lemonade, ice tea and chocolate milk."

Lynn hid her smile. "Lemonade will be great."

Taylor took off for the kitchen. Lynn swung her

gaze to Davis and saw that he was closely monitoring her reactions.

"So far so good?" he whispered.

Lynn nodded. "So far, so good."

But one of the things she couldn't help noticing was that Taylor most definitely had a proprietary hold on her father. She smiled up at him in a coquettish fashion and never hesitated to hug Davis, or lean against him, or in other ways clearly show her place in his life. Lynn was charmed and amused more than anything else. And it said much about Davis that his daughter adored him.

When they sat down to dinner, Lynn offered to serve. Davis said he'd do it. Then Taylor declared that *she* would because she was the lady of the house. Lynn could see that Davis, too, was surprised by his daughter's comment.

"Daddy, can I say grace?" Taylor asked her father.

Lynn could see that the notion made Davis a little uncomfortable, but he consented.

"My grandmother taught me," Taylor said, sitting forward on the edge of her chair, pressing her hands together and closing her eyes. "God is good, God is great, and we thank Him for our food. Amen."

"I know that one, too," Lynn smiled at Taylor as she opened her napkin. "I learned it when I was a little girl like you."

Chapter Seven

Lynn was trying not to think about the fact that Shawn was once again missing in action. He'd shown up early in the day and helped to unload the equipment and supplies needed by the performance troupe who'd volunteered to do a Saturday program for the neighborhood kids. Also on the agenda was a children's book writer and illustrator, who was going to read from his books and demonstrate some of his art. And there was going to be food. Shawn was to have returned after the library officially closed to help rearrange the furniture to create a space for the performers and room for the children to sit on the floor around the author. Instead,

Lynn was forced to accept Mr. Benjamin's help, all the while hoping that the older man wouldn't collapse on her. She glanced at him to see how he was managing. Behind him, through the locked front doors of the library, Lynn was vaguely aware of the eerie blinking lights of an emergency vehicle, and she wondered if something had happened, or if the emergency vehicle was just passing through.

"Miss Lynn, where you want this to go?" Mr. Benjamin asked, pointing to a giant globe and its base.

Lynn turned her attention to him. She'd just pushed two study tables together to be used to serve refreshments. "Put it outside my office. It'll be out of the way there."

The phone rang in her office, and Lynn hurried to answer, hoping it was Shawn, but it was her mother reporting on an earlier doctor's appointment. After the call Lynn returned to setting up for her program. Again she heard the sound of an ambulance, muffled through the doors, but it was not an unusual sound in the neighborhood.

She went through a mental list of other things that had to get done that night, but she couldn't help but wonder about what had happened to Shawn. Whenever he was late or seemed to disappear, the first thing that went through her mind was the possibility that he had returned to his friends and their influence.

But there hadn't been any real proof that that was the case.

Actually, in the three weeks since Shawn had accepted the terms in return for not being charged in the mugging, Lynn had to admit that he'd been working out better than she'd hoped for. He had trouble with authority, and he could be impatient. But he tried hard and was mostly respectful. The kids coming to use the library had learned to pay attention to what he said, and order prevailed. So what was she to think about his current absence?

The phone rang again, but Lynn and Mr. Benjamin were in the basement looking for a supply of paper cups and napkins. Lynn couldn't reach it in time to answer.

It was getting late, and she turned to her elderly volunteer.

"Mr. Benjamin, why don't you go on home. I think I can finish up tomorrow."

Mr. Benjamin, looking a little tired, shook his head. "Miss Lynn, I ain't leavin' 'til you leave."

"I'm not going to stay too much longer. I'm pretty—"

There was suddenly a loud crash, and Lynn realized something was pounding on the exit door that led out from the building to the alley. She and Mr. Benjamin exchanged wary glances. Lynn thought she could hear someone calling, but she couldn't distinguish the voice or the words.

"Somethin' goin' on," Mr. Benjamin said fatalistically.

The banging started up again, thunderous and urgent.

"I'm going to see who's out there," Lynn said, heading toward the corridor.

"I wouldn't if I was you. Could be someone dangerous."

Lynn hesitated but then started forward again, resolved. "Maybe someone needs help."

"Lord, have mercy. Call the police, Miss Lynn," Mr. Benjamin muttered.

Lynn stood behind the door, her heart racing as her instincts debated her common sense. Her safety and that of an old man against the unknown intentions of whoever was in the alley. Lynn pushed against the crash bar, opening the door.

Shawn lunged into the entrance, stumbling as he came through the door. Lynn jumped back, gasping as he grabbed the door to close it behind him.

"Shawn! What's going on? Did something happen? Oh, my God. Did you—"

"I ain't do *nothin'*," Shawn panted. He was sweating, and he kept shifting nervously from one foot to the other.

"Miss Lynn, there's a bunch of police and people out on the street," Mr. Benjamin announced. "Probably lookin' for that boy." He pointed to Shawn.

Lynn studied Shawn, trying to detect guilt or innocence, but she couldn't. "Mr. Benjamin, please turn out the lights in the front."

"But, Miss Lynn . . ."

"Shawn, come over here and sit down." She touched his arm to guide him. The muscle was taut. "You have to tell me what happened."

Shawn turned mulish and silent, although he kept bouncing his knee rapidly up and down, a sign of agitation. He shook his head and wouldn't speak.

"Probably tried to mug somebody else," Mr. Benjamin said righteously.

"What you know, old man?"

"Shawn . . ."

"I ain't do nothin', Miss Hayes. I swear it wasn't me."

"Something must have happened. I hear squad cars and an ambulance. Did someone get hurt? You know anything about it?"

Shawn reluctantly nodded. "But I didn't have nothing to do with it."

"Why should we believe you?" Mr. Benjamin challenged.

Lynn, watching the boy's face, suddenly saw not a swaggering street-smart punk but a confused teenager. It reminded her of the night Shawn had been involved with the mugging and how he'd kept urging his friends to let her go, not do anything more.

"Shawn has never lied to me," she said to Mr. Benjamin. Then she turned to Shawn. "At least, I don't think you have," Lynn said to the boy.

Shawn looked at her. "Miss Hayes, I didn't do it."

Lynn's stomach nevertheless turned over. *Do what?* she silently asked herself.

Someone was now pounding on the front door. Everyone jumped, and Lynn put her hand on Shawn's arm, as if she expected him to bolt. But he only looked at her, his gaze wary. "It's all right. I don't think it's the police."

Lynn got up and hurried to the front door. Through the meshed glass she found Davis peering in at her anxiously. She unlocked the door and let him in.

"Why didn't you answer your phone? I've been calling for the last hour. Don't you know what's going on outside?"

Lynn couldn't get a word in. Suddenly, Davis pulled her briefly into his arms, as if to make sure she was whole and okay, before releasing her.

"Maybe you better ask him," Mr. Benjamin said, nodding toward Shawn.

Shawn stood up. He looked to Lynn for help. She stared at Davis. "I heard the police cars. What is it?"

Davis was staring at Shawn. "There was a holdup at the Chinese takeout down the block. A female customer is dead. She wasn't shot or stabbed, so it must have been some other kind of trauma. Did you have anything to do with it?"

"Naw, man. I wasn't no place near that."

"Davis, I believe him," Lynn said, holding his arm as if she thought he would go after the teen and shake the truth out of him.

"Do you know who was involved?"

Shawn's demeanor changed. He stared at the floor and stuffed his hands in the pockets of his jeans. He only shook his head. Lynn felt her stomach coil. This time she knew he was lying.

"The police are probably going to canvass the neighborhood and talk to people. I'm not going to cover for you, Shawn, and I'm not going to let Lynn do it, either. You have a choice."

"If you weren't involved you have nothing to worry about," Lynn tried to reassure the boy. She could see him withdrawing defensively.

Davis put his hand out to quiet Lynn. He focused on the teen. "Listen to me. I want to believe you, but someone died tonight. What if it was your grandmother?"

"I can't. My boys, they got my back. I got theirs. I can't roll on them to the cops."

"So you know who was there, right? Look, I'm hearing your name on the street. Everybody knows about what happened six weeks ago with Miss Hayes.

If the cops come for you, there's nothing we can do. You understand?"

The boy looked confused, and Lynn felt sorry for him. But before any more could be said, Shawn turned and took off for the door he'd banged on just moments ago.

"Shawn, don't run!" Lynn cried out and started to go after him. Davis held her fast.

"Stay here. Let him go, Lynn. There's nothing more you can do for him."

Lynn listened to the door closing, afraid that this time Davis was right.

Lynn smiled as the kids laughed with excitement at the sounds the author made to accompany his own story. He commanded their attention, which was no small feat, for most of them had never been disciplined to sit still for long. But they were definitely having a good time.

She glanced over to the side of the room and saw Taylor seated on the floor next to another little girl with whom she'd bonded. The girls had all been given pink plastic sunglasses, the lenses shaped like stars. The boys had magic wands, long Lucite tubes filled with clear oil and glitter. Unfortunately, the boys had a tendency to brandish the wands at each other, as if they were sword fighting. She located Davis leaning against the wall next to the refreshment table, sipping

Hawaiian Punch from a paper cup. He caught her staring and gave her a thumbs-up.

For Lynn the one noticeable thing was Shawn's absence. She was worried about him and prayed that nothing more would happen to him. He was just a troubled boy who needed help, and a break.

The library was filled with adults and toddlers and a few restless, whining babies. People wandered in and out to see the entertainment, or they stood around just to hear their children laugh. Earlier, a local TV network affiliate had shown up with a crew to interview Lynn about the library and the special children's event. She'd wisely used the opportunity to mention the tremendous financial needs of the library and how it was a valuable resource to the community. She told the interviewer that she hoped the city would not renege on a past promise to fund innovations and upgrades. She had a suspicion that Davis was responsible for the TV crew's showing up, but there'd been no time to ask.

Lynn walked around the periphery of the room, making sure that everything was going well. There were deflated balloons littering the floor along with crumbs from cupcakes and brownies and a squashed and forgotten hot dog. She scooped it up and threw it in the garbage. The punch was almost gone, which she was sure pleased Mr. Benjamin, who'd stood at the ready to mop up any spills, and there had been plenty.

But despite the gratification of having staged a successful event, Lynn knew that half of her attention had remained alert to the possibility of seeing Shawn in the crowd. Not being sure of his whereabouts presented her with a huge problem. Should she report to the police that he might not return to fulfill his part of the arrangement that was a condition of his release? Would they think he'd had something to do with the tragedy of the night before? Would the police put out a warrant for his arrest?

"Lynette, I think I'm going to leave now."

Lynn turned to her mother, who'd arrived in the middle of the activities, declared them too noisy, but had stayed for the past two hours anyway.

"If you wait another hour until this is over, I'll take you home."

"No, no. Don't bother. I could be home by the time you're ready to leave. I'll be fine." She looked around. "I met that reporter, Davis. I talked with him for quite a while."

"Yes, I noticed."

"Don't worry. I didn't go into that when-you-were-a-little-girl thing. Davis seems really nice. And he's smart. He had a lot of questions about you, you know."

"No, I didn't."

"How well do you know him? Besides the fact that he took a bullet for you."

Lynn smiled at her mother but didn't respond. Alice shrugged.

"Well, that's all I had to say. For what it's worth, I like him. Call me later."

Lynn kissed her mother's cheek and waved goodbye to her. When she turned to look for Davis, he was gone. A quick glance around showed that Taylor was still engaged with the reading but her father was nowhere in sight. Lynn had no time to wonder where he'd disappeared to. She had one more hour to get through before the afternoon was over.

When the children finally began filing out of the library, Lynn was relieved to see that there was no damage and only minimal mess. Davis finally returned to collect his daughter and take her home. Lynn was telling Mr. Benjamin he could take any leftover food if he wished, when she felt someone tapping her back. Lynn turned around to see Davis's daughter.

"Thank you for inviting me to the program. I had a good time," she said.

"You're welcome, Taylor. Thank you for coming."

"Are you going to have another one?"

"Maybe late in the summer, before school starts again. I'll certainly invite you if I do."

Lynn looked at Davis. He directed his daughter to wait for him by the door.

"You did a great job. Better you than me."

Lynn laughed. "Coward. They're just little kids."

"More than three and it's a gang. But they were good." His voice dropped and he was suddenly serious. "Lynn, I have to talk to you."

"What's wrong?"

"Nothing. Actually, I think it's good news. It has to do with Shawn."

"Did you see him?"

"I saw him sort of sneak in about an hour ago. He stopped by to plead his case, but you were too busy taking care of your program. I told him he'd have to talk to me instead. He still feels he has to convince you he had nothing to do with that holdup last night. We went out and we talked. But I'll tell you all about it later."

"When?" she asked, annoyed that Davis would leave her hanging.

"Tomorrow okay? I have a deadline to make tonight and I haven't written anything yet. I'm driving Taylor over to her grandparents' in the morning for a two-week visit. I could stop by when I get back to the city."

"Please do."

Davis looked around for Taylor, found her at the door staring out at the activity on the street, and turned back to Lynn.

"I was going to kiss you, but I better not risk it."

She grinned at him. "Afraid of what Taylor will think?"

"Afraid Mr. Benjamin will come after me. I'll call you."

Lynn was so engrossed in the Sunday paper that when she heard the doorbell she blindly reached for the cordless on the end table next to the sofa, where she was comfortably curled up. Realizing her mistake, she scrambled up and hurried to the door, newspaper still in hand.

She opened the door and found Davis on the doorstep. It was pouring rain, and she'd expected him to call at some point and cancel getting together. But there he stood, under an umbrella that was too small to provide adequate protection, and carrying a small bag.

"Hurry. Come on in. It was getting late, and I thought maybe you had changed your mind."

Davis closed the umbrella and stepped inside, holding the umbrella out the door to shake off the excess water. He laid it on the doormat to dry out. "Traffic. I guess I should have called. I was hoping we could go out for brunch."

"Why don't we stay here instead? I could pull something together."

"Bet," Davis agreed, following her into the kitchen.

She immediately poured him coffee as he sat on a stool at the island.

"Taylor enjoyed your program."

"I'm so glad," Lynn said. "You're very fortunate."

"I know," he agreed. "Taylor asked me if I was going to date you."

Lynn calmly broke two eggs into a bowl and added a little milk. "What was your answer?"

"I'd like to." Davis was leaning forward on his folded arms, watching her. "Without the drama, muggings, dysfunctional teenagers, and if no one else has a claim."

Lynn looked at him with a gaze that was warm. "No one."

"Good. That's part one. Part two later."

"What are you talking about?"

Davis got off the stool and returned briefly to her entrance. "I have something for you." He held out the brown bag he'd arrived with, which was so wet it was falling apart.

"Davis, you didn't have to get me anything," Lynn said, accepting the package and taking it to the counter to open.

"I didn't," he said as she pulled out a small potted plant, an African violet already in bloom. "It's from Shawn."

"Shawn? When did you see him? Is that why you're late?"

"After our long talk yesterday I told him he owed

you for believing in him. I suggested he show his appreciation. He was the one who suggested flowers . . . but he had no money. I loaned him a few bucks."

Lynn, deeply moved, slowly rotated the plant as she examined the flowers. "It's beautiful, and very thoughtful. Will I get a chance to thank him?"

"I think so."

Brunch temporarily forgotten, Lynn sat opposite Davis while he told her about the conversation with Shawn the day before. She wasn't the least surprised that the boy had been concerned that he'd really go to jail, this time for something he hadn't done. But Davis said he'd assured him he wouldn't let that happen if Shawn would be straight with him. Once Shawn had revealed the truth about the holdup, Davis had persuaded Shawn that if he went to the police and told what he knew, Davis would go with him and even bring along a lawyer friend.

"Bless you, Davis," Lynn said fervently.

"Wait, I'm not finished," he said, holding up his hand imperially, making her laugh. "He wasn't sure if you believed him. I reminded him that you gave him a chance before anyone else did." He took hold of one of her hands.

"So, what's going to happen?" Lynn asked.

"Well, two things. Shawn and I are meeting with the police Monday morning. We'll get it straightened out that he wasn't involved. Second, I promised that I'd check into getting him a part-time job at the paper. But he *had* to return to school. That condition was nonnegotiable."

Lynn shook her head and said ruefully, "I couldn't get him to do that."

"Yeah, well . . . I'm bigger than you are and capable of kicking his behind. Sorry, but he understood that."

Lynn laughed. "No need to apologize if it works."

Davis sat staring at her closely with a look in his eyes that made Lynn want to blush, or turn away, or wonder if she was dreaming.

"I told Shawn things happen. You've gone through some hard times, I've gone through some hard times. That's life. But I have to say his survival instincts are pretty sharp. Misdirected, maybe, but for the first time I think there may be hope for him."

"Thank you, Davis. I'm really grateful that you've been so understanding."

"And I'm so grateful I met you, despite getting shot."

"Grateful to who?" she asked, arching a brow.

"Oh, here we go. Lynn, I don't know and I honestly don't care. I just believe we were supposed to meet."

"Well, that's a start," she grinned.

"Maybe there is some great force out there," he said, waving his hand widely in the general direction of the sky. "Some kind of universal being, a God. I'm skeptical, but I've seen how your belief has given you a real peace. I envy that. You've found a way to survive all the things about life and the world that don't make a bit of sense. I admire *your* survival instincts most of all. It works."

"I only know what works for me. I believe that's pretty much how it is for everyone. I still think of myself as a spiritual work-in-progress."

"I hope whatever you're doing rubs off on me. Do you think I'll get points for trying?"

"I'll pray on it. It can't hurt."

About the Authors

ReShonda Tate Billingsley's #1 bestselling novels include the NAACP Image Award–winner *Say Amen, Again* and *Let the Church Say Amen*, adapted as a BET original movie.

Visit reshondatatebillingsley.com or go to Facebook (reshondatatebillingsley) or Twitter @Reshondat.

Jacquelin Thomas is a national bestselling author and a two-time winner of the Ethnic Multicultural Media Academy (EMMA) Award. *Divine Confidential*, from one of her young adult series, was a 2008 NAACP Image Award nominee.

Visit www.jacquelinthomas.com.

J. D. Mason is an *Essence* bestselling author whose novels include *That Devil's No Friend of Mine, Don't Want No Sugar*, and *One Day I Saw a Black King*, winner of the Atlanta Choice Award. Her short fiction appears in the Zane anthology *Blackgentlemen.com*.

Visit authors.aalbc.com/jd_mason.htm.

Sandra Kitt, an *Essence* bestselling author, has won Lifetime Achievement Awards from *Romantic Times* and the Romance Writers of America. Her novel *The Color of Love* was optioned by HBO and Lifetime, while *Significant Others* was one of Amazon's top twenty-five romances of the twentieth century.

Visit www.sandrakitt.com.